SAVING THE WEST

BY
PETER R. DECKER

Published by
WESTERN SLOPE PRESS
750 Pennsylvania St.,
Denver, CO 80203

www.westernslopepress.com

All persons appearing in this work are fictitious.
Any resemblance to real people, living or dead,
is entirely coincidental.

Peter R. Decker

ISBN: 978-1-887805-32-2
Library of Congress Control Number: 2010929428

Cover watercolor by William Matthews

Printed in Korea

to: Deedee, once again

CHAPTER ONE

Jodi Marlow appeared at the breakfast table in her work clothes—dirty jeans, a torn snap-buttoned cotton shirt worn through at the elbows and scarred work boots. She'd assembled her sandy hair, streaked with gray, into a braided ponytail; her dour countenance suggested she'd spent the entire evening in her single bed sucking lemons. She acknowledged neither the presence of her husband, John, or the fried eggs he had prepared. Her blue eyes, once so bright, had dulled in the past few years to a cloudy gray, and her lined face and callused hands reflected the 20 years of hard labor on the working end of an irrigation shovel. She'd given the energy of her youth to the Marlow family and their 65,000-acre Colorado cattle ranch, the Diamond J. Now in her middle years, her exterior scowl reflected her internal depression.

John watched as Jodi glanced around the kitchen. It needed major repairs, a task he had postponed every year until winter but never undertaken. The inside of the 1940s G.E. refrigerator, still referred to by John as the "ice box," and the coils on top of it invited a thorough scrubbing. The cast iron sink, always filled with dirty dishes and pans, required a new sturdy stand. And the linoleum in front of the sink and wood cook stove had worn through to the floor boards. Circle burns and severe knife cuts scarred the matching linoleum counters. Jodi had pleaded repeatedly for new appliances—an electric toaster and a modern refrigerator—but the family's small savings always went to the repair of a rusted bailer or 20-year-old pickup. In fact, very few improvements had been made to the ranch house since John's father built it with the help of his brother right after his marriage in the late 1920s.

Without acknowledging Jodi's presence, John allowed her a sip of coffee before he greeted her with a sharp question.

"Have you finished the fencing job in the winter feeding pasture yet?"

Jodi took him by surprise with a quick and emphatic "No." He didn't ask for an explanation because he knew the question had set her off like a fire alarm.

"I could sure use some help from somebody on this outfit to dig and set new corner posts; it's like trying to set posts in concrete," Jody said with some anger. Recently, she talked with so little energy, John wasn't sure she'd finish her thought or the sentence. "You know John, I didn't enter this marriage to be a fence builder, equipment operator, irrigator, which is to say the ranch slave, while you spend hours in town on your errands."

Another one of her pissy moods, John said to himself. "What in hell has put you in such a foul mood this morning?" he asked in as sarcastic a tone as he could muster.

"Let's just say I no longer have patience for seven-day work weeks and twelve- to-fourteen-hour workdays and nights in mud, rain and snow. I've had it with this ranch, you and your precious cows. I need a break, John."

Jodi took a breath." You don't seem to understand that not everyone can work as long and hard as you do. Not me, not Josh," and then Jodi hesitated and added, "or Johnnny," referring to their 18-year-old son.

"After Josh finishes helping me fix the backhoe, I'll send him up to give you a hand on the fence." Maybe Josh's assistance will relieve her of some burdensome fence work, John thought to himself.

Jodi turned and faced John, with a severe frown. "Forget it. I've decided to leave today, go to Cheyenne and move in with my sister. I've talked it over with Johnny. He'd like to come with me. He can play football in Cheyenne. He's tired of early morning chores before driving to school and then after practice, more chores."

Jodi's announcement came as no surprise to John, only it's timing over breakfast, and the absence of angry preliminaries which usually preceded Jodi's recent blowups. The real surprise to John was not her decision to leave, but that his son had participated in her decision and apparently agreed with it. The news that Johnny would move out with his mother hit John hard, like a swift kick to the shin from a young colt. It was one thing to understand that a separation was inevitable at some future date, but another matter to accept that his son would also be part of the decision. Yes, he'd admit that their marriage had eroded into a series of boring routines, but he thought they'd made a few small personal compromises necessary to keep the relationship together, if not for the sake of the marriage, at least for the benefit of their son—or so they convinced themselves.

"I'll talk with Johnny and see what he thinks about all of this," John responded and then added, "In your selfish way, you don't understand the disruption to Johnny's life."

"Forget it. He's already made up his mind and, as you probably know, he's talked with the football coach in Cheyenne. They're really recruiting him."

"And who is recruiting you?" John snapped back.

Jodi sat silent. Ignore the comment, she said to herself. He'll only add fuel to this flaming marriage and, in the end, take it out on Johnny. Jodi had learned long ago that any complaints she voiced only solicited silence from John and his parents when they were alive. The silent message remained the same: just suck it up and work though whatever bothers you. Consequently Jodi performed her ranch chores with skill and without complaint, though recently with little enthusiasm. Still she had labored on, hoping a renewed marriage might spring to life like a newborn calf, even in the face of the ranch's bankruptcy more than a year ago.

"Need I remind you that this ranch supports you and Johnny?"

"Sure, look at all my fancy clothes," Jodi said, tugging on her frayed and torn shirt, "and do let me know when you see a picture of this kitchen in *Good Housekeeping*. One more thing. If I continue to eat beef every day, I expect I'll start to bawl like a cow. John, you know as well as I do that the only folks who are supported by this ranch are the bankers, and they've about lawyered us into poverty. I feel like I've been branded with the Diamond J just like the other 800 females in your herd. I'm leaving and no one is going to talk me out of it."

John's repeated attempts to placate Jodi's resentment only managed to elicit more reasons why she wanted to escape. He tried to humor her but ranch work had destroyed what little humor she had brought to the marriage; he pleaded on Johnny's behalf to remain, but Jodi again used Cheyenne football as an excuse. John reminded Jodi of the earlier days of their marriage, right after he'd come back from Vietnam.

"You loved ranch life on your parents' place, and for years, you loved your work on this ranch and took pride in it. You have to admit we've had some good times, Jodi, like the fishing and camping trips in the mountains and our trips to the Dakotas after fall work. And as a family we've shared a joy in the quality of the calves we've sold every fall."

John admitted to Jodi, "I know I placed extra work and responsibilities on you after Dad's stroke, and then when we went into bankruptcy, you worried yourself half to death, not knowing if the lawyers would throw us off the ranch." He continued, "I hired Josh to lighten the workload for everyone, but we only found more projects that needed work to make up for my dad's neglect of the irrigation ditches, the corrals, equipment and particularly fences. What if I hired some part-time help to give you more time for yourself and trips to town?" John hoped the offer might put a temporary hold on their marriage, while Jodi gathered a new perspective on her work and the ranch, and maybe even their marriage.

"We can't even afford a new shower curtain much less an electric stove. And what if we need a new part for the pickup or tractor? How in hell do you think you have the money for part-time help? And besides you're not even sure you'll have a job next week with a new owner. It won't work, John, and you sure as hell know it," Jodi said, throwing her hands in the air.

"So are you suggesting a divorce?" John wanted to flush out all her thoughts.

"We'll see. I just want some time alone, away from this place." Jodi stomped out of the kitchen into the adjoining living room. She turned on the old black and white Dumont television with the aluminum foil curled around the rabbit-ears antenna. As usual, a screen of snow served as the background for a voice reporting the national news.

John had to admit to himself that they went to town less frequently, and too often they had to cancel vacation plans because of some ranch emergency. The few holidays they chose to celebrate frequently conflicted with a contractor whose schedule could only allow him to replace the well pump on the 4th of July or to doze 2 feet of sediment from a water hole on Labor Day. More recently Jodi had suggested selling the ranch to escape from the daily chores and demands of the bank, but John would hear none of it. Maybe that was the problem, John said to himself. If and when it came to a choice between the ranch and his marriage, he'd save the ranch. Jodi knew it, and John knew that she knew it.

Until a year ago, they followed the same routine after a 10-hour work day—supper with little conversation except for a discussion of some ranch matter, or a comment from Johnny about his school day. John would read the paper or the latest edition of *Western Horseman* and Jodi would work on the ranch accounts, then they'd retire around 9 p.m. for bed; Johnny instead attended to his homework in his room. But after Jodi decided on a separate bedroom within the last year, she'd head for the basement right after supper, turn out the light and immediately fall asleep. She allowed no visitors, no TV or radio, not even a photo of her immediate family. She kept it as bare as a prison, except for an alarm clock and two old issues of *Family Circle.* After John's father left over a year ago for the assisted-living facility in Gunnison, she seemed to lose all enthusiasm for cooking and knitting, and constantly shouted at John or Johnny to turn off the TV. "I can't stand that damned program; besides, I'm trying to work on the ranch books." It came to a point where John and his son would have to make up an excuse to go to town on Sundays to watch the Broncos at the VFW bar. About the only time John spent with her was over breakfast and supper or when they, out of necessity, had to work together on a ranch chore. Their love for each other had slipped away towards silence as if their batteries had lost their juice. Neither of them seemed in any rush to recharge them.

Jodi reentered the kitchen. "And one more thing John, I want to be left alone in Cheyenne."

"I can see you've made up your mind, Jodi."

"Sure have," she shouted, annoyed that John had once again read her mind, as she spat the words into his face like bullets.

A week after Jodi announced her departure and John began his bachelor existence, Charles DePuyster Devlin III breakfasted with Amanda, his young attractive wife of two years, in their New York City, Park Avenue penthouse. After breakfast, Charles was scheduled to meet with his advisors to sign documents to purchase the Diamond J Ranch.

They stood together in the lavishly appointed living room. Two deep couches covered in a floral design faced each other in front of the fireplace. Silver-framed family photos covered the mantel and the baby grand Steinway sat off in the corner. On the opposite wall, an English antique buffet served as the host for three porcelain animals, a silver bowl and two decanters, one of port, the other sherry, and a signed photograph, "to Charles, with appreciation" from the President standing with Charles in the Oval Office.

Amanda was dressed in red velvet slacks that fit tightly against her flat stomach; her ample breasts bulged beneath an oriental silk blouse, the three top gold buttons of which she left open. Her shoulder-length, blond-streaked hair was pulled back and fastened with two silver barrettes to frame her beautiful face—deep green eyes, perfect skin, high cheek bones and full lips. She stood on her toes, wrapped her arms around Charles and pecked his cheek with a soft kiss.

Amanda pulled back and looked him in the eyes. "You look so handsome in your new tie," she said, referring to her birthday present to Charles, a red silk tie with embroidered buffalo. "Forty-nine years old and still a hunk, but I've heard that after 49 it's all downhill. True?"

Charles responded by grasping her tight muscular ass and pulled her tight against his body. "Don't believe a word you hear or read. I'll prove you wrong after the closing when we're in Colorado tonight."

"I can't wait to see the ranch again, smell the fresh air, and look out on those beautiful pastures. What a life! Darling, I do hope the closing goes well," she said, adding another kiss for emphasis.

"I'm not expecting any surprises. There better not be for all the legal fees I've accumulated in trying to put this deal together. After the closing, I'll come get you in the limousine, probably about ten o'clock, and then out to Teterboro for the flight to Colorado." The limo and the Gulfstream Four were only a few of the perks Charles received as Chairman of Goodman Samson, the city's leading investment bank.

"Remind me again, who's flying out with us?"

"Just Rigby, you, me. I had thought of bringing our lawyer, but as you know, the ranch isn't set up for visitors currently." Charles always referred to his personal accountant, Rigby, the one person responsible for overseeing all of his personal properties, by his last name. The mention of Rigby reminded Charles he needed to phone him.

Charles pulled out his cell phone and walked into the book-lined library just off the living room.

"Rigby, don't forget to bring the draft of the personnel contract with you. We may need it in Colorado if we hire John Marlow as the ranch manager. Also remember to bring along the ranch maps from the closing."

"I'll have the contract with me." Then after a long pause Rigby continued. "Charles, are you certain you want to go through with this purchase? I know you've spent considerable time on structuring the deal, but it's not too late to back out. It's not like you're an expert when it comes to ranching. Corporate equity evaluations, yes. But cattle, no. Remember, we're talking about over 35 million dollars, not pocket change, even for you. I know you get a nice tax break on the transaction, but you'll be carrying over 15 million in debt. If the economy turns south, you'll be right on the edge, if not off the cliff."

"For Christ sakes, Rigby, we've been over this a hundred times. I know you think the debt is excessive, but remember I have those stock options from Goodman and I'll have more coming at the end of this year. I know what I'm doing! I didn't get to where I am at Goodman Samson by making dumb decisions. I'm diversifying my assets, plus some huge tax benefits."

"Oh, I thought it was all about saving open space," Rigby replied in a sarcastic tone of voice.

"Well … it's that, also. But remember I also get a 10 million dollar tax credit, thanks to your good advice and the way you've structured the purchase."

"It's the debt I'm worried about," Rigby shot back.

Charles didn't lack for self-confidence or optimism about the ongoing, long-term profitability of Goodman Samson. He'd grown with the investment bank and, since becoming Chairman, guided it on a steady and profitable course. Charles' exquisite manners hid a competitive spirit and assertiveness that he used, when necessary, to cut throats and twist arms with his Darwinian competitors. His secretary referred to him behind his back as "a kitten that can act like a pit bull." He relegated distasteful decisions to others, in particular Rigby, when it came to personnel matters outside the bank.

Charles recognized Rigby's brilliance when it came to the manipulation of numbers. But at the same time, he thought Rigby too cautious and unwilling to take risks on Charles' behalf. "Just calm down and I'll see you at the closing," Charles said to end the conversation, "and don't forget to bring your cowboy boots. The current ranch manager, John Marlow, tells me he has a horse for you, real gentle. He goes by the name of Dynamite."

"I can't wait," Rigby replied. And to have the last word, he continued, "I hope you understand, Charles, we're going to need a first-class ranch manager, not to mention the additional time I'll have to give to this new endeavor to assure its profitability, which I believe we can attain within the first two years."

Charles stepped into the elevator and looked again at the black buffalo on his new tie. He believed the birthday gift complimented his hand-tailored tweed jacket and gray slacks that partially hid his new alligator leather Lucchese cowboy boots. His clothes fit comfortably on his slim 6-foot body, and the white shirt set off what remained of his summer tan. As always, his sandy hair, perfectly combed with not a single hair out of place, gave definition to a handsome, unlined face, marred only by a small scar on the right side of his upper lip acquired last winter in a squash game. Charles thought of himself in excellent physical condition, a fine athlete on the court, the links and on the slopes. He had the small hands and clean, well manicured nails of someone accustomed to inside work—turning pages of corporate reports or manipulating a computer mouse. The one callus on his right hand came from assisting Amanda with pruning the privet hedges that enclosed the family compound at East Hampton on Long Island.

He arrived at the front door exactly at 8:30 a.m., the time his Lincoln town car regularly appeared to take him to his downtown office. Billy, the doorman, outfitted in his gray gabardine uniform, held the door open. "Morning, Mr. Devlin, your car's not here yet."

"That's alright, Billy, I've cancelled it. I'm walking to an appointment on Fifty-Seventh Street. Over on Fifth Avenue."

Charles prided himself on tailoring his dress for meetings. With European bankers he preferred Italian suits, silk ties and black shoes. For Silicon Valley visitors or Kansas City bankers, he dressed more casually in a blazer or sports jacket, but never without a tie. On this crisp autumn day, Charles decided on a western appearance for his meeting at the headquarters office of the National Open Land Conservancy (NOLC), a nonprofit national conservation organization on whose board Charles served as Chairman.

He had joined the organization five years ago at the urging of Goodman's directors, who believed the investment bank should be associated with one of the nation's leading conservation organizations. Such an affiliation, the directors advised Charles, would signal to important corporate clients the investment bank's interest in and support for a cleaner environment—specifically open space and wildlife preservation, the two major focuses of NOLC. Important corporate clients such as Exxon, Georgia Pacific, Peabody Coal and Dow Chemical, frequently the target of conservationists, could enhance their public relations with a connection with an investment bank, like Goodman, known to have close ties with conservation organizations. Charles' position as Chairman of NOLC could only boost Goodman's reputation with clients whose anti-environmental practices came under increasing public scrutiny. These and other clients would, it was hoped, continue to look to Goodman Samson for advice on mergers and acquisitions, in addition to equity and bond underwriting.

Charles' conservation views could hardly be considered comprehensive or deeply considered. He did not share, for example, the passion or more radical views and tactics of many conservation organizations and their leaders. A strong believer that competitive markets in a capitalist system could and should dictate solutions to environmental problems, Charles' interest in conservation and the environment focused on the preservation of open space, not only for aesthetic purposes but for the recreational needs of his family and his friends. His wife volunteered for various conservation fund raisers, benefit dinners and gala events. One month it was "Save the Whales," the next month, "Save the Redwoods" and the month after, "Save Central Park," the latter Amanda's passionate cause. While her commitment to and knowledge of conservation issues was deeper than her husband's, it was also true that she thrived on the social recognition and status she garnered with her energy and Charles' money in addressing environmental problems.

Just across from Central Park on Fifth Avenue, Charles entered a well-preserved 19th century stone mansion, the former home of a railroad tycoon, which now served as the national headquarters for NOLC. The sound of splashing water from a ceiling-high stone waterfall greeted Charles at the entrance. Large color photographs on the walls displayed scenes of a western grassland filled with grazing buffalo and cowboys. Another photograph pictured two grizzlies fishing for salmon, and the largest blowup captured hundreds of Sandhill cranes gliding in for a landing on an isolated river island. Charles passed the receptionist and took the stairs that spiraled around the waterfall to the administrative offices on the second floor. The stained-glass windows in the conference room, a former library, cast a multi-colored mosaic onto a 20-foot-long mahogany table, where a silver coffee service and pastries awaited the attendees. Here Charles was joined by the NOLC's Executive Director, Ambrose ("Andy") Chase, its legal counsel, William Blodgett, together with Charles's personal lawyer, Carlton Whitman and Rigby, whose bald head reflected the window's colorful patterns.

In his role as Chairman of NOLC, Charles had approved the purchase of large parcels of critical wildlife habitat throughout the United States. NOLC's stated purpose was "to preserve open land" in order to "save critical habitat for endangered species." Recently, NOLC spent over $80 million to acquire miles of shoreline on Chesapeake Bay's eastern shore of Maryland. This purchase foiled a rapacious developer who planned to build inexpensive condos for weekenders out of Washington, D.C.

Charles had inside knowledge of future open land purchases that the organization hoped to initiate throughout the country, and he let it be known to NOLC that he would be interested, depending on the land, location and price, in purchasing land identified as "critical." After the Marlow family declared bankruptcy and the Diamond J Ranch was taken over by an insurance company and a bank, NOLC purchased the ranch east of Gunnison, Colorado, at the base of the Continental Divide and approached Charles as a potential "conservation buyer."

Charles and Amanda and her two sons had flown out in the early summer to inspect the Diamond J. They had fished for native rainbow trout in the stream that flowed within the ranch and ridden horseback with John Marlow across vast, lush meadows and then climbed through aspen groves and stands of Engelmann spruce in the Gunnison National Forest to above tree line. It seemed that all of Colorado had spread itself before them. On the way back to the ranch, the riders viewed a herd of 60 elk.

Amanda's teenage boys enjoyed the half-day journey and expressed the hope they might spend summers working on the ranch. To Charles, Amanda had always expressed her enthusiasm for the West, where she'd spent summers as a teenager on a guest ranch in Montana. The open space, the smell of wet sage, the natural beauty of snow-covered mountains, and the log ranch house, all fit comfortably into her romantic vision of the perfect summer retreat. For Charles, he believed the addition of a western cattle ranch to his already hefty assets would serve as a prudent investment, not to mention a glorious vacation spot.

Over dinners in New York the Devlins had discussed the pros and cons of owning a ranch.

"Darling, you know the boys loved it. How much better it would be for them to be working on a Colorado ranch in the summer than sailing or playing tennis at the country club in East Hampton. I could take up riding again since we left Sussex two years ago, and you, my dear, can literally run with the bulls, as they say on Wall Street. With our interest in conservation, we can, as you have suggested, make important changes to the ranch that would be a major statement for all to see, in much the same way that we've done here with Central Park in the city. And if nothing else, the ranch could serve as a safe haven for us should New York once again, God forbid be attacked by terrorists."

Charles believed that to own part of the West while preserving, and maybe enhancing, its natural beauty could be an enjoyable endeavor. In his view, the West was slowly destroying itself by allowing uncontrolled development, including mining, drilling and timber cutting associated with development. He had long urged NOLC to take the initiative in preserving western ranch land. The June inspection trip to the Diamond J convinced Charles that the property met all of the aesthetic characteristics he looked for in a critical piece of open space. "It is a worthwhile undertaking," Charles had said to Amanda over dinner one evening, "and with our money, we can make the necessary changes to make the ranch a sustainable operation and a significant conservation statement in the West."

"Darling, you've given your life to Goodman. As I've said many times, you need to find more time to relax, get away from your job, stop worrying about your investments here and in Argentina, spend more time with the boys, who adore you, and more time with me, who also adores you. We seem to have less and less time for each other. The Hamptons don't excite me anymore. The frantic social scene is nothing but an extension of the city, and God knows the number of functions we attend in both places is exhausting."

"We'd be free of scores of boring benefit dinners, and think of all the money you'd save in new outfits," Charles added for emphasis.

"Also, I could do my conservation work just as well from Colorado as I can from Park Avenue. In fact, I could see the fruits of our efforts right on our own property. Oh, Charles, please let's buy the ranch."

Charles also hoped that the ranch purchase might also strengthen his marriage, which he felt had declined from a passionate relationship into something more conventional, exactly the reason he exited his first marriage. Maybe a new summer vacation spot, he thought, could revive the initial infatuation and, at the same time, bring him closer to his stepsons. Besides, the $10 million tax write-off looked particularly attractive to offset Charles' multi-million dollar income at Goodman. As Andy Case had exclaimed to Charles when he first presented the property to him, "Let the IRS help you buy your dream property. At the same time, you'll save thousands, maybe millions, in taxes and preserve land all in one transaction. It is a win-win arrangement, except, of course, for Uncle Sam."

NOLC's lawyer reviewed for those assembled around the table the structure of the ranch purchase. He explained: "We purchased the 65 thousand acre ranch, including the 25 thousand acre Forest Service lease, cattle, equipment and improvements, for $37 million from the First National Bank in Cheyenne and the Metropolitan Insurance Company, the joint owners of the ranch after the Marlow bankruptcy. We then placed a 'conservation easement' on the ranch to prevent any future development, including mining and timbering on the property, plus some other minor restrictions. The easement also stipulates that the ranch must be operated as it has in the past, which is to say—as a cattle ranch. The valuable water rights that go with the ranch cannot be sold off. The water must be used on the hay meadows as in the past." Then pointing to the ranch map pasted on the wall, the lawyer went on to explain, "Only two additional housing structures are allowed to be built in the future, both of which must be placed within the designated areas, identified on the map as the 'building envelopes.' We recognize that these easement restrictions have devalued the market value of the ranch. Therefore our sale price to Mr. and Mrs. Devlin has been adjusted to $27 million. And in order that NORC does not lose money on the transaction, Mr. and Mrs. Devlin have agreed, in a letter of intent, to make a $10 million donation to NORC. The donation, plus an additional $200,000 fee for closing and administrative costs, is considered a tax credit for the Devlins. In the end, NORC saves the ranch from development with the easement and without any out-of-pocket cash loss, and the Devlins receive a very generous tax deduction." There were smiles around the table except for Rigby who, without expression, gave a slight nod in agreement.

Charles interrupted and asked, "Are there any limits to the size of these structures?"

"None whatsoever."

Again, Rigby nodded in agreement as he reviewed the final closing documents, including a water lawyer's opinion. Charles' lawyer then instructed him to sign the appropriate documents.

As everyone gathered up their papers and pushed back from the conference table, Andy leaned over to Charles and expressed his appreciation for preserving this "very special property in one of Colorado's most beautiful and historic valleys."

Pleased that the closing had concluded without complications, Charles suggested to Andy that he make a summer inspection visit "to see that the ranch is conforming to the provisions of the conservation easement. In addition, I'm certain you'll be interested in some of the conservation measures my wife and I plan for the ranch operation. We believe they'll positively affect the bottom line very quickly."

"I can't wait to visit and cast a fly into the Silver River," Andy responded, "and check out those 800 Angus lawnmowers you just purchased."

Almost before Charles and Rigby had settled into the leathered comfort of the limousine, Rigby said in a tone of resignation, "Well, you got it done; now you'll have to find someone to milk all those cows."

Charles immediately responded with an edge to his voice, "If you're going to oversee the management of the ranch for me Rigby, you'll have to learn the difference between beef cattle and dairy cows."

"I was just kidding," Rigby responded.

Charles didn't think so.

They picked up Amanda at the coop. She was dressed in walking shoes, faded jeans, a floppy straw hat, and a shoulder bag shaped like an over-the-head horse feeder with a polo player embroidered into the canvas. The doorman loaded two Gucci bags into the back, and said to the Devlins, "Have a pleasant trip. See you in two days."

The pilot checked everyone's seat belt. Rigby's belt barely made it around his exploding waist. Charles and Amanda sat together holding hands. With everyone settled, the pilot announced, "we're facing a slight head-wind this morning, which means a flight of four hours and fifteen minutes. It should be smooth until we approach the Rocky Mountains. Mr. Devlin, you know where the sandwiches and drinks are stored. Any questions?"

From the front seat of his pickup, John heard the jet as it appeared over the mountains to the east and followed it to its landing in Gunnison. The pilot opened the door and let down the steps to the runway. Charles jumped out first and was greeted by John Marlow.

"Sir, good to see you and Mrs. Devlin again. Pleasant flight? I trust the closing went well?"

"A good flight except for Rigby's snoring," Charles said as he threw his head in Rigby's direction. "And yes, the closing went off without a hitch."

Charles then turned to Rigby and introduced him to Marlow. John had never before seen such a bald head, which he likened to a ball of wax that he hoped wouldn't melt in the bright Colorado sunshine. Must have worked it over with furniture polish in preparation for the visit, he thought. Rigby stood on the tarmac in his white patent leather loafers and khaki shorts and Hawaiian shirt breathing with difficulty at Gunnison's 8,700-foot elevation.

John turned to Amanda and greeted her. But because her gold-framed designer glasses hid her eyes, John found it impossible to judge her reaction either to the flight or her surroundings. Her streaked blond hair, perfectly coiffed, and her painted nails seemed as out of place in the Colorado mountains as did Charles' brown tweed jacket, dress shirt and silk tie.

Charles thought John looked and dressed like the stereotypical cowboy—dirty jeans, scuffed riding boots, a work jacket frayed at the cuffs—except for the sweat-stained baseball cap he wore advertising "Silver Valley Ready Mix." Amanda thought John handsome, despite his short stature, with his clear blue eyes, tanned face and strong jaw. Charles for the first time noticed a slight limp in John's walk and also a jagged 3-inch scar on his left cheek. It took nothing away from his good looks; instead, the purple scar added a signal, of sorts, that if one wanted to cross John in a fight, he was more than capable of holding his own. A thick neck, broad shoulders and a hard, callused handshake gave Charles further evidence that the "acting manager" had grown up working outside.

John directed Rigby to the seat in the rear of the crew cab, and then squeezed Charles and Amanda into the front seat. Rigby immediately noticed the rifles in the gun rack over the rear window.

"What are the guns for?" Rigby inquired.

"Prairie dogs, coyotes and trespassers, more often than not, Texans. You get 'em out in the open, and they're an easy shot for that 30-caliber with the scope."

Amanda laughed. Rigby said nothing. He took an immediate dislike to John; it had nothing to do with Texans, more with what appeared to be a wise-ass attitude. He'd keep a close eye on him, if he should become the permanent manager.

CHAPTER TWO

Two days before Charles Devlin signed the papers to take possession of the Diamond J Ranch and his arrival at the ranch, John Marlow conducted the fall roundup of cows and calves on the ranch's 25,000 acres leased from the Forest Service.

John headed up the roundup, a job he had learned under his grandfather and father when they ran the ranch. The crew consisted of Josh and his wife, neighbors and friends. They assembled at the Diamond J corrals at sunup. Everyone knew the drill from years past, where the cattle hid from the riders, and once collected, where to move them for the final drive to the ranch. Only the weather changed. Last year, the crew rode up into the forest amidst a torrential rainstorm, and didn't return until early evening with the aid of heat lightning—nature's strobe lights—illuminating the main trail back to the pastures adjacent to ranch headquarters. This year John commented on the cold wind out of the north that threatened snow. "If the roundup goes off without a hitch, we should be back at headquarters with the cattle before the storm hits."

All the riders wore shotgun chaps except for Josh, who favored the old-fashioned bat-wing design. A few wore spurs, and everyone tied a slicker to their saddle and a coiled rope. As was the custom, everyone had wrapped their saddle horns with rubber strips cut from old inner tubes. John wore a tan vest that leaked feathers despite the patchwork of duct tape. Out of habit, he wore a frayed red silk scarf double-wrapped around his neck for warmth or, in an emergency, for use as a tourniquet. No one would mistake John for the Marlboro Man. He wore his sweat-stained ball cap, and he hadn't bothered with gloves, his hands long ago had leathered into thick calluses. One rider, Zeke Baylor, who'd suffered a recent horse accident, donned a white bike helmet decorated with iridescent, red plastic strips and a decal advertising Jim Beam, the source of the accident.

John's body matched the thick muscling of Bando, his dun-colored quarter horse. Following along at Bando's heels was Dixie, John's canine assistant, a black and white Kelpie stock dog. The saddle bags carried bottles of penicillin and LA 200, another medicine, plus two syringes and spare needles, a Milky Way candy bar, and a pair of fencing pliers.

John gathered all the riders around him and announced, "Josh and I'll clear the 'Hell Hole,'" Everyone cheered for having avoided the dreaded assignment. "We'll gather all the cows, calves and bulls to this gate and then trail everything into the ranch. Cut the ear tags off any dead cows or calves you find. Leave all the gates open on the way out so that whatever animals we miss can drift back to the ranch."

Everyone rode off towards the forest. John inspected the cow/calf pairs with an eye for the calf's size and the cow's condition. His thoughts also turned to Jodi and Johnny in Cheyenne. How were they faring? Was Jodi working? And Johnny, how had he settled into his new high school? He missed them both. Then he thought about the new owners and what they had in mind for the ranch. Was John included in their plans? Except for Uncle Sam, he'd never worked for anyone else except his family and himself, and only briefly for the bank after the bankruptcy. How could he relate to New Yorkers? Damned if my life hasn't become more complicated, John thought.

Within four hours, the crew had gathered the cows and calves and assembled them at the designated gate. They let the mother cows pair up with their calves and drink at a nearby spring before moving them through the gate and eventually back to where they'd spend the next nine months at the Diamond J. John inspected the cattle as they passed through. One of the riders handed John four cow tags as Josh made the cow count. John turned to Josh, "They're in good flesh." Josh nodded and then said, "Yeah. We're six short on the cow side. We'll wait till they pair up to get a count on the calves. I did see that Red Angus bull we couldn't find in August. He's a bit lame, probably foot rot, but otherwise he appears healthy and in good flesh."

The Forest Service grazing permit had come to the ranch in the early 20th century when John's grandfather ran the Diamond J. The permit specified the number of cattle allowed to graze (700 cows, 120 heifers, and the bulls to service them) and the time on the forest land (four months). In return, the Diamond J paid a monthly fee for each animal, and maintained all fences and other improvements. John's grandfather had split the permit into four separate pastures, not pastures in the normal sense, but fenced enclosures of timber, grass and steep hillsides and, in one instance, a rocky escarpment with a deep canyon, flat at the bottom with an elongated grassy meadow, known affectionately as the "Hell Hole." But each "pasture," identified by name, had ample grass and water. When John estimated that a group of cows had consumed about three-quarters of the grass in one pasture, he and Josh moved the cows and calves to another. By the end of the summer, they'd grazed in all four pastures.

John saved the roughest pasture for his yearling heifers. Right after he artificially inseminated the heifers in June, they'd be trailed to the "Hell Hole"—4,000-acre piece of rugged landscape that gained 3,000 feet in elevation from the south end to the north. Josh called it "one rocky son-of-a-bitch," a description no man or heifer would disagree with. John intended that the yearlings learn to walk in rough country to find their grass and water. "By God, these heifers are going to work for the ranch, not the other way around," John would say to anyone who asked why he sent these yearling heifers to suffer three months in what the ranch called "bovine boot camp." By September, John knew they'd have learned how to forage on their own, where to find ample grass and water and, in the process, toughen their feet. They were survivors, and after their first calf there'd be no need to baby them.

As the truck pulled up in front of the log-homestead cabin that the Devlins had enjoyed on their previous visit, John saw that Rigby had pulled a note pad from his briefcase and started taking notes on what John referred to as "headquarters." The corrals defined the western edge, and an equipment shed and barn sat across a dirt yard opposite the corrals, with the three-bay garage/shop building close by. A small well house squatted behind five tall spruce trees. The headquarters probably could use some tidying up, John thought to himself, looking out into the yard where rolls of rusted barbed wire kept company with some cedar posts, steel posts and a wheel barrow with a flat tire.

After dropping Charles and Amanda at the cabin, John carried Rigby's bag to his son's room. The accountant wore shorts and his Hawaiian shirt, both stretched uncomfortably across his bulging midsection.

"I'll see you in the kitchen," John said as he thought about his first meeting with his new boss and his accountant.

Charles appeared in the kitchen in a pair of artificially faded, pressed jeans and hiking boots and a cell phone to his ear. John heard him say into the phone, "Why tomorrow?" and then a loud "shit, OK." He snapped the phone shut and said in annoyed tone to Rigby, "I have to be in New York tomorrow to meet with the Argentinean finance minister. So let's get started." After John poured some black coffee, Charles sat at the table and opened the conversation.

"John, we've come out to the ranch today specifically to talk with you, learn more about the ranch and determine if you're the right person to be our manager. I know from your resume that you grew up on the ranch, worked for your father, and before that your grandfather. That's an indication to me that you know every acre of the ranch and every cow on it. I see also you served in Vietnam, were awarded the Purple Heart and a Bronze Star, and attended a community college for a year."

John nodded. Charles continued. "I don't claim to know much about cattle or ranching, nor does Mr. Rigby who, by the way, is my right-hand man and personal accountant. But what we're both looking for is someone we can trust to run the ranch efficiently in our absence, and within our budget. Rigby will be the key person when it comes to the budget, and therefore will oversee the entire financial operation of the ranch. It is critical that we feel comfortable with the manager and he with us."

John immediately recognized the importance of the ball of wax sitting across the table from him. "I understand," he replied, looking at Rigby.

"Let me ask you," Charles continued, "what do YOU look for in a worker when YOU hire someone to work on the ranch?"

He's never been asked the question before but he'd accumulated some knowledge over the years. "I always say to a new employee, 'If you can't smell your sweat, you're not working hard enough,' and if they don't damned well sweat, they'll find themselves sent down the road without a check. I want that person to know, within a couple of months, every facet of the ranch routine, and that includes the cattle operation, irrigation requirements, putting up the hay crop and the maintenance of the ranch equipment. It'd be nice if, like me, he could break a colt, shoe a horse and maybe even repair a saddle. I like to reward good performance with a raise or maybe to allow the man to have an additional stock horse on the place, but only a gelding, never a mare."

"Anything else?" Rigby asked.

John continued. "You'll need to remember, Mr. Rigby, that stock out here means Angus or a European breed, like Charlois, or Limousine, not IBM or General Motors. A blue chip stock to me is a healthy crossbred calf weighing 500 pounds at weaning time in September. Options are a range of actions available to save a calf's life, and the best is the one that guarantees the calf a better than 50-50 chance of survival. My Dad always said that to be a good cowman you need to 'work like a dog, and think like a cow.' So I'm looking for a good cowman. Cows, unlike sheep, have intelligence and you need to allow their natural instincts and intelligence to guide their behavior. For example, in a snowstorm the cows on this ranch know where to seek shelter. They have memories. The older cows remember the location of every patch of grass and water hole here and on the forest permit."

It was not John's habit to be so loquacious, especially with a relative stranger. But if he were to be kept on as manager, he knew he had to impress Devlin, and probably Rigby, with his knowledge of the ranch and what it took to manage it.

"One other thing," John said. "I have no use for what I call 'dukin' the cattle. You seen how in John Wayne movies the cattle are always at a gallop, but if he worked for me, I'd shit-can his ass. There's no hootin' and a hollerin', and throwin' ropes around on this outfit. I just tell the men to be quiet and the cows will figure out what you want them to do, and the calves will follow."

"I assume the rodeo cowboys we see on TV are not what you're looking for? The cowboys I once saw at a rodeo in Madison Square Garden sure could ride and rope and handle those big bulls," Rigby commented as sweat trickled down from beneath his hat.

"Personally I don't have no use for 'em. I remember one cowboy who pulled up to the ranch with his horse trailer looking for a job. He was wearing one of those trophy rodeo buckles, the size of a dinner plate, and a sweat-stained cowboy hat. His waxed mustache had grown out beyond his tobacco-filled cheeks and drooped down just short of his shirt pocket. He sashayed over to Dad, who took one look at his trophy belt buckle and said, 'Buckaroo, if you're looking for a job here, forget it. On this outfit we don't ride bulls, the bulls here ride the cows, just like God intended. As for bucking horses, if we find one and it can't be trained, we either eat it or send it off to the glue factory. Finally, you won't find no buckle bunnies within a hundred miles of here. Good luck down the road, son.' The old man always said he much preferred a good cowboy from Mexico, where the skills originated, than those rodeo types. We use to hire Indians, usually Utes. They made damn good cowboys; best riders you've ever seen. But keeping 'em sober after pay day, that's a problem."

"I won't hesitate, myself, to fire the ass of a cowboy who leaves large dry spots in the middle of an irrigated pasture. And what really pisses me off is anyone who tears up the equipment. You can bet they're gone by sundown, and without a positive reference," John said with conviction.

"Sounds as if you had some good teachers in your Dad and Granddad," Charles offered.

"You bet. They taught me things you won't learn in school or get out of a book, like the technicalities of water rights, how to site an irrigation ditch without a transit so that the water drops exactly one foot for every hundred feet in length. You'll come to understand that water here is gold. You've got to use it efficiently through flood irrigation."

"I see a lot of equipment here. Can you fix it when it needs repair?" Rigby inquired.

"Both Josh and I can operate and repair a tractor, baler or swather, fix seals, hydraulic hoses, valves, and almost any moving part except a transmission. We can weld, solder and rewire about anything on the hay equipment, a tractor or pickup. I've replaced the rotten hand-hewn beams, rafters and cottonwood floor planks in the horse barn my great-grandfather built in the 1890s. This last winter Josh and I built a loafing shed for the first calf heifers to give them better protection for calving during spring storms and, I'm happy to say, we dug and buried the water and electric lines to the structure without causing a brownout in the valley. I'm damned proud of what Josh and I can build and fix without hiring some extra help from town."

"What's a swather?" Charles asked.

"It's the mowing machine that cuts the tall grass hay and, in the process, breaks the stems so the hay dries quicker."

Neither Charles nor Rigby knew enough to ask about animal health and John didn't volunteer that he could identify and treat foot rot, a blistered udder, cancer eye, various strains of scours, diphtheria, pneumonia, intestinal blockages, mastitis and plant poisons ingested by the cows. For each problem, he had a medical solution, some of which were not taught at veterinary schools. John also had learned from his dad how to fashion a small loop when chasing a calf at a full gallop through the high country timber, rope the calf, dally the rope onto his saddle horn, pull the calf to the ground, dismount and run down the rope held taut by his horse, grab the syringe of penicillin from his mouth, hold the calf to the ground with his left knee, and inject the medicine in the calf's butt all in one continuous motion. If asked, Josh would confirm all of John's talents and add one more: his skill with a bull whip. Josh once bragged on his boss, "He can kill a horsefly in mid-flight with that weapon."

"What do you do in your free time? You must have family responsibilities?" Charles offered as a leading question to discover how much time John spent off the ranch.

"Don't have no family here anymore. My wife took off a couple of weeks ago. My 18-year old son lives with her in Cheyenne. What free time I have, usually after supper, I'll work in the shop making saddles or other cowboy gear such as spur straps, bridles, chaps, saddle bags, a quirt or a pair of leather hobbles. I get a lot of orders for that stuff from folks around here and it helps with the bills. Some nights I'll work with Scruffy and Dixie, my Kelpie stock dogs, on arm and whistle signals. With the three steers I keep in the corral, I teach the dogs how to heel cattle through a gate. I also have two colts I'm working with."

"I'm curious," Charles asked, "how do you train a horse, say like Dynamite, the one Rigby will be riding?" John caught the wink from Charles.

"First thing I look for in a horse, aside from his muscle pattern and bone structure, is his eye. Dad always said the whiter the eye, the meaner the horse. That Dynamite horse, he's got a lot of white."

Laughing, Charles interrupted and said, "Rigby, look at me." Rigby turned to his boss, who said, "I can tell you're also one mean son-of-a-bitch." Charles' joke only confirmed what John had already decided about Rigby.

"Sorry," Charles said. "Please finish your horse training session."

John went into a long description of how he trained a horse, quick to point out, "I never let a horse buck if I can avoid it. I train my horses to be partners, not adversaries. My Dad used to say, 'take care of your horse like it was a close relative.' Nothin' worse than to be fightin' your horse all day when you're workin' cattle."

"Can you train Rigby?" Charles asked. "He could use some manners and a good workout to slim down his flanks."

Rigby sat stone-faced silent. John thought better of responding to the comment. Instead, he changed the subject. "You asked about my free time. I assume you mean vacations. I'm not much on taking vacations or a holiday off. The cattle don't celebrate the fourth of July, any more than turkeys celebrate Thanksgiving. Only when I can hire a good hand to help Josh, usually during the fall slack season, do I leave the ranch for more than a day. The best vacation I remember was the time when my son was young, and my wife and I took off for Mount Rushmore. We saw buffalo herds on an Indian reservation in South Dakota, caught 12 fat rainbows in Wyoming, and bought some saddle pads, ropes and ox-bow stirrups at King's Saddle Shop in Sheridan. Sometimes I'll take an extra day on a bull-buying trip, but with a trailer load of bulls, I'm usually pressed to get them home and settled. I did make a special trip to Durango two years ago for a wedding, rode the antique train with Johnny up into the mountains and back to Durango, but all the booze at the wedding gave me a monstrous hangover. Haven't had champagne or bourbon since. I would, however, like two weeks of vacation a year, though I probably won't take the full two weeks."

"Don't you get into town to shop, pick up supplies or have a meal?"

"Now I go into town when I tire of my own microwave meals. My wife used to say I specialized in three main food groups: macaroni and cheese, hash and pizza. When I have the urge for greens, I dress up and splurge on a chicken-fried steak and large salad at the Wagon Wheel, the steak house in town. I recommend it. Usually I'll coordinate a dinner in town with a meeting at the Silver Valley Volunteer Fire Department, the Veterans of Foreign Wars or the Silver Valley Cattlemen's Association. You'll see that there ain't too much to do in Silver Valley after five, except if you're a drinker; then you can hang out at the VFW till midnight."

John stopped, took a long sip of coffee, shifted in his chair and looked directly at Charles.

"Mr. Devlin, I'd sure like to stay on this ranch. As you know it's my home, and these cattle, I help birth them, feed them through winter storms and care for them when they're sick. I've tried to maintain it to the standards of my father, grandfather and more recently, the bank. They've trusted my judgment and knowledge of the ranch and allowed me free rein, except for some financial restraints. I'm use to working on my own, unsupervised. I know this place as well as anyone. I think I can do you a good job."

"I'm sure you can," Charles said as he stood up. "I want some time to think this over and also confer with Rigby. We'll be flying back to New York this afternoon. I had hoped to look at the prospective housing sites where we're allowed to build, but I'll have to do that on another trip, probably next week if I can arrange it. I'd like to bring my architect with me."

"I know you're rushed for time," John said as Rigby nodded to confirm John's observation, "but I'd like to know something about this conservation easement you talked about on the phone, and what it means for the ranch."

"Aside from the tax considerations, the easement requires that the meadows have to be preserved and irrigated as they were under the former owners. That means the water cannot be sold off from the ranch. No timber can be cut for commercial purposes, nor is mining allowed. Any new road within the ranch, in fact any construction or activity which changes the nature of the ranch, will have to be approved by NOLC. Even the barns, corrals, storage sheds and the pump house must be preserved. I don't believe the easement agreement will impact the ranch operation in any major way," Charles said and then stood up and concluded, "I'm sorry to have to cut this meeting short, but we need to be at the airport in an hour. I do wish Rigby had the time to ride Dynamite before we left."

John had questions he wanted to ask of Devlin and Rigby but they hadn't given him a chance. Or maybe I talked too much, John thought to himself. All he knew about Devlin was that he ran a bank in New York, appeared to have money and had a pleasant family. Would the job be permanent or conditional, and what about health insurance? Would he be given a free hand or would they be issuing weekly orders from 2,000 miles away about what equipment to buy, the composition of the feed ration for the replacement heifers and if and where to sell the calves in the fall? Was Devlin interested in the cattle operation or did the cows represent for him little more than decorative objects—a bovine backdrop for the family's recreational needs? John could accept that but only as long as he was left alone to run and improve the cattle herd. He certainly didn't want to put himself into a position where he was made to feel like a guest on the ranch. Maybe he'd have to seek another line of work? Two years in the Army had taken him away from home to the jungles of Vietnam, but at his age, returning to the Army was not an option. He could make saddles and get a good price for them, or hire out to another ranch. But it was the Diamond J land and the cattle that centered his life. He would have to await word from New York.

While the men talked in John's kitchen, Amanda had taken a walk through the meadow where cows and calves grazed. At first she had feared that one might take a run at her but as she appeared non-threatening, sitting quietly among the cattle, the cows only lifted their heads and stared at her. Amanda stood up and took a step towards the calf with her hand held out as if to offer feed. The calf bolted. The cow stood her ground ready to protect her calf. What a wonderful life they have, Amanda thought. Eat and sleep on lush meadows that look out at the mountains with not a care in the world. How uncomplicated and beautiful. I can be happy here where the air is so light and clean, away from New York and its constant demands. She laid down in the meadow and absorbed the smell of the grass and sight of seven snow geese gliding over the yellowing cottonwoods.

Amanda's mood changed immediately upon return to headquarters where

Charles announced to her that they had to return to New York this afternoon due to Charles' important meeting with the Argentinean finance minister tomorrow morning.

"You've been to Argentina three times in the last two months. What's the problem?"

"Dear, there's no problem. We've some investments down there that will help pay for this ranch," Charles responded. Amanda's scowl expressed her disappointment as she walked to the cabin to pack.

CHAPTER THREE

The New York office of Goodman Samson occupied the top 20 floors of its 45-story building on Broad Street in lower Manhattan. Massive marble Greek columns circled the great hall and extended to the high ceiling where small gold-trimmed rosettes hid the security cameras. In the reception area visitors awaited their meetings in the deep burgundy-colored leather chairs grouped near a mahogany table, where a collection of daily newspapers and financial periodicals shared space with a pot of coffee and Danish pastries. The security office, a delivery and pickup window and a glass-enclosed conference room occupied the rest of the ground floor. The entire entrance area, with its high ceiling and vacant space, gave the impression, as intended, of a successful money temple.

The armed security officer at the check-in desk close to the elevator nodded in recognition to Charles as the Chairman strode to one of two manned elevators. On the 45th floor, Charles entered his own private world. An original Monet and other French impressionist paintings, mostly rural scenes, lined the walls, a reminder to visitors that Goodman could afford to own a multi-million dollar art collection. The attractive middle-aged receptionist/secretary, whose language skills allowed her to greet international visitors in French or German, handed Charles some telephone messages. "Your meeting with the Argentine finance minister is scheduled for ten in the conference room."

"Did he give any indication why he requested this meeting at the last minute?"

"No, just said it was very important that he see you as soon as possible."

In addition to Charles' suite of offices, the Executive Dining Room occupied much of the north end of the floor, its kitchen the envy of some of the city's finest restaurants. The boardroom, adjacent to Charles' office, accommodated all 16 directors, plus necessary staff at quarterly meetings. The directors, Goodman's senior partners and five CEOs of corporations with which Goodman had long-standing relationships sat beneath the portraits of former Goodman chairmen and the founders, Marvin Goodman and Earl Samson. They glowered from the walls like the fierce animals they had mimicked in life.

Charles' office overlooked the New York harbor to the west and the vacant site of the World Trade Center. Silver framed photos of his family graced a mahogany credenza. The art tended towards landscapes, which kept company on the wall with a small but exquisite Germantown Navajo rug. A signed photograph of President Reagan and Charles standing in the Oval Office adorned its own antique side table.

It had taken Charles 22 years to climb the company ladder to the chairman's office. After Choate, Yale and then Harvard Business School, Goodman had recruited him, first as a research analyst specializing in energy companies, then to the corporate finance department where for 60 hours a week he crunched numbers preparing the critical figures for a merger or acquisition, or an IPO. After five years as an apprentice to Goodman's foremost merger and acquisition partner, the senior partners rewarded Charles' flair for figures and relentless energy by appointing him the lead banker on some of their most important transactions. He led the acquisition team, advising Chevron in its complicated merger with Gulf Oil and later its absorption into Texaco. He then went on to enhance his reputation with other mega-deals, in the U.S. and overseas, involving European banks, telecommunications and manufacturing companies.

At the relatively young age of 39, Charles had been appointed a managing partner, one of the youngest in the 120-year history of the firm. The firm's management committee sent Charles off to London, where he headed its expanding European operations and led the successful efforts to solicit new clients within the maturing European Union.

Three years later, after Charles had brought in business from throughout Europe, including former communist countries, the management committee transferred Charles back to New York as Vice Chairman. With the retirement of Frederick Whitenburg, Charles moved to the Chairman's office on the 45th floor.

Charles fit the part of Chairman, with his waspish good looks and background. He was the image of what senior partners referred to as the "Goodman style." He dressed conservatively in European styled suits, spoke with precision, participated generously in charitable organizations, and worked at being collegial to all within the firm. Yet outside the firm he could be, when necessary, a cut-throat and independent competitor amidst the hustle and bustle of the national and international marketplace. He appeared happily married to his young, attractive second wife, who through her own family had important social and financial connections valuable to Goodman. In short, Charles had proved to be not only a money maker for Goodman, but a man of trust and integrity.

By virtue of his position as Chairman, he'd been asked to serve as the spokesman for the nation's investment banking community in Washington. Two past chairmen of Goodman had served as Secretary of Treasury, one under a Republican president and the other in a Democratic administration. The nation's business community recognized the possibility of Charles being tapped by the current administration for a high post in Washington or an ambassadorship overseas.

At his desk, Charles used the time before his meeting with the Argentine finance minister to place phone calls. He contacted Goodman's office head in Hong Kong about the details of their forthcoming investment in China's largest bank, and the status of Goodman's currency hedge against the "inflated" Japanese yen. He reviewed his calendar with his secretary regarding a dinner reception for the head of Poland's Central Bank, and ensured the presence of a discreet interpreter. He placed a call to Goodman's CFO about the record travel expenses run up by the equities department last quarter.

"Why all the travel expenses by the equity boys? It's an all-time record for them. I'm assuming they're going business class?"

"They probably assumed they were entitled to first class," the CFO responded.

"I'll let them know when they're damned well entitled to it. In the meantime, it is business class or they can walk."

Charles then called a vice president and directed him to dismiss Goodman's head of retail sales, whose performance Charles had found inadequate. Charles never liked to dirty his hands or his reputation with unpleasant personnel matters, preferring instead to leave such matters to subordinates. After the call, Charles commented to his secretary, "And to think I had to read about our drop in sales and commission income in the *Wall Street Journal*. What happened to the monthly reports they had promised to send me?"

Charles turned his attention to his upcoming appointment. What could the finance minister want on such short notice? We've already made a $550-million loan to his government, and I've personally made a $5 million investment in Central Banco de la Republica de Argentina to demonstrate my confidence in the country's new fiscal and monetary reforms. Charles's personal fondness for Argentina started in the summer of 1968, after his sophomore year at Yale, when he lost his virginity to a beautiful Argentinean athlete he'd fallen in love with at Baraloche, a ski resort in the Andes. Later, on business trips to Buenos Aires, he came to appreciate the city's night life, its restaurants and sports venues, especially soccer.

At 10 a.m., Charles greeted the minister in the conference room. Petro Escobal's thick, dark framed glasses overwhelmed a handsome face. He was elegantly dressed in a dark suit. A pearl stick pin anchored his silk tie to a pale blue shirt. "Good morning, Senor Escobal. Some coffee? My secretary tells me it's from Argentina."

After passing on the personal regards of the Argentinean President, the minister thanked Charles for rearranging his schedule to meet on such short notice.

"My purpose in wanting to meet with you is to report our decision to default next week on our 20-million euro loan from France. We are now in the process of attempting to restructure the debt with Paris. But as you can well understand, the news of the default will affect our worldwide credit standing and certainly the value of our bonds held by Goldman. Tax revenues for the last quarter did not meet our expectation, primarily in the energy and agricultural sectors. However, we believe this is only a temporary situation, and by the end of calendar year, we will be reporting revenues in line with our projections."

In the course of giving this unexpected news to Charles, Escobal had crossed and recrossed his legs several times, while fidgeting with the knot in his tie. Charles thought about the unfavorable news stories that were bound to appear when the *Wall Street Journal* connected Goodman's investment in Argentina with that country's bond default. Charles also knew the default would severely devalue the Argentine bonds that Goodman held as collateral on their loan.

"Have you gone to the International Monetary Fund for assistance?" Charles asked, worried about the dreaded consequences for Goodman and also his own personal investment in Argentina.

"Yes, but they've demanded reforms we're unable to make in the time table they've set for us."

Charles asked a few additional questions and thought the answers evasive, if not misleading, without signaling his true feelings to Escobal. Charles continued, "I very much appreciate your taking the time to report this news to me in person. Your personal presence, I believe, strengthens our relationship with your government. If you tell me revenues will improve, I have no reason to doubt it." If fact, Goodman's recent research report made it abundantly clear that Argentina's recent economic downturn was more serious than first thought. Increasing inflation kept eating away at the country's gross national product. Goodman multi-million dollar loans were at risk, maybe even Charles' position as Chairman, and also Charles' personal investments in the country.

After the finance minister left, Charles wanted to relieve himself of his problems with Argentina and turned his attention to his newest investment. He put in a call to the ranch.

"John," Charles greeted the manager, when he answered the call at the ranch office. "On our flight back yesterday, Rigby brought up some issues we neglected to mention at our meeting. He will need a comprehensive inventory of all ranch improvements—barns, sheds, houses, buildings of any description, the estimated date of construction of each improvement and their estimated value. In addition, he's asked for an inventory of all livestock, number of horses, cows, calves, bulls, etc. and their combined value. It would probably make sense, John, to put this information into your computer for our ranch records and e-mail the data to Rigby with a copy to me."

"I can but it's going to take some time," John said.

"Not a problem; just so that we have it well before tax time, say in February. By the way, how many cows do we have?"

"As of last week it was 733, today it's 729."

"You mean four died?"

"Found 'em dead up in the forest two days after our fall gather earlier this week. Not a mark on any of them and, in two cases, with their calves standing right beside them."

"And you can't tell how they died?"

"It wasn't lightning and it didn't look like larkspur. They weren't bloated, just dead."

"Is Larkspur a neighbor?"

"No, it's a plant. If cows eat it in large amounts, it thickens their blood and they die. Not common in the fall, like now, but more likely to occur in May and June."

"But you don't know what killed the cows? Can't we have an autopsy so that we can have some assurance the rest of the herd is not at risk?"

"Look, Mr. Devlin, it's been my experience that a cow can die for any number of unexplained reasons. It could be brisket disease, or maybe a heart attack, or a piece of barbed wire in the stomach, or it could have been a virus. But if I had to have an autopsy for every cow on this ranch that died, you and I would be in hock to the vet into the next century."

"Well, that's not very reassuring," Charles responded in an exasperated tone.

John wanted to answer by saying that he'd damned well better get used to death since it was part and parcel of the cattle business. He thought better of it and asked Charles, "When are you planning to come to the ranch, Mr. Devlin?"

"John, please call me by my first name, Charles, not Charlie or Chuck, just plain Charles. I do want to get out to the ranch again as soon as possible. I've got some commitments here in New York and a trip to Chicago coming up. But I could come out the week after next. How does that work for you?"

"Fine. It's actually a good time to come since we'll be weaning calves and shipping."

"What will you do with the calves?"

"Well, we need to talk about that. We can ship them off to a feedlot and feed them up to slaughter weight, then sell them in the spring to a packer; or we can sell them off now to folks who specialize in feeding calves to slaughter weight. But if we send them off to a feedlot, we'll have another $400–$500 in each critter—that's the feed cost—maybe a total of as much as $250,000 by my quick figuring."

"What do you recommend?"

"Depends how this market is going to look next April. To be on the safe side, I'd recommend selling off all the calves, except for the replacement heifers. Let someone else take the risk."

"OK, but is there money to be made by retaining ownership, feeding the cattle, and selling them next spring?"

"Sure, but it all depends on the market."

"Sounds like the racket I'm in," Charles responded. "Let's wait to make the decision until I get to the ranch. In the meantime, I'd like you to prepare some figures on a spread sheet showing me what options we have for the cattle. While you're preparing figures for me, I'd also like to see a ranch budget for next year. I never saw one for this year, which I assume you prepared for National Open Land Conservancy. By the way, you mentioned replacement heifers. What are these?"

"These are the female calves we'll keep to replace some of the older cows who are no longer producing."

"Yes, we certainly need to be replacing the older cows. I'll get back to you in a day or so with my schedule. When I get to the ranch, I want to visit the house sites approved by NOLC in the easement."

John was beginning to understand that Devlin's business schedule took precedent over John's ranch schedule. Also, John recognized that the owner had much to learn about how a cattle ranch operated.

"Let me know your schedule when you've got it settled. I'm not going anywhere."

Charles detected a slight frostiness in the tone of John's response. He looked at the thick Argentinean file on his desk and thought of the possible disastrous scenarios that he might have to face in the months ahead.

CHAPTER FOUR

John Marlow didn't have the slightest idea how to prepare ranch expenses and income figures on a spread sheet. In fact, the computer provided to him by his former employer, the bank, remained something of a mystery. And when it came to assembling a comprehensive budget, he'd never encountered such a request. Yes, he could make some quick budget projections on a piece of paper, but as to transferring it into the computer, he remained clueless. He'd have asked his wife but, as John learned from his son, Jodi was now hooked up with the head of the parts department at the John Deere dealership in Cheyenne. Together, with her boyfriend's two teenage sons, she and Johnny had crowded themselves into a double wide trailer in Indian Hills, advertised as "Cheyenne's only gated mobile home park."

Ranch budgets had never guided the Diamond J Ranch. John's father and his grandfather before him knew what the ranch required in the way of equipment, feed and supplies, and had a fair idea of what price their cattle would sell for in the fall. Certainly they had made some major miscalculations over the years, particularly when the bottom dropped out of the cattle market in the late 80s, a catastrophe that forced the Diamond J into debt with an insurance company and the local bank. When the family hit rock bottom with their creditors, John's father had tried to explain to them that "even the best budget in the world couldn't have predicted the drop in the cattle market."

After the Marlows lost the ranch, John never put much faith in budgets. Those he prepared for the National Open Lands Conservancy, after they asked John to stay on as manager, was bare bones, less a guide for himself and the ranch than a document to satisfy the sharp pencils in New York. They told him to keep doing what he'd always done and do it the same way, but any expense over $1,000 had to be approved in New York. All bills went to NOLC and only occasionally did an unknown voice over the phone question him about an expense. It became very complicated when he tried to explain the necessity for a new and expensive drive sprocket on the New Holland baler. But after a while the accountant at NOLC stopped questioning John's decisions, in part, John thought, because he never could understand the answers. As John complained to the accountant after he repeatedly questioned the high cost of feed bills last winter, John reminded New York that "cattle have a tendency to die if not fed every day."

Devlin's Gulf Stream Five touched down at the Gunnison airport exactly on time. In preparation for Devlin's visit, John had washed the Dodge Ram diesel pickup, cleared out the tools from the truck's cab, which served as John's mobile office, and swept out the dirt, spent shell casings and used injection needles.

"A good flight, sir?" John asked, careful to add the "sir" to show deference to his new boss, who was dressed in his artificially faded, pressed blue jeans and a clean white Stetson.

"Right on time and no problems with the weather or the refueling stop in Kansas City," Charles responded, climbing into the truck, while the pilot followed behind, placing Charles' Gucci leather bag in the bed of the truck before returning to the plane.

They drove away in silence before John asked about Mrs. Devlin.

"She had to stay in New York for some meeting concerning her work with Central Park," Charles responded. Then he asked what was on the schedule for the next two days.

"We're going to start weaning the calves early tomorrow before it gets too hot, give the calves their shots, cull some old cows and ship the calves off by late morning when the trucks arrive. Then I'd like to show you around the ranch some more. You and Mrs. Devlin really didn't get to see everything when you came out last summer or last week. Also, tonight I thought we could go over some figures. We need to make a decision about the calves, whether to maintain ownership in a feedlot or sell them straight out at the sale barn this Friday. I told the trucker I'd let him know tonight if the calves were going to the Nebraska feedlot or the sale barn in La Junta."

"What about looking at the house sites?" Charles asked.

"We'll have time day after tomorrow. With the trucks ordered, I need to get these calves out of here tomorrow morning."

"I've already made the decision to maintain ownership. My people in New York think the cattle market will only strengthen into next year, aided primarily by a strong export market. What do you think?"

"Myself, I'd sell 'em right off. Folks I talk to think there'll be a drop in the market this winter; it's already dropped three dollars in the last two weeks and the futures market, I understand, don't look too good. Why pump more money into these calves with that kind of news?"

"I'm putting my trust in the judgment of my commodity people back in New York; they track these things on computer programs for a living. Plus, I'm a gambler," Charles concluded as he smiled over to John.

John was surprised by the decision and especially its timing. He had been led to believe from NOLC that Charles would thoroughly evaluate ranch matters before making changes, particularly personnel matters. Such was his style at Goodman, they assured him, and one expected it to be no different at the ranch. Why had Devlin, or was it Rigby, wasted my time asking me to put together these figures, John thought, if he was going to listen only to the advice of his "commodity boys"?

They drove on in silence until John announced: "I hope you'll find the homestead house comfortable during your stay." Charles knew from his last visit that the small, single-story log house was the oldest structure on the ranch, built by John's grandfather in the 1890s. "I had the wife of our hired man, Josh, clean it this week; also moved a sitting chair and desk in from my house to make it more comfortable. There's food in the fridge for breakfast, and Qwest is due out in the morning to fix the phone."

"I'm sure it will be fine," Charles answered, hiding his annoyance that he'd be without a phone until at least mid-morning at the earliest. His cell phone connection at the ranch proved unreliable on his last visit, and for Charles, a phone was as vital to his existence as food. To be without it in Colorado put him at great risk back in New York, a situation Charles knew his manager would not understand.

Charles reminded himself before he departed for the ranch that he'd have to show patience, not one of his renowned qualities, as his wife constantly reminded him. He knew the homestead house would be uncomfortable, with the warped door that wouldn't shut and windows that leaked the constant wind. On his previous visit after the closing, he had opened the drawer of the oak dresser and found a clump of cotton and wool hairballs, clearly the winter headquarters for some rodent, probably a rat. The cabin, Charles figured, hadn't seen a repair since the day it served as an "improvement" for Caleb Marlow's homestead claim back in the late 19th century. And, after an afternoon bumping about in a pickup, the sagging double bed would aggravate the lower back strain he suffered two weeks ago playing golf. John's culinary skills, he remembered, consisted of whatever Mr. Campbell put in a soup can or Mrs. Swanson's newest creation for John's mini-microwave. John said last summer that his "cooking was better than the meals served in town at the Qwick Stop," a gourmet comparison Charles did not wish to test.

Charles put his mind to the purpose of the trip. He wanted to get a better sense of his manager: how would he take suggestions, particularly about the appearance of the ranch? To Charles's eye, the headquarters appeared untidy, an unattractive mess. John's two-story frame house desperately needed a paint job. The weathered siding had warped and in places peeled away from the house, like blistered skin off a sunbather. Little clumps of dead grass and weeds surrounded two unattended and thirsty fruit trees. Tall untrimmed lilac bushes hid the dirty front windows while the front porch had long ago detached itself from the house and slid off in the direction of Kansas City. The second story windows were covered by sheets of thin plastic, what John proudly referred to as "cowboy insulation." A discarded mattress with an empty dog bowl rested against the outer wall of the unpainted wooden, two-car garage. An old low slung log barn, with its sagging roof, stood across the rutted dirt yard, more out of habit than in conformance with any law of physics. Old equipment—a rusted plow, a hay rake missing most of its teeth, and the bed off a faded red pickup—was scattered about the yard along with rolls of wire and a pile of fence posts—all arranged, no doubt, by one of the valley's infamous wind storms.

Charles needed to learn from John more about the operation of the ranch—the method of irrigation, the equipment and the cattle. He would also need to locate the site for the family's new ranch house, a promise he had made to his wife before closing on the ranch. Once the site was selected, Charles would fly out the architect from New York, and together they'd put together a house plan, a tentative budget, and then arrange for construction to start in late spring.

Yet above all, Charles wanted to establish a workable and friendly arrangement with John, something he hadn't found time for on his two previous visits. He hoped that the arrangement would quickly translate into personal loyalty, a trait Charles demanded from his employees in New York. In short, he needed to hire, as he said to Amanda before he left New York, a "stock manager with a saddle and a horse. Someone who won't lose me a pile of money and who can bring a profit to the bottom line, hopefully within a year." He had also reminded her: "I employ professionals in New York almost every month without knowing the nitty gritty details of their work—the same applies to John Marlow. Running a ranch is not rocket science. God grows the grass and the cows eat it. Very basic, my dear."

At dinner that evening over what was for Charles, a too-well done T-bone, John asked if he found the cabin comfortable.

"Looks like you brought in Martha Stewart," Charles said.

"Who's Martha Stewart?"

"Never mind," Charles replied, waving his hand to dismiss his unappreciated humor.

"One matter I need to explain to you is the importance of Rigby to the oversight of all of my properties. He will be involved, as I believe I told you at our last meeting, in many of the financial decisions regarding the ranch operation. In many ways, you'll be in contact with Rigby more often than me."

"Charles, I really don't need much direction or supervision. I know how to run this place. What I learned from my granddad and dad still applies today. When I worked for Dad, the hours went from sunup in New York to sundown in Hawaii. I know every inch of this ranch, including fences, buildings, irrigation ditches, hay meadows and the dry spots that go with them. I can tell you which head gate was built when and by whom, which cows weaned off 500-pound calves, and what neighbor will lend a hand during branding and who comes only for the beer. There's not much that needs to be changed around here, except the water every day, maybe some fences, a few repairs and the replacement of some very old equipment. But I don't need direction. I know what to do and when to do it, and sometimes what not to do." John hoped the statement would be carried back to New York, especially to Rigby's office.

Then Charles put the hard question to John. "How, with all the ranching experience you and your family had accumulated over the years, did you manage to lose the Diamond J to your creditors?"

John was prepared for the question. "You have to go back to my granddad who, with his brother, put this place together with borrowed money. After the death of Granddad and the departure of my uncle, those debts passed to Dad, and he added to them with some questionable land purchases. In hindsight, he told me once, 'I probably shouldn't have bought the Pierce Place.' At the time he thought the neighboring ranch, a 7,000-acre place that adjoined us, could make us a better operation. Good water, meadows and spring pasture, which we were short of. The debt on that Pierce place hung over us, and we had to mortgage the rest of the ranch to make the payments. We only dug ourselves deeper into debt. Then, in the mid-80s the cattle market went to hell, prices dropped 30 percent, then more debt, even after selling off 350 cows. Then Dad had his stroke. My wife and I couldn't take care of him properly so we put him in an assisted living facility in Gunnison. More expenses. They just seemed to overwhelm us. That's when we were forced to declare bankruptcy. The rest you probably know. The First National in Cheyenne took title to part of the ranch, including the cattle, and the insurance company took the rest. Dad and I were left with virtually nothing. That's when NOLC showed up and put the ranch back together with their purchase from the bank and the insurance company.

They damned well got themselves a good ranch at a good price. Then you purchased it, and here we are."

"Couldn't you and your dad have sold off part of the ranch to keep it going?" Charles asked.

"Yes, but Dad wouldn't hear of it. Every time we looked at what to sell off, he'd say we couldn't do that. 'It'd ruin the whole operation.' He had it worked out in his mind that every acre had its use at a particular time of year. Couldn't sell off this piece because it was critical spring pasture. Couldn't sell off that piece because it was important to our hay production. And couldn't part with the bull pasture—where would they go when not with the cows?"

"How long did your dad live in the assisted living facility?"

"Just over a year. He died a vegetable, weighed about 90 pounds. I couldn't stand visiting him. It seemed every time I saw him he looked more wasted. For the last year, I don't think he recognized me; he just stared at the ceiling with tubes dangling from his arm and nose. Doctors told me he had a chance of recovery, so we kept praying, but he just got worse and, with the miserable insurance we had, his condition just sucked up a lot more money. It is amazing how a body can waste away. Before his stroke he was a strapping hulk of muscle that no young man would want to challenge, Hell, he had muscles in his fingers that most men would be proud of in their arms. He threw 80-pound hay bales around as if they were lumps of coal. Then, two years later he just melted away and stopped breathing. Painless, really, but sad. I miss him very much."

Charles could see the tears forming in John's eyes, and immediately changed the subject.

As the two finished their conversation over dinner, Charles announced, "Time for me to turn in. What time tomorrow morning?"

"Plan to be at the corrals at six-thirty, and dress warm, it'll be chilly. We'll gather the cattle on horseback, and then separate off the calves in the sorting alley and give them their shots. I'm hoping we can begin loading the trucks by about ten-thirty"

"Thanks for supper, see you at six-thirty."

Charles returned to the cabin, found his cell phone actually worked and called Amanda to check in. After receiving news that everything at home sounded normal, he lay on the uneven mattress worrying about his minimal riding skills and how they might be challenged the following day. Then Charles remembered that a good cowman, according to John's father, was someone who could "think like a cow." But, for lack of experience or any reference point, that might be difficult, Charles thought. It wasn't as if he could call upon one of his former professors at the Harvard Business School, and ask if he could recommend some reading on how to "think like a cow." An entrepreneur, yes. But a cow, no.

Without coming up with an answer, Charles fell asleep in the cool mountain air of the Rockies.

CHAPTER FIVE

The next morning, Charles' horse was saddled and waiting for him at the corrals. John stood with two men sipping hot coffee and leaning against their saddled horses.

"Charles, this is Josh Webster. Been with us for almost two years. Lives with his family in the double-wide down behind the corrals." As he gave Charles a close inspection, Josh's glum countenance hid his usual buoyant and jovial nature. His short frame appeared ill-suited for his broad chest and muscular arms. Charles couldn't help but notice his green eyes staring directly at him. Then John turned and said, "And this here is Jeff, a neighbor, comes over to help when the coffee's hot and the beer is plentiful. Been known to take a trophy elk off this ranch and not always in season. Right, Jeff?"

Jeff smiled and took a sip of coffee as Charles shook hands with Josh and Jeff. He noticed their tough callused hands as the two men put a hard squeeze on Charles' soft hand. Pointing to a saddled horse and addressing Charles, John said: "And this is Ginger. She's a gentle sweetheart and smart with cow sense. Just give her a loose rein and point her towards the cows, she'll do the rest. We're going out into the home pasture, where we put the cattle we gathered off the forest last week. It will be an easy gather. Move 'em slowly and they'll go right towards the corrals. Anything real lame that can't keep up, let 'em drop back and we'll pick'em up later."

Charles inspected Ginger, not knowing exactly what to look for in an equine, except maybe for ears laid back, a wild look in white eyes, and snot blowing from its nose. He hadn't been on a horse in over a year, not since he rode one on a beach in Mexico during the boys' spring vacation. Ginger looked gentle enough and, like Charles, didn't show a great deal of enthusiasm for the work at hand. Charles did notice what appeared to be a new saddle on her, and commented about it to John.

"Just finished it last week," John said. "It's 15 inches in the seat, I hope it's comfortable. Check the stirrups. Look a little short from here. See how they feel."

Charles threw his left leg up towards the stirrup and missed. He caught it on the second try and then mounted the horse as if he were climbing a 6-foot wall off a short step ladder. Josh only added to Charles' embarrassment when he had to boost him into the saddle.

John had Charles stand in the stirrups. "Yep, a bit short. I'll let them out two notches, they'll feel more comfortable." Off they trotted into the home pasture with Charles unable to coordinate his weight and balance with Ginger's gentle trot.

Charles watched as the other men circled around the outside of the cattle with the two work dogs. The two cowboys gave a quick whistle to get the cow's attention and then moved slowly towards the cows and their calves. When one calf broke from the herd, a dog instantly ran up behind it nipping at its heels, a lesson to the calf to stay with its mother. Charles rode up close to John, from whom he could take a lead. John was careful like the other riders to not push too aggressively and close to the cows. They were moving towards the corral gate at their own leisurely pace when all of a sudden, one cow that had momentarily lost sight of her calf turned back and broke from the herd. Ginger, in an instinctive reaction, moved sharply to her left to cut off the cow's retreat. The horse's quick spin off its back legs caught Charles by surprise. He grabbed the saddle horn and barely remained mounted. For the rest of the morning, he rode with one hand wrapped tightly around the horn and the other held tightly to the rein while mumbling sweet messages to Ginger.

John noticed the near accident and figured he'd be giving riding lessons in the future. He rode up to Charles and casually commented "nice recovery." As they continued pushing the herd towards the corrals, Josh rode ahead to open the gate for the cattle. They headed directly to the hole. From the back of the herd, the riders continued to put gentle pressure on the cows and calves to move on ahead. Again, another cow broke back against the riders. John wheeled his horse quickly into the cow's path to push her back to the herd. Charles noticed that John had performed the small task quickly and quietly, without the hoopla he'd come to expect from watching Hollywood westerns at the cinema on New York's Lexington Avenue.

Once in the corral, the cows bawled for their calves, and amid the noise and dust, the cowboy crew pushed about a quarter of the herd into the sorting alley, where the riders dismounted. John placed Charles at the back of the cattle in the sorting alley where he believed his boss could cause the least amount of havoc during the sorting and weaning process.

John directed his instructions to everyone, but primarily to Charles. "Just keep gentle pressure from the back of the herd, while I sort off the calves from the cows at the front. The mommas will pretty much peel themselves off, slide along the edge of the sorting alley and find the open gate into their own pen. It's the calves that can cause the headaches. Just take it slow, boys, and we'll be finished in an hour or so."

Again, Charles watched closely to observe the work. On foot, he and Josh walked up on the cattle, snapping their whips at the cattle to make them move in John's direction where he, with a sorting stick and a gate behind him, quickly and efficiently peeled the calves off into their own pen. After working half the herd, John suggested a coffee break and then, to break the monotony of the work, asked Charles if he might want to work with him at the front of the herd. All he needed to do was work the Powder River steel gate, keep the cows from entering the calves' pen and throw the gate quickly against the side of the alley, to close the opening and prevent a cow from following its calf. It looked easy enough, Charles thought. "Yes, let me give it a try," he replied and exchanged places with Jeff.

The men went back to sorting. Almost immediately, a cow slipped through Charles' guard, then another, and another. John tried to help and calm the frustrated gate keeper. "Charles, you've got to anticipate how a cow will think. It will usually want to follow a calf. So you need to think like a cow, which is to say, not too fast," John advised with a slight smile.

"I'm working at it," Charles responded as he attempted to regain his composure at the gate. Once again, a renegade cow made for the opening to the calf pen. Charles threw the gate to close off the calf pen and stop the cow. Instead, the gate caught the cow on its neck and pinned her to the side of the alley. He moved quickly to pull the gate back off the cow. As he did, the cow kicked hard at the gate. It swung back fast and caught Charles on the bridge of his nose. Blood flew off in the direction of his hat, as Charles lay semi-conscious on the ground. John rushed over, retrieved Charles' hat and asked, "You OK?"

"Yeah, I think the cow's mental process was a bit quicker than mine." He pulled a handkerchief from his pocket, dabbed at the wound, and said: "Let's get back at it." John had Josh take Charles' place at the gate, and within minutes had fashioned a butterfly bandage for the cut over the swollen bridge of Charles' nose. After an hour, the calves and cows had been separated.

The sorting process continued as the steer calves were separated from the heifers. John explained to Charles that he needed to select about 130 heifers to replace the older cows that would be culled later in the day. "The culls," John explained, "are typically nine-year-old cows or older; they've raised a calf every year though after they reach seven or eight, their milk production begins to drop and their calves are smaller. We'll cull cows also with a cancer eye, a bad bag, missing teeth, and those, like the two we dropped back in the pasture this morning, that come up lame after the summer grazing season."

He continued his cattle lesson for Charles' benefit. "I'm looking for heifers that I believe will eventually make good cows. I know most of the heifer calves. And from their ear-tag number, I can tell the age of their momma. In most cases, I know the momma and her past production, so I'm looking for a good-sized heifer that is long in the flank, has a good hip for calving ease, is feminine in looks, and has some good breeding behind her."

"They all look the same to me except for the color," Charles said, referring to the pen of 370 heifers, most solid red or black, and a few with a patch of white on their head.

John entered the pen of heifers and selected replacements one at a time, transferring each calf to Josh, who guided the heifer into a separate holding pen for the replacements tended by Jeff. The selection process lasted an hour, before John called for a count.

"One-twenty-five," Jeff shouted above the noise of the bawling calves.

John slipped into the pen and culled out six more heifers, placed them with the larger group of heifers destined for the feedlot, and then moved the group into the shipping pen with the steers. The shipping pen led into a narrow alley and extended to the loading ramp against which a cattle truck had backed. "We'll give them their shots in the alley before loading," John announced to his crew. From a box behind the squeeze chute, John brought out the injection guns, and from the Coleman cooler, the medicine bottles. Josh and Jeff began filling the glass canisters with medicine.

"What's the medicine?" Charles asked.

"It's a seven-way medicine for shipping fever, black leg, pneumonia and a bunch of other stuff I can't remember," John responded. "Better we give the shots here than in the feedlot. At least we know it's done and it's far less expensive for us this way."

Josh and Jeff moved quickly along the outside alley ramp, leaning over to inject each calf as it moved down the line. As the calves loaded slowly onto the trucks, urged on by John with an electric prod, Josh and Jeff reloaded the alley with calves and again commenced giving shots. Charles looked on in amazement at the smooth process, how everyone knew his job and moved accordingly, as if in a choreographed dance. For Charles the work in the corrals differed considerably from his romantic vision of cowboys galloping across the horizon on their steeds. The noise, dust and smell of fresh manure only added to the danger of working close to 500-pound calves, whose anxiety had been heightened by the separation from their mothers and the numerous needles stuck into their necks or flanks.

It was eleven-thirty when the trucks pulled out of the ranch headed for the Nebraska feedlot. The replacement heifers bawled in their pen in an octave higher than the cows, which had crowded back into the corral looking unsuccessfully for their calves, all of which, except for the replacement heifers, were headed to the feedlot.

The men retired to the barn, where they unsaddled their horses.

"How's the nose?" John shouted over the noise of the bawling calves.

"Throbs a bit but the bleeding has stopped. That saddle you made, it's comfortable."

"I'm glad you like it. I love making a good working saddle. Besides, they bring me in some extra income, especially the trophy saddles. The All-Around Cowboy at the county's Labor Day rodeo gets one every year. I sell 'em to the rodeo association for $3,500 a piece. Nice piece of change. Also, I sell less expensive ones, like the one you rode this morning, to local cowboys. They're custom-ordered—style, seat size, rigging, amount of tool work and type of leather. Mostly roper models, nothing too fancy, that's the demand, at least around these parts."

"Where'd you learn the saddle-making skill?" Charles inquired.

"My granddad mostly and also my dad. My granddad was famous for his saddles and horses. A couple of his trophy saddles are in the Cowboy Hall of Fame in Oklahoma, and some of his quarter horses won cutting events. But he mostly sold to the Army until McArthur decided to exchange horses for tanks after World War One. Granddad always said it was a damned foolish decision by the Army."

"Yeah, I remember that General Patton was an old cavalry officer before he mounted a tank," Charles answered.

"That's right. In the house, I'll show you a photograph of Major Patton on one of Granddad's horses at Fort Riley in Kansas. 'A fine polo pony,' Patton wrote on the signed photograph. I've got the picture to this day."

"Your family goes back a long way here in Colorado," Charles said, hoping the observation might solicit more family history.

"Yes, my great-granddad came out here from western Iowa to mine in the 1870s, got himself an eye injury in a mining accident and decided to take up ranching. When the Ute Indians were removed from here in 1879, he filed on a homestead; you're staying in the original homestead house. Soon afterwards, his brother joined him and filed on another adjacent homestead up above us near the forest; I'll show it to you this afternoon. The hired man, as a condition of his employment, filed on yet another homestead. By the turn of the century, the ranch had expanded to 2,400 acres. My granddad, with money from his cattle, but primarily from his horse sales to the Army and some borrowed money from the bank, bought out some of his neighbors and doubled the size of the ranch. Right after Dad inherited the place, the cow market headed south, and it kept going in that direction for longer than the family cares to remember. In addition, he made some mistakes, as you know, and combined with some bad luck, the rest is history."

John hesitated before concluding: "And now it's yours." Wishing to change the subject, John suggested they head to his house for a sandwich before touring the ranch.

The clapboard house sat at the center of what was considered the ranch headquarters. Close by, a weathered wooden barn protected stacks of horse hay, bags of grain and mineral block for the cattle. An adjacent storage shed housed two old John Deere tractors, a disabled '57 Ford pickup on blocks, a baler and hay rake. To the east, the small wooden pump house squatted in the spruce trees and the tack room and covered saddling area sat just off the east end of the corrals.

The four men entered the house through the back mudroom. "Excuse the mess, the cleaning lady comes tomorrow," John said with a smile. "First time in a couple of years," Josh added. With empty dog bowls scattered about, the enclosed porch had the appearance of a kennel but the smell of a corral on a hot summer day. Galoshes and boots, crusted with manure, competed for room on the dirty floor with two pairs of muddy and frayed coveralls that served as bedding for the dogs. An empty Swanson frozen food carton and an empty Alpo can sat atop the brimming trash container. Sweat-stained cowboy hats, straw and felt, and caps advertising Wilson Angus Bulls, Silver Valley Ready Mix, John Deere, and King Ropes clung to walls like splattered mud balls.

They entered the kitchen that John had managed to put in some semblance of order after his early breakfast. "Nice home you have here," Charles said as he looked from the kitchen into what John used as an office and TV lounge.

"Yeah, it's comfortable and certainly big enough for me to rattle around in now that Jodi, my ex, and my boy are gone. Been a bachelor for over a month now. My son comes down from Cheyenne from time to time to help out when we need an extra hand. Good kid, smart, too. He's off to college next year; wants to be a forester. I tell him, it's one hell of a lot better than being a cowboy."

"You got that right," Josh chimed in.

John put together some bologna and cheese sandwiches and laid out the work for the afternoon.

"Mr. Devlin and I are off on a tour of the ranch. I want you two to sort off the cows we've already identified for culling. If you forget, the ear-tag numbers are in the cow book in the tack room. Also, I want that red baldy with the broken horn to go. She's a mean little bitch who'll get someone hurt. If you see any others that look like they should go down the road, put them in the pen with the culled bulls and mark their numbers in the cow book. Put some hay in there and be sure the cattle fill up on water. I'll look at them tomorrow before the truck shows up to take them to the Brush sale barn."

After Charles and John finished their meal, Charles said he wanted to put a new dressing on his wound and also get the ranch maps he had brought out from New York. He walked back to the cabin feeling a bit embarrassed by his ineptitude on horseback and in the sorting alley. But regardless of the day's accident, he felt exhilarated by participating in the ranch's activities. As he changed the bloody bandage on his nose, collected up maps and his camera, Charles reminded himself how he must focus on thinking like a cow.

"There are two spots I'd like to spend some time at this afternoon," Charles announced. "The conservation easement only allows two building sites for new construction. They're red-lined on the maps I brought with me. We're allowed to build or add onto ranch structures here at the headquarters complex. But my preference is to be away from headquarters, its noise and dust, and be off somewhere secluded with good views of the mountains. I've been told by NOLC that the two sites they selected fit that description."

Charles again reviewed the conditions of the easement with John. "I think I forgot to tell you that the water can't be sold off, no mining and no logging for commercial purposes."

"Yes, you already mentioned that to me. Hell, as far as I know, there ain't any minerals around here or my granddad would have discovered 'em. As for timber, it's mostly aspen and scrub oak, some black timber up high, but not very much. Sounds to me like you didn't have to give up much to get the tax benefits."

"That's the way I figured," Charles said.

"Here are the places I want to inspect closely," Charles said leaning close to the map and pointing at the red-lined areas.

John looked at the designated areas on the map and immediately recognized one of the building sites.

"Oh shit," he said under his breath.

CHAPTER SIX

The two men made their way out through the home pasture past the bellowing cows crowding the corral fence. They drove the pickup to the far end of the hay meadow, up and across an irrigation ditch, through another meadow with its fenced stack yard filled with baled hay, and then onto a rutted ranch road that led higher into an aspen grove.

Charles looked at his map to orient himself.

"Here?" Charles asked pointing to the map.

"No," John responded as he pointed to a different location. "Right here where the road enters the southern edge of Section Fourteen." Charles looked at the map, oriented himself again and noticed the indicated elevation at 7,500 feet. He also noticed for the first time that John had lost the tip of his index finger on his left hand.

"OK, just ahead then is the first of the two designated building sites." About a hundred yards ahead, Charles saw a clearing and above it a small flat-top hill. "That must be it there," he announced. John pulled the truck to the base of the hill, and Charles jumped out with his camera. Surrounded by aspens, the site had gorgeous views in three directions, particularly to the north where in the distance the snow-capped Rocky Mountains broke above a timbered hillside in the foreground. Charles photographed the site and its views from all angles.

"What a beautiful setting! Look at the sun on those snow-covered mountains," Charles declared. "To gain even better views, we could build up on that hill and not endanger any of the surrounding trees."

"Much of it will depend upon where you find water up here," John answered. "You'll have to dig a well, or pump it up from the irrigation ditch down below. In any event, it could be an expensive proposition. Fortunately, there's a road into here. It's not very good but it can be improved, and it's an easy grade allowing for winter access."

"Winter access is important," Charles responded, "since I hope to spend time here skiing." He continued," I love the views and so will Amanda and the boys."

John asked when he planned to start construction.

"As soon as we have plans. We should be ready certainly by next spring," Charles answered.

It figured, right when we're busy with calving, the busiest time of year, John thought.

"Now I want to see the other site," Charles announced.

"It's a special place," John responded as he continued down the ranch road and then onto what appeared to be a narrow jeep path. He geared down and shifted into four-wheel drive as they began to climb through the timber. They came to a good-sized stream that flowed through a wooden irrigation box.

"This is Wapiti Creek, the maps call it Cabin Creek, but we've always referred to it as Wapiti. That wooden structure is the divider box where we divert our irrigation water for the south end of the ranch," John announced as Charles looked at the map. They crossed over a log bridge to the uphill side, stopped, and got out.

"This is the other building site marked on your map," John said. He knew the site well. The tall grass clearing with its southern exposure was surrounded by aspens just beginning to turn color and in the background, an expansive view to the mountains. The rock-lined creek bisected the lush meadow before meandering off to the east through another aspen grove.

"This was my granddad's favorite spot on the Diamond J," John declared. "His brother, my great-uncle, homesteaded this part of the ranch. Granddad called this place 'the birthing chamber.' He wouldn't allow cattle to graze in here, always wanted to save it for the elk. Every spring, they'd move in here to birth their calves. Here, in the protection of these giant aspens, they're sheltered from the wind, and with plenty of feed and no folks around to bother 'em." John continued: "On holidays, when I was kid, we'd come here for picnics. That tree over there has my initials carved on it from when I was eight. My brother's initials are just above mine and above his, Dad's and Granddad's." Charles walked over to inspect the blackened initials on the white bark. Other trees were similarly scarred by the teeth marks of elk that had, over the years, chewed into the bark for winter nutrients.

As John continued, it was as if he was recounting memories for himself rather than Charles. "On the fourth of July every year, Granddad would organize a fishing derby for me and my brother Clyde. After flipping a coin, I'd go in one direction along Wapiti Creek and my brother would go in the opposite direction. The rules were that we'd fish for three hours and then return here to the picnic site for the official weigh in. My granddad always warned us: 'No worms allowed, only bugs, flies or grasshoppers.' He always presented the winner with a terrific present. One year, I remember, it was a horse-hair head stall made by the Crow up in Montana. My brother got that one. Another year, I won a pair of tooled spur straps made by Granddad. That was the year I thought my brother had won. But Granddad cut into the stomach of a fat brown trout only to find an undigested worm. He carefully extracted it from the fish's gullet, held it up and wiggled it before Clyde's nose and gave him a killer stare. 'Don't ever do that again.' he said. Naturally I was delighted to win the spur straps. There're a bit worn, but I still use 'em to this day. We had some good times here, with family and neighbors."

"Sounds like your granddad taught you more than fishing," Charles added.

The question dug deep into John's memories of his granddad. "Yeah, he was a hard task master but a good teacher. When he laid out a line for us to fence, he wanted it straight, the posts exactly 12 feet apart and the corner posts dug no less than 4 feet into the ground. One summer after my brother and I put in a line of fence, Granddad came along in his jeep to inspect our work. One of the corner posts looked to him as if it had been sawed off at the top, which it had, and that it might not be set to his 4-foot standard. To test his theory, he backed up his jeep and hit the post with the bumper. Sure enough, the post popped out of the ground. He ordered us to reset all the corner posts and added for emphasis, 'this time be sure to set them 4 feet in the ground like I told you.'"

John continued, "Up until he was 80, he could rope a calf running through the timber. And the spring before he died, I watched him do a C-section on a cow; he saved both the cow and calf. There wasn't much he couldn't do on the ranch and if he couldn't do it, he always said, 'it wasn't worth doing in the first place.' A tough old bird. Dad always said of his father that he was born with the bark on his hide and died with it still in place but only thicker. It'd be 20 years ago this August that Granddad said he needed to ride up here to check this irrigation box. When he didn't return for dinner, Dad went looking for him. Found him right over there, leaned up against a tree with his shovel, dead of a heart attack, and his horse standing right by him. Dad laid him over the saddle and led him back home."

John neglected to inform Charles that his grandfather was buried beneath a large flat stone about 20 feet from where they were standing. John's dad had wanted to keep it a secret within the family; he marked the grave with a flat stone where the family would lay flowers every Fourth of July. Sometimes, when the snow wasn't too deep, they'd ride up on Memorial Day and take lilacs to honor their ancestor, a World War I veteran. John, like his father before him, thought the "birthing chamber" a special place, where God delivered life and took some lives back and returned them to his pocket. John sure as hell wasn't going to share with Mr. Devlin the secrets of the ground. Devlin wouldn't understand the sacred nature of this "building site."

As Charles and John bumped along the rutted road back to ranch headquarters, John broke the silence, "What's your thought on the sites?"

"I sure like the last site, fantastic views, it has access, though it will have to be improved, there's water nearby, and I'm sure the elk can find themselves another calving spot."

It was all that John could do to control his anger. The thought of a house in the "birthing chamber" violated every memory John had of the sacred site, I have no intention of reburying my grandfather, father and mother, John thought. What in hell is wrong with the other site and what did a bunch of New York conservationists know about the history of the Diamond J and the family who founded it? Why hadn't they asked me about this small meadow before they selected it as a building site? Careful, don't say anything that might jeopardize a job offer, John reminded himself. Maybe Charles could be dissuaded this evening over dinner, he thought.

Charles changed into a clean pair of pressed jeans and then poured himself a generous portion of Johnny Walker from the flask he pulled from his Gucci briefcase. His head throbbed as he replaced the bandage and noticed in the mirror the discoloration beginning to form beneath both eyes. At dinner in John's kitchen he picked at his venison steak as if it were a jellyfish, turned to John and asked: "What sort of salary are you looking for?"

"Fifty-thousand would suit me fine," and then John added, "plus some health benefits, and the opportunity to run 40 cows of my own, run them together with yours. I'd pay the vet bills and reimburse you the cost of any supplemental feed; they'd have my brand on 'em, the bar M."

"Sounds reasonable to me. What about help?"

"I'd like to keep Josh on. He's a good hand. Thirty-thousand would keep him, plus health benefits. Other help I need seasonally, I usually hire by the hour and provide room and board if they're any good. I use the homestead cabin during haying season and other occasions when I need some extra help."

"I'll have New York send out the necessary paperwork. Rigby will find a medical and insurance plan for you and Josh and he'll set up an IRA account for you. As for running your own cattle, I see no problem as long as the numbers and the associated expenses are reasonable. Have you figured these labor costs into your new budget?" Charles asked.

"For sure," John responded as he pulled from his pocket the budget he'd worked up just for the occasion. He handed it to Charles, who gave it a careful review.

He noticed the large expenditure under the heading, "capital costs."

"What's this for?"

"We're going to need a new baler, and we could sure use a replacement for the 1955 John Deere that has seen better days, something powerful enough to pull a high capacity baler. We're puttin' more money into that tractor with repairs than what we originally paid for it. The other big item is for fencing. We can do it cheaper if we hire a fence crew, have them replace some fences, charge us time and materials, rather than hire some extra help and do it ourselves, which we don't have time for. We can, however, continue to do the maintenance. Some fences are over 80 years old, standing up only out of habit."

"On the income side, I see you've projected cattle sales considerably higher than last year. Why is that?" Charles asked.

"Well, you remember you made the decision to maintain ownership of the calves through the winter at the feedlot. They'll be worth a lot more when they're ready for sale and slaughter next April. But you'll see the extra feed costs on the expense side."

Charles had missed the extra costs in the expense column. "Yeah, looks like a big ticket item, those feed costs."

"They sure are," John responded. "I hope your projections about the market come true. If they do, I figure we're looking at a profit of close to $80,000."

"My commodity boys in New York are sharp," Charles responded with an air of confidence. He was disappointed with the profit figure but had enough confidence in his business acumen that he could, over the years, improve the margin. After their budget discussion, Charles felt added confidence in his manager.

"A couple of other issues. My lawyer is concerned about liability matters. He advises us not to allow outsiders to help or hunt on the ranch, like the neighbor who helped us this morning. There are other neighbors, I understand, who come in every year to hunt. The liability exposure for me is immense."

John looked hard at his new boss. No, it wasn't a suggestion, he thought, rather an order. "I let neighbors who help us on the ranch from time to time come in to hunt. They wouldn't accept money if I pushed it on them. Everyone wants to help at branding time and roundups. It is the neighborly thing to do … been doin' it for years. I do it for my neighbors when they're shorthanded, Dad did it and so did Granddad. The guys who help at branding and roundup have come to expect the hunting privilege. It'd be hard to stop."

"Well," Charles responded with curtness, "It's got to stop. Another thing, these neighbors who come on the ranch, what happens if they get injured like I did this morning? They could, as I understand from my attorney, sue me and the ranch. One major lawsuit could bring me down—loss of the ranch and other assets. I'm not willing to run that risk just to placate the neighbors and I don't think you should either."

"Charles, believe me. I know my neighbors well enough not to have to worry about them. I just worry about gettin' the work done. We've not had the money to hire extra hands when we needed them. I depend on my neighbors the same way they depend on me. It's the way we do things around here, have for generations."

"I'm sorry but you're going to have to change your ways, and I'm going to have to pay for the extra hands. There's no other way around it."

John tried to hide his irritation. How would he explain these new ridiculous rules to his friends and neighbors?

"Shit."

Charles witnessed for the first time John's temper. He tried to humor his new manager. "Amanda would be horrified to know that our neighbors come onto the ranch to kill our elk. Besides, think of all the elk you'll have for yourself."

John hesitated to respond, recognizing that Charles wouldn't understand that a mature cow or bull elk eats as much grass as a cow. The reason John wanted his neighbors to hunt on the ranch was to keep the elk herd to a manageable size. In the winter they were a constant annoyance around the stack yards, breaking through the wooden panels to get to the hay. And in the spring they could graze through some pastures and clean out the new grass in a matter of days. He'd have to educate the Devlins at some later date about the damage caused by wildlife.

Charles then turned the conversation to the site for his home. "I much preferred the second site, the one your grandfather named the 'birthing chamber.' The views are fabulous, there is water nearby and, I believe, the access is easier than the first site."

John mentioned the disturbance to the elk, to which Charles responded without hesitation, "They'll just have to find another place to calve. There must be other places on the ranch or up in the forest." Then John exaggerated the difficulties with the access and the possibility of an intermittent supply of water from an unreliable spring. Charles responded, "I'm sure we can make it work." John wanted to mention the graves at the "calving chamber" site, but he could not bring himself to talk about them. He feared Charles would demand that they too be moved, like wild animals to another site.

Charles broke the silence with the suggestion that it was time to turn in.

John stood to clear the dishes from the table and then reminded Charles, "We need to leave here by eight to make your departure time at nine."

"I'll be ready."

Charles used the driving time to the airport to ask questions about the cattle, their genetic background, the location and ownership of the feedlot, the process by which the cattle would sell in the spring, and the issue of cattle brands. But foremost on Charles' mind continued to be the issue of his new dwelling. He let it be known to John that he and his family could not enjoy the ranch if they were confined to the homestead cabin for any length of time. Also, Charles felt he could not ask John to vacate his home for the Devlin family, given the physical and emotional disruption the move would cause.

Charles addressed his manager while trying to pencil some notes in the moving truck. "After I get back to New York, I'll be talking with my architect about the house and then send him out here in about two weeks. I could tell you're not happy with the 'birthing chamber' site but it is far better than the first one we looked at. You do understand, I hope, that our choices of where to build are limited by the easement restrictions."

"Couldn't the easement restrictions be changed to another site? I can show you dozens of similar sites on the ranch."

"It would be difficult, not to mention the time it would take with lawyers. I need a house in place by the end of next summer at the latest."

For John, the issue seemed decided. He let Charles know that house construction was not one of his skills, and that come spring, he didn't have time to pound nails when he'd be busy calving.

"You won't have to worry about the construction. The architect will hire a full crew and supervisor. I'll need your recommendation, however, for sub-contractors."

"Depends on how fancy you want to get, and the size of the house."

Charles then explained his thoughts for a house. "Something that blends into the natural environment, log and stone construction, with large picture windows to let in light and the spectacular views, and a comfortable porch facing the mountains. At least four bedrooms, each with its own bath, a country kitchen, a 'great room' arched by huge timbers, a small cozy library with a wet bar adjacent to the living room, and a large rock double fireplace which can heat both the library and the living room. In all, I figure about 10,000 square feet, excluding the three-car garage. Also, I'd like to have a separate office. I haven't decided yet about a guest house and swimming pool."

"Heated, I assume?" John added.

"Of course." Charles couldn't help notice the bite of sarcasm in John's last comment.

As they pulled up to the airstrip, Charles' plane and pilot awaited him.

"We're fueled and ready to go, Mr. Devlin," the pilot announced.

Charles turned to John to say his goodbyes. "John, thanks so much for all your help. I look forward to working with you, watching the ranch grow and improve, and spending more time here with my family and guests. It will be a challenge, but I thrive on challenges, as I know you do. I'll talk with you in a couple of days. If anything comes up, remember I'm only a phone call away."

John began to have real doubts about whether he could work with or satisfy Devlin and his accountant. His thoughts were disrupted by the roar of the plane as it took off to the west, and then banked steeply in a vapor trail of cotton and disappeared to the east.

CHAPTER SEVEN

Before returning to the ranch, John ran some errands in town. Silver River served as the county's only town, hence the county seat, for a population that numbered about a tenth of Pine County's 6,735-foot elevation. The town came into existence in the early1880s with the discovery of silver. It took its original name from the owner of the largest mine, who named the collection of shacks and tents after his wife, Harriet. For its first five years the mines pumped prosperity into Harriet, distributed, however, with increasing inequality throughout the county. By the late 1880s, the mineral wealth had played out before the local miners and merchants could afford to replace Harriet's original wooden buildings with more substantial brick structures. In 1891, a fire started in the hardware store and quickly spread through half the town's wooden buildings before the volunteer fire department, with its single horse-drawn pumper, could bring it under control. The local miners eventually used dynamite to control the conflagration but in the process, pulverized most of Harriet's south end. The fire forced some new brick construction, primarily the courthouse and brick school building, but wooden false-front shops continued to dominate Main Street, which was wide enough for a wagon team to make a U-turn before heading for the mines. The final blow to Harriet's livelihood occurred with the election of President Grover Cleveland, who took the country off the silver standard. Residents would never again vote for a Democrat, believing in what the Populist William Jennings Bryan predicted: the country would be "crucified upon a cross of gold."

When the Depression came in the 1930s, everyone lost what little they had accumulated over two generations. The pioneer habits of the community revived but in a different form. Instead of working towards community prosperity, those in the Depression directed their limited energy towards survival. It was not until tourists "discovered" the valley in the early 1960s that Harriet witnessed any renewed growth. But once again the hand of Washington struck the community. The Bureau of Reclamation planned a dam for water storage and recreation downstream of town that would flood Harriet. The small community only survived because Congress kept delaying the appropriation. Then in 1978, President Carter put the Silver Valley Dam on his "hit list," declaring the project too expensive. Soon thereafter, Harriet's family relatives became tired, if not embarrassed by the constant message from outlying residents that they were "headed into Harriet for a little fun." The family petitioned the county commissioners and the new Chamber of Commerce to change the town's name; and so, in 1986, three years before the mine closed, Harriet became Silver River.

The town was old enough to have an American Legion Post for World War II, Korean, and later Vietnam and Desert Storm war veterans, but not big enough to sustain a fast-food franchise. The Legion's "Miller Lite" neon sign provided the only illumination along the main thoroughfare, though Attorney Tucker's desk lamp also lit up the sidewalk on the first Tuesday of each month when he worked late in his office to avoid his wife's Tupperware parties. The two-man police department occupied the building two doors down from the American Legion. A two-cell jail in the back alley served as the sober-up pen for the Legion's Friday night's dusk-to-midnight "happy hour." A small wooden garage leaned against the jail protecting the 1978 Chevy Impala police cruiser, with its bald tires and rusted fenders.

The American Legion, the town's only watering hole, served as a sports bar, dance hall and community center. The Broncos or the Rockies dominated the TV screen. Notices of meetings, farm auctions, lost-and-found animals and "bargain sales" plastered the wall by the entrance. No one bothered to remove the older notices for fear the town's history might be compromised. Out-of-towners marveled at the Friday night crowds and their attempt to dance on a space the size of a hubcap. Once, when an out-of-town visitor demanded a channel change to "Dancing with the Stars," the sheriff had to be called to restore order by returning the channel to the Rockies' losing effort against Atlanta.

With no traffic light in town, the captain and his sidekick sergeant spent their entire time ticketing speeders, assuming their cruiser could catch the vehicles before they exited Silver River's incorporated boundaries. Speeders supplied the town with almost 40 percent of its operating budget, thus insuring the captain's tenure. Local speeders knew enough to request a trial for their hearing, recognizing that the town lacked the funds for a jury. Tourist dollars made up what locals refused to pay. No one had to tell the police force that a new bridge across the river in town would require more vigorous enforcement of the 10 mph zone in front of the school.

When in the 1970s the tourist traffic increased, particularly in the summer, and a few residents petitioned for a traffic light, both police officers recognized the threat to the town's revenue base and argued vehemently against the traffic control measure. The police captain, Buss Calloway, testified at a hearing: "The light will only clog Main Street with more traffic and carbon dioxide fumes, which would present a major threat to the town's air quality, and hence our public health." Sensitive always to "the environmental concerns and expert testimony of our police force," the town council turned down the request.

Just down the street from the guardians of the law was Sam's Variety Store. It stocked kitchen wares, film, camping equipment, souvenirs of the area, kid's toys and a wide assortment of moderately priced clothing, all short on fashion but long on utility. Newspapers for sale consisted of day-old *Denver Posts* and copies of the neighboring county's weekly, which included a page devoted to Silver Valley news, primarily the police blotter, school sports scores and an occasional obituary. The newspaper worked hard at avoiding compound sentences, less out of concern for its readers than because of the grammatical skills of the editor.

Next to Sam's, Sarah Boynton guarded the antiques in her store, Sally's Treasure House, as if they were her children. In an extraordinary exhibition of entrepreneurship never before seen in town, Sarah removed all the furniture and household items from her mother's house after her death, and those items that remained after the Nearly New Shoppe in Montrose picked through the furnishings, gained "antique" status. Most of the furniture could be traced back to 1930s Sears Roebuck catalogues. Six old kerosene lamps kept company with a cracked marble-topped table. Close by, a dining room table with a matching mahogany-laminated sideboard occupied much of the shop's dusty space. Three uncomfortable Victorian chairs crowded one corner of the shop, and a red velvet love seat greeted visitors with horse hair pricks. All prices were negotiable and included an extensive oral history of each "antique."

Valley Market, the general and grocery store, stocked all the basic food items, though usually no more than three of any single item. Shoppers learned to show up early on Tuesdays and Fridays to snatch the best of the fresh produce. Afterwards, it was slim pickings even in the frozen food section. Fresh bakery items rarely lasted beyond Wednesday mornings, the day they hit the shelf. Big sellers were milk, beef and eggs shipped in from Denver, canned hash from Kansas City, Idaho potatoes and fresh fruit in season from Texas and Mexico. The only available local items were the scented candles produced by the owner's wife and the over-priced pies from his sister-in-law's oven.

Most of the town's other shops catered to the tourists and the increasing number of retirees who'd settled into one of the three new housing developments along the river. An old saddle shop had given way to a crafts store, and Jim's Clothing Emporium had recently closed when it could no longer compete with K-Mart in Gunnison and Wal-Mart in Montrose.

John first stopped at the Valley Hardware store. The usual gang of six retirees was huddled around the potbellied stove with their coffee and spit cans. The group traced its origins to an invitation some years ago from hardware store owner, Jake Kerrick to Slim Warren, an elderly local customer. Jake had suggested that Slim warm up by the potbellied stove and have a cup of coffee. Within a week, five of Slim's friends, hearing about the free coffee, joined the gathering: a retired miner, a former ranch hand, a retired heavy-equipment operator for the county, the retired manager of the county dump and the high school history teacher who, town folks claimed, had retired the day after he taught his first class 35 years ago The group prided themselves on knowing everything that was worth knowing in Pine County. The men viewed strangers to the store with deep suspicion, recognizing that "outsiders" brought with them unwelcome change which, like a virus, could devastate a community. They called themselves, as did everyone in town, the "Circle of Knowledge." When pressed, the Circle often bragged that they could predict the future even though they found it difficult to remember the past.

The Circle greeted John that chilly autumn morning with the sound of tobacco juice splattering in the vicinity of the spit can next to the wood burning stove. Phil, the ex-miner, looked up from the stove, wiped his moist mouth with the cuff of his cotton-plaid shirt and announced: "Lookee here boys, if it ain't John Marlow. Haven't seen your skinny ass in about a month. How's things out at the ranch?"

"Bout the same as last month, except I've got a new boss," he replied.

"Yeah, heard your place sold to some dude from back east," another old-timer added.

"Mr. Devlin is the name, a New York banker."

"Bet he's got some bucks; they all do, at least the ones who've been comin' out to this part of the country recently. My God, look at what that guy out of Chicago done with the old Porter place, or what that Los Angeles lawyer done with the Henley homestead by incorporating it with three adjoining ranches. Shit, you should see the million-dollar post-and-rail fence that circles the outfit."

The ex-miner continued, "Now it's called the 'Broken Arrow Ranch,' with large NO TRESPASSING signs. Too bad there aren't some Utes still around here. You can bet your ass they'd disregard the sign, take it home and use it for fire wood."

Another member of the Circle joined the conversation. "All these new city cowboys can afford to throw a pile of money at their outfits every week to make up for the mistakes they made the week before. One of them came in here last week, showed up in a big brand new yellow Hummer looking for some wire pliers. From the way he was dressed, I thought he might be going to a wedding. New, clean boots, a black Stetson and, if you can believe it, wearing a pair of pressed Levis. Damned if there ain't more of the pressed Levis set moving into our county every day. We took the land from the Indians, and now the city folks are taking it from us. Where will it end? It sure is nice to have money."

"What's your man like?" Cliff, another Circle regular, asked as he scratched his tobacco-stained beard.

John didn't want to offer too much detail for fear it might elicit more questions, but at the same time he'd volunteer just enough information to satisfy the ex-miner's curiosity. Whatever he told them, John knew it would be revised, altered and packaged into an exciting rumor. Truth was not a high priority with the Circle. And if it took rumors and falsehoods to keep the Circle enlivened and the town entertained, then one or all members would work diligently to gather pieces of information and then package them into beautifully crafted rumors that flew through town as if propelled by a rocket. One member, who had it out for the local Baptist minister after the cleric testified on his wife's behalf in their divorce case, started the rumor that the good reverend was poking the choir mistress after Wednesday evening rehearsals. The rumor moved through town as the "gospel truth," and ultimately hurt the attendance at the First Baptist Church, not to mention its collection plate. John measured his words carefully before declaring, "I suspect we'll see some changes at the Diamond J; maybe even some improvements."

"Yeah, the last time I looked, you could sure use some new equipment."

"You've always had a sharp eye for someone else's place." The group couldn't help but pick up on John's sarcasm.

He then went off looking for a sharp rasp, to replace the one he'd dulled on hundreds of horse hoofs.

"You guys behave yourself in my absence and don't be chasing no virgins down Main Street in your running shoes," John said as he walked towards the counter pointing the rasp at the group.

"Ain't no virgins left in this town," Cliff responded and then added, "We've been workin' overtime to guarantee it."

John headed for the feed store to pick up two mineral blocks for his horses. Next, he headed to the variety store, which also served as the town's UPS pickup and delivery point, and signed for a large package that he knew to be the fiberglass saddle frame he had ordered weeks ago from Denver. At the market, he bought up some basics, including four frozen pizzas and a couple of Mrs. Swanson's TV dinners.

John headed back to the ranch thinking about Devlin. He seemed pleasant enough, John thought to himself, but he sure as hell is going to take some babysitting when it comes to ranch matters. As for "conservation improvements," whatever the hell they were, he'd deal with them when they presented themselves. At the ranch, John walked into the shop and encountered Josh, who had a truck distributor disassembled on the scarred work bench.

"How'd it go with Mr. Devlin?" Josh asked.

"OK. I think I got you a raise."

"Thanks, John. You're the best." Josh said as if he really meant it.

"One thing I didn't want to hear from Devlin is the construction schedule for his new house. They'll be building next spring when we're running around here in circles trying to catch our ass during calving season."

"Did you tell him you'd forgotten how to pound nails?"

"No but I told him we had over 700 cows to look after, and 120 heifers to calve. He understands, but we'll have to keep an eye on the project so they don't tear up the place." John didn't mention the problems with the site.

"It's going to be one big mansion, 10,000 square feet. Think of the maintenance on that little sucker. And you can bet your ass who'll be called on to fix the cranky heater at three in the morning when it's 30 below."

"Me," Josh responded. John nodded.

"Hell, the kitchen and master bedroom will probably be in two separate time zones. And there'll be a swimming pool to take care of."

"We can use it as a dipping vat for the cattle," Josh suggested.

John appreciated the humor but still couldn't rid his thoughts of the family burial ground.

He walked to his kitchen, grabbed a cold beer and sorted through his mail. A few bills, a note from the Qwest repair man saying he'd fixed the phone line, a flier from the sale barn in Brush advertising its upcoming weekly sale of high-quality feeder calves and a letter from Clyde, his brother, who worked as the manager of a big cattle outfit north of Cheyenne.

He hadn't heard from Clyde since early in the summer, when he called looking for a good saddle horse for his son Cody, John's favorite nephew. John said he didn't know of anything for sale that he could recommend and they chatted about cattle prices, the lack of moisture, the impending sale of the Diamond J and whether John might visit for Thanksgiving.

The letter from Clyde again mentioned Thanksgiving and asked if John he could bring with him a photo of the homestead cabin. "It's a way of being reminded of the ranch," he'd written.

He called Clyde to say he'd drive up the day before Thanksgiving.

"Good that'll give us some time for you to look at my new mouse herd."

"What in hell are you smokin' up there?" John asked.

"I'm not smokin' anything. It's just that when I had a grass and weed inventory done by the Wyoming Extension Service, they discovered part of our ranch had become home to the Preble Jumping Mouse. The Extension Service called the U.S. Fish and Wildlife Service and they were up here in a shot. They saw the mice, said they were 'threatened' or 'endangered,' I forget which. Anyway, the land where the relatives of Mickey Mouse now make home is considered to be 'critical habitat.' And that means no permanent building can be constructed on that part of the ranch. That's got my owner in California goin' ape shit, screaming at me, 'it's private property.' Apparently he called Wyoming's two senators, the Speaker of the House in Cheyenne, and they all said 'Forget it.'"

"Clyde, you and I have a lot to talk about. See you next week and in the meantime take good care of your mice herd."

Before leaving for Thanksgiving, John arranged for the trucks to haul the cull cows to the Brush sale barn, made another sort and cut on the replacement heifers, gathered up the hay bales that remained in the meadow after the front-end loader broke down in October and spent two days driving to Nebraska to check on the weaned calves and confer with the feedlot owner about a feed ration.

By comparison, the drive on the interstate up to Clyde's place in Wyoming was relaxing. He thought of Jodi and Johnny in Cheyenne as he drove through the city, wanting to stop for a visit with his son. Jodi had prohibited unannounced visits, however, saying they only served to "disrupt her household," whatever the hell that meant.

Clyde's ranch was headquartered in a protected valley along Beaver Creek, the site where, according to Clyde, the absentee owner, a computer genius out of Silicon Valley, planned to build his residence.

Clyde, three years younger than John, was thick-muscled but in a shorter package than his brother. The reason his hair had turned prematurely white, Clyde explained, was because "I've spent too much time in snow country." He had never worked well alongside their father and left the ranch the week after John returned from Vietnam, taking a ranch job in Wyoming, where five years later he moved into the manager's position. The brothers rarely communicated with each other and did so only through the efforts of John's wife, now his ex.

As John pulled into the ranch, Clyde came out from the barn. The brothers greeted each other warmly, asking about each other's family before discussing the prospects for much needed moisture in the winter months ahead.

"Damned dry here, and with so little rain the Forest Service kicked me off our permit two weeks early. All our pasture is gone here at the ranch, and if we don't get some moisture soon, I'll have to start feeding hay, or selling some cattle. I could use a heavy winter," Clyde said looking to the sky.

"We've got the same situation in Colorado, with hay prices expected to top $90 a ton, and that's without the freight. Can't feed cows at that price and make any money."

"For sure," Clyde added for emphasis.

They walked across the yard towards the kitchen, past the machine shed and shop, and the small calving shed with its squeeze chute and hot box for sick calves. Clyde's wife, Irma, her red hair pulled back in a bun, greeted her brother-in-law with a peck on his cheek, and offered the brothers a beer.

"Supper's ready in about an hour. I'm sure you must be starving, John?"

"You bet, and I'm lookin' forward to that turkey tomorrow."

"It's a big fellow, a butterball from Safeway. Sure better than that wild turkey Clyde shot two years ago."

"Yeah, tasted like piñon bark peppered with lead shot," John said looking at his brother.

"Well, beats the hell out of those Swedish meatballs I've had at your place two years in a row. They must have had a special on them in Silver Valley."

"You're mistaken. Those were Rocky Mountain oysters in my special sauce."

"Sure, and calf prices are going to two dollars."

Clyde changed the subject to the home ranch.

"So those conservationists back in New York found a buyer? What's he like?"

"You've seen the type. City boy born and bred, a banker out of New York. Doesn't have a clue about what the cattle business is all about, or ranching for that matter. Bought the place, I think, as a vacation retreat for his family and friends. So he's pretty much left everything up to me, except for big ticket items, at least that's the impression I get. I'll just keep running the place like before but hopefully without the debt. Good intentions, though. We'll see how long they last when he sees the first winter feed bill and calf prices drop below 80 cents."

"Sounds like my new boss," Clyde responded.

"I have a real problem with my boss, and I think you can help. You know the 'birthing chamber' where Dad and Granddad are buried? Well, my new owner, Mr. Devlin, wants to build his new house there. I haven't told him about the graves, but if I did he'd demand that they be moved. Just like he said the elk could find another place to calve. I've been thinking about those mice of yours, maybe taking some down to Colorado with me and placing them in the 'birthing chamber.' When the Fish and Game boys find the mice, with my help of course, presto, they'll say we have 'a critical habitat' that translates into no permanent structures. What do think?"

"John, you're one smart dude."

"What do these micc look like?" John asked.

"They look just like any other mouse I've seen, but they have a dark stripe down the middle of their back, and they do jump."

"How high, a couple of feet?"

"No, maybe 5 to 6 inches off the grass."

"So what's the big deal with these jumping mice? Most mice I seen jump. Doesn't the President have enough to worry about? Wish to hell that sorry son-of-a bitch would do something about declining cattle prices and my outrageous health care costs."

"You've heard of the Endangered Species Act? Well, these little furry jumpers are protected by the government, which means if you hurt them or injure their habitat, you're in deep, over-your-head shit," Clyde explained, and then continued, "The feds explained how the government had to protect the mice to pacify the environmentalists, said that there were additional mice on similar creek beds up north and south into parts of Colorado. The good news was that I could continue to use the meadow to graze cattle but, as I said, no new structures."

"Got any ideas how I can gather up some of these little fellows?"

"The wildlife folks tell me they use a small metal live trap like the ones I use to catch muskrats along the irrigation ditch. Just bait it with some rolled oats and corn mixed with molasses and they'll jump right in. The bait is the same feed we give to our first calf heifers in the spring. Got some in the barn. Come to think of it, that's why I find so damned many mice in the feed bins. You should see the rib eyes on the mice and my barn cats, which feed on those mice all winter. They're fatter than an open cow in spring time."

Clyde continued. "You'll want males and females so that they breed and multiply. The wildlife guys told me they have two or three litters a year if properly fed."

"Any idea how to sex a mouse?" John asked.

"I'm guessing, if you lift them up by the tail, you'll find everything you need to know. The testicles will be between the hind legs, smaller than Rocky Mountain oysters but bigger than yours."

"Try for once to be helpful, will you?" John pleaded.

At supper, the two men put down three beers apiece and cheerfully exchanged embarrassing stories about each other. Slightly drunk, John decided that the mouse transfer might be a fitting climax to the Devlins' conservation ethic. Yes, John thought, they and their friends wanted to save the jumping mouse, but if its presence blocked their personal plans, would they adhere to the ethic or tell the mouse to "bug off?" The brothers loaded up two traps, a sack of the molasses-covered grain, and with some additional long-necked Coors they headed for Beaver Creek. Clyde stopped his pickup at the exact location where he'd last seen the mice.

"Right here in this meadow and along the bank of the creek," he pointed to John. And then warned: "Watch your step. We don't want to be destroying 'critical habitat.'"

"Look, right there," Clyde said excitedly, pointing ahead off to his right.

Sure enough, in the glare of the pickup headlights they could see two pairs of beady eyes looking in their direction

"Yeah I see 'em. But they're not jumping."

"I'm sure if you put 'em on some good feed and they'll jump all night," Clyde said, as he moved to the back of the pickup to unload the small traps. "Let's get these traps set before they jump their way north to Horse Creek. I understand they've got some relatives up that way."

John went along with Clyde's suggestion as they baited the traps and placed one in the meadow and the other along the creek bank.

"Pretty spot in daytime?" John asked as he returned to the pickup for a beer.

"Sure is, that's why the owner wanted to build here. Close to water, nice views to the south and relatively easy access."

"Same as the birthing chamber at home," John commented.

"Yep, and now both plots will be home to Mighty Mouse!" Clyde exclaimed with a look of supreme satisfaction.

"I'm violating the law by moving these mice, aren't I?" John asked of his brother.

"Technically speaking, you're probably right. But look at it this way. You'd be violating a small, dumb-ass law to save the family grave sites. What's more important? The mice or Dad, Mom and Granddad?"

"You're right. But it will be just my luck that after getting these furry fellows settled and fucking like rabbits that a pack of coyotes will move in and chow down on them."

"Not to worry," Clyde assured John, "My environmental skills also include coyote eradication and removal."

John reached for another beer, pleased with his inventive plan to protect his family's graves.

CHAPTER EIGHT

The next morning the Marlow brothers returned to their traps. Clyde moved over to the one closest to the river and shouted to John, "We've got mice, looks to be about 10 of 'em." John meanwhile located the trap farthest in the meadow. "Only three here," he said, clearly disappointed.

Clyde gathered some tall wet grass by the river, picked up John's trap and placed the grass in a deep cardboard box in the pickup. Unceremoniously, he dumped the mice out of John's trap into the grass floor of the box. Then he went over to his trap and emptied the other furry captives on top of John's harvest and sprinkled in some sweet feed.

"Not enough for a breeding herd, you'll need more than we have here," Clyde declared. "Let's reset the traps and see what we have by mid-afternoon."

"How many you think I should take home?" John asked.

"It's not like you're going to overload the springs of your pickup. Take all that we can catch, and hope they're evenly divided, male and female."

"How can you tell?" John asked.

"I told you, pick 'em up by the tail and do an inspection," Clyde said as he reached into the box and pulled out a mouse by its tail. He held it up to eye level, gave it a close inspection and said, "Must be a baby. Can't tell."

John, disappointed by the news, observed, "You're holding it as if it were a dog turd. Give it a closer look."

"Here," Clyde said as he handed the dangling mouse to his brother, "you give it an inspection."

John flinched. "I don't want to touch the thing. It might be carrying bubonic plague."

"Mice don't carry the plague; it's prairie dogs that carry it."

"Yeah, but them mice and prairie dogs hang out together. No telling what they're carryin', could be the plague, rabies, maybe even AIDS."

"So where did you get your medical training?"

"Look, just give them a sex inspection and be done with it. You're the specialist. Remember, I need some horny mice so we can build a herd."

Clyde tried to put his brother at ease. "I figure we got thirteen mice, and by all odds, six are female, six are male."

"And what about the thirteenth?" John asked.

"We can't be certain."

"Probably gay," John added with a frown.

"Could be. But with the other 12 you have the basis of your breeding herd. We just need to capture some more to ensure an exponential increase in their numbers."

"What kind of increase?" John asked.

"Big," Clyde added with a look of exasperation.

The two men reset the traps with more sweet feed, and then returned to Clyde's house for some coffee.

"How about helpin' me with some small chores before we return to the traps?"

"Nothing too strenuous, I hope."

"Fix some gate latches and then we'll go look at some cattle. I've got a bull I want to show you."

While the two men worked the bent latch on a Powder River alley gate, John told Clyde about the gate that had injured Devlin's nose. And how Devlin insisted that no visitors be allowed to assist with ranch work in case they injured themselves. And how he also prohibited hunting to outsiders, except for ranch employees.

"How the hell are you going to control the elk herd from eating you out of house and home?" Clyde asked. And then he added, "You mean no neighbors can help you with brandings, or cattle drives to and from the forest?"

"That's right! The guy's afraid of a lawsuit and losing everything."

"You're going to have a lot of explaining to do in town," Clyde added.

John nodded, all the while thinking about how he'd have to inform his friends and neighbors that they were no longer welcome at the Diamond J. For generations, local ranchers had come on to the ranch to help his grandfather, his father and John move cattle in May and October on and off the forest, assisting with the multiple tasks involved with branding, and on one occasion coming to the assistance of John's father to help control a dangerous grass fire that threatened the headquarters buildings. Sure, people suffered injuries from time to time, like the young Hessler boy who received a nasty burn on his leg from a branding iron, or his neighbor Ben Watson who, in the process of roping a calf, had his horse come over on top of him and broke his arm. He never thought of asking the Diamond J to pay the doctor bills. Nor did he even imagine bringing a lawsuit against John or the ranch. Besides, the town's single lawyer would have refused to take the case.

To change the subject, Clyde asked: "How you getting along without Jodi?"

"Can't say I miss her, except maybe as an irrigator. She's working at Wal-Mart in Cheyenne and is hooked up, I understand, with some guy at the John Deere dealership."

"How about young Johnny, how's he doing?"

"He's in his last year of high school with grades off the chart. He got his scores back from the tests he had to take for college entrance, and his counselor said the scores put him in the top 2 percent in the country. Besides his grades, he's the star on the Cheyenne football team."

"Just like his Dad, but clearly a lot smarter. Is he off to college next year?"

"I hope so. His biology teacher has him all excited about the western pine beetle, the one that has destroyed 10 million acres of forest land here in the West."

"Around here," Clyde added, "lightning's hit the dead trees and burned half the lodge pole forest south of Cheyenne. Same story, I understand, in Montana, Wyoming, New Mexico and Colorado."

"In Silver City, the nearby fires sure scared the hell out of the tourists. The County Business Alliance estimated the loss of business at close to a half-million dollars."

John continued: "The biology teacher managed to find some research money and has asked Johnny to help him with his pine beetle research. He's been pushing Johnny towards Yale University back East, where the teacher went in the

'80s. Apparently, it's got a first-rate biology department plus a forestry school. He thinks Johnny can get a scholarship, he talked with an entomologist there, but it will have to be a damned big one. Costs over 40 grand to go to Yale. Put travel on top of that, plus books, we're probably looking at close to 45 grand."

"Johnny can get a football scholarship, right?" Clyde asked.

"Not at Yale. They don't give athletic scholarships. Sure, at places like Colorado or Wyoming, but he's too small to be playing against those 300-pound linemen and monster linebackers they recruit these days." John added that with his son's grades and football skills, Yale had indicated the boy had a good chance of being admitted early with an academic scholarship. "But it's still expensive."

Clyde reminded John how their dad had gone off to Colorado A & M in the Depression and without any money. "Granddad didn't have the tuition money but he made an arrangement with the college where the ranch swapped some hay and cattle to pay Dad's fees. Then after two years, they couldn't afford either the cattle or the hay and Dad had to drop out. Maybe you could work out something like that with Yale," Clyde suggested.

"It's not like Yale is an aggie school, it's not Yale A & M. I can't just pull up to the college with a trailer load of cattle, dump them out in front of the treasurer's office and announce: 'Now here's my son's tuition—40 pairs of good Colorado-raised cows and calves.'"

"If they got a forest and a school to take care of it, they must have some cattle to graze off the grass, like we do around here."

"Look Clyde, it is probably a small forest and the school studies trees, how to keep them healthy and how to reproduce them. The college produces doctors, lawyers and even a couple of presidents, not cattle or cowboys."

"Well, maybe they'd take some jumping mice instead."

"Forget I even mentioned Yale. Let's go look at your bulls," John said, exhaling deeply.

After lunch, Clyde took John out into the bull pasture where Clyde pointed out his newest bull, the one he paid $4,000 for in the spring.

John stepped out of the pickup to give the bull a closer look.

"He sure is put together. Nice top line, small head, good rib eye and butt. And look at his hardware!" Seldom had Clyde received such an enthusiastic compliment from his brother.

Clyde suggested they go check the mousetraps. As they drove back towards the river, the two men continued to talk about the single subject that defined their work: cattle —the comparative advantage of different breeds, the prices for calves and cull cows at the La Junta sale barn compared with those at the recent sale in Torrington, the price outlook for finished cattle in the spring and the forecast for a tough winter.

They parked by the river and together walked through the tall grass to the traps, where they counted eight more mice.

"They're not jumping," John whispered.

"Probably tired," Clyde explained. "You'd be too, if you were trying to get out of a trap. Wait till they get to Colorado, and you give them some cheese soufflés—they'll perk up."

They dumped the new mice in with the others, removed the old grass and replaced it with new grass and some feed, and then splashed some water over both. "That'll keep them happy until they're at their new home." Clyde added.

Back at the house, they watched the Cowboys play the Packers on TV before retiring to the Thanksgiving Day dinner table. John appreciated the wholesome meal, the kind of meal John never experienced with his own cooking. He debated with himself about spending another evening with his brother or leaving immediately for Colorado. With four hours of good light he could make it home before dark.

"Think I'll try to get home tonight. I'll have enough time to get the mice settled in the birthing chamber," John decided

"You sure? You could leave in the morning. The mice will be OK in that box over night."

"I don't want to risk losing them. I'll get them settled tonight and they'll be ready to jump all over the meadow tomorrow."

"Don't forget to let the Wildlife boys in Colorado know you've got this big problem with mice."

"Don't worry, I'll bring them action photos even if I have to hire a camera crew," John declared.

He placed the box of mice in the truck cab, put the seatbelt around the box and turned to Clyde. "Wouldn't want them to get injured, or windblown or wet in the back of the truck." At the house, he thanked his sister-in-law for the "delicious butterball. "You keep in touch now," she said as she kissed John on the cheek.

He drove out of the ranch slowly to see how his furry passengers took to the bumps on the dirt road. Once on the interstate, he kept his eye on the speedometer, imagining the conversation he'd have with the police officer who caught him speeding.

"And what do we have here?" the officer might ask as he looked into the front seat of the pickup after checking John's driver's license and registration.

"Just some mice," carefully adding "sir" to his response.

"What, you got a shortage of them in Colorado?"

"Not really, they're for my daughter's science project. Captured them up at my brother's ranch on Beaver Creek."

"Well I bet your brother is happy to part with them. They wouldn't be the jumping mice I've been reading about, would they?"

"Just common ordinary barn mice you find anywhere. No sir, these mice can't jump. Their legs are too short. I checked."

"OK cowboy, be on your way then, and watch the speed limit."

"Yes, Sir!"

The time passed slowly as he listened to the radio out of Cheyenne. The commodity news announced cattle prices steady while corn futures advanced, and pork bellies were slightly down. The weatherman predicted no letup in the dry, windy weather. As always, John found the national news depressing—hurricanes in Florida, more corruption in Washington, and the president's announcement that he "would not standby idle" as gas prices reached record levels. From the sports announcer, the updated injury report on the Bronco's quarterback put John's bet against the Pittsburgh Steelers in jeopardy.

By the time he arrived at the Diamond J, the sun cast long shadows off the yellowing cottonwoods leading to headquarters. John headed immediately for the birthing chamber, where he distributed the mice in the tall Timothy grass, placing them far enough from the creek so that if the mice became disoriented in their new surroundings they wouldn't drown. Couldn't take too many precautions, John thought, after going to the trouble of transporting the critters from Wyoming. He wished them good night and headed back to his house, all the while rehearsing the phone call he'd make the next morning to the Fish and Wildlife folks announcing the presence of Mr. Preble's extended family in the neighborhood.

CHAPTER NINE

"You know those mice we've been reading about in the papers, the jumping ones that the environmentalists want to save?" John said to Cal Ashton, a former high school classmate and now the local state game warden.

"Yeah, you mean the Preble's jumping mouse?" Cal responded.

"I don't know their name but the ones I got up at the Diamond J are jumpin' all over the upper pasture along Cabin Creek, and having the time of their life. Personally, I don't give a shit about the mice. But I've heard that where you have a concentration of mice, they'll attract coyotes. That's my concern. I don't need no more coyotes around here, especially at calving time."

"You sure you saw them jump? There are some of those mice up north, mostly in Wyoming and some out on the Front Range on streams near Denver, but none in these parts of Colorado, at least none that I've heard of."

"Well, a pack of them must have jumped all the way down here from Wyoming or come over the Rockies from the east. Frisky little things, they are. If they are what I think they are, should I trap them and send them on to you or the Sierra Club?"

"Don't touch them, John. I'll notify the U.S. Fish and Wildlife Service. They'll want to come up to the ranch and give them a look. If they are the threatened mouse, they'll look at the extent of their habitat, map it, and identify it as 'critical habitat.' Not the entire ranch, mind you, just where they hang out. Now John, I know how much you love government regulations, but please don't be messing with those mice before they get there."

"What if I herd 'em on over to my neighbor? Or maybe you could bring in some bobcats to feed on them?"

"I don't have any bobcats and don't even think of moving them. You'd be violating federal law and they'd fine you, maybe even lock you up. The presence of the mice won't trouble you. They don't bite and they don't eat much grass. You can continue to use the area for grazing. But the major restriction is you can't build a structure in their 'critical habitat.'"

The next day, three Fish and Wildlife officers, including a biologist, showed up unannounced at the Diamond J in their new Dodge pickup. John knew the head official from previous visits to the ranch.

"Where they located, John?"

John led them to the area where he'd deposited the mice and pointed towards the creek. As the three men shuffled through the tall grass, they spotted a jumper within 10 feet. It jumped above the grass, its tiny brown eyes staring directly at the men.

The biologist stopped in his tracks, reaching for his camera and said, "That's a Preble, all right. Besides jumping he's got those long back legs and a tell-tale stripe down his back." An assistant took notes in a small notebook. The biologist aimed his digital camera in the direction of the jumping mouse, as he waited impatiently for additional action.

As they waited for another jumper, the biologist turned to John and asked, "How many do you think you saw yesterday?"

John, trying to look as if he were giving the question his deepest concentration, said: "At least 40, maybe 50," and then added, "They're not jumping like yesterday. Probably tired from that long trek across the Rockies. I'd be sleeping also if I had to hop, skip and jump my way over here from Denver or Wyoming, or wherever the hell they came from."

"No doubt," the biologist confirmed.

"Well I sure hope they don't spread themselves across the entire ranch. Why is it, by the way, we have to protect these critters?"

"The environmentalists want to protect and enhance biodiversity, like saving the wolf and the prairie dog," the head official responded in the most authoritative voice he could muster.

"And why is it that all threatened or endangered species show up in Colorado, Wyoming and Montana—you know, the bald eagle, mountain sheep, the grizzly, gray wolves, the sage hen, the black- tailed prairie dog, the Gunnison sage grouse and now some fucking jumping mice?" John asked.

"It's not just Colorado, Wyoming and Montana. We've got the cave beetle in Texas, the snail darter in Tennessee and the pygmy owl in Arizona, plus other species all over the United States."

"Well, you tell your environmental friends, I don't need any of their fucking wolves coming onto our ranch to chow down on some helpless mice or our defenseless calves. If those city folks had a real job, maybe they'd leave working ranchers alone and take their threatened or endangered species, or whatever the hell they are, and pack them off to Central Park. Rather than hiking through the woods in search of some spotted owls and palliated wood fuckers, they need to keep their nose and laws out of our business."

"You're sure fired up this morning, John."

"One more thing, while I'm at it. You and the environmentalists talk about endangered, or threatened, species. What about us ranchers—we're endangered—calves bringing 80 cents a pound when it costs us over a dollar to produce them. Also, I don't see anyone out there trying to protect our critical habitat except the ranchers themselves. And it's ok for wolves and coyotes to feast on our sheep, but it's not ok if we shoot one of the little darlings. I tell you, I'm goddamned sick and tired of their bitching and moaning. Put a bunch of tree huggers on this ranch for a week and they'd starve to death."

"I'll be happy to tell them, John. And when I do, I'm sure the Sierra Club will offer you a free lifetime membership."

"Thanks. I'd rather push a wet noodle up the ass of a rabid wildcat than have to deal with them environmentalists. What the hell am I going to say to my new boss who wants to build his house where the mice now make home."

"He probably pays you big money to give him bad news. Tell him he'll have to build elsewhere if we have to designate the meadow as 'critical habitat,' meaning there can be no permanent structures on the site. It's not as if there aren't other sites on your ranch, right?"

"True."

"Better he knows now than later when, in the middle of construction, he, his manager, that's you, and his contractor would be arrested, fined and then spend some time in prison."

John asked him for some more details about the mice and if, in the event they multiplied, might the remainder of the 65,000-acre ranch be classified "critical habitat."

"Not likely. They carve out a small area and tend to stay within it."

"And to be certain they don't reproduce, can we spray then to make them impotent? Or maybe we should castrate them?"

The biologist saw no humor in John's response." Don't even think about either option. I've got to go back to the office and file a report to headquarters in Denver. You'll be getting a letter shortly from Washington informing you of this critical habitat and the restrictions you'll have to follow. As I said, nothing drastic, you can still graze here, but no permanent structures or disturbance of the ground. Got it?"

"Got it. But I'd sure like to get rid of them. Understand they attract coyotes and I already have plenty of them already."

"There's no evidence that I know of that these mice will attract coyotes," the biologist said as he and his assistants strolled towards their truck.

As John drove off towards his house, he gave some thought to the phone call he'd have to make to Mr. Devlin.

In the kitchen, John opened a beer to assist with the call.

"Hello, Mr. Devlin, John here at the ranch."

"Glad you called. I met with my architect today. He wants to fly out to the ranch next week. If I can arrange it, I'll join him. What's going on?"

"Well sir, it's a bit of a long story." And then John explained to Devlin what he had learned from the wildlife officer about the Endangered Species Act, and its impact on ranches all over the West.

Devlin broke into the conversation, clearly impatient. "John you don't have to lecture me about the Endangered Species Act, I know all about it. Now what is it you're calling about?"

John explained how and where he discovered the Preble's jumping mice on the Diamond J. Because the mice attract coyotes, John explained, he felt obliged to inform the Fish and Wildlife folks so that they could get rid of them. "I'd have poisoned them myself, but I remembered reading somewhere about large fines for disturbing them." John was careful not to criticize the environmentalists with whom Devlin consorted. After John explained the prohibition against building in the "critical habitat," he held his breath and waited for the explosion.

"You're telling me I can't build on my own property because of a goddamned jumping mouse?"

"Yes sir, that about sums it up."

"I'll contact our environmental lawyers at NOLC, and see what they have to say about the situation. By the way, how many of these mice are jumping around?"

"As a conservative estimate, I'd say we saw about 50 to 60 this afternoon. I asked the feds if we could somehow get rid of them, like spraying or burning. They warned me not to harm them. If I did, you and I would be fined and possibly jailed."

"I'm going to call Colorado Senator Barlow. Maybe he can get this little rodent delisted from the 'threatened' category. He's got an election next year, and I'm sure he'd appreciate a generous campaign contribution. In the meantime, sit tight. We'll get this solved one way or another. And don't forget, no outside hunters on the ranch. Just you and the hired man, understand? No unauthorized visitors either, and I'm talking about the folks who show up to help you brand and move cattle. If they had an accident, I'd be dead meat to my insurance company. Plus, they hold a big mortgage on the ranch."

"Yes, sir, I understand."

John had forgotten about the hunters, friends who considered it almost an entitlement to bag an elk for winter meat or cut some firewood. How to tell these guys? The fastest and most efficient way to spread the word, John knew, was announce it before the Circle of Knowledge.

CHAPTER TEN

After finishing his morning chores, John drove into town and pulled up in front of the hardware store, where the Circle had already assembled. Brad Kemper, the high school's retired history teacher, a wispy man in his sixties with a serious sinus problem, was holding court with a story about an Indian attack on the town's silver mine. Born and brought up on a local ranch, Brad always dressed in the same frayed flannel shirt in which, out of habit, he carried a small notepad and pencil. He wore his graying hair in a ponytail, and had a slight swagger to his walk. His metal-framed glasses magnified hazel eyes in a ruddy, but attractive face.

Brad prided himself as the town's unofficial historian, a title he gained by publishing, at his own expense, *The History of Silver Valley*, an edited version of his master's thesis at the state teachers college in Gunnison. No matter that Brad didn't always get all the facts correct, like when he wrote that the town of Silver Valley came into existence with the discovery of gold in 1858. In fact, the town wasn't settled until 1875 with the discovery of silver. Still, the locals deferred to Brad as THE authority on the history of the town and the surrounding area. If the reader took seriously Brad's history, and most residents and tourists did, the county in the 19th century specialized in general mayhem—wild Indians, cowboys, murders and a monthly lynching. Zeke's Variety Store, which also served as the local bookstore, found it difficult to keep Brad's book in stock during tourist season. Straw cowboy hats, offered in colors not seen in nature, John Wayne T-shirts and the finest selection of rubber tomahawks west of the Mississippi adjoined the book shelf where Brad's book kept company with the works of Louis L'Amour and a wide collection of sex and violence titles.

The only blemish to Brad's reputation as an historian occurred two years ago when he reported to the public, by way of the Circle, that he'd read about two Spanish missionaries who traveled through the area in the 18th century on their way to California. When traveling through the Rocky Mountains, near present-day Gunnison, the clerics lightened the burdens of their pack horses by unloading two chests of gold and some weapons and body armor. Brad confirmed, with considerable authority, the burial of two chests of gold, on the Harris Place, a ranch ten miles from town. Within a week, and before old man Harris scared off local gold seekers with his shotgun, the cratered landscape looked as if the Air Force had used it for bombing practice.

"And what brings you into town today, Cowboy?" asked the history teacher.

"Just some errands, food and supplies. Also wanted to learn of any new rumors you boys might be starting."

"Nothing new today but give us some time. We might have something by late afternoon. Check back at closing time."

"I've got work to do but I do have some news for you. Some of you won't be too happy with it, I can assure you, but it isn't a rumor," John declared. "I'm sorry to have to announce this, but my boss said to me yesterday, there's to be no outside hunters on the ranch this year, except for employees. I know those who have helped during brandings and fall roundups have always been welcome to hunt on the Diamond J. But I'm sorry to say, no more."

"Hell, folks around here have hunted that ranch for three or more generations," the retired teacher said. "You know that trophy elk down at the Legion, the one over the bar? My uncle shot that eight-pointer back in the early 50's. And your granddad allowed some of the less fortunate folks in town, including my granddad, to hunt so they had some meat to carry them over through the winter."

"What's this all about, John?" the ex-miner asked. "Why the no trespassing all of a sudden? I bet it's got something to do with lawyers. Right?"

"Part of it, yes," John replied. "For the owner, Mr. Devlin, it's a liability issue. He's been advised by his New York lawyer that someone might get injured on the ranch and bring a lawsuit against him. He's got a lot of money to lose. He's also concerned with conservation, preserving the wildlife in the area."

"That's the craziest thing I've heard around these parts in a long time. Hell, John, you know as well as I, that we've got more elk and deer here than we did 20 years ago. If the herds aren't kept to manageable size, they'll eat you out of house and home. As for the liability issue, if I were to shoot anyone hunting, it wouldn't be by accident, but intentionally, like maybe the sheriff's assistant who ticketed me the other night for not coming to a complete stop at three o'clock in the fucking morning. But then he wouldn't be around to bring a lawsuit against me or your boss, right?"

"I'm sure your sharp-shooting skills will be appreciated by my boss," John replied.

The man who once managed the town dump, recently renamed the Silver Valley Recycle Center, chimed in: "John, I don't know your new boss but it seems to me you need to do a little educatin'. You know as well as all of us here that we got too many elk. Also, if there was any accident, major or minor, do you think any of us would bring a lawsuit against the ranch or your boss? That's not our way. We come onto the ranch and accept the risk of being hurt, either in hunting, or a horse accident or even food poisoning from one of those foul bologna sandwiches you offer up after the fall roundup. Remember last spring when your hired hand, that Webster boy, burned a perfect "M" on my left calf with the branding iron rather than the critter on the ground? Well, I didn't go flying off to Tucker, the lawyer, so I could sue the bejesus out of Webster or the ranch. Hell, Tucker wouldn't have accepted the case anyway. Lawsuits may be the way of city folks, but they ain't our way. You know that. I take responsibility for my actions and I don't need no lawyer tellin' me how to act and who to sue."

There were nods of agreement all around the Circle.

"I'm not particularly happy with the news myself," John said.

"I'm sure you're not, but that doesn't change anything as far as I'm concerned. I'll still be there to help you and the ranch when you call. But don't let me work alongside of your boss. What's his name, again?"

"Charles Devlin," John said. "Not only does he not want hunters, he's saying he doesn't want anyone coming onto the ranch who is not employed there. In other words, no one comes onto the ranch, even to help—just personal guests and family. Again, for him it's a matter of liability, security and privacy."

"That's going to make it real hard on you, John, when you need help." You need to tell your boss what it means to 'neighbor.' People who got money can hire help. But those of us without have to depend on our neighbors. I can understand he wants to come out here, not be bothered and be left alone. But if he's concerned about security, no one around here is going to be threatenin' his life or be peekin' in his bedroom window."

"I'll be sure to educate him about your ways," John answered.

John slipped away from the Circle, and no one said a word as he walked towards the door. John asked himself if maybe he had handled the situation improperly. Maybe he was too blunt with them, but he also had a responsibility to Devlin and what the owner wanted for himself and his family and the ranch.

As expected, the news of Devlin's restrictions flew through town so fast that even before John returned to his ranch, three angry phone messages from his neighbors awaited his attention.

For two days the Circle discussed the folly of Devlin's decision. Sure, he had the right to his privacy, but by his definition, "privacy" excluded the reciprocal responsibility of neighboring.

Such an interpretation of a word so infrequently used in Silver Valley hit the Circle as unfriendly, foreign and certainly inappropriate. Three days after John's surprise announcement, Brad produced one of his own Circle colleagues.

"You remember a couple of years ago, I told you about the Spanish missionaries, Dominguez and Escalante and how they came through this country in 1776 on their way to set up missions in California?"

"Sure do," the miner said, "and you said that when they came to these mountains guided by some Ute Indians in the winter, they had to lighten their loads. Buried some equipment and two chests of gold. Planned to retrieve the gold on their return from California."

A member of the Circle broke in. "They sure as hell took a wrong turn if they came through these mountains on their way to California. You can always trust the Catholics to get lost and then turn to heathens for guidance."

Brad went on to explain the miseries the Dominguez-Escalante Expedition experienced as it climbed into the Rocky Mountains. "Their food supply ran out, and their horses weakened under the heavy loads in the deepening snow." The Circle listened carefully to their certified historian as his voice took on a more serious tone.

"As I mentioned to you a couple of years ago, the expedition came right over these mountains on an Indian trail leading west over the divide. When they crossed over the summit and came to this side, that's when they unloaded two chests of Spanish doubloons. According to the English translation of Escalante's journal, discovered two years ago in Madrid, the burial spot was 1,000 meters from the top of the divide and marked by a 3-foot-high pile of rocks. Finally, we know from other sources that the Utes annihilated the recovery team the following year. The gold is still lying buried somewhere out there on the north end of the Diamond J Ranch." Brad hated to do this to the Diamond J and especially John, but for Brad the issue transcended personal friendship.

"Brad, you're full of shit," the ex-miner said. "You said the same thing to us two years ago about the gold being buried on the Harris place. That poor ranch on the east end now looks like a bombing range after we all went to the Harris place and started diggin'. No gold turned up. Now you tell us there's two chests of gold buried somewhere out there on the Diamond J Ranch. How do you know all this?"

"The reason they never found the gold on the Harris Ranch is that folks, including myself, were looking in the wrong place. Like everyone, I measured a thousand meters from the crest of the current highway thinking all the while that the highway followed the old Indian trail. I've done some more research and the summit of the current highway is at least one-half mile distant from the Indian trail. The Colorado Highway Department confirmed that to me after they checked some of their old maps." What Brad failed to mention is that he had no use for the Harris family after the son was caught dealing drugs at the high school, hence the invention of the burial site.

"You're suggesting that if you marked off 1,000 meters from the summit, you'd be on the north end of the Diamond J?"

"Cliff, you used to have shit for brains. What happened?" Brad answered.

No member of the circle questioned the integrity of the history teacher's report, hoping it was true. He was, after all, their authority on the past in spite of his false gold report two years ago. Every Circle member knew that no one within the ranks could keep a secret. The question in everyone's mind became: Who would they tell first?

Cliff was so excited he swallowed his Red Man, and when he started to speak, his dentures rattled like a set of castanets. Someone told him to calm down and "control those rattlesnakes in your mouth." Cliff put two fingers in his mouth to reset his rattlers.

"What are we going to do?" Cliff asked the Circle.

"One thing is for sure," another member answered. "The north end of the Diamond J will look like an open pit mine after we spread the news through town. Mr. Devlin can forget about unauthorized visitors or his privacy on his ranch. Of course, the news we spread will not mention the 3-foot pile of rocks."

Visits and phone calls to the Valley Hardware store increased as word of the buried treasure seeped through the county.

"No, we have none in stock," Jake, the owner, responded to the callers seeking metal detectors. One of the county commissioners offered to pay double the value for a mine detector at the Army Reserve unit in Gunnison. Another enterprising citizen went on the Internet and purchased 50 metal detectors for an average price of $72.00. He advertised his new supply in the local newspaper ("For Sale: Bounty Hunter and Colorado Gold Stick, the best metal detectors money can buy, $149.99"). Within one week, the young entrepreneur had doubled his money.

The Forest Service public-access road through the Diamond J became as busy as Silver River's Main Street as locals drove up to the north end of the ranch, got out their metal detectors and began scouring the landscape off to the side of the road and well onto the ranch's private property.

John pleaded with the county sheriff to control the invaders. The overweight sheriff was in no condition to hike across the north end of the Diamond J looking for trespassers when he could rest comfortably in his cruiser at the school crossing, holding his inoperative radar gun and a cup of coffee. He reminded John, "We went through this same routine a couple of years back when folks were somehow convinced that there was some buried gold on the Harris place. Remember? I was powerless to stop the trespassers with only a three-man force, and usually only one man on duty on any eight-hour shift. Our first responsibility is to stop speeders through town and at the school."

The sheriff suggested to John, "You should post your property along the Forest Service road. Maybe that'll keep them off." The sheriff knew very well, as did John, that no amount of "Private Property, Keep Out" signs would discourage the fortune seekers.

In addition to John's other chores, he took time out to patrol the road during the day and evening, reminding trespassers they were on private property. One evening on the Forest Service road, John encountered a brigade of locals walking down the road with shovels over their shoulders as if they were on a work detail.

"Out for an evening stroll?" John asked the lead man.

"Lookin' for that gold," responded a young man with a pick and shovel.

"I need to remind you're on private property. See the sign?"

John knew most of the gold bugs—two high school classmates, a hired hand from a neighboring ranch, a couple of county employees, two shopkeepers and their clerks, the basketball coach, even the head of the Ladies Silver Valley Garden Club. When John asked them to please leave, they did so without complaint out of respect to John.

The situation reached a critical stage late one evening, when John discovered a backhoe at work in a small hay field off the forest road. As he approached the backhoe, the operator turned off its lights, thinking, no doubt, that the yellow machine was invisible in the half-moon light.

"And what might we be diggin' up here this evening?" John asked.

"Oh, I thought I'd dig around. Understand there's gold somewhere around here, and my metal detector buzzed at this spot like a wasp nest."

"Don't you know you're on private property?" John said firmly.

"Not here, it's Forest Service land," the digger responded.

"Their road is over there," John said as he pointed in the direction of the road, "but once you're off the road you're on private property. See that sign?" John added as he nodded to the moonlit "NO TRESSPASSING" sign facing the two men from the road.

"What's your name?" John asked the bearded, heavy-set backhoe operator.

"Jerry Griffin," the young man said as he let go a stream of tobacco juice.

John recognized Griffin as the local electrician's helper, and then asked, "You read English?"

"Guess I lost my bearing," Griffin said, as he rolled down the sleeves over his beefy tattooed arms.

"You'll lose more than that if you don't fill in the hole and move your machine and butt out of here pronto."

"No reason for you to get a hair up your ass."

"Look Griffin, I'll put that bucket up yours where the sun don't shine if you don't start filling in that hole and smoothing it out. And I mean NOW. Understand?" John said as the blood rushed to his face. "Come in here again, and I'll dig a hole in your chest big enough for a bear to hibernate in."

Griffin quickly moved all of his 200 pounds as he jumped back into the seat of the backhoe, turned on the lights and began filling in the cavity. After 20 minutes he was rolling back down the Forest Service road towards the main highway.

Within five days of the initial report of Spanish treasure, the gold hunters had discovered a wide array of items with their metal detectors—broken sickle sections from a hay-mowing machine, spent .30 caliber shells, half an exhaust pipe, a harness buckle attached to a piece of dried leather, a windshield wiper blade and a couple of old Copenhagen snuff cans, one containing a well-preserved "Hoover for President" campaign button—but no chests of gold.

CHAPTER ELEVEN

The volume of gold hunters into and thru the Diamond J Ranch increased in the weeks following the Circle's news of the Spanish missionaries. Neither John nor the county's Sheriff's Department could stop the invaders.

John decided it would be best to talk with Mr. Devlin in New York. Maybe he could come up with a solution to keep gold seekers off the ranch.

John dialed Devlin in New York, only to discover from his secretary that he was in Argentina on a business trip. "If you're in contact with him, would you please ask him to call me at the ranch? It's very important."

Devlin returned the call that evening, and John explained the situation, the story of the gold and the problem with trespassers.

"What do I do?" John pleaded.

"How did you let this rumor, and I trust it is just that, spread and take on a life of its own? Couldn't you have prevented it?"

"Sir, I'm not certain it is a rumor. But whatever it is, it sure as hell got the town folks all excited. In this town, if it's a rumor with just enough credibility, it is transformed into a true fact, and then it takes on a life of its own, as you've suggested. You don't know this town. Any rumor, no matter how small or insignificant, propels itself through this place as if carried by a tornado. For folks around here rumors provide excitement, like entertainment. The TV offerings are pretty bad, and the picture show closed 10 years ago." John tried to explain.

"Yeah, entertainment at my expense," Devlin replied.

He then he went on to give John some direction on how to deal with the situation. "For starters, I don't want any trespassers on the ranch. If they come onto the ranch, they need to know they'll be arrested. If you can't count on the sheriff, and it sounds as if he may be part of the problem, then I want you to go out and hire a private security force. There probably isn't one in the county so you may have to locate one in Denver. They can stay at ranch headquarters for as long as necessary and I don't care what it costs. I want to be absolutely certain YOU understand my concern on this, John. There is a big liability issue here and also it's about the sanctity of private property. No trespassers. And I mean NONE. Period."

"Yes sir," John answered. "But I can assure you, we will more than fill the county jail, plus one or two other pens in adjoining counties."

"I don't care if we fill every jail in Colorado. I'm not going to have a bunch of gold-seeking locals walking helter skelter through my ranch. As you know, I've given new computers to the high school. You'd think the town's people would respect my wishes for privacy. The ranch isn't a public park, it's private property. Understand? Now go locate a security service, and I'll check back with you tomorrow night. I have more than enough to worry about with these damned Argentine bankers and politicians, who seem incapable of running a smooth economy. I don't need more problems in Colorado. A good ranch manager would have taken care of these problems. Good night."

John was about to respond but the receiver clicked dead. John wanted to tell Devlin that he and Josh had spent countless hours attempting to keep trespassers off the ranch.

He pulled out the ranch map and determined where guards should be posted. He counted three critical locations on the north end, plus a guard at the juncture of the Forest Service road just off the highway. A quick Internet search on the library's computer, with the help of the local librarian, identified two services: Valhalla Guard Service, whose advertisement highlighted tough looking veteran Army Rangers and Navy Seals armed with rifles, side arms and guard dogs baring sharp teeth. The other service, The Happy Security Service, advertised itself as "protectors to the rich and famous all over the world," and prided itself on its use of the latest technology. "Our advanced technology will set off fireworks (grenades and land mines can be substituted) when sensors detect unauthorized intruders in areas under our protection. We also provide armed escorts for executive motorcades and air travel."

John went with the Valhalla folks, fearing that the Happy Security's fireworks could start fires and that their grenade and their land mine option might solicit those lawsuits Mr. Devlin so feared. Captain Jack, the Valhalla owner, said the company could have 12 armed men at the ranch in two days. The charges would be $400 a day per man (including a per diem food allowance, but not board). If Valhalla was hired for a week, assuming three eight-hour shifts, the estimated cost would run to about $34,000. The cost, Jack said, included ammunition and incidental supplies. However, if the men could not stay at the ranch, the cost of motel rooms would be an additional expense. "We also offer our gold service," Captain Jack added. "That option is everything I have mentioned, plus guard dogs and tear gas."

John explained that with hunting season about to start, the local motel, the Lazy K, would no doubt be booked. "In that event, I'll have the boys bring a nine-man squad tent. There's no additional charge for that," the captain explained, and then added, "Rest assured these men are professionals, good shots when they have to be, and forbidden to drink when on duty."

How reassuring John thought, and then asked "Do they have to be armed?"

"Sir, our experience is that when a man is armed, both with a dog and a weapon, the combination is a very, very effective deterrent to trespassers; and I gather that is why you are hiring us. So what option do you prefer? Our regular service or the gold service?"

"What is the added cost for the dogs and gas? John asked.

"The cost for the dogs is $50 a day per dog. If you opt for the gold, I'll throw in the tear gas for free," Captain Jack offered.

"Damned if they don't eat a lot." John responded.

"Sir, these aren't toy poodles but big ferocious animals, like pit bulls and German shepherds."

"Yes, I'm sure they are. Look, I just don't want anyone shot or chewed to death or gassed. We have some insurance concerns here."

"Understood, sir," Jack replied, "but you want us to prevent trespassers, correct?"

"OK, fax me a contract but figure the costs without the dogs, and please, no assault weapons. They'd only unnerve the locals," John said.

"I'll have the contract to you by late afternoon, and you can expect your armed-guard contingent to be at the ranch by noon on Friday. They will look to you for instructions," Captain Jack responded.

Early the next morning Charles Devlin called from Argentina.

"What is going on?"

"The same problem, sir. But I did contact a guard service. They are expensive but also experienced at this sort of thing. They guarantee they'll get rid of the trespassers."

"Good. Thankfully I'm about to leave this financial snake pit at the end of this week for New York. I talked with the office today, including Rigby. John, I think it would be useful for all concerned if you came east to New York the middle of next week. We have a number of things to go over, and Rigby's got a bunch of financial questions for you. I'll send my plane out for you and you'll be in the city by dinner. Then a full day of work in New York, and I'll have you back to Colorado the next afternoon. Can you arrange your schedule accordingly?"

"I could, yes, sir. But I've arranged for the guard service to start tomorrow. I'd like to be here the entire time they're present on the ranch in the event of any trouble. I've contracted them for a week. Hopefully by then the problem with the gold hunters will have vanished. Can I delay my trip to New York by a week?"

"I'm counting on you to make damned sure the problem does vanish and quickly. I'll see you in a week."

CHAPTER TWELVE

From the tone of Charles' voice, John understood well enough that he had to solve the problem of the gold-seeking trespassers. He hoped that the guards would, no doubt, perform their "mission," as Captain Jack referred to their task.

John placed a call to the history department at the university and was directed to Professor Juan Gutierrez, a specialist in 18th century Spanish colonial history. John related the story of Dominguez and Escalante, as explained by Brad.

"Is there any truth to this expedition?" John asked.

"Most certainly," the professor announced with some authority. "With the discovery of the Escalante journal three years ago, we do know that the expedition buried some gold and heavy arms. Your local historian obviously learned about the buried gold from the publication of the journal."

Clearly, the story possessed some validity, John thought. Yes, there might be two chests of gold buried somewhere on the north end of the ranch, but where? John figured he couldn't kill the rumor, true or false, but he could put a scare into the trespassing gold bugs. John drove to town to meet with the news department of the Circle of Knowledge.

"Look who's here," the ex-miner said, looking up at John as he entered the store. "Pull up a chair and have a cup of Jim's crank case oil; it's warm and fresh."

John pulled a chair into the Circle. "I'll pass on the oil, thanks."

"What brings you to the big city? Lookin' for a metal detector or maybe some ammunition for them guards of yours? You know, John, those armed guys sure as hell have pissed off a lot of locals. Handcuffing folks and then having them arrested at the Sheriff's Office. Nasty dispositions they have. I guess that's why they're guards. And I hear they sure don't tip very well at the café or the VFW."

"They're about to leave," John announced, "but only after they bury some anti-personnel mines to discourage trespassers on the ranch. Not even with the most advanced mine detector would I venture across parts of our ranch."

"What part?" the ex-sheriff asked.

"That's for me to know and you to discover, but don't blow yourself up in the process."

"John, what's gotten into you? You're sure making it dangerous for them cows," the Circle member volunteered.

"We've taken out land mine insurance," John responded, while having difficulty containing his laughter at the Circle's gullibility.

"What's this we hear about your problem with jumping mice up on your place?" Carl asked.

John was more than happy to change the subject and oblige in a discussion of mice.

"Fish and Wildlife guys came out last week and discovered a whole bunch of them. Say they jumped in here from Wyoming. The Feds tell me that wherever the mice live is 'critical habitat,' which means it has to be protected for the mice."

"That's those damned environmentalists for you," Phil said. "You watch out John, they'll close down ranching when they learn your cattle are taking a shit in the stream; and if the wolves, which they've introduced around here, don't multiply like rabbits, you can bet they'll blame you and your cattle for their impotence. They closed the silver mines and the lumber mills around here and never gave a rat's ass how many miners or lumberjacks they laid off."

Another Circle member volunteered, "Damn, John you've had a busy fall, what with dealing with the gold seekers and now the Fish and Game idiots."

"That's for sure," John said, and then added, "I hope to get some work done as soon as I get back from New York."

"New York?"

"Going there to see my boss, Mr. Devlin. He's sending his private plane to pick me up."

As John signed for a new socket wrench at the counter, the Circle wished him a good trip.

Two days later, John wasn't certain what to pack for his trip to New York. He had no suit, and only one real dress shirt, a pair of green wool pants and an old sports jacket he'd last worn to his dad's funeral. He hoped the bolo tie would be acceptable to the Devlins in New York. John stuffed the financial reports and inventories that Rigby wanted into a plastic satchel, a promotional gift he'd received at an agricultural seminar. Once packed, he talked with Captain Jack about the guard situation and how he was pleased with Valhalla. No one had been hurt and only three arrests had been made.

"One other thing, Jack. I wish you'd tell your men to spread the word in town that they've planted some anti-personnel mines in the area they're patrolling. I've mentioned that to a few of the gold seekers I know in town. It sure got their attention."

"What a great idea. Count on it done," Jack replied without asking any questions.

John then headed to the Valley State Bank for some cash and finally on to the airport in Gunnison.

He heard the jet plane taxi up to the door of the waiting room. The young pilot, with four braided gold stripes on each sleeve, introduced himself and carried John's bag to the aircraft. "This is a Gulfstream Five," the pilot said, "which only last month replaced our smaller Gulfstream Four. This one can fly to Europe, Latin America and even Asia without refueling, plus it can carry more passengers, has a far more advanced climate control system and a shower. Mr. Devlin also likes it because he can stand up in it."

"It's nice not having to refuel," John said, as if he'd experienced the inconvenience of having to make a stop on the way to Buenos Aires.

The co-pilot and an attractive middle-aged woman, Trish Jackson, introduced themselves at the steps to the plane's cabin. The pilot said, "We picked up Trish in Durango on our way here. She'll be flying to New York with us to meet with Mr. Devlin. Anything you want in the way of food or drinks, you'll find in the small refrigerator. There's a good selection of newspapers and magazines on board plus wireless Internet. We also have a few movies. They are mostly westerns, at Mr. Devlin's insistence. We'll be cruising at 35,000 feet and our flying time to Teterboro Airport, just outside of New York, is four hours and seven minutes, assuming a slight tail wind. Now, up we go," the pilot said as he pointed to the stairs. The pilots followed John and Trish into the cabin.

The last time John had flown was in the hospital plane he rode with other injured soldiers back to the states from Saigon in 1970. The military plane smelled of vomit, and most of the injured servicemen had been so drugged, they hadn't a clue if they were on a roller coaster, a boat or an armored personnel carrier. On his flight over to Vietnam in 1969, John remembered, the plane had to make an emergency stop in Anchorage to remove a hysterical soldier who'd been placed in a straitjacket after he'd screamed he didn't want to return to Vietnam for a second tour.

John thumbed through the newspaper collection but decided to review the reports he had prepared for Rigby. He'd have to explain some large losses from last year, which he was prepared to do, and the estimates for this year's budget, which would also need explaining. John recognized that Rigby knew little, if anything, about ranching. Then he thought about the approaching winter and hoped the weather would be mild for the feeder calves, but with enough snow in the mountains to supply irrigation water for next summer.

John wanted to get another look at Trish and her spectacular sky-blue blue eyes, slightly magnified by her reading glasses. To John her slim but well-muscled body, particularly her legs, suggested an athlete, and an attractive one at that. He unbuckled his seatbelt and went forward to the galley where Trish had prepared a pot of coffee. "Want some?" she asked John.

"No thanks, but I would take a beer if you can find one," John said.

Trish reached in the small refrigerator, pulled out a German lager, and snapped off the top. She poured it too quickly into a glass, and the foam flowed onto the counter and dripped onto the floor. "I need lessons in bartending," she said as she wiped the counter and floor dry.

"This sure is a nice plane that Mr. Devlin owns," John said hoping to start a conversation.

"He told me it's the company plane, but since he's the chairman, I suspect he gets to use it often. Nice place to do business, at 35,000 feet, wouldn't you say."

"Sure beats the hell out of my office—front seat of my pickup."

"The pilots tell me you're Mr. Devlin's ranch manager. What takes you to New York?"

"I'm his new manager. Have some meetings with Mr. Devlin and his accountant. And you, what takes you to New York?"

"Mr. Devlin is thinking of hosting a conservation conference in Colorado just north of Durango. I work for the Durango-Silverton Railroad, which may transport the conference attendees from Durango to the conference site. I'm to meet with Mr. Devlin regarding all the details of the conference, including the transportation."

"When is the conference scheduled?" John asked.

"Probably in late May or early June. It's not been decided yet."

I hope I'm not involved, John thought to himself. That's the busiest time of the year, with calving, cleaning irrigation ditches, repairing fences and attending to sick calves.

"Do you want to watch some TV? I can find an all-news channel, maybe some sports or maybe CNBC with the latest stock prices."

"Can we check the stock prices for a minute?" John asked, hoping he could get a quote from the Chicago Mercantile Exchange on finished cattle for May. If they were steady, he could report the good news to Rigby.

As Trish approached the TV, the plane encountered some rough turbulence. The captain asked everyone to take their seats and put on their seatbelts. Trish staggered to her seat, almost in tears, as she buckled her seatbelt and looked nervously out the window.

"I hope this plane stays together," she said clearly frightened by the turbulence.

"Don't worry," John said, "I'm sure Mr. Devlin had them use super glue."

Still frightened, Trish only starred at John.

After five minutes, the plane resumed its smooth flight. Trish sat frozen in her seat.

"How about some TV?" John suggested as an antidote to Trish's fear. She nodded.

The color set flickered for a minute and then came on in the middle of a report on October's car sales. Another announcer summed up the performance of the Dow Jones average at mid-day, industrials up, Internet stocks weak, with energy stocks "showing some strength after yesterday's drop."

"Can't find anything else. Reception is a little cranky. Probably the altitude," John said, facing the television. "This station seems to be reporting about Wall Street stocks. I was hoping to find quotes on farm stock, you know, things like cows, steers, pigs and maybe even some grain prices."

"Can't help you with that. Sorry." Trish said.

To lighten the situation, John smiled and suggested a sports channel. "We could watch an ice-fishing contest on ESPN. If that's not available, what about the stereo beneath the TV?"

"OK, but I get to pick the music. What about a sandwich?"

They sat side by side eating and listening to the Dixie Chicks. Damn, it doesn't get much better than this, John thought to himself, as he settled into another German lager and looked into Trish's blue eyes. Maybe there are, after all, some benefits to working for a New York rancher with some money.

CHAPTER THIRTEEN

As they prepared to land at Teteboro, Trish leaned across John to adjust and then attach his seatbelt. He couldn't help but notice her firm breasts floating inside her loose white blouse. She then sat down beside him for the landing and crossed her gorgeous legs. As the plane pulled up to the Executive terminal, Trish turned to John and offered, "I do hope I'll have the pleasure of seeing you on the plane again or in Colorado."

"I fly back in two days," John responded quickly. "Will I see you on the return flight?"

"I'll try to arrange it with Mr. Devlin."

"I'd like that. You should also see if you can arrange a visit to the ranch. I'll see to it you have a horse that doesn't buck."

The driver of Devlin's limousine introduced himself inside the terminal, and then picked up Trish's small suitcase and led the couple to the Lincoln Town Car. "I'll drop you off first, Mr. Marlow, and then go onto the hotel where Ms. Jackson is staying.

As they approached the Holland Tunnel on the way into the city, John asked the driver, "Do we go through this hole to get to the city?"

"Yes, it's the Holland Tunnel, goes under the Hudson River."

"Never been in an underwater tunnel. I trust it don't leak."

"Hasn't in over 50 years," the driver responded.

"Bout time you built a new one, I'd say. I have a buddy back in Colorado whose father was a sandhog. He told me his father helped dig this hole."

"I think I'd rather drive it than dig it," the driver responded.

"That's for sure."

John turned to Trish to ask why she wasn't staying at the Devlin's guest apartment.

"He's put me up a hotel within walking distance of his office."

"Damn, I was hoping we could get better acquainted." Trish's silence let John know he was out of line.

As the limousine pulled up in front of the apartment house where Goodman Samson kept guest quarters on Central Park South, the uniformed doorman opened the door for John, greeted him by name, and took his plastic briefcase. The driver fetched his canvas overnight bag from the trunk before John could retrieve it himself. John leaned over to Trish, resisting the temptation to give her a kiss and said, "Hope to see you on the return flight."

He entered the apartment building's foyer, aware of light reflecting off the white marble floor and the brass wall fixtures bracketing large prints of stationary ducks and geese. At the elevator, the doorman handed John an envelope with a key and a note inside.

Dear John,

Please make yourself at home. The west bedroom is made up for your use. The maid will fix your breakfast around nine. We'll be here at 7:30 this evening to pick you up for dinner. Dress casual.

Welcome to New York.

Amanda Devlin

PS. If you need to call, our telephone # is: BU-8-3561

The fifth floor apartment looked out to Central Park. English antiques and large stuffed chairs filled the living room. Landscape painting and two Currier and Ives prints complimented the view from the large picture window. The flower pattern on the slipcovers picked up the off-green and tans in a large Larry Rivers landscape hung directly behind the sofa. To the rear of the galley kitchen was a bedroom and adjoining bath, with another bedroom and bath to the left of the living room. Which was the west bedroom? John tried to locate the sun to get his bearings, but it was lost in the hazy sky. Both bedrooms had king-sized beds. Should he call Mrs. Devlin? No. It'd look stupid if the ranch manager couldn't tell east from west. Finally he figured that if the apartment was located at Central Park South, he must be looking north out the window, so he went to the bedroom to the left, unpacked his "casual" clothes and popped open a beer in the kitchen.

John wasn't certain what the note meant by "casual" dress. Maybe they had expected he'd show up in New York in a suit and tie? Would a clean pair of jeans be considered too casual?

When the Devlins appeared at seven-thirty, Charles was wearing a tweed sports jacket and a large silver and turquoise bolo tie. His alligator cowboy boots complimented his western attire. Amanda wore a long peasant skirt with a tooled leather belt decorated with silver conches, and a silver-buttoned low-cut cotton blouse that managed to show off her considerable cleavage. Some exotic animal, probably endangered, had given up its life for her footwear. They exchanged pleasantries at the door before walking to the large picture window overlooking the park. Charles mixed a drink for himself and Amanda and then asked John what he'd have.

"I'll just continue to sip on this beer, thanks," John replied.

Amanda's immediate impression of John, given his dress, his swigs from the beer bottle and even his slack stance before the window suggested someone not given to social graces. She had felt his callused hands at the front door and as he slouched on the couch she noticed the dirt beneath his chipped fingernails and his poorly trimmed hair. His ill-fitting jacket showed wear around the cuffs and collar, and the wrinkled pants on his slim waist seemed a bit long as they creased severely over the top of his semi-polished cowboy boots.

Standing before the picture window, Amanda observed, "Isn't it beautiful? This park serves as the lungs of our city. It's a real treasure, the last wild space in a city of 10 million people. We're committed to maintaining this park in its original state."

Their conversation turned to the ranch. John reported the gold hunt had about ended with three arrests and the rumor of the minefield.

"A minefield rumor?" asked Amanda.

"Yes, the town thrives on rumors. With poor TV reception in the valley, it's their entertainment, and for some, their livelihood. I thought the story might stop the trespassers. And it did."

"Well done, John," Charles volunteered with a wide smile.

John went on to report that the cattle were doing fine. The same for the yearlings in the feedlot, though cattle futures did not look promising for their sale in May. John also brought the Devlins up to date with the mouse problem and the need to select another site for their house. "If we so much as disturb one of these critters, we'd be in big trouble with the Feds and the conservationists," John reported. Amanda asked about "the conservationists"—who they were and if they had caused problems for the ranch. "Mostly outsiders," John responded, "folks from Denver and the East who keep telling us how to run things." He wanted to say they were a real pain in the ass but knew enough, for the moment, to hold his tongue.

Amanda turned to Charles and asked how he planned to solve the problem of the "threatened" mice on their potential house site.

"Dear, I'm sure we can find a solution here. I'm working with Senator Barlow in Colorado to see if we can't get an exemption."

Amanda then asked about the ranch horses and their dispositions. "I've heard about Dynamite but for myself and the boys I want safe horses. They don't have much riding experience, mostly at a summer camp in Maine two years ago and some limited riding at a stable in the Hamptons last summer and of course, our visit to the ranch. Charles considers himself an experienced rider, but he could use something gentle also."

"I can handle myself far better than you think," Charles responded abruptly. Amanda smiled and suggested they leave for dinner.

At the French bistro, John had a problem with the French menu. Rather than cause any embarrassment by asking for an English version, he said "the same" after the waiter took Amanda's order. He was surprised to learn that the "escargot" turned out to be snails, not John's usual fare, and that "sweet breads" had no relation to sugared potatoes.

Amanda led the dinner conversation and let it be known that she wanted the ranch to be a showcase for conservation in the West. She didn't have much respect for those Westerners who were "fouling their nest with mining, over grazing, clear-cut timbering, and drilling. The West will become an environmental disaster, if it isn't already, unless some drastic conservation measures are undertaken. My view is that Westerners need to save the beauty of their land, their wildlife, their water and minerals, and before they destroy their environment, which belongs to all of us, they need to think seriously about biodiversity."

John usually had little patience with conservationists and their misinformed opinions. But with Amanda, here on her own home turf, he attempted to be more thoughtful. "Westerners do appreciate the beauty of their land," John explained, "but at the same time we do need jobs. Those jobs are in the mines, forests and on the land. I would argue that ranchers are some of the best conservationists in the West. We're not about to destroy or waste the grass and the water that provide us our livelihoods."

But before Amanda could respond, Charles, fearing the escalation of Amanda's aggressive opinions, changed the subject to some business matters. "You're meeting with Rigby tomorrow, and I'm sure you will find him helpful in the financial affairs of the ranch." He expressed the hope that he'd get out to the ranch in a couple of months with his architect to select an alternative site for the house. In the meantime, he had some important business in Argentina.

Over coffee, Amanda again returned to the subject of conservation by way of suggesting to John that he take a walk through the park in the morning. "It is the symbol of what conservation can do in the city. Our Park Conservancy raised almost 10 million dollars last year in private donations to keep the 800 acres in tip-top shape. Lawns need to be cared for, ball fields and playgrounds maintained, shrubs and flowers planted, trees fertilized and pruned, graffiti removed, monuments, bridges, buildings, and the zoo maintained, in addition to looking after the park's lakes and woodlands. I devote over half my time to the Conservancy and its operation, and I believe that some of our methods are applicable to the West. In our meetings with the Nature Conservancy and the National Open Lands Conservancy, of which Charles is the chairman, they both have suggested that some of our methods and ideas can be applied to the western landscape, including our new ranch."

They walked John back to the front door of the apartment building, where Charles's chauffeured limousine awaited them. As they said good night, John asked if Radio City Music Hall was nearby. He'd like to see it tomorrow after a walk in Central Park.

"Just down Sixth Avenue, about eight blocks," Charles said. "You can walk it in no time at all. When you get there, you might want to return by way of Fifth Avenue. You'll see many of New York's fancy shops. He then described the route for John and reminded him of his late-morning appointment with Rigby.

Coming in from the cool evening air, John found the heat in the apartment suffocating. He couldn't find the thermostat, nor could he find a window that opened. Instead he opened the front door, hoping for a small breeze to cool the hot apartment for a night's sleep.

The street noise from vehicle horns, the screeching firetrucks and the screaming police sirens leaked through the closed windows and added to John's sleeplessness. Finally, after another beer he dozed off on top of the covers. When he woke he heard someone moving about in the kitchen. A woman who introduced herself as Shelia was preparing breakfast.

"I found the door open when I arrived this morning. Did you hear anyone come into the apartment last evening?"

"No, but I left the door open to get some air in this place. It was hotter than an oven."

"Sir, you can't be doing that around here. You'll have every rapist in the park dropping in for cold beer. I'll turn the air conditioner on but it's best you keep the door locked during the night. You have any laundry I can do for you?" Shelia asked.

"Haven't been here long enough to get anything dirty."

"It doesn't take long in this city, even in an apartment like this. I can't keep up with the dirt, and the cockroaches and mice."

"Mice?" John asked.

"Yes. I trap them under the sink and in the food closet with Skippy's peanut butter. They seem to prefer the chunky kind, but I can't seem to get rid of them."

"Well I can tell you they're a problem in Colorado, also. The ones we have like to jump around and are protected by our government. They call them 'threatened.' Do yours jump?" John asked.

Shelia shrugged. "Caught one here this morning," she said as she went to the garbage bag in the kitchen and lifted out a mouse by its tail.

"Looks just like the ones we have in Colorado. You sure they don't jump?"

John asked, and then added, "Mind if I take it from you? I'd like to carry it back to Colorado."

"Mon, you can take him and all his cousins for all I care."

John took the mouse, wrapped it in a plastic bag and placed it in his overnight bag.

After breakfast, John strolled over to Central Park. He encountered a statue of some general of yore mounted on a horse that had reared onto its hind legs. John studied the conformation of the well-muscled horse. Too big for a Morgan or a quarter horse, he thought, and too thickly muscled for a thoroughbred. It bothered him he couldn't identify the breed. He noted the pigeon droppings all over the horse's head and most of the general's hat and shoulder epaulets. He'd have to report the situation to Mrs. Devlin, who'd spoken at length about the park's cleanliness.

As John walked further into the park, the smoky sunlight peeked through the bare limbs of the ginkgo trees. The elms and pin oaks still carried most of their mustard-yellow leaves in anticipation of the first frost. Joggers ran past with their headsets and blank stares. The exhaust from passing traffic caught John's attention. The frolicking squirrels seemed oblivious to the fumes. Further down the paved path, John noticed a group of mostly elderly women with binoculars looking up at a tall maple tree. Was it a mugger or a bird, John asked himself. As he approached the group, he heard one of the women say, "it's got a red breast."

"Leave him alone, ladies, and stay back. He's obviously wounded, and probably armed and dangerous," John said in a loud, serious voice.

"Darn it, he just took off north. Let's head to the brambles," the leader said to her binocular'd flock. She then turned abruptly to John, clearly annoyed. "This is a private birding group. We're out here every morning, and we don't need strangers disturbing our bird habitat."

John wanted to ask if the park had a mouse habitat but only responded, "Sorry ma'am," and walked on towards a lake.

Mothers with baby carriages sat on concrete benches absorbing the hazy sun filtering through the pin oak trees. A young boy tried to skip a stone across the black water. One mother with some popcorn had attracted a flock of pigeons. The pigeons flapped into flight when a small child ran at them with a stick. On a nearby bench, a bearded man in rags, homeless no doubt, shifted his sleeping position. A wheeled grocery cart transported his earthly possessions—two bulging plastic bags, a pair of dirty sneakers without laces and a child's broken pinwheel.

Not much in the way of wildlife, John thought. Just some squirrels, filthy pigeons and a red-breasted what-ever. Why is it that Mrs. Devlin and the conservancy folks wanted the West, and its national parks, to look like this park? Everything so perfectly manicured, paved walkways and even a few roads. Where are the wild animals—deer, elk, coyotes, bear, moose, mountain sheep and lions? In the park zoo safely behind bars, he knew. If Mrs. Devlin and her friends want to reintroduce the grizzly and the wolf throughout the West, why shouldn't they be reintroduced in the East, and maybe even into Central Park? Not in my back yard, they'd say, where hikers, children and their pets would be at risk. After all, the West has all those sheep to keep the wild critters well fed.

John fantasized about trapping a grizzly and a pack of coyotes, maybe a mountain lion and a wolf or two, plus a few feral dogs, and trucking them to New York, then dumping them in Central Park some summer evening. They'd certainly scare the hell out of the muggers and rapists who'd be forced to find safer ground outside the park. The coyotes and wolves would keep the squirrel and Canadian geese population in balance, not to mention the pigeons, which meant that the mounted general wouldn't have to change his uniform every day. Also, the city's dog population, which appeared to be mostly white toy poodles, would be returned to a manageable size. Surely the city would be happy with less dog shit.

And what if some prairie dogs could be transplanted. They could serve as appetizers for the coyotes and might even attract a few eagles for the bird watchers. These "cute little furry fellows," so described by Mrs. Devlin at dinner, could aerate all the ball fields and open grass meadows in the park while spreading the bubonic plague to muggers and rapists, assuming they could distinguish the bad guys from the general population. As for the male and female grizzlies, would New Yorkers kill them, feed them or cuddle them? Clearly, John believed, the bears would have all the berry bushes for themselves, grow fat and happy and breed like rabbits. Isn't that what Mrs. Devlin wanted? A balance in the natural world, especially in the West. Why not in the East, also? How perfect, John thought. He needed to suggest his plan to Mrs. Devlin.

John walked on and crossed a bridle path where three women rode by in their English riding habits and polished knee-high boots. They were accompanied by a mounted policeman. "Hi cowboy," one of the riders greeted John, as she and the other riders reined in their mounts. "Good morning girls," John replied as he tipped his cowboy hat. "Nice looking horses."

Then John looked at the policeman's scrawny horse and said, "Sir, that gelding of yours could sure use some groceries. I wouldn't want to be chasing muggers on that bag of bones," John offered.

"We've got some squad cars as back up," the sergeant reassured John.

"Have a good ride, ladies," John said as he walked away in the direction of a park bench. In the sunlight, John sat thinking about the city and his sheltered life on the ranch. What would it be like to live and work somewhere else? When he was in the Army and recovering from his Vietnam injuries at Letterman Army Hospital in San Francisco, he'd ride the cable cars, walk among the small fishing vessels by the wharf and take in the sounds and smells of the sea. He thought then that he might work as a seaman on a fishing boat, or as a brakeman on a cable car; maybe even stay in the Army if they'd promise to keep him in San Francisco. John thought of a trip he'd made to Billings, Montana, to a bull sale with his father just before his Army call up. Nice country, he thought; no mountains and deep snows, just blue-sky days and green grass. No, he reminded himself, same work but different grass.

Denver held no attraction for him—a city, unlike San Francisco, without charm, dry and filling up with folks pushed off their farms and ranches with the help of banks and insurance companies, who defined the economics of agriculture. The Broncos weren't bad, but the Rockies couldn't beat a good American Legion team, even if given a five-run lead in the ninth inning. After only one day in New York, John found the people to be interested in matters he knew nothing about or, if he did, he disagreed with them. Like Mrs. Devlin and her conservation ideas—wanting the West to look and live like the East. Or Rigby and his accountant mentality—thinking that everything could and should be measured in dollars and cents. Besides, John asked himself, what could I do in New York? I have no skills to match the city, except maybe as a mounted policeman in Central Park. But he'd be damned if he'd be seen riding one of those aged nags looking for muggers and rapists.

No, he'd just have to be satisfied with the world of Pine Valley and the Diamond J. Not a bad life, John had to admit, sometimes a bit lonely, and the winters often stretched out into May. But the West was changing. No longer the home of independent, self-sufficient workers and owners, it was becoming a region increasingly owned by easterners and their man servants, wage-slaves like John—skilled but no longer the owners. All John really wanted was his own ranch. But given the economics of ranching, he'd have to inherit it, and it was too late for that. Or win enough in the lottery to purchase a place, which meant he'd have to start buying lottery tickets. In the meantime, all he asked was an owner who left him alone to do what he did best, and who kept Rigby locked up in his urban cage.

A pack of joggers interrupted John's thoughts. Why so many of them in New York? Don't they have better things to do than to run around wasting their energy and ruining their health as they trotted behind exhaust pipes? I could put that energy to a useful purpose on the ranch, he thought, "like building a head gate, cleaning irrigation ditches, or putting shoes on a young colt ready to crack your chest open with a thousand-pound kick. After that little task, I'd ask them to mount the hurricane deck of the mustang and ride the buck out of the frightened animal. If they had any energy left over for a jog, I'd send them to town for some food shopping and a lesson in survival amidst the Circle of Knowledge.

John walked on over towards Columbus Circle and passed a statue of Ballion the sled dog. Why memorialize a dog, John asked himself? Just another thing he didn't understand about New York. He followed Devlin's directions to Radio City Music Hall. On the way, he noticed that the pedestrians thought nothing of bumping into him on the crowded sidewalk. Street vendors hawked silk scarves and gigantic pretzels the size of steering wheels, while pigeons fluttered about searching for crumbs. John couldn't understand why the city would spend money on those lighted DON'T WALK signs when nobody seemed to pay them any attention. He crossed a street with a green light only to have a speeding bike messenger bounce off his hip. He finally came to Radio City Music Hall. Its gray exterior looked like most other buildings in the city, dirt-streaked stone or concrete in need of a good scrubbing. He looked at the movie advertisement along with a photo of the Rockettes on stage. Maybe he'd catch a glimpse of one of those long-legged beauties. He could then report back to the Circle of Knowledge about his sighting. A 10-minute wait produced only more traffic and noise but no Rockette.

He felt restricted, almost claustrophobic, in the city. In every direction, he viewed only the sides of buildings or the canyons they created, which prevented him from seeing the sun, and certainly not a horizon, but only infrequent sightings of the sky, the color of galvanized metal with the bitter odor of vehicle exhaust.

John turned east on 51st Street and headed towards Rockefeller Center, a site Charles Devlin had suggested. As he walked on, he heard voices over the traffic shouting, "Stop the Horse." John looked up the street and saw a lanky, coal-black horse pulling a carriage trotting towards him. The reins were wrapped around a short post at the driver's seat, currently vacant. The horse, outfitted in a fancy black leather harness highlighted by polished brass fittings, trotted no faster or slower than the yellow taxies that surrounded the rig to the front and rear. A small group of pedestrians on the sidewalk ran alongside the horse shouting, as taxi drivers worked their horns, and the horse merrily moved with the traffic, clearly oblivious to the clamor and excitement that it had caused. John quickly stepped off the sidewalk and casually stepped in front of the horse. With his left hand he caught the reins up close by the steel bit. The horse came to an easy stop when John pulled him up by the slack reins.

The horse's warm breath felt soothing on John's cold hand. The horse was a big boned, tall Standard Bred gelding which, as he came to a stop, started to take a leak. He stood calmly under John's firm hand, taking a nibble at his hat, no doubt confused by the identity of his new handler. The sidewalk contingent stared in amazement at John and the ease with which he had captured the horse; John was now talking to the horse as if they were old friends. John expected someone to emerge from the crowd, not to offer a hand that he didn't need or expect, but to claim the horse, or lacking that, maybe provide some information as to the owner of the horse and carriage. No, they just silently stared at the horse, its shrinking penis, the puddle of urine, and John dressed in his hat and boots.

John asked himself, what in hell do I do with a horse and carriage in the middle of New York on a busy street with a bunch of irate taxi drivers and unhelpful pedestrians? He thought about driving the rig to his destination at Rigby's office. But that would mean doing a U-turn on a one-way street. Or, he could go around the block, over to Fifth Avenue, pull up to a fancy store and tell the doorman "Hold my horse and carriage while I pick up a diamond bracelet for my wife." No, that wouldn't work either; he'd probably get lost and miss his appointment with Rigby. He thought about perhaps driving the rig to the park, locating a policeman and handing the horse and carriage over to him. He'd probably be given a summons for disrupting traffic with a horse, but that would be a small price to pay in return for an escape from this predicament. John asked an onlooker, "Is there a policeman around here?" The well-dressed gentleman remained mute and immediately broke eye contact and walked east.

With John holding the horse and carriage near the curb, street traffic had all but stopped as taxis, trucks and cars moved slowly and cautiously around John. One taxi driver adjacent to the horse and carriage continued to lean on his horn. Recognizing the growing nervousness of the horse, John shouted at the driver, "You're not moving the traffic any faster with your horn, buddy." The driver leaned out the window and in his best Brooklyn accent yelled at John, "Fuck you and the horse you rode to town on." Nice folks, these New Yorkers, John thought and replied to the cabbie, "You must be the head of the city's Tourist Bureau." Another driver from the rear yelled, "Hey buddy, keep moving west.

Kansas City is just across the bridge."

Suddenly, a man in a heavy dark overcoat, scarf and leather gloves appeared on the scene holding a cup of steaming coffee. Out of breath, he ran up to John and gasped, "That's my horse you're holding, and I sure appreciate your assistance, buddy." The owner explained that he'd stopped at a coffee shop up the block, made a call to the hospital where his wife was expecting a baby, went to the toilet, and then returned outside only to find his horse and carriage missing. He asked a pedestrian if she'd seen his rig, and she said it was two blocks west and stuck in traffic. The owner was obviously relieved to locate the means of his livelihood. He told John about the horse Harry, which he leased from a stable near Central Park, said he drove Harry six days a week, also in the evenings sometimes, and made a decent wage, "even after the terrible insurance, feed and farrier costs." The driver commuted in from Queens Village every day, and had grown up around horses further out on Long Island. "I started this work about five years ago after my uncle said he'd made some good money doing the same line of work back in the 50s. I like the work, particularly the customers. They tip well, especially on holidays and anniversaries. It'd be a lot more pleasant if it weren't for the cabbies. They sure can be real pains in the ass."

"I know what you mean," John said as he passed the reins over to the owner.

As John left Harry and his driver, he turned his thoughts to the upcoming meeting with Rigby. He walked east, past Rockefeller Center and its ice rink, and over to Fifth Avenue. He looked in some of the store windows and wondered if people actually wore the clothing on display—like the spiked, high-heeled shoes. Someone could easily break a leg if they fell off the heel. Or the long fur coat which, if worn anywhere near Silver Valley during hunting season, would attract a .30–06 bullet.

John found Rigby's office on the 16th floor of the Madison Avenue office building. The receptionist said, "You must be John Marlow."

"That's me," John replied as he took off his cowboy hat and looked around the area at some plastic plants and uncomfortable chairs.

"Hi, John, good to see you again." Rigby, attired in an expensive suit too small for his overweight body, did not offer his stubby hand. Instead he pointed John to an office with three computers and a small conference table surrounded by red leather chairs. "Have a seat, Marlow. Coffee?"

"No thanks," John said as he studied Rigby. The thickness of his glasses turned his eyes into tiny brown beads, and his bald head had, once again, the high gloss of a glass bowl. More hair emerged from his ears than grew on his head. John thought that someone might have stuck an air hose up Rigby's ass to inflate his overblown, blubbery torso that at the moment put considerable pressure on the buttons of his coffee-stained white shirt. John imagined the buttons popping off like rifle bullets. He disliked Rigby, his soft fleshy appearance, his abrupt manner, and particularly his smell—a potent combination of Old Spice and sweat strong enough to stagger a pen of feedlot cattle.

"Let's get started," Rigby offered.

"Fire away," John responded.

"What's that supposed to mean?"

"I thought you had a lot of questions about the ranch and its operation.

That's what Mr. Devlin told me."

"Well, yes and no. I pretty much understand the operation of the ranch from talking with the accountant over at NOLC. And I've looked over the books from the time NOLC took possession of the ranch from the bank and the insurance company until Mr. Devlin bought it three months ago. But I do have some questions. For example, for the last fiscal year, there is a sum of $4,500 for fuel. What kind of fuel and for what purpose?"

John explained the number of vehicles on the ranch, the additional gas and diesel used during haying season and the added expense for the D-4 Caterpillar used during the winter months for snow removal and in the spring for ditch and water hole repairs. Rigby then asked about "excessive" repair costs, veterinarian and medical costs, and why the $10,000 for miscellaneous costs. What the hell are they? John went through all the costs by category and item by item from Rigby's ledger.

"And what about these feed costs that show up in the summer? Is God charging more for his grass?"

"No, but the Forest Service is."

"What Forest Service?"

John went into a long explanation about the ranch's arrangement with the U.S. Forest Service. The Forest Service leases grazing rights to grass on its land for the ranchers' livestock each summer. The fee varies according to the length of the summer lease and the number of cattle placed on the forest. Usually the numbers of cattle and the days on the forest don't vary from year to year except when there's a drought. "That's when they cut us back," John added.

"How many acres do we lease from the Forest Service?" Rigby asked.

"About 20,000 acres, though last summer we picked up another 5,000 acres when we bought the lease from a neighbor. That's the reason we paid more to Uncle Sam for grass last summer than we did the summer before. You'll notice also there is a capital charge for $250,000 for last year that includes $100,000 for the purchase of a Forest Service permit."

"Yes, I wanted to ask you about that."

"Forest Service leases, or permits, are bought and sold among ranchers. The lease/permit we purchased allows for 100 cows to graze four months on the forest. The lease was for sale at $800 an animal unit, or in our case a cow-calf pair. That equaled almost a $100,000 after the legal fees and closing costs were included."

"That's a hell of a lot of money the insurance company put out for just 100 cows. I can't see how, after you pay the monthly lease fee, which is $17 a cow I believe, and then figure the interest on your capital, you can make any money in this crazy business."

"Actually, we picked up that lease at a bargain rate. Our neighbor really needed cash," John explained.

"Still doesn't make sense. Did you recommend this purchase to the insurance company? I assume you did. And I assume we, the Diamond J, currently own this lease/permit?"

"Yes, in both instances."

"Now I want to move to the summary figures. You remember two years ago, the ranch lost almost $300,000. A year ago when the bank and insurance company repossessed the ranch from your family, the ranch lost almost $250,000. And if my projection is correct for this year, based on the first three months, it looks as if you'll be in the hole another $250,000, assuming the feeder cattle sell well in May. If not it could be much worse. And now, Mr. Devlin told me last week, you need some new equipment, fences and a new building, a utility building I think he said."

"Correct, and on top of that I recently contracted with a guard service for about 30 grand."

"What's this about a guard service?" John explained the circumstances and quoted Mr. Devlin: "I don't care what it costs." Then John added, as if to turn the knife in the wound, "We still haven't accounted for the costs we'll have for Mr. Devlin's new house."

"He may be living in the barn for a few years," Rigby replied without a smile.

"I assume you'll make that suggestion to Mr. Devlin," John said half in jest.

Rigby saw no humor in the response. He then glared directly at John through his thick glasses and said: "Look Marlow, this situation can't go on, understand? Either we start making some money on our investment, or we'll find someone who can turn this operation around. Mr. Devlin is a tolerant man, but not when it comes to hemorrhaging money. He's got himself a serious problem in Argentina. He doesn't need, nor do I need, additional problems in Colorado. This is a place for him to relax, enjoy his family, do a little riding and entertain some friends and business associates. We need to cut expenses and raise some more income."

After a slight pause, Rigby continued. "Don't forget you work for Mr. Devlin. This isn't your ranch anymore. It is the Devlin family's ranch and you're the hired hand. Do I make myself clear, Marlow?"

"I don't need to be reminded of who I work for. By the way, if you knew the ranch was losing so much money, why did Mr. Devlin buy it?"

"We looked at the ranch as a turnaround situation, a large enough ranch to provide some economies of scale. We're not expecting large profits immediately, but at a minimum we're expecting you to stop the financial bleeding. Mr. Devlin and I see the ranch as a good long-term investment, and we're counting on you to enhance Mr. Devlin's investment."

John didn't feel like getting into a discussion or an explanation of the economics of ranching with an accountant who'd have a hard time distinguishing a cow from a steer.

He stood, put on his hat, placed his papers in his plastic satchel and said: "I've got a plane to catch, Rigby. Maybe you can write me with your ideas on how to cut costs and increase income. And by the way, you might find it easier to do this on the ranch in Colorado rather than from your desk on Madison Avenue."

John marched out the door, took the gum from his mouth and pinched it onto a leaf of one of the plastic plants in the reception area.

CHAPTER FOURTEEN

When John arrived at Teteboro's Executive Flight Terminal's waiting room, he was both surprised and pleased to see Trish talking with the two pilots.

He took the same seat he had on the flight east, and Trish, as he had hoped, sat next to him. He fumbled with his seatbelt, hoping for some assistance from his cabin mate. All she said was, "you are a slow learner. Pull the strap down to your right and snap it in the red receptacle." John noticed Trish was wearing another loose blouse and tight slacks that accentuated her small but firm ass. Today she had pulled her auburn hair behind her head into a small knot, held in place by a silver barrette. She reached over and gently removed John's hat. "Hey cowboy, you won't need this on the flight, and if you feel naked, it's right above you."

For almost an hour they talked—about her youth in Toledo, two years of college, a failed marriage at too young an age, and her disappointment at not being promoted within the ballet corps at the American Ballet Theatre in New York in the 80s. "They said I was too busty to be a lead dancer."

"What a way to fail," John observed with something of a smile on his face as he took a peek at her breasts.

She enjoyed her work with the railroad in Durango. "They pay me well and offer good health benefits. I get time off to ski all over the West and, on occasion, sunbathe in Mexico. Not a bad life really, though I'm ready, I think, to settle down. I just haven't met Mr. Perfect yet. I know I'm a bit spoiled so it would be nice to find someone who could understand my habits."

"You mean like someone with a Gulfstream Five and residences scattered around the world?"

"Yes, something like that; I'm sure I could adjust to it."

"You make it sound as if you're an expensive keeper."

"Not really. I just broke up with a guy who lives in New York who clerked in a bookstore. A very sweet man. The trouble was, he kept changing jobs every year and refused to settle down. Also, his parents didn't help the relationship. They thought I was an airhead."

Trish looked over at John. "What about you?"

He talked about his life on the ranch, his failed marriage, his service in Vietnam, his hobby of saddle making and his great pleasure in spending time with his very talented son. "He's a good athlete and an excellent horseman," John explained, "plus a good student." He told her about the loss of the ranch to creditors and Mr. Devlin's purchase of it four months ago. "I'm happy to be working on what was our family's cattle ranch for four generations," John said. "I'm kind of stuck in my ways. My skills all relate to ranching or what I learned in the Army. The only things I do well are ride a horse and fire a weapon. Not skills that are in high demand these days."

"But you work outside, with cattle and horses. It sounds so healthy."

"You've been watching too many movies. Ranch work is not as pleasant as you might imagine. It's not all riding the range where the deer and the antelope roam."

"What did you do in the Army," Trish asked?

"I served in an Air Cavalry unit. We, the infantry, would fly around in a chopper like a pack of wasps and then go sting Charlie and the pajama boys on the ground."

"How'd you end up in the Army?"

"Drafted with some buddies right out of high school. With no college deferment, off I went to basic infantry training and then to jump school. The second time I was wounded, they sent me home.

"The second time?" Trish asked.

"The first was because of a dumb mistake on my part. I got my index finger caught in the chamber of a .50 caliber machine gun. It became infected and the doc had to chop it off at the first joint." John held out his left hand. "The second injury was the real one. We put down in open field. Charlie greeted us with his usual welcome wagon, otherwise known as an ambush—mortars, grenades and machine gun fire. Shrapnel about tore off my ankle. The docs reconstructed it so that I walk almost normal. It's hard to get a boot on because the ankle joint is partially frozen." He lifted his foot to show Trish his boot. "See? It's got a zipper on the inside like all my other boots. I just slip my left foot into the boot, zip it up and off I go."

"You're carrying some horrible memories. Any pain?"

"Only if I ride all day, it'll give me some pain. Advil mixed with bourbon at dinner usually takes care of the demons and the pain."

"You need bourbon now?" Trish asked, looking at John with a perfect smile. He nodded and threw her a kiss as she moved to the wet bar, poured two stiff bourbons on the rocks, handed one to John, and then held her glass up. "To my favorite cowboy and soldier." John stood up and kissed her. Trish moved her hand behind John's neck and pulled him close.

When they returned to their seats, she noticed him wiping his brow with his handkerchief. "Look at this," he said, holding out the handkerchief, which had collected some sweat and grime.

"That's New York for you. Maybe you need to shower," she suggested, referring to the small shower in the rear of the plane.

"How about joining me? I could drown in there alone."

It took a few seconds to absorb what he had suggested. He was handsome even though she figured there was a 20-year age difference. Nevertheless, she felt very attracted to John. But in a shower, she asked herself? She looked seriously into his eyes, and shook her head gently, saying "no."

John nodded affirmatively in response. He stood up from his seat, grabbed Trish's hand and pulled her out of her seat towards him. He pressed against her breasts and then moved his head slowly towards her lips. They kissed and then opened their mouths to each other's tongues; she placed both hands on the back of John's head and held him tight, and pressed into John's growing erection.

She pulled away when he took her hand to lead her towards the back of the plane.

"No John, not here. You take your shower and I'll have a drink waiting for you."

Clearly disappointed, John walked alone to the shower.

Within 15 minutes, he returned in bare feet with his wet hair combed.

"You look refreshed," Trish said as John sat beside her.

"I'd be more refreshed if you had joined me."

"I prefer the lower altitudes and without the water. Now, here's your drink."

They toasted one another before John asked Trish about her meeting with Devlin.

"He outlined the plan for the conference and asked how it might be coordinated with the train trip to the conference site. I went over some of the details with him, the logistics and cost. We kept being interrupted by phone calls from Argentina. He said he'd put together the names and addresses of the invitees and be in touch in a couple of weeks after his trip to Argentina."

"What is it that takes Devlin to Argentina, did he say?"

"Goodman has made some large loans to two Argentinean banks. I overheard Devlin talking about it on the phone. He also told me he's made a large personal investment in one of the banks. Apparently, Devlin thinks it's a good investment with the Argentinean peso tied to the dollar. Devlin's been down there three times now in the past four months, with another trip coming up. From what I could gather from his phone conversations, it sounded as if they're having some serious political problems in Argentina that may be affecting Goodman's loan and Devlin's investment."

"I'm sure Devlin will survive, with his deep pockets and the help of that son-of-a-bitch Rigby."

"You met with Rigby, didn't you?" Trish asked.

"Yes, this morning. It didn't go well. He's clueless about ranching. Just doesn't get the unpredictable nature of cattle markets and weather. He even threatened me with my job if I didn't turn things around and start to show a profit. To me he's nothing more than a REMF, which in the Army means 'a rear echelon mother-fucker.' Excuse my French. A REMF has the capacity to really mess up your life."

"Can you do what Rigby wants?"

"Yes, but it will take a while and a little luck, like better cattle prices and good weather. After we land, why don't you come to the ranch? I'd like to show you around." John added, "We might even have time for a shower."

"I'd love to spend time with you at the ranch but I can't right now. I have to work tomorrow. Damn it."

"Tell him you have some ranch chores to finish."

Trish laughed. "I've got too much work. Besides, I bet your shower stall is too small. Will you let me know when you'll be in the Durango area?"

"You bet. And will you call me from time to time and let me know how much you miss me?"

The plane landed in Gunnison. As John and Trish embraced, she whispered into his ear, "I'll miss you, cowboy."

"If you get lonely down there in Durango and can't find a shower, come up for a visit. Plenty of hot water," John said with a wide grin.

"You can count on it."

John drove from the airport to the ranch, stopping at the hardware store to pick up some supplies.

"Any new rumors been created in my absence?" he asked the Circle of Knowledge.

"Three town folks stepped on some land mines while you were gone. Hard even to find their remains," the ex-sheriff reported. As the Circle broke into laughter, Clyde's dentures fell to the floor. As John leaned over to pick them up, Slim shouted, "Don't touch 'em John. They're infected!"

John walked over to the medical supply section of the store. In the cooler he picked up a small bottle of fresh penicillin. For a cow with pink eye he found the proper medicated powder and a black eye patch.

He felt happy to be back on home territory where he could see the sky, breathe the fresh air and not be bothered by WALK and DON'T WALK signs. Back at the ranch, Josh reported he had placed the cow with pink eye in the corral for doctoring, but no other problems.

The next morning, John started Josh on winterizing all the vehicles and then rode through the cattle, grazing in the recently cut hay meadows. Two bald eagles had made their winter move from their fishing perch atop the large cottonwoods on the river to similar outposts at the edge of the hay meadows. Instead of fish, they swooped down to catch field mice and an occasional young prairie dog. Their annual arrival at the ranch signaled to John the official start of winter. It would be an early winter this year, John thought. He loved to watch the eagles glide in the thermals above the pastures and then dive quickly for their meal. He had to admit that the conservationists had helped the ranch in their successful efforts to save the eagles. John turned his attention to the cattle. They had come off the forest in good flesh. The heifers, too, looked especially fit after three months at boot camp. He hoped it would be a mild winter with no need for supplemental feed other than their daily hay ration. That would be a savings in Rigby's book.

John returned to resume chores with Josh. They easily fixed a broken water pump with a freshly soldered connection to the engine's coil. They then turned their attention to the broken set of tire chains for John's pickup. Also, John noticed the cracked hydraulic line on the tractor. Until he could pick up a new one in town, the line would have to function with a couple of wraps of duct tape. If not for baling wire and duct tape, this ranch would have failed long ago, John reminded himself. He made a mental note that he'd also have to order a new battery for Josh's truck; it just wouldn't hold a charge. After two days and the winterizing of all the vehicles, the men readied themselves for their annual elk hunt.

John knew where the bulls hung out at this time of year. He'd never failed to bag a bull elk except for three years ago, when the drought hit the country and disturbed the elks' usual migration. John and Josh placed the pack saddle and the two pack panyards on the same stout, bay gelding they used in summer to haul salt blocks to the cattle on the forest permit. As a precaution, they tied some orange tape to the manes and tails of their horses, a safeguard against a trespassing hunter who might mistake their mounts for elk, like the Texan who shot the horse out from under John's neighbor. They tied to their saddles the scabbards that held their .30 cal semi-automatic rifles and, with their panyards filled with sandwiches, ammunition, binoculars, two dressing knives and a meat saw, they rode off into the forest.

Within two hours they had gained about 2,000 feet in altitude as they rode through aspen groves, turned gold with the first frost. They let the horses blow before they came into the area where the bull elks normally hung out after their summer breeding activity. Fresh manure gave away their location. The two hunters tied up their horses well below where they planned to station themselves for a kill. John took up his position behind a large spruce next to the same game trail he always hunted. Josh did likewise about 30 yards away. They had agreed that if a bull appeared, John would take the first shot. If more than one bull appeared, as they sometimes did, John would take the bull closest to his firing position.

John rarely missed a shot to the heart. He hated, like any good hunter, to injure an animal and let it escape. As a youth, he had injured a bull through the lungs and failed, at first, to locate it. When he reported the incident to his father that evening, he was ordered to return the next morning with a pack horse and track the blood trail. "Don't come home until you find it," his father demanded. It took John most of the morning to pick up the trail and by mid-afternoon, he found the bull lying on its side in an aspen grove breathing with difficulty. He put a bullet into its heart, gutted and quartered the half-ton animal and packed it out by horse on two round trips to the ranch. He learned his lesson: either take a good shot or no shot at all. Nor did his father allow the use of a scope on any rifle. "A scope only magnifies the chance of wounding an animal," he once told John. "To assure a clean kill, you have to get close to the animal."

John and Josh were careful to place themselves downwind of where they believed the bulls were bedded. By mid-afternoon, John knew the elk would move down from their beds along the game trail to a small water spring below the men's camouflaged position. Sure enough, as the shadows lengthened from the tall Engelmann spruces, a six-point bull appeared at the top of the game trail. John held his fire, waiting patiently for the bull to move closer and broadside to John's position. After a long wait, the bull turned with his flank facing John. John slowly and methodically squeezed off a round. The bull dropped instantly, with a bullet to its heart.

The two men dressed out the animal, quartered it and loaded up the two panyards. "Nice shot, John," Josh said admiringly. John responded, "I was afraid he'd stand there facing me for the rest of the day. Finally he turned broadside for a good clean shot. Next couple of days we'll come up here again and get you one."

"Hope it's a six-pointer like yours."

"There's plenty more up there, I know," John replied, pointing up the hill. "On our ride up here, did you see the amount of elk manure scattered on the trail?"

Late in the afternoon, they rode into the ranch corrals, unsaddled, grained and thoroughly brushed their horses and turned them out. John and Josh hefted the elk quarters into the back of John's pickup. The next day he'd take the carcass to an old timer in town who'd hang the carcass, butcher the quarters into various cuts, wrap each portion separately, mark and date the individual packages. The meat would fill almost half of John's freezer and last until next summer.

Back at the house, John called the Fish and Wildlife office to report his kill. He didn't have to by regulation, but it helped them in their kill count for the season.

The biologist, the same one same one who had come up to the Diamond J to investigate the mouse situation, couldn't resist asking John about the mice.

"I checked in on them on our way up to our hunting site. They must be horny little buggers. They were jumping all over the place having a hell of time, an honest-to-goodness orgy it looked like." John reported.

"You haven't disturbed them, have you?" Ted asked.

"Wouldn't think of it." John responded. "Why, I saw one huge mouse yesterday; you could have saddled him and rode him to town. Another one had a rib-eye on him that Swift would pay a premium for. If I could sell them by the pound, I could retire tomorrow."

"Thanks for your call, and don't you be selling any of those critters to the packing houses for Marlow's Mouse Fillets."

"Why, that's a great idea. I never thought of that," John chuckled as they ended their conversation.

In late November, the morning frosts lasted well into the afternoon. The gray skies day after day and the overhead migration of geese suggested an early winter. The equipment was ready, John thought to himself, but were the cattle?

CHAPTER FIFTEEN

Winter backed into late November, with the season's first snow two days after John bagged his bull elk. The first three inches soaked quickly into the unfrozen ground. It was the way John had hoped the winter would start: a wet, early winter snow covering the meadows followed by a hard freeze to capture the internal moisture until spring. After the spring thaw, the stored moisture would kick-start the new grass into the growing season.

Days after that first snow and with nighttime temperatures dropping into the high teens, the winter feeding season for the ranch had officially begun. The frost-covered brown grass lacked nutrition and so to maintain the cattle's flesh, John started to feed a light ration of hay. He figured that with the 1,600 tons of hay put up in the fall, there would be enough feed, assuming a normal winter, to carry the 800 cows and heifers through spring calving and into the summer grass season. He liked to augment the cow's hay ration with a little protein supplement if the winter turned severe and extended beyond Easter. If they fell a bit short of hay, John knew he could purchase some at a reasonable price from a neighbor. Yet, he also knew the protein blocks added to operating costs, which would mean, no doubt, bitter complaints from Rigby. But the extra cost assured healthier calves and a smaller death loss.

By the end of the first week in December, 22 inches of snow had already fallen. The tractor pulling the feed wagon, loaded with round bales, managed to keep the paths open through the deep snow in the meadows. Every morning the cows met the wagon and after the bales were rolled out, they consumed their 20-pound hay ration. It was the same drill every morning. Load the hay wagon, roll out the hay, look for any sickness in the cows and then chip ice and break open water holes in those irrigation ditches that carried stock water in winter. The only break in the daily routine occurred when Johnny came down from Cheyenne on vacation to help out, which allowed one man a day off from the cold boredom of feeding.

Two days before Christmas, a major blizzard hit western Colorado. By the time it ended late on Christmas morning, 38 inches had piled up on the snow already on the ground. Lying in bed, John knew this was a nasty storm, with small flakes and strong winds out of the northwest, the direction all livestock men most feared. "The smaller the flakes, the worse the storm," his father always said. When John awoke just after midnight to feed the fires in the kitchen and sitting room, he noticed that the power had gone off at 11, according to the electric clock. He rose with first light and saw that the snow continued to come down sideways and that some drifts had already reached above the window sills. He dressed in cotton and wool layers before stuffing himself into his insulated Carhart coveralls, fired up the gas stove in the kitchen for some coffee and fried a frozen waffle in bacon grease before adding a generous helping of lumpy peanut butter. He was prepared to meet the day but without great enthusiasm. It would not be a pleasant one, he knew from surviving countless winters in the mountains.

John had learned long ago that one couldn't fight a storm any more than he could fight a battalion of armed Viet Cong with a penknife. Winter was God's test of a person's fortitude, patience and strength. Sometimes Mother Nature took the upper hand. John had learned it was prudent to let her have her way. If you resisted, a person could waste a lot of energy and get beat up real bad. Granddad Marlow advised John years ago during a spring flood, "that the Silver Valley River has the right-of-way, and she never hesitates to take it."

John struggled to make his way through the snow from his house to the equipment barn. Without even checking, he knew the electric block heaters for the tractor and the pickups had shut down, which meant the engine oils would have thickened into a glop, the consistency of paste. He also knew that neither the tractor nor the pickup engines would start; they'd only groan as the batteries tried unsuccessfully to push the tie rods and pistons through the frigid oil.

Josh came out from his house bundled in his winter coveralls, the frayed pants pulled over a pair of waterproof work boots, and the earflaps of his wool cap tied under his chin. He had a red silk scarf wrapped across his nose and mouth to cover his lips already discolored with a heavy application of bag balm. He moved stiff-legged in the snow towards the equipment shed with a jug of hot coffee.

"Merry Christmas," Josh offered. "One hell of a storm. My nostrils froze to the inside of my nose walking over from the house."

"Sure is. Probably the worst in my lifetime," John answered. "Dad always talked about the one in '48 when they had 6 feet on the level, right up to the fifth wire on the fences and 20 below."

"Well it's 20 below right now, and I measured over 5 feet in a drift by my back door, so we're pushing up against that record. It's at least a five-wire blizzard by my reckoning. That wind feels like a blow torch against my face. Don't be shedding any tears about the cattle, or your eyes will freeze shut. This one looks to be a competition between Mother Nature and her children, and assuming I'm one of the latter, I'd put the odds on Big Momma right now."

"Yeah, it's a nasty one all right, Cold enough to freeze the balls off a brass monkey," John said. "I have no idea when the power company will get us up and going again but I can bet, given the winds last night, they've got lines down from here north to the Wyoming border. And out here, we're always the last to get any attention."

"What are we going to do about the tractor and pickups?" Josh asked, recognizing the seriousness of not being able to get feed to the cattle.

"I'll go to the house and see if I can reach the power company. Maybe they can give us an estimate when we'll have some juice."

"Forget it," Josh said, "The phones are out." John reached for his cell phone, only to greeted with the message, "No service available."

If the ranch only had that Honda generator John had asked the NOLC for last winter. The cows would soon need water. If the men were unable to get to the ditch to break ice, they would quickly dehydrate and weaken in the sub-zero weather.

"My Dad once had a tractor frozen like ours," said Josh. "He took some hot charcoals, put them in his cooking grill and placed it under the oil pan of his John Deere. Had to watch out he didn't burn up some wires, or ignite some oil or diesel on the tractor's frame, but within two hours he had the engine started.

Then he connected jumper cables to a pickup and we were in business for the day."

"I'll get my grill and charcoal and we'll have a barbeque," John added with a smile. "You fetch some hot dogs and a fire extinguisher."

Within 30 minutes, the men had the coals red hot, but without a dangerous flame. They placed the grill under the tractor, propped it up close to the oil pan on some cinder blocks and hung plastic tarps from the tractor's hood to fashion a makeshift tent to keep the heat trapped against the bottom of the tractor. They waited with their hot coffee for the heat to warm and thin the oil.

"I'd sure as hell like to experience some of that global warming we hear so much about," John said.

"That's for sure. Who's that guy who's always complaining about global warming?" Josh asked.

"You mean the former Vice President, Al Gore."

"Yeah, that's the guy."

"Give him a call, wish him Merry Christmas and tell him we need the National Guard to help us feed this morning, and could he please arrange for a small heat wave to arrive in Colorado within the next 24 hours?"

"This is about the time I wish we had a team of horses like Dad's," John offered. "You never had to plug those guys in an electrical socket to warm their engines. They always started on a cold morning like this, a bucket of grain and they'd be ready to move out and work all morning."

Josh nodded. "My Dad used to say the dumbest damned thing he'd ever done on the ranch in Fraser was to sell his Belgian work horses."

The two men listened to the weather report on a portable radio. The news was not encouraging: "The mountains can expect more snow and sub-zero temperatures throughout the day and into the weekend. Record lows have been recorded in Gunnison and Fraser, and snow depths in parts of the state have measured over 6 feet, with drifts up to 12 feet. Large cattle losses are expected in the western part of the state from the San Juans in the south and north into Wyoming. Blowing snow and mounting drifts are forecast for the eastern plains. The Highway Patrol has closed all interstates within Colorado and most county roads are reported impassable. The Colorado Cattlemen's Association has requested the Governor to declare the hardest hit counties as 'disaster areas.' All major highways, airports and most municipal services are closed, while hospitals in most areas remain operational with auxiliary generators."

After two hours of sitting next to the tractor holding a fire extinguisher, Josh announced, "I think this beast is well done, or at least medium rare. Maybe we should give it a try."

"John, give the carburetor a shot of ether. That should help."

On the first attempt, the tractor's engine turned over and wheezed as all pistons fired up. With the tractor running, John attached the jumper cables from the tractor to the Dodge pickup. It too sputtered to life. After Josh adjusted the tractor chains, he jumped up into the coved cab with John. They headed to the stack yard for hay.

The ten o'clock agricultural report on the tractor's radio announced more bad news. Livestock losses were mounting, particularly among some of the state's largest sheep operators. All sale barns had closed because sellers couldn't transport their livestock to the yards. The Governor, after flying over much of the state with the Commanding General of the Colorado National Guard, had declared 22 counties "disaster areas." The announcer admitted he'd never reported such a storm in his 35 years on the air. As usual, he ended his program with, "Have a Good DAY." Josh looked at the radio, gave it the bird and then said, "Fuck OFF."

The chained-up tractor with the feed wagon made slow progress towards the stack yard, bucking drifts that came up to and, in some cases, over the radiator. The falling snow muted all sound from the bawling cows but not the whap, whap, whap from the tractor's engine. At the stack yard, guarded by a high fence, a drift on the west side had allowed some elk easy access to the hay. They had fed there all evening, leaving behind a 3-inch layer of frozen elk manure. It took both men 20 minutes to shovel open the gate to the yard. The tractor's forklift easily loaded 8,000-pound bales onto the wagon. Normally, the cows stood together in the meadow awaiting their hay, but on this morning after the blizzard they'd sought shelter under trees, behind large bushes, or in the dry irrigation ditches left empty of water during the winter. John noticed the two bald eagles in the cottonwoods by the ditch. It would be awhile before their winter feed source—prairie dogs, rabbits and field mice—would make their appearance from under the snow. The coyotes, too, would have difficulty chasing rabbits that could scamper atop the snow with feet designed like snowshoes.

As John looked off to the east end of the meadow,, he thought he noticed a large number of cows, maybe as many as 50, that had drifted with the wind to the meadow's east end. He pulled out his binoculars. The cows had drifted up against the wire fence, where they had piled on top of each other. They had either smothered or were trampled to death. Through the glasses John saw no movement in or near the pile of Black Angus hides that stood out against the snow. He noticed a few frozen carcasses, their legs stuck high in the air like flagpoles announcing surrender.

To keep the main herd of cows from following them to the east, the men quickly unloaded their hay as the survivors appeared from their cover. They moved slowly in single paths, humped up against the cold with icicles hanging from the hair beneath their bellies, to the rolled-out cured hay. John noted some runny noses; he could expect some respiratory problems in the next couple of days.

As the men moved towards the east fence, they could tell the ranch had suffered a major loss. The mass of carcasses extended for 30 yards along the fence and in some places the cows had piled up three deep. If only the fence had broken rather than acting as a barrier, John thought, the losses would have been minimal. Instead, he estimated at least 40 dead.

With the tractor's forklift and a heavy chain, they disentangled the frozen carcasses, and then clipped off the identifying ear tags. They counted 48 tags from mostly young cows that had never learned survival techniques in a blizzard. Coyotes had already feasted on the loins of some of the animals, the open wounds too frozen to add blood to the reddish snow. Surely the eagles and neighborhood hawks, and maybe a mountain lion or two, would join the feast and survive the blizzard, John thought.

The only communications between the men were the hand signals they exchanged. John would give the wrap sign from the tractor's cab and Josh, with his scarf covering his nose to protect against the smell, stood amidst the dead cows, wrapping the chain around the leg of one cow, then another, as he gave a thumb up to John to lift the dead animal. He'd slowly lift the bloated carcass and place it beside the others, then signal to Josh to unhook the chain. For over an hour they continued to disassemble the pile of dead cows. John knew the rendering truck could not make it through the snow to collect the carcasses for the dog food processors. They'd have to remain there until spring, when the internal gases of the animals would bloat the carcasses into gruesome shapes. By then, no rendering outfit would touch them. John would have to come out in the spring with his backhoe, dig a large pit and bury them. He'd fashion a marker, onto which he'd attach the useless ear tags.

They moved to the irrigation ditches that carried winter stock water; they were frozen solid. John looked at Josh and muttered, "Just our luck. When we get back to headquarters, we'll see if we can get the snowmobile going. If so, you'll need to go up to the head gate on the river, chip the ice from around the gate, and open it higher so we can get some more water down to these ditches for the cattle. If that doesn't work, we'll have to build some fires in the ditch and hopefully melt enough ice to satisfy the cattle. Now let's get going over to the bulls, feed them and check their water. Same problem, you can be sure." To their surprise, all the bulls were accounted for, but because they were on the lower end of the same frozen ditch, they too lacked water.

By the time both men had finished feeding, chipping ice and counting their losses, it was well after noon. They unhitched the hay wagon and parked the tractor inside the barn close to the hot wood stove. They hauled more wood in from the shed, and then John poured some hot coffee from his thermos into two cups. He lifted his cup. "Merry Christmas. Your father would have been proud of the way we cooked that John Deere this morning. Let's go and get warm."

"You're going to join us for Christmas dinner? Mary is expecting you and the kids have a present for you," Josh said.

"Let me clean up at my place first. I've got to feed the fire to keep the pipes from freezing. Give me 15 minutes and I'll be right over."

The cold had not yet frozen John's water. Why, he wasn't quite sure, except he knew that it helped to leave the gas stove on in the kitchen.

The phone rang. That the phone had sprung to life surprised John more than the caller. He hoped it was his son.

"Merry Christmas," Charles Devlin announced in a cheerful voice. John returned the greeting without much enthusiasm.

"I see on the television news that you had a big storm out your way," Charles said, leaving an opening for John to fill in the details.

"It's big all right. A blizzard by any definition. About 5 feet on the level and drifts above your head in some places, and below zero only adds to the misery. Makes it hard to feed. We just got finished."

"Sounds unpleasant," Charles said from his penthouse apartment in New

York.

"I can assure you, sir, it is more than unpleasant when the temperatures drop to 20 below and we suffer some bad losses."

"Bad losses?"

"Yeah, some 42 pregnant cows dead and quite a few sick and weakened by the storm."

"My God, what happened?" Charles asked.

John explained how the cows had drifted into the fence during the blizzard, piled up on each other and had either smothered or had been trampled to death.

"Is there no place we can provide them protection from these storms?" Charles asked.

"Not unless you want to build a giant barn for over 700 cows. This was an unusual storm. We haven't seen one like this since '48, so it's uncommon to have these huge losses."

"That's not particularly comforting. What do you estimate the loss in terms of dollars?"

"They were all young pregnant cows probably worth $1,200 apiece."

Charles paused but a moment. "Christ that's $50,000."

"And that doesn't include our losses at the feedlot, which I expect we'll have," John added.

"Are we covered by any insurance on these cattle?"

"Not that I'm aware of. It's very expensive but you might want to check with Rigby," John responded, knowing the answer.

Charles changed the subject and asked about the weather forecast for the next few days. Then the real purpose of his phone call became obvious when Charles announced: "Look, I know you're busy, but I want to bring the boys out for a couple of days of skiing. I understand the snow conditions are excellent. You must ski—join us for a day."

John took a long breath to calm himself. As for the skiing invitation, John thought it best not to remind Devlin that the cows hadn't yet learned to feed themselves in the deep snow. He then said, "If I have to work in the snow, I don't have much inclination to play in it." He questioned Devlin as to where everyone would stay.

"I can sleep in the cabin, and if you don't mind, maybe the boys could stay in your house, which I assume would be warmer. They don't need anything fancy, some empty floor space that's all. They'll have their sleeping bags. For them it will be like camping out."

And for me, they'll be a pain in the ass, John thought.

"What about the pilot? Should I try and find him a room at the motel in town?"

"No need to," Charles replied, "he's flying on to Denver, where he'll spend the night after dropping us off in Gunnison, and then he'll fly some clients back to New York the next morning."

John knew he had more important things to do than babysit and cook for some teenagers who, if they found the temperatures unbearable for skiing, would stick around the ranch, and be in the way of John and Josh's efforts to keep over 700 cows alive.

"Mr. Devlin, this is a hard time for me to be entertaining guests. Maybe you and the boys could wait a week until things, you know, settle down here, and the roads are plowed," John said. Rather than a week he wanted to say a month.

"That wouldn't work, given their vacation schedule and my planned trip to Argentina. We won't be in your way, all we need is a four-wheel drive vehicle and we'll be out of your hair all day. Without bragging, I'm also a pretty good cook. Anything I can bring out to you?"

"Yeah, I could use a good stiff drink right now and a good generator. Our power is out, though I expect it back by tomorrow. Also, we're a bit short on working vehicles at the ranch right now. It'd be best if you could rent an SUV at the airport."

"I'll arrange it and also bring some booze. As for a generator, can't you find one in town?"

"My problem right now is I can't get to town. Most of the county roads are impassable and the road into the ranch is drifted closed. I'll have it plowed by nightfall. I expect the county roads will be passable by the time you arrive here tomorrow afternoon. If not, you'll have to parachute in. As for the generator, I'm sure Rigby will complain loudly about the expense," John said in a curt manner.

"You care for the ranch and its needs, and I'll deal with Rigby. Get yourself whatever size generator you need. We'll see you tomorrow afternoon, and I'll be carrying your Christmas present."

Damn, I wish he'd bring me Trish. That would be enough of a present.

CHAPTER SIXTEEN

By the following morning, the snow had stopped, the electricity was restored and the county roads plowed. Josh's work at the head gate had provided the livestock with running water. Only the health of the cows and the feedlot yearlings worried John. He felt fortunate that they had suffered only two deaths, though the feedlot manager did report considerable weight loss among the cattle, plus the placement of four steers in the sick pen. But the agricultural news on the radio reported some good news. In reaction to the storm, cattle futures had jumped 10 cents a 100 weight. We might make a nice profit this spring on the feedlot yearlings, John thought.

The Devlins enjoyed their skiing days at Crested Butte, and Charles had proven to be a decent cook. His cheese omelets were a welcome change from John's usual cold cereal and toast. And he particularly enjoyed the steaks Charles had brought out from New York. Why was it, John wondered, that New York beef always tasted so much better than the tough, tasteless leather strips available locally?

On their third day at the ranch, when a cold wind returned from the north, the Devlins decided to forego skiing. The break allowed John to discuss some ranch matters with Charles over breakfast, specifically about where on the ranch he wanted to build his home and the summer construction schedule. "I'm assuming, because of the mouse problem, you'll want to build at the first site we looked at?"

John's question clearly changed Charles' mood.

"John, you need to know there have been some major changes in my plans. All my recent trips to Argentina are the result of some very large investments my company has made in two Argentinean banks. I've also made some large personal investments in the country, mostly banks, but also in some real estate ventures. Only two weeks ago, however, the Argentine government announced it could not repay its international loans, including interest payments to my investment bank. The Argentinean economy currently is in a nose dive with its currency depreciated 40 percent in only one week. The loss to my company, after writing off the debts, will be in the neighborhood of $200 million. Consequently, the value of Goodman's stock has plummeted and the value of my stock options with Goodman has lost value. In addition, my personal Argentinean investments have similarly suffered. What all this means, right now, I can't predict, but I do know that I may have some difficulty paying off the loan on this ranch. Therefore, I've decided to delay the construction of our ranch house. Recently, I've needed to get away from New York, clear my head and spend some time with the boys. That's the reason for our ski trip. Mrs. Devlin is, as you can imagine, very upset with the news and that's the reason she remained in New York. I'd much appreciate it if you could keep this information confidential. I'm having enough problems answering questions to the press and to my corporate directors in New York. I don't need to be doing so in Colorado."

"I'm sorry to hear the news. We can keep everything going here as if Argentina didn't exist," John assured Charles. Then John realized Devlin could lose the ranch and John his job because of some incompetent and crooked finance minister 10,000 miles away.

"I very much appreciate your efforts and loyalty," Charles responded. "We need to watch our expenses and hopefully increase the income."

"I'm working at it, Mr. Devlin."

Charles moved the conversation away from business matters and asked John about his family.

"They're in Cheyenne, doing OK I guess. Johnny, my boy, made all-state football this fall and is working hard to get into Yale. He's got the grades and hopes for a big scholarship."

"Yale, that's where I went," Charles said excitedly. "I'd like to write a letter of recommendation for him."

"Thanks. That would help."

"Send me the boy's resume."

After breakfast, John went to join Josh for their usual feeding routine. Charles spent his morning reading reports when not on his cell phone with New York. The teenage boys, dressed in their ski outfits, joined John and Josh during their feeding chores and asked innumerable questions about the tractor, the cattle and their feed requirements, and the presence of the carcasses at the far end of the snow-covered pasture. An answer to one question only encouraged a host of additional questions. Finally, John announced, "Any more talk and the cows will be spooked by the noise. We need to be quiet for a while." About the time they had finished feeding and chipping ice at the ditch, the boys began to complain of the cold wind.

On their return to headquarters, Chris, a tall lanky boy, the oldest of Charles' stepsons, asked if there were any chores he and his brother might do. Before John could answer, Josh offered his suggestion. "I could sure use some fire wood at my house, and I'm sure John could also." John looked at Josh, shook his head and said, "They've probably never handled a chain saw." Randy, the youngest boy, piped up and answered, "Oh yes we have."

John walked over to Charles' cabin, where Charles had set up his work on a table next to his unmade bed and asked if the boys might use the chain saw to cut some wood. John said to Charles, "We could sure use it, but only if you feel comfortable with them operating a chain saw. They tell me they've used one before." Charles put on his down ski jacket and insulated boots and walked out to where the boys stood over a pile of logs and a saw buck. Josh was showing the boys how to start the saw using the manual choke for cold weather. Charles looked at the situation and said to the boys, "Now I know you've used one of these saws before out in the Hamptons, but I want you to be careful. Be sure you're wearing gloves and put on your ski goggles for protection."

John suggested they all take a break and after lunch the boys could begin their work at the woodpile. Over steak sandwiches, the boys had more questions for John, indicating they'd not spent much time around livestock or in the out-of-doors, except maybe skiing. Living in New York too long, John thought, the city had flushed out of them all the basic human survival instincts: how to prevent frostbite in sub-zero temperatures, where to find protection in a blizzard, how to stay warm without electricity or even what to eat and how to dress. But then John recognized that the boys possessed survival skills he'd never acquired:

how to move around New York on its complicated subway system, how to avoid the crossfire of gang wars, where to have a computer fixed or even how to use one.

After lunch, John and Josh lit a fire in the equipment shed's wood burning stove before cleaning the carburetor on the snowmobile. Meanwhile the boys worked at the woodpile. The whine of the chain saw indicated they were progressing without any trouble through the pile of spruce and scrub oak logs. Right after John heard the chain saw stop, Randy ran into the shop where John was huddled over the snowmobile's engine. The youngest Devlin boy blurted out: "Chris had an accident with the saw, come quickly."

John and Josh ran to the woodpile to find Chris sitting in the snow with his left pant leg ripped and bloodied. Chris looked up, tears in his eyes, and said, "The saw slipped, hit a knot I think, bounced up and came down on my leg right here," pointing to a bloody cut on his left leg. "Hurts really bad," the boy declared with tears beginning to flow down his cheeks. Josh and John picked Chris up and carried him into the shop. Josh ran to find Mr. Devlin, while John cut through Chris' ski pants. Devlin came running into the shop and immediately eyed the bloody pants. John said quickly, "A lot of blood but not too deep."

"How you doing?" Charles asked his stepson.

"It hurts. Will I be able to walk?"

"Of course you will," John responded, preempting anything that Charles might say.

Charles looked at the wound and then turned his head away from the gash as John swabbed the blood that continued to flow from the ragged wound.

"We need to get him to a hospital as soon as possible to have the gash looked at and stitched," Charles said, his voice strained. "Also, a specialist could tell whether there is any muscle, nerve or ligament damage. We can fly Chris back to New York and have him at Columbia Presbyterian Hospital with a specialist in five hours."

"There's a hospital nearby in Gunnison," John suggested.

"Are they capable of dealing with something this serious?" Charles asked.

"Look, Charles, this isn't serious. It may look so with all the blood, but I don't see that the cut went very deep, maybe slightly into the muscle; really only a nasty flesh wound. I'll put a tourniquet on his leg to help stop the bleeding and then we can take him in the SUV to the Gunnison hospital."

"I still think we need a specialist," Charles insisted.

"There may be one in Gunnison, I don't really know," John replied.

"Are the doctors there any good?" Charles asked.

"Well, they've all been to medical school, except for those witch doctors who are called upon to do heart transplants."

"This is no time for humor, John," Charles snapped.

"Sorry, Charles, but believe me this is not a serious wound. I could sew him up myself; it's a simple procedure. I've done it on cows when I've had to do emergency C-sections."

Chris' teary eyes bulged at the suggestion. He looked for help from his father.

"Do you mean to say, you operate on cows from time to time?" Charles asked.

"Of course. When I can't get a vet in an emergency, we'll do a C-section ourselves to save the calf and the mother. It's not too difficult; I learned by watching our veterinarian. The tough part is keeping the incision clean while sewing up the cow. Also learned how to deal with combat wounds in the Army much more serious than what Chris has suffered. It takes patience, that's all. Chris here has only a deep cut, no big deal. I have the Novocain to kill the pain if you want me to sew him up."

"John, I appreciate your medical skills, but I still think we need a specialist. By the way, how successful have you been on the cows?" Charles asked out of curiosity.

"Saved four out of five cows and all the calves," John responded. "The fifth died of peritonitis, an infection, always a danger with an open wound. That's why we need to get Chris to Gunnison," John said in a voice that suggested some immediate action.

Chris, who recognized from John's comments that any delay in attending to his wound might be life-threatening, pleaded with his father to take him to Gunnison.

"OK," Charles said as John used his silk scarf for the tourniquet on the boy's leg, "let's get going."

Within 40 minutes, Chris was through the admittance process and in the emergency room with an attending physician. Charles barged in and asked the doctor, "How's it look?"

"Not serious. Really, a deep flesh wound with some minor muscle damage, that's all. We'll have him fixed up shortly. Now sir, if you'd please return to the visitor's waiting area, we can go about our business," the doctor said as he turned to the attending nurse. John half expected Charles to ask the doctor if this were his first experience with this kind of wound. Thankfully he didn't. He leaned over, gave his stepson a kiss on the top of his head and then turned from the gurney towards the door.

Fifteen minutes later, Chris came limping out from the treatment room without the aid of a cane or crutch. The doctor accompanied the boy and reported to Charles, "Fifteen stitches, actually staples. He should be back to normal in about three weeks. In the meantime, he should keep off the leg as much as possible, and elevate it for the next 48 hours. He'll find it to be more comfortable if he puts a pillow under the leg in bed." Turning directly to Chris, the doctor said, "You're a lucky young man. I've seen some nasty chain saw injuries. You always need to be careful around them."

"Yes, sir," Chris answered. "Thank you very much."

The next morning, John followed the Devlins to the airport in his pickup. While he was in town, he'd locate that generator. At the airport, John helped the pilots load the skis and baggage, and then leaned through the plane's door and said to the boys, "Thanks for your help guys, and Chris, take care of that leg. See you out this way in June."

The plane climbed quickly into the clear blue sky, leaving an exhaust trail behind the deep growl of the jet engines.

John headed to the hardware store to price out a large portable generator and purchase some additional medicine. The Circle of Knowledge had already assembled around the stove. Brad had finished reading the police blotter in the local paper to the members and had turned to the classified listings.

Refrigerators, a 10-year old, 8-cylinder '64 Chevy truck with a horse trailer, a dining room set, and five piglets caught the attention of the Circle. Brad read aloud the date and place of the Lions' Annual Auction. Highlighted items included: a handyman jack, a 16-piece socket set, a 20-gauge Winchester shotgun, a carburetor repair kit, a free meal for four donated by Domino's Pizza and a brand new checkers set. Then Brad announced in a voice that suggested special attention, "Gentle horses wanted by local rancher. Call John Marlow, evenings at: 729-8311." All eyes turned to John.

"Yeah, I'm looking for some gentle riding horses for the Devlin family. Know of any?"

"I got two Appaloosas I could part with for a fair price," said the old rancher, "long-legged geldings, and gentle too. They'd get you through this snow without a sweat."

"The reason there're so gentle is that they're two months short of death," said Brad, the history teacher.

"Dead my ass! How do you know?"

"Cause I sold you those two Appys 'bout 20 years ago. That's why."

"How'd you get through the blizzard out at the ranch?" the rancher asked John.

"Busier than a one-legged cowboy in an ass-kicking contest," John replied. "We had some real problems with the cows. Wind blew about 43 of 'em into the east fence, where they stacked up and died." John didn't have to explain any more details. Everyone in the Circle was familiar with the different ways livestock died in a storm.

"We got some sickness in the cows, but we're getting it under control. Hard to get around on horseback to doctor the critters in 5 feet of snow."

"What you need are some long-legged camels," Brad suggested.

"Yeah, I checked with Hertz and they told me they're all rented out," John replied.

"Call if you need assistance," the former sheriff said. John knew he meant it. He could count on any of the Circle members to help him in an emergency, in the same way they could count on John if called. The habit of neighborly cooperation, especially in an emergency, ran deep in Silver Valley, especially in the winter.

John went off to look for a portable generator. The Honda Deluxe he knew to be reliable but at 200 pounds it came in a bit heavy, and at $2,799 it would raise a red flag to Rigby. But his brother Clyde in Wyoming bragged about his Honda. John asked the store owner if there might be a discount on the machine. "John, we've already marked it down from almost $3,000," the owner responded. "It's the best one on the market. It'll start at 40 below and put out all the power you need, guaranteed."

"OK, I'll take it. Charge it to the ranch account." John and the owner wheeled it to the door where the two men lifted it and walked it to John's pickup.

John and the cattle passed through the rest of the winter without any additional major storms. With Josh's help, John had cleared up the respiratory problems among the cows. The last cow to respond to the penicillin was also one of the two cows to abort her calf. The coyotes had fed on the fetuses, and what they left behind, the eagles cleaned up.

The weather hesitated to follow the calendar as it moved towards spring. Wet March snows came about the time the cows began to calve. The calving season, a narrow window between what John called "blizzards and bugs" always exhausted everyone—feeding the cows in the morning while vaccinating and ear tagging the newborn calves in the afternoon. The two-year old heifers needed to be checked every three hours throughout the night in case one encountered trouble birthing her first calf. John and Josh alternated on the heifer shift, and after a few weeks, fatigue began to take its toll on the men.

More often than not, Josh or John would have to assist at least 10 heifers during the calving season. One of the men would attach a small chain onto the front legs of the emerging calf, and then, taking hold of the loop in the chain, together they'd slowly pull the calf out through the birth canal. Sometimes an oversized calf would need to be ratcheted out of the uterus with a calf puller. If that procedure failed, John would reach into the uterus and reposition the calf for another attempt at extraction. Infrequently, a C-section would be necessary. John much preferred to call a veterinarian rather than have to perform the stressful operation himself. Extracting the calf was the easy part; the most difficult task was keeping the incision clean, particularly when sewing it back up through four layers of tissue—first the uterus, then two tissue layers and finally the hide. The stress on the cow often discouraged her from accepting and nursing her calf, but with patience and a little "mother-up" powder, the cow would claim the calf. The procedure John and Josh most detested involved extracting an oversized dead calf from a cow's uterus. Carefully, John would have to reach in with a small OB serrated wire and cut the calf into pieces before pulling the bloody body parts out through the birth canal.

Yet, for all its problems, for John calving was the most rewarding of all his ranch responsibilities. He never ceased to be amazed by the magical beauty of a calf coming to life and instantly seeking the cow's teat to suck the rich colostrum, so important to the calf's health. Despite the inevitable calving losses, to see hundreds of cows with their baby calves filled John and Josh with pride for all the year's work that led up to the culmination of a live birth. A spring storm with 6 inches of snow, like the one that hit the ranch in early April, could quickly turn joy into sorrow.

During the morning feeding, the men noticed many of the young calves had suffered in the storm. Even huddled up to their mamas, they could not stay warm or dry. Most suffered scours, what John called "the squirts," a form of diarrhea that quickly debilitated a calf with dehydration. After feeding, the men mounted up with syringes and medicine in their saddle bags. Some medicines worked depending on the strain of scours. Last year, John discovered a medicine designed for pig scours to be the most effective with his calves. He complained bitterly when the FDA took it off the market. "Wouldn't you know it. Just when we had something working, the dumb bureaucrats in Washington say we can't use it. Something about getting in the human food chain. It's OK in pork, but not in beef." He turned to Josh and continued, "those Scour Guard shots we gave the cows last fall didn't work worth a damn this season. What a waste."

"Yeah, they sure got the squirts this morning," Josh answered.

"I reached into the mouths of two sick calves and could tell their body temperatures had dropped. We should probably bring them into headquarters and put 'em in the hot box." John identified the calves for Josh, who dismounted, picked one up and placed it on the front of John's saddle. Josh picked up the second calf, placed it up on his saddle and then swung himself up behind the calf. The two men rode the weak calves back to headquarters and placed the animals in the 10-square-foot wooden box kept warm by an electric heater.

"Let 'em set in there for a couple of hours. They'll dry out and regain their body temperature. One of them looks as if we should give him some electrolyte to hydrate him. Josh, mix up a batch, then we'll tube him. Also, check to see if we have any of that Adolph's Meat Tenderizer; we're sure as hell going to have some diphtheria with this storm." John was referring to what a local rancher had discovered, probably by accident, that Mr. Adolph's product when mixed with a little hot water and squirted into a calf's throat, was the quickest cure for diphtheria. The owner of the local grocery store in town never figured out why so many ranchers all of a sudden emptied the shelves of Mr. Adolph's recipe, a powder more often applied to the road kill the store sold over the meat counter.

John's day ended after dark but he had the night to himself, with Josh on the late shift to keep an eye on the three heifers yet to calf. He sat down to a hash dinner about the time the phone rang.

"Hi cowboy," Trish's voice was immediately recognizable to John.

"How's my favorite flying partner?" he asked.

"Fighting snow and cold weather here in Durango. Great weather. How's yours?"

"Don't ask. You should see my nose, the only part of my body not wrapped in goose down."

"Sounds miserable."

"That about sums up it up."

"Have you read the papers recently? The Argentineans have reneged on their international loans."

"I know. Devlin told me all about it when he came out with his boys for a short skiing vacation."

"I didn't know you skied."

"No, it was their vacation, not mine. I had to cancel my vacation to Bali given the blizzard here. Any chance of you getting up here soon?"

"Probably not. I'm off next week to visit my mother in Indianapolis. She's in poor health and needing some attention. Could you get down here for a weekend after you're finished calving?"

"I'll work on that. We've taken some big cattle losses this winter. I'm guessing I'll be ordered back to New York to do some explaining, especially to Rigby.

I'm expecting a nasty call from him any day now. It may be late spring before I can shake loose of the ranch."

Rigby had a week to review John's most recent report, which included figures on the death losses and the weight losses suffered by the feedlot cattle. John didn't have to wait long. The day after his conversation with Trish, Rigby left a message on John's answering machine. "Call back at noon mountain time."

"Hello Rigby, Marlow here."

"I've read over your report for the last month and reviewed the ranch expenses. I can see it was a bad month," Rigby said with an emphasis on "bad month."

"That doesn't begin to describe it," John replied.

"Before we discuss the cattle losses, I thought we had an understanding that any ranch expense over $1,000 would need to be approved first here in New York."

"Are you referring to the portable generator?" John asked.

"Damned right I am," Rigby snapped back.

"Well Mr. Devlin approved the request when he and the boys were out here skiing."

"Next time, I need to be informed BEFORE the purchase. Remember John, money doesn't grow on trees around here."

I thought that was the whole purpose of Central Park, he wanted to say but held his tongue.

"As for the cattle losses," Rigby added, "I can only think you weren't properly prepared for the storm, that all precautions were not taken."

"And what kind of precautions do you have in mind?"

"Look John, you're the manager, not me. That's why we've hired you. It is not my job to come up with solutions to your problems. These losses are unacceptable. It's your job to see that they don't happen," Rigby said, as his voice raised another octave.

"If we had a heated barn on the ranch the size of a football field, I would have brought the cattle in, made them comfortable with some warm hot chocolate and soft music."

"Don't be a wise ass with me, Marlow," Rigby shouted.

No one had ever seriously questioned John's competence. Even after the family lost the ranch, the bank had high praise for his managerial skills. Now a pea-brained, number-crunching accountant, whose only experience with cattle was the beef he stuffed into his lower intestine, had suggested that John didn't know his job by ignoring the welfare of his cattle.

"Maybe you think I should have made a phone call to cancel the storm? If you'd please send me God's 800 number, I'll be sure to call Him when the next storm hits. In the likely event I'm put on hold, I'm sure the background music of harps and violins will, no doubt, soothe my nerves. Or if I get a recorded announcement such as: 'our angels are out assisting other customers. Please try back later when our lines are not so busy. Your call is important to us, you can be assured I'll run out and tell the cows to please be patient and stand stiff to the wind. Help is on the way."

"I don't much appreciate your sarcasm," Rigby replied.

"And I don't much appreciate your fucking criticism from your warm, cozy office 2,000 miles away."

Before he hung up and walked to the refrigerator for a beer, John thought he could smell Rigby's Old Spice over the phone.

He could see some trouble ahead. He didn't know what relationship Rigby had with Devlin, but the accountant's sharp pencil and know-it-all attitude continued to challenge John's patience. Could he survive the constant irritations from someone who believed humans had absolute control over the forces of nature? Submission to a greater power was not a characteristic in Rigby's DNA, except for maybe taking orders from Devlin. And Devlin's problems with the Argentineans might very well end with the sale of the ranch and, with that, John's connection to the Diamond J. How did it come to be, John asked himself, that his livelihood was dependent upon a corrupt Latin American politician and a fat slob of an accountant in New York?

CHAPTER SEVENTEEN

John put Rigby's call behind him and went on about his work, with highest priority to finishing the calving season. The weather finally managed to cooperate, with sunny days and cool but not freezing temperatures at night. With only three more heifers and 20 more cows to calf, the evening watch could end within 10 days. By John's count, the ranch had lost 16 calves from the older cows and heifers, not counting the unborn calves lost with the 43 cows in the blizzard. He now turned his thoughts to the feedlot cattle that he hadn't seen since before the blizzard

John called his son, Johnny, to see if he might drive down from Cheyenne to join him at the Greeley feedlot. They arranged to meet on Thursday at the adjacent sale barn café.

"See you at noon. Also, I have some news for you, Dad."

What kind of news, John wondered. He didn't dare ask his son for fear they'd have a disagreement on the phone. Had he volunteered for the Army or Marines, or worse yet, planned to get married after knocking up some cheerleader? About the military, I can talk some sense into the kid, John thought. You might get to see parts of the world you wouldn't otherwise visit, but when they unload you in a country you've never heard of, the foreign Chamber of Commerce will greet you with a couple of mortar rounds, followed by a burst of machine gun fire. As for marriage, don't rush into it, son. Take your time, go to college, get some education so that you won't have to spend your life looking up the ass end of cow, like your father.

John left at dawn for the Greeley feedlot. The town specialized in feeding cattle and then slaughtering them at the old Monfort plant. You didn't need a map to get to Greeley. "Just follow the smell of cow shit," his father used to say. When he arrived at the feedlot, filled to capacity with 10,000 head of cattle, he found to his surprise the pens dry and without their usual mud holes. He went to the office where he located the owner/manager. The aroma of cow manure was only slightly weakened by the smell of burnt coffee.

Harlan Schneider, an overweight hulk of a man in his 50s dressed in manure-covered overalls, greeted him and they talked about the toll the storm had taken on the cattle.

"We fared OK, with death losses," Schneider reported," but we had to doctor night and day for three days straight. Finally got everything under control. As you know from the death slips I sent you, you lost two. Not bad really, considering the weather. The storm, particularly the cold, did set them back. They probably lost 40 to 50 pounds each, which will push back their finishing by about a month. Unfortunately, the futures don't look so good for June."

"We'll need 72 cents to break even," John declared.

"You probably won't get but 68, if the market holds steady. That's what the futures market is telling us. I don't know what to suggest," Harlan said as he looked out into the feed pens.

"What if we sold them now?" John suggested.

"I don't know anyone who'd buy 'em and give you what you need. The cattle have been stressed and are only now beginning to come around. No one wants the risk of finishing them out right now. Plus, we're not through with the bad weather. You know what it's like around here in April."

"Shit, we should have sold them last fall, but my boss said his commodity boys back in New York thought we could look forward to a stronger market this spring."

"I don't know who they've been talking to, but with rising corn prices, a drop-off in foreign demand, particularly from Japan, due to that one mad cow up in the State of Washington, the market is nervous."

"One mad cow and the market turns south. You got a calculator handy?" John asked.

"Here. Use this one." Harlan handed John a small calculator from his breast pocket. John started punching in some numbers. He groaned at the result and said to Harlan, "We're looking at a loss of about $100,000. Wait till they hear that back in New York."

"We could cheapen up the feed ration, but that would only push their finishing date into late June, when the market traditionally takes a dip."

"Let's hope the demand increases and prices recover. How're you doing with our account?" John asked. "Up to date I hope?"

"No problem there. The check comes in every month from New York."

"I'll give you a call from time to time, to see how the cattle are doing. If any emergency comes up, let me know."

"You bet," Harlan replied.

When John arrived at the auction barn, he could hear on the outside loudspeaker that the sale was underway. He looked in at the auction arena to see the familiar buyers from the three large packing houses. They'd nod their head to indicate to the auctioneer a bid on an old broken mouth, crippled, or cancer-eyed cow which, in a day or two, would be packaged into hamburger. Old bulls whose breeding life had come to an end, either because of age or injury, followed singularly into the sale ring after the canners and cutters. They, too, would end up in the hamburger display cases at supermarkets across the country.

John walked into the smoke-filled café, where he found Johnny already seated in a booth. He was warming his hands around a cup of weak coffee.

"Hi, Dad, you're looking OK for someone on the tail end of calving season. How's it going?"

Every time John saw Johnny he seemed to have grown another 2 inches and put some additional muscle on his stocky frame. Other than needing a shave, he looked well.

"Can't complain. I still got my job, and the beer truck still stops at Silver Valley. Suffered some bad losses in that big storm and the feedlot cattle took a hit in terms of their weight."

"How will they sell?"

"Right now, the futures don't look too bright. We're facing a big loss."

"Good thing your boss can afford it."

"I hope he can. I hear he's got some problems with his investments."

"What kind of problems?"

"Something to do with Argentina. I don't know the details. Now what's the news you have for me?"

"I heard from some colleges last week. Got into Yale with a nice scholarship; also a scholarship to Wyoming and Colorado State."

"That's great news. You've had a terrific school record in Cheyenne, good grades and All-State Football. I'm real proud of you for what you've accomplished, considering you're now living in a crowded double-wide with your mother and new boyfriend, plus your two stepbrothers. So what's it going to be: Colorado or Wyoming?"

"Most everyone tells me I should go to Yale Forestry School. I'm told it's got the best program in forest management and they're the leaders in pine beetle research. Also, I had a meeting with two Yale grads in Cheyenne. They were really helpful. But, as you know, the problem is the cost."

"How much is it" John asked.

"Forty-four thousand dollars, and that's without books and travel."

"Whew. At that price, I assume the beer is free. And where do you think you can find that kind of money?"

Johnny pulled from his pocket a sheet of paper with some figures and read off the list "Yale offered $25,000 for an academic scholarship plus a job waiting tables for another $4,000. I won an Elks scholarship of $1,000, plus another $1,500 from the Cheyenne VFW. Mom says she's got $2,500, and I have $3,000 saved from my summer job. I figure I'm short about $10,000 after I count in travel, books and clothes. Yale tells me I could make that up with a low-interest rate loan they'd make available."

John responded without hesitation, "and that's only the first year. What about next year? Are you planning to rob a bank, or is that what you want me to do? I do have a good roping horse that should bring maybe four grand, but that's about all. Little in the way of savings, as you can imagine." John took a deep breath and continued.

"Look, Johnny, you're looking at a total college bill of almost $200,000, and that's assuming the tuition, room and board don't go up. Hell, for that kind of money, you could buy a nice little ranch, plus some livestock. Look at the alternatives. What's the matter with Colorado State or even Wyoming? They're good schools and at a fifth the price and close to home. What's Yale got for 45 grand that you can't get in Laramie or Fort Collins for less than 10?"

"Like I said, Dad, Yale is the premier forestry school in the country, doing the leading research on the pine beetle, which I've been working on at school. Also, I know I can play football there, at least I think so, since they've recruited me."

"Then why aren't they offering you a football scholarship?"

"The Ivy League schools don't give athletic scholarships."

"I don't get it. Colorado and Wyoming both have trees to study; there can't be that many of them in Connecticut, and who the hell ever heard of Yale football, except maybe for Harvard?"

"Dad, it may not be the Big Twelve but at least I get to play."

"Yeah, and for 45 grand. One hell of a deal."

"But you'll get free tickets and a cold beer when you get to New Haven."

"Including transportation?"

"Can't guarantee it."

John felt helpless to assist his son get a college education, something that no family member had ever experienced. Financially, John thought himself a failure when it came to helping his son, and even his ex-wife.

"Look Johnny, if you've got your heart set on this, I'll support you. My problem, as you know, is I can't be of much help financially. I'll help in any way I can. Maybe Yale would take some roping horses or saddles in lieu of your fees."

"Not likely, Dad."

As they finished their meal, John suggested they wander into the auction arena to watch some sales and catch up on the market. "They should be into the yearlings and calves about now," John said as he gulped down the rest of his coffee.

The small smoke-filled arena had filled up with sellers and buyers. Up on the block, the auctioneer tapped his mallet to the cadence of his calls.

"I got 74.50, looking for 60; do I have 60? Need 60 for these good-looking heifers weighing 550 pounds. Sixty, thanks Sam, now I need 74.75 for 44 of these fine crossbreds out of North Park. Come on boys, these feeders are worth more, look at the frame on them. Long stretchy calves, the kind that will make you some money in the feedlot, or better yet some nice replacements in your herd. I need 70, got 70 in back, anyone give 80, 80, got 80 right here, now 90, need 74.90." Pause. "Going once, going twice, gone for 74.80 eighty, up there in back, number 713. Thank you, Roger. Put 'em in with them other heifers? Thanks."

The Marlows watched a couple more sales of calves. John's interest lay with the yearlings that came up after the calves. When a fancy set of 35 crossbred Angus steers brought 65 cents a pound, John knew immediately that the market had not recovered. "They should have brought at least 73," John said to his son, referring to the per pound price he hoped his cattle would bring in June.

The two walked out of the sales arena and at Johnny's truck, his father turned to him: "Keep me informed on your college plans. I'll send you a check when I get that roping horse sold. I know someone who wants him real bad. Also, if I can find the time, I need to finish a saddle for a neighbor. That'll bring in two grand, enough for books but probably not enough for beer." He gave his son a big smile and a playful punch to the chest.

On the drive back to the ranch, John thought over their conversation. The boy knew what he wanted, like always, and he never failed to accomplish what he set out to do. As a youngster, Johnny would stay loyal to an ornery horse, one John would have shot or shipped off to the glue factory. He never tired of irrigation and took pride in his meadows. He always put up the most hay per acre on the ranch. In school, he'd have the best project at the science fair and the highest grades in his class, besides being a damned fine quarterback who'd led his team to the state championship. I'll come up with the money somehow to help Johnny, even if he's going east to college, John thought. The kid has his head screwed on. Try as they might, Yale can't ruin his western upbringing.

John thought about how he'd pass on the bad news to Mr. Devlin about the feeder cattle and the anticipated $100,000 loss. The news would certainly travel fast to Rigby's computer, with a nasty phone call certain to follow.

John stopped in Gunnison for supper and returned home after dark. The sudden appearance of Josh at his door with a beer immediately suggested to John some emergency.

"What brings you over here at this time of night, Josh?"

"Couldn't sleep, plus I've got some bad news. How'd the feeder cattle look?"

"Not good, lost some weight in that storm, plus the market is down for feeder cattle. Little likelihood we'll make any money on them. Now tell me about the bad news. But first, let me guess. Three cows were blown up by land mines."

"No, but I did come across three dead calves. The teeth marks on their bodies, particularly around the neck, suggest coyotes. I waited around for about an hour and sure enough one showed up to finish off the carcass. He's hanging in the barn with a bad case of lead poisoning in his skull."

"See any others?"

"No, but I've seen their tracks. I'm guessing a small pack of four or five."

John wondered if the coyotes might also have dined on some of the mice. He'd wait till tomorrow to find out.

CHAPTER EIGHTEEN

John opened a beer and read the postcard from Trish on the top of the mail pile. She reminded him of his promise to visit Durango. He'd thought of her often but it wasn't his habit to make unsolicited calls to women. What the hell, he said, and went to the phone.

"How's my cowboy doing up in the wild country?"

"Waiting for spring, when I hope to get to Durango. And what about you?"

"Nothing new, except a lot of work for your boss." Then she brought John up to date on the plans for the conservation conference north of Durango. John related his problem with the feedlot cattle.

"Then are you going to come up for a visit?

"It's hard to get away from this job with summer approaching. That's when the tourist season starts and that's when the railroad makes its money." The Durango-Silverton Railroad, which originally hauled ore from the mines in Silverton to a smelter in Durango, continued operating after the mines closed in the early 20th century. But now the railroad catered to railroad buffs and tourists wanting to ride the open cars through the spectacular San Juan Mountains.

"After October things slow down but by then you're into sub-zero weather and snow up to your chin. Right?"

"Depends on how tall you are. However, the skiing is good and the food is delicious."

"I can ski here in Durango. I don't need to travel 200 miles to break my leg and eat your food. However, I would like to come up soon and see you. I'll bring my own food."

"Sounds good to me."

John walked into his kitchen, put on some coffee and reviewed the serious problems he faced. How in hell could he tell Devlin and Rigby about the anticipated $100,000 loss on the feeder cattle, in addition to losses caused by the coyotes? Rigby will recommend that he be fired for sure, and Devlin will no doubt agree. In addition, as Rigby mentioned, the future of the ranch is unclear, given Devlin's financial problems at Goodman and his own personal investment losses in Argentina. Will Devlin be forced to sell the ranch? And if so, what's my future? All due to some corrupt Argentine politician who's been milking the country for his personal profit. I bet he has no problem financing his son's college education. And how to help Johnny with his tuition? There's plenty of money for all those players who aspire to a post-college career in the NFL but very little for those who choose to devote their lives to research. "I've got to help him," John said aloud, "and I will."

Together, John and Josh doctored the Angus bull in the squeeze chute with a shot of penicillin. "He already looks better after the dose we gave him two days ago," John volunteered.

"Yeah, he'll be ready to hump some cows by the time we go to the forest. That's assuming the sun can crack through the gray sky and melt what remains of the snow."

The men discussed which irrigation ditches needed cleaning, a new splitter box for the north meadow and some backhoe work on a ditch bank that needed repair. "I figure we're about three weeks away from when the water commissioner will allow us to turn water into the ditches. Should be good water this summer, with all that snow in the mountains."

"We could use some extra hay as a backup," Josh commented.

"Yeah, sure could've used it this winter, especially when the price went to $90, not including freight. Doesn't make a hell of a lot of sense to be putting $90 hay into cows when their calves are at 80 cents a pound and a new pickup will cost you 30 grand."

When John returned to the house he noticed his message light blinking. It was Rigby summoning him to New York for an "important" meeting in two days. What was so important that it couldn't be discussed on the phone? Rigby's message said the company plane was booked for the week so he'd have to fly commercial. Also Ms. Jackson was coming to Denver to meet with Mr. Devlin. "See if you can coordinate flight plans with her so the limo can meet both of you."

John called Trish to coordinate her flight from Durango for a connecting flight from Denver to New York. He'd purposefully reserved seats on a late flight so he'd miss any chance of a dinner invitation from the Devlins and a plate of snails.

"So, why are you going back there? I thought you hated New York."

"I do," John responded, but "Rigby wants to see on some important matter. I've made us reservations on United flight 245, leaves Denver at 4:10 in the afternoon. I've arranged for Devlin's limo to pick us up at LaGuardia. Rigby has me staying at Mr. Devlin's guest apartment. What about you?"

"The same hotel close to Mr. Devlin's office."

"Damn, I was hoping we could shower together at the guest apartment. Nice digs, really. I can't get a flight out of Gunnison, so I'll drive down. See you at the gate in two days. Bring your shower cap."

On the flight to New York, John explained his problems at the ranch, the cattle deaths through the winter and the projected loss on the feeder cattle.

"The losses could have been worse, right? Maybe that will take the sting out of the news for Rigby and Devlin."

"Maybe."

John put his arm around Trish. She leaned over and kissed him softly on the cheek. "Everything will work out, I'm sure."

"I want to know more about this conference," John said in a serious tone.

"Devlin's had this idea about a national conference for over a year. He wants to bring conservation leaders and wealthy donors from all over the country together to discuss the topic, 'Saving the West.' I gather he and his wife feel strongly that the West is destroying itself, mainly its environment, with open pit mining, clear cutting forests, wasting water and any number of other unmentionable horrors I can't remember. The plan is that once the guests are in Durango, they'll get on the train, make a lunch stop and then go on to the resort. They'll have gambling there the first evening, assuming Devlin can get permission from the county commissioners. The profits will go to a national coalition of environmental organizations. Mr. Devlin thinks that between the gambling and a private auction of Indian blankets and jewelry, the conference will clear about $200,000. He tells me there'll be some big hitters in attendance."

"So what's your role in all this?" John asked.

"I'm setting up all the arrangements for the train ride, including the lunch, and the arrangements at the resort, you know, like food, reservations, golf tee times, and seeing to it we hire folks who can run the auction and the gambling tables, assuming we get the go-ahead from the county commissioners. I expect we will. Devlin has greased the system by financing a new wing of the LaPlata County Library that will include the Charles and Amanda Devlin Western History Room."

"Hell, I can run the tables. Besides I'm one damned good poker player. Five-card stud or Texas draw are my favorites. You let me run the poker table and it'll take Devlin over a day to count his profits. Of course, I'll take my cut before he counts."

"Are you bonded?"

"That might be a problem, given my credit rating with the Silver Valley Bank," John admitted.

Trish and John spent the rest of the flight trying to find a time for Trish to visit the Diamond J. Her position with the railroad tied her to Durango for the entire summer. Instead, Trish suggested John visit Durango.

"It's a nice town, with a small theatre and concerts offered from time to time at the college." Then she thought to add, more to John's interest, "and good restaurants."

John pulled out a paper bag from his satchel beneath his seat and offered Trish one of the two sandwiches he'd prepared. She pried the bread off the sandwich and eyed the gray meat partially covered with mayonnaise.

"Think I'll pass. Thanks. John you must do something about your eating habits and cooking skills. No wonder you're so thin."

"Then come on up to the ranch for an extended visit and give me cooking lessons."

At the LaGuardia terminal, John recognized Devlin's driver, who picked up the two small bags and led John and Trish to the limousine.

"Different rig from what you had last time I was in New York," John observed.

"That's right. Mr. Devlin traded in the last Town Car for this new one. Only had 30,000 miles on it. Almost like new. But this model has a nicer interior, all wood paneling, and even a small wet bar."

"How about a shower?" John asked with a smile turning to Trish.

"No shower. Maybe next year's model."

They drove through the light traffic into the city and up to the front door of Devlin's guest apartment across from Central Park.

"I want you to see this apartment—quite fancy and a great view of the park. Then we can go out for a bite to eat."

"I'd like to see it. But then I need to get checked in at my hotel."

The doorman greeted John by name, handed him a set of keys and an envelope, and carried both sets of bags to the elevator.

"You can leave Ms. Marlow's bags downstairs. She'll be leaving for her hotel after dinner. Can you tell me if there's a small, quiet restaurant nearby with a menu in English? The doorman smiled and suggested a bistro around the corner on Sixth Avenue. John handed the doorman fifty-cents, thanked him and entered the elevator with Trish. In the apartment he headed straight for the refrigerator for a cold beer, and joined Trish at the picture window looking out at the park.

"That's Mrs. Devlin's preserve, probably filled with hundreds of muggers and perverts." John went on to explain Mrs. Devlin's work with the Central Park Conservancy, for which she was "the major fund-raiser, protector and Mother Superior."

Devlin's note to John said to be at his office at 10:30, followed by a meeting with Rigby at noon. Devlin also noted that he had a noon lunch meeting with Ms. Jackson at the Yale Club.

Trish continued to look out at the Park as dusk light engulfed the trees.

"Hey Trish," John shouted from the west bedroom, "come in here and look at this room. Someone copied the décor of my boudoir in Colorado."

"Pretty nice. I see you're fond of silk pillow cases, flowered wall paper and French antiques."

"Of course, and what I like most are the two pink overstuffed chairs."

Trish laughed and gave John a peck on his cheek, leaned back and said, "You cowboys sure have good taste."

"And especially in women." He caught Trish around the waist and pulled her to his side. She opened her mouth to his tongue. His erection pushed against her crotch. Within seconds they grappled with each other on the queen-sized bed. Trish kicked off her shoes as John unbuttoned her blouse and then reached beneath her dress for her panties. She assisted his fumbling hand with her own and slipped them down her legs before kicking them off. John stood, pulled off his boots, jeans, shirt, and underclothes and stood naked before Trish.

He walked towards the bathroom, turned to Trish and said, "I'll be right back, need to be sure there's warm water in the shower. Also need to put on my spurs."

When he returned to the bedroom, Trish had finished undressing and had slipped between the pale blue silk sheets, her auburn hair beautifully arranged across the pillows. John moved in next to her warm, contoured body. Trish wrapped her arms around him and whispered, "So where are the spurs?"

"I sent them out to be sharpened. Wait till after dinner." He kissed her breast, and then they made passionate love for an hour.

"Before you tear all the skin off my back, maybe we should take a break for dinner."

"I could use a good meal and maybe a drink," Trish said.

They climbed into the shower, washed each other, and dressed.

The bistro was a pleasant respite from the street noise, though John wished they'd turn down the background music from the speaker directly behind him. At dinner, John answered Trish's questions about his ranch routine and the ranch's history. His questions to Trish focused on her life away from her job. After dinner, they took a short walk before returning to the apartment. They strolled over to Columbus Circle, where John pointed out the statue of the mounted general on his rearing horse. "The poor guy is still covered in pigeon shit," John said, looking at the bronze statue. "I mentioned it to Mrs. Devlin on my last visit to New York. I'd have thought she would have had the old boy cleaned up by now. That's no way to treat a general," John said with some annoyance.

Back at the apartment, they talked over beers. Trish wanted to know more about John's life at the ranch and his broken marriage. "Must be something of a lonely existence," Trish observed.

"Don't have much time to be lonely. Josh is great company. And what with the truckload of girls we bring in from town every Friday night, there's plenty of action over the weekend. I need to rest during the week."

"And you brought in the girls even when you were married?" Trish asked. "No wonder your marriage fell apart."

"For me it had nothing to do with other women. My ex hated the ranch, missed town, even though she'd been raised on a ranch. Besides, she couldn't get along with my parents when they were alive. Good thing she left when she did. The tough part for me is not having Johnny around. He loves the ranch and the work. Believe me, it's not hard work after you get used to it."

"I'd love to come up to the ranch and follow you around for a couple of days. I want to know your life better, what makes you tick. Also I might be able to help out."

"I always need extra help fixing fence and breaking a wild colt or two," John answered. Then he put down his half-finished beer, went over to Trish and kissed her on the top of her head.

"Before you get all excited again and put on those sharpened spurs, I need to be going. Quite honestly I'm exhausted, and I need to get ready for my lunch with Mr. Devlin. You stay where you are. I'll catch a cab to the hotel," Trish said. John wanted to accompany her but she insisted he remain at the apartment. "You'd probably trip over your spurs getting in and out of the taxi."

John woke with the sun the next morning and heard someone in the kitchen. The maid, he thought, probably trying to catch some mice. He got up, showered, dressed and followed his nose to the smell of fresh coffee.

"Here, Mr. Marlow," the Jamaican maid said to John as she handed him a mug. "You look like you could use this. Sugar or cream?"

"No thanks. By the way, are you still catching mice around here?"

"It never stops. If it isn't mice it's cockroaches. See?" she said, pointing to a good sized roach making its way from under the refrigerator.

"Hell, I should put a saddle on that thing and ride him down to Mr. Devlin's office."

"They come bigger, believe me. That mouse I gave you last time you were here, did he make it to Colorado OK?"

"Sure did. I showed him to the Fish and Game folks when they came up to the ranch. He was a bit shriveled but still recognizable as a mouse. They said your New York mice were different from our Colorado mice. That kind of surprised me. They want to protect the Colorado mice because they jump."

"Never seen mice jump around here. Must be their diet in Colorado," the maid said, throwing up her hands.

John ate at a small table overlooking the park. With its new spring foliage of lime green leaves, John thought the park could be mistaken for a Colorado forest, if it weren't for the roads winding through the trees and mothers pushing those Hummer-sized baby carriages along the asphalt paths.

John stood up from the breakfast table and said to himself, it's about time I left for the execution chamber. Probably death by a firing squad after a meal of broccoli. Or maybe they'll hang me out of an upper story window and then cut the rope. Splat.

By taxi, John made his way down to Charles' office building, where he was stopped by a security guard, who looked suspiciously at John's attire, particularly the cowboy hat and bull-hide boots, and asked in a clipped tone: "May I help you, cowboy?"

"I'm here to see Mr. Devlin."

"Do you have an appointment?"

John was quick to pick up the guard's dismissive countenance. "I wouldn't be standing here if I didn't. Come all the way from Colorado with instructions to see Mr. Devlin. OK?"

The guard picked up a phone, mumbled something into the receiver, and then said, "Take the elevators to the right," pointing in that direction, "to the 45th floor." John thought to himself, that's a ways up there; and a fall from that height could do serious harm to his body.

The receptionist greeted John by name and said, "Mr. Devlin is expecting you. Please follow me." She led him to the spacious office. Two men came out with large stacks of papers in their arms. Then Devlin appeared in a perfectly tailored suit and cowboy boots. "Welcome to New York, John. Come in, have a seat. How about a cup of coffee?"

"Yes, thanks."

John stared out the window, taking in the view of New York harbor, the bridges he didn't know the names of nor the adjacent buildings, many of which rose higher than Devlin's. He looked straight down and immediately felt a siege of vertigo, the same feeling he had as a paratrooper in the Army when he looked out from the door of a C-46. But here he was at twice or three times the height from which he jumped in Vietnam, usually into a thick forest clearing. Here and without a chute. Ouch, he thought.

John reported on the ranch operation, and then moved to the subject of losses. Devlin knew of the cow losses on the ranch from his ski visit in December, but the calf and feedlot losses came as a total surprise. He showed no anger at the news of an anticipated $120,000 loss; he asked only if there was any way to avoid further losses, or the possibility of compensating for them.

"Not really," John explained. "The market is down, which only makes things worse. The yearlings are gaining the weight back that they lost during the winter storms, but it is costing us money. This is about the time, under normal conditions, we'd expect the cattle to be 1,100 pounds and ready for sale to a packer. Right now I'm guessing the cattle average about 900 pounds. They'll need another two months on feed. That's where the loss is. The feedlot did a good job, however, keeping them alive during the storms. We were lucky to have lost only two steers. Not bad, really. As for the calf losses to the coyotes, we're trying our best to control them."

"Rigby, I know, won't be happy with the losses. I guess we should have sold the calves in the fall, as you suggested," Devlin volunteered.

"Twenty-twenty hindsight."

"I've become a specialist in that," Charles volunteered, and then he continued, "The reason I wanted to see you is to warn you because my company is taking a real beating in Argentina; not only the company but also me, personally. You may have heard some rumors or read in the papers that my Board of Directors may replace me. I hope not, for our sake." John couldn't fail to hear "our" in Devlin's statement, tying Devlin's fate to that of the ranch and John's employment. At least, he didn't say "your sake," John thought.

Then John went to the heart of the matter when he asked Devlin if his financial problems might put the ranch at risk.

"Could be if things get any worse. Obviously I'm trying to work out of these problems. We'll have to wait and see how things settle out."

John was surprised by Devlin's apparent calm in the face of his loses, including the possibility of his job and the ranch.

"I understand you have an appointment with Rigby. I need to be off to the Yale Club for a luncheon with Ms. Jackson to firm up the arrangements for our conservation conference this fall. I trust you know about the conference?"

"Ms. Jackson has told me about it. If the West continues to degrade its environment, it will get to a point where no one will want to visit the West or invest in it ever again. Something must be done."

So why do we have to "save the West" for tourists, John wanted to ask. About the only thing they bring is money so they can buy our land, cut our timber, close our mines and overwhelm us with lawyers. All this because of a series of insulting stereotypes of Westerners as environmental destructionists. Maybe Easterners want to save us in the same way Westerners saved the Indians by putting them on reservations? I'm certain I don't want to be saved by folks back east, especially if it means taking orders from assholes like Rigby.

CHAPTER NINETEEN

John arrived at Rigby's office five minutes early. He flipped through *Accounting Today* and *Practical Accountant* displayed on the coffee table, sipped some weak coffee offered by the heavily made-up receptionist, and noticed that the gum from his last visit was still stuck to one of the leaves on the plastic tree. John was made to wait another 10 minutes before Rigby appeared. As gracious as ever, Rigby offered not his hand but only a curt greeting, "Come in, Marlow, and have a seat."

For the first time, Rigby noticed John's slight limp as he moved towards the chair. Rigby knew that all cowboys, at least on the screen, limped like John Wayne.

"I see you're over budget again on fuel, medicines and feed," Rigby said, dispensing with any small talk and peering down at a spreadsheet.

"The heavy snows accounted for the extra fuel," John explained, "and the sickness brought on by the storms required extra medicine. As for the extra feed," John said, "it resulted again from the storm when the yearlings lost considerable weight in the feedlot. We now need to carry them on feed an additional 60 days. The calf losses at the ranch are due to sickness and some coyotes."

"Why don't we sell the feedlot cattle now rather than pumping more money into them?" Rigby asked. "As for those coyotes, I thought that's why you carried that rifle in your pickup."

Cool it, John said to himself. He pulled out a copy of his current account and flipped to the third page. As he did, Rigby noticed the tip of John's index finger missing to the first joint. Probably cut it off opening a beer can, Rigby thought, as he waited impatiently for John's reply.

"We'd lose even more money. Also there's a slight chance the market could improve over the next 60 days."

"For you, John, it is always tomorrow and things will get better. I'm sure I need not remind you this winter has been a disaster for the cattle, the ranch and certainly for you. I don't like to repeat myself, but these losses are unacceptable to me, and especially to Mr. Devlin. John, you need to act less like a cowboy and more like a business manager. A good manager would have taken preventative action to avoid the situations that have led to these losses. Right?"

"Rigby, there are certain things I can control on the ranch but the weather is not one of them. Nor do I have any control over the cattle market, or the dietary habits of coyotes. Also, you may not know I recommended to Mr. Devlin that we sell the calves last fall and not carry them over the winter in the feedlot."

"I'm looking for solutions, not excuses. And unless I get some from you very soon, it will be my recommendation that Mr. Devlin replace you. Obviously, you have what I would call an 'attitude problem.' You've had it ever since we first met."

Rigby stood up from the table, his face red and his double chin bubbling up from beneath the front of his buttoned collar, and leaned over towards John. "Maybe you don't understand. It is my responsibility to see that Mr. Devlin's investments are profitable, or in the case of the Diamond J, not bleeding to death. And I will see to it that the ranch stops hemorrhaging money, even if that means finding a new manager."

"What about the blood loss in Argentina?" John's rejoinder only managed to increase Rigby's blood pressure.

"We're dealing with that problem in due course. But to add the problems of the ranch on top of Argentina is more than Mr. Devlin can handle at one time." After a long pause, Rigby continued.

"I've discussed the ranch problems at length with Mr. and Mrs. Devlin and it is their recommendation, upon my advice, that you begin to enact some conservation practices on the ranch, Both of the Devlins have talked with two conservation advisors at the Nature Conservancy and it is their opinion, given their own experience running cattle ranches, that they can be profitable if managed properly. We recognize that you may not be familiar with most of these conservation practices, since many of them were developed in the East. With that in mind, we are going to be sending out to the ranch a 'conservation advisor' to work along with you and suggest necessary changes in the ranch operation. We believe we have the advisor selected, but I need to meet with her one more time."

"It's a her?" John asked.

"That's what I said. She's been recommended to us by the Conservancy; an honors undergraduate and graduate student of a first-class environmental program. She's worked and advised on two other ranches, both owned by the Conservancy."

"And when can I expect my advisor at the ranch?"

"Probably within two weeks. During her time at the ranch, she can stay in the old homestead cabin, where I understand there is a primitive kitchen. You can expect she'll have any number of questions about the ranch operation. I ask that you be patient and helpful to her during her stay, which will probably be no longer than a month or a month and a half."

"It sounds to me as if you and the Devlins have already made the decision about an advisor."

"Correct."

"Does she know anything about cattle? How to handle them? How to doctor them? How to irrigate? Right now, I'd kill for someone who could repair fences."

"Again, John, her responsibility is not to help you with your daily chores, but to look at the overall operation—the bigger picture—and make some specific money-saving, environmentally-friendly recommendations to me and the Devlins, and ultimately to you."

John saw no use in arguing about what had already been decided. If he did show any resistance to the arrangement, Rigby would, sure as hell, recommend that he be replaced. Why didn't Devlin mention the conservation advisor in their meeting, John asked himself.

"Any further questions?" Rigby said in a curt tone, as a way of bringing closure to the meeting.

"Not at the moment, but I'm sure I will soon," John replied.

John took a cab back to the apartment where he waited for Trish to return from her luncheon with Devlin. He tried to contemplate what would be the working arrangement with the advisor: would she follow Josh and John around on their daily chores all the while asking dumb questions, or would she go off on her own looking at the ranch, its fences, meadows, the irrigation system, equipment, cattle and improvements? He only hoped he wouldn't have to babysit this unnecessary intruder. He had neither the time nor the patience.

Trish arrived from her lunch. "So how did it go?"

"Could have been worse, I suppose."

"They didn't fire you or hang you out the window?"

"Neither. I'll tell you all about it on the way out to the airport. We better get going. Is the limousine downstairs?"

"He's at the front door waiting for us."

On the drive out to LaGuardia, John relayed his conversations with Devlin and Rigby. "That son-of-a-bitch about tore me a new asshole. Not happy about the losses and expected me to somehow take measures to prevent a snow storm, and somehow make coyotes disappear. Such arrogance. He needs to get himself outside from time to time and meet Mother Nature up close and personal. If things don't improve, Rigby assured me I'd be replaced. Also they're sending out an environmental advisor to recommend changes in the ranch operation that might make it more profitable."

"Did you meet her?"

"Not yet. She's due out at the ranch in about a week. Can't wait. Rigby says she looks like Julia Roberts, can ride like an Indian and rope like a cowboy."

"Well, at least you have something to look forward to," Trish said, clearly not pleased to hear about John's new helper.

Airport security had John remove his hat, boots, belt buckle, undo the brass button above the zipper on his Wranglers, remove the loose change and keys from his pockets and the silver clip from his bolo tie. But when he went through the metal detector, he still buzzed like a rattlesnake. The guard pointed to John and directed him, "over here, cowboy." He then moved the hand-held metal detector over John's legs and torso, setting off more buzzing. John explained, "It's probably the screws and wire in my ankle or the brass buttons on my Wranglers."

"The screws are right here," John said, pointing to his ankle, "but they don't come out easily without a screw driver. I assume you have one? Maybe you want me to take my pants off?"

The guard could see Trish trying to control her laughter. He then told John to recover his belongings and move along to his flight.

On the plane, Trish commented: "One of these times you're going to get yourself arrested for hassling a security agent."

"Could happen, I suppose, but I'm sure the prison food beats anything we get on the plane."

"Don't worry, I brought some sandwiches. Some fresh ham and cheese, unlike that gray mystery meat you offered on the flight yesterday."

"Anything to drink?"

"Not allowed to bring it on a plane. Could be gasoline, you know."

"I had a drink like that once on an Indian reservation in Montana. Cost me two dollars, and an intestinal bypass."

Soon, the cabin attendant came around asking for drink orders.

Trish ordered a Bloody Mary and John ordered double bourbon.

"Sir, we don't serve double bourbons."

"Well, do you have a single bourbon?"

"Yes, sir."

"Then give me two singles, please."

The attendant offered up some bagged pretzels. John told Trish as he bit into one, "I'm sure the airline bought these at a discount from Air Vietnam 20 years ago. Let's talk about this conference Devlin has planned. Tell me more about it."

"He wants it to be big and fancy, given the topic, Saving the West, and the important people who will attend. He wanted to invite 400 including spouses, but the train will only accommodate about half that number.

"The plan is for folks to fly into Durango on Thursday evening. Most will arrive on their own planes. Those poor souls without a private jet will have to fly commercial to Denver and then connect to Durango. They'll overnight in Durango, virtually taking up two entire hotels. The next morning they all board the Durango-Silverton train, which will take them to a picnic spot, and finally on to Tamarron, the site of the conference. Saturday is the conference, with environmental experts from all over the country presenting their views. I'll have to coordinate all this madness with the railroad, and be in contact with the resort management. When the invitation list is finalized, hopefully by the end of next week, the invitations will go out with a brochure specifying each day's schedule, the various panel discussions and speakers, and the available recreational activities like golf, tennis, riding, hiking, fishing and even a glider ride for those crazy enough to want to do it. It sounds like a wonderful vacation to me."

"Do you know if Mrs. Devlin and the boys plan to attend?"

"I understand only Mrs. Devlin. But your buddy Rigby will be there. I think they plan to come to the ranch after the conference."

"Can't wait to get Rigby on Dynamite, the meanest, nastiest equine in the West."

After they landed in Denver, John walked Trish to her gate. He promised he'd get down to Durango for a visit after the pressure of spring work let up. He also promised to bring Julia Roberts, his conservationist advisor, with him.

"Safe drive home, cowboy."

It was dark when John arrived back at the ranch. Josh must have seen the truck's headlights because he was at John's backdoor within minutes. Without knocking, he joined John with a beer in the kitchen,

"How'd it go?"

"We still have our jobs. But it's clear they want to see more of a profit from the ranch." Josh wasn't privy to the ranch finances but he knew enough about the economics of ranching to recognize the costs of winter storms and cattle deaths.

"Did you explain what we went through this winter?" Josh asked.

"Sure did, but they think of snow as something to play in rather than an agent of death and disease. If I'd asked them how to deal with the coyotes, I'm sure they'd have told me to put out some canned dog food so they'd leave the calves alone."

"Also, New York is sending us a conservation advisor. She'll be making suggestions on how to improve the ranch operation and, presumably, ways to make it more profitable."

"We could sure use some additional help with fence repairs, we're way behind. Also nice to have an additional hand for irrigating," Josh volunteered.

"Sure could, but I don't think she knows one end of a shovel from the other or the difference between a set of fencing pliers and a church key. She's supposed to look at the 'big picture' rather than help with everyday chores."

"The only 'big picture' on this ranch is work, followed by more work."

"You be sure to tell her that," John said as they finished their beers.

Spring came quickly in the Rockies and lasted as long as it took the snow to disappear. The spring work for Josh and John fell into a familiar routine. They'd ride the cattle in the morning, on the lookout for scours among the calves, doctor those that had the "squirts," and for the rest of the morning they'd repair fences damaged by snow drifts. Their afternoons were given to clearing tree limbs, leaves and excessive silt from irrigation ditches. They also built and installed new irrigation boxes and repaired the main head gates. Together they shared the task of dragging all the meadows with a shallow-spiked harrow that broke up the manure pies and aerated the ground.

As expected, Rigby called to say that Gretchen Harris, the conservation advisor, would be arriving in two days. "She has no special needs, and I think you'll find her a pleasant person to be around. She'll be in charge of her own meals, so you won't have to cook for her. Also, I have asked her to go over the budget with you as soon as possible, so that she has a sense of the scale of the ranch operation and its various components."

Gretchen arrived on the Goodman plane with enough baggage, including a tennis racquet and a fishing pole, for an entire family. She deplaned and introduced herself to John, who, with Gretchen's assistance, loaded the four bags into the pickup bed amidst the two work dogs. Only about 5 feet 3 inches in hiking boots, she stood no taller than John's shoulder. Her metal-rimmed glasses gave her a studious appearance that was reinforced by her frizzy red hair, flat chest and small, delicate hands. Clusters of freckles added the only color to her pale skin.

"What beautiful country," Gretchen said as she looked south towards the mountains, which were still covered with snow.

"The views are even better at the ranch," John responded.

She looked through the cab window to see the dogs making themselves comfortable on her duffle bag.

"Your dogs?"

"Yeah, Kelteys. Good work dogs with cattle, but they can't drive a tractor worth a damn. You'll come to learn that most stock dogs around here have the same first name: 'God-damn-it.' Gretchen failed to catch John's humor.

"Tell me a little about yourself. Rigby filled me in to some extent, but not much detail. Said you were a real cowboy."

"You can be sure he didn't mean that as a compliment."

"Given his tone and his frown, I think you're right."

"Enough of that horse's ass. First I want to know more about YOU," John said, trying change the subject.

"I was born and raised in Connecticut, attended Wellesley College in Massachusetts, on to graduate school at Harvard in Environmental Studies, and then went to work for the Nature Conservancy. Worked on two ranches they own, one in Wyoming along the Wind River and another near Craig, Colorado. I helped mostly with budgets, and improving the wildlife habitat. Can't say I know much about cattle, but I'm willing to learn. I can drive a tractor but I'm short on maintenance skills. All in all, I like to work outside, particularly in the West. Now it's you turn."

"Born and raised on the Diamond J, know almost every tree and rock on the place. It's been my home and my livelihood my entire life, except for a stint in the Army. My college education consisted of listening to my grandfather and working alongside my father, now both dead. I have a son, who lives with his mother in Cheyenne, visits from time to time to help us out. But most of the time it's only me, Josh and 800 cows and heifers with their calves, 35 bulls, some 15 horses, and 2 dogs. Not much of a social life out here, 40 miles from the city lights of Gunnison. The TV reception is worthless—all snow—about the same for the programs. The boys in town say the best program is NFL football and Desperate Housewives. I only watch the football. Ranch work keeps us plenty busy in all seasons, especially winter. We like to say around here, 'it's nine months of winter and three months of poor skiing.' The cows have yet to learn how to put on skis. That about sums it up."

At the ranch, John showed Gretchen the homestead cabin, her new home, and helped her with her bags.

"Not much in the way of closets. If you need to store some stuff, let me know and I'll put it over in my house. The mice like to make their home here so keep your bags closed and all food covered. I've set some traps under the sink. Also, the bears will hang around if there's food they can smell outside. You'll notice it takes a while for the hot water to come on. If it doesn't, check to see if the water heater is lit. It works off the propane tank in back of the cabin. So does the stove. The icebox here is electric. The phone only works when Qwest pays attention to their lines, which is not very often. I'm making dinner this evening and afterwards we can go over the budget. OK? I forgot to mention, if you need to go to town for anything, like food, we have a jeep you can use. The mail is delivered three times a week out at the box on the county road. You'll want to keep your door closed at night so my dogs don't come for a visit."

"Any bears around?"

"Like I said, there are always a few around here hunting up food scraps. So you do want to keep your garbage covered. See you over at the house in about an hour. I hope you like macaroni and cheese."

"I adore it."

After supper, John hauled out the budget sheets. Gretchen had scores of questions. By their nature, John could tell she knew something about ranching. For that, he was thankful, even appreciative.

The next morning Gretchen followed the men out into the pasture as they checked cows and calves from horseback. She followed behind at a distance in the jeep.

They roped and doctored a calf, and then John looked up and pointed to an animal moving from the tree line into the meadow. He whistled to Gretchen who also saw the animal. She pulled out a pair of binoculars, and stood there transfixed by the slow moving object.

"A beautiful wolf," she shouted over to John.

"Damned well better not be," John said, walking over to Gretchen, "or we'll give him a couple of shots of lead poisoning."

"How do you do that?"

"With the tip of a .30 caliber bullet," John said with emphasis on the last word.

"You mean kill it?"

"That's what I mean. I still can't understand why the government has reintroduced wolves around here."

"I can understand why ranchers don't want them around their livestock."

John looked into his binoculars again and said, "It's not a wolf, but a coyote probably looking for a dead or weak calf to feast on."

"You shoot them, too?" Gretchen asked.

"Not unless they're causing us problems with the calves. For the most part, I like to have them around. They control the field mice and even the prairie dogs that have survived our poor marksmanship."

"So you shoot those innocent little prairie dogs and any 'endangered' wolves that might show up?"

"That's about it, except we'll also shoot house dogs that chase the cattle. And during hunting season we'll harvest deer, elk and even sometimes a Texan. I have one, a two-pointer, mounted over my fireplace at home. Did you notice him last evening?"

Gretchen failed to find any humor in John's hunting habits. "Why is it necessary to kill all this wildlife? I'm horrified to learn you refer to killing wildlife as if it were a crop that needed to be harvested."

John explained about the damage caused by the elk in the winter and the amount of grass they consumed at the expense of the cattle, in the spring and summer. "Besides, the animals provide Josh and me meat through the winter and spring. As for those 'innocent' prairie dogs, they dig large holes in pastures into which a horse can break a leg. Besides, their holes interrupt the even flow of irrigation water across a meadow."

"That's no reason to kill them," Gretchen implored.

"If you had to put down a good cow horse with a broken leg, you might think differently."

She said nothing as the men mounted their horses. She followed them in her jeep as they continued to ride through the cattle. She noticed one calf that looked as if it had a blanket tied to its back. The binoculars showed it to be an animal skin tied on the calf. When the riders stopped to check a calf, Gretchen pointed out the calf with the extra skin and asked about it.

John explained that the calf was nursing from a cow that had lost its calf at birth, and the calf's natural mother also died at birth. "That calf is what we call a 'grafted' calf. We skinned the dead calf, tied that skin to the live calf, sprayed some 'mother up' powder onto the hide and placed the live calf up against the cow. She recognized the smell of the hide as being her calf, and then allowed the 'grafted' calf to nurse from her enlarged bag. So you can see, we're in the adoption business also."

"I suppose you think that makes up for all your killing habits," she responded.

"Not necessarily, but it helps put food on the table and cuts the financial losses of the ranch. Isn't that why you're here?"

Gretchen didn't respond.

John wanted to talk more about what Gretchen called his killing habits but knew he'd lose his temper and, with Gretchen's report back to Rigby, probably his job.

That afternoon, Gretchen took a map of the ranch and went off on her own. John and Josh worked together in the shop, welding a new metal head gate. "I keep thinking of all that gold buried out there," Josh remarked, pointing towards the west.

"Stop thinking about it. Even if you found it, you'd probably piss it away in a week instead of buying what you really need, like a new pair of irrigating boots, a shovel and a new pair of Carharts.."

"Why am I so lucky to have the opportunity to work on this snowbound ranch beside you?"

"Must be divine intervention."

They had almost completed the welding job when they discovered they'd run out of welding rods.

"I'll go into town tomorrow morning and pick up some more rods and refill the oxygen bottle. I need to get away from this place for a few hours," John said in an exasperated tone.

"Will you be taking Little Miss Muffet with you?" Josh asked

"She's all yours, and be sure to answer all her questions politely."

John first stopped at the hardware store for the welding rods and some more penicillin. The Circle of Knowledge had already assembled and was working on their third cup of tar.

"I'll be damned; if it isn't John Marlow," the ex-miner declared. "What's this we hear about you having a new girlfriend out at the ranch? She's a bit young for you, don't you think? I never knew you were partial to redheads."

John didn't want to explain why Gretchen had come to the ranch, especially the conservation part. "Friend of Devlins, the owners. She'll be at the ranch for about a month."

"Does she cook or perform any other house duties?" someone asked.

"She cooks for herself and I cook for myself, which is best for her own health. And, one other thing. Don't be starting any rumors about her."

"We've got some cooking and you're at the center of them, John," another member added.

"Can't wait to hear 'em. What else is going on around here of interest?" John asked, changing the subject.

"Did you see the paper this morning? The story about your boss, Mr. Devlin, and how he's going to host a big conference near Durango for some city folks. They'll be taking the Durango-Silverton train to some fancy resort where there'll be a gambling casino. Seems Mr. Devlin wants to save the West with the conference. Not a bad idea. I hope he plans to save this little shit-burg of a town and our little Circle."

"John, what does your boss have in mind saving?" another Circle member asked.

"I'm not quite certain, but I am certain that the Circle of Knowledge is not high on his list of priorities."

"Them conservationists don't save nuttin'. All they do is close mines and logging operations and put county folks out of work," Jake the ex-miner added.

"This here article in the newspaper goes on to list some of the rich dudes who'll be attending, like the chairman of Exxon-Mobil, the head of Georgia Pacific, someone from Newmont Mining and a whole herd of bankers and Wall Street tycoons."

The ex-sheriff, a Circle member, observed that the train from Durango would be loaded with rich folks. "Think of the money they'll have on them," he declared, as if he were announcing the combination to a bank safe. Then Jake offered his opinion: "Imagine a train robber relieving them of all that cash."

CHAPTER TWENTY

As John sauntered towards the hardware store counter to sign for his purchases, one Circle member shouted out, "Now John, you go easy with that little redhead you have out there at the ranch. She came in here a couple of days ago looking for some duct tape, you know that stuff that keeps your ranch together. She looked as if she'd been ridden hard and put up wet. I'm ashamed of you for messing around with such a young lass."

"I'll call you for reinforcements, if I need 'em," John replied.

John drove to the grocery store for provisions and a copy of the local paper. Sure enough, it reported that Charles Devlin, "a local rancher," would be hosting a "national conference in Colorado for conservationists who wished to 'Save the West.'" As he rode back to the ranch, John gave some thought to the Circle's discussion, indeed Jake's vague suggestion about a robbery. A fanciful idea, yes. But realistic? Probably not for someone without criminal DNA and some experience in that line of work, John thought. Still, the idea appealed to his playful nature, in much the same way as the mouse relocation project had. Yes, it went against his respect for the law, but hadn't Devlin suggested breaking the law by eradicating the mice? Hypocrites all. And their toadies—Miss Muffitt and Rigby—made his job all the more difficult and unpleasant. Wouldn't some extra money provide Johnny with a first-class education, something he'd never afford on wages? His son wouldn't have to follow in his father's footsteps—an ass kisser and caretaker to the rich—or spend the rest his life wading in cow shit like his father, grandfather and great-grandfather. Also, a successful robbery might deflate the arrogance of those folks who are so quick to tell westerners how to live their lives. And to play to eastern stereotypes of westerners—wild Indians and gun-toting cowboys—might be a lesson to Devlin and his friends that stereotypes can have dangerous consequences. To pull off the heist, and with no one hurt, would be an accomplishment John could take pride in. No, he thought, someone could get hurt.

At ranch headquarters, he dropped off the oxygen bottle and welding rods in the shop and then headed to his kitchen with his groceries. Gretchen came out from the homestead cabin and greeted him in the yard. John suggested she join him in the kitchen for a cup of coffee.

"How's it been going?" he asked.

"I've spent the last couple of days driving around the ranch, though I didn't get up on to the forest permit because of the snow. The meadows look lush with the grass starting to come up. You must have fertilized them," Gretchen commented.

"The fertilizer truck from the co-op came out and fertilized all the irrigated meadows two weeks ago. We do it every year; it helps boost the hay tonnage, but it's getting expensive as hell. As you probably know, fertilizer costs always track with fuel prices—up 15 percent from last year."

"Why use that chemical fertilizer? It costs a fortune, and besides, it kills all the microorganisms in the soil that help aerate the it, and the chemicals eventually work their way into the rivers and water supply," Gretchen responded with some authority.

"No one's come up with a better substitute," John replied.

"Golf courses use a chemical-free fertilizer," Gretchen suggested.

"I've looked into it. Only golfers can afford it."

"How about all that fertilizer the cows produce?"

"Even if we could collect it efficiently, there's not enough of it to cover all the meadows. I tried it one year on a portion of one meadow. Took me forever to transport it from the corrals to the manure spreader to the pasture. Plus, the fuel we used for the tractors hardly made it cost effective."

"It'd sure be better for the soil, and the runoff from the meadows with the chemical fertilizers wouldn't be poisoning the streams."

"Who says our fertilizer is poisoning the streams?" John asked.

"There is some very good scientific evidence that shows the poisonous effect of chemical fertilizers in streams and rivers. Not only are you poisoning our streams but your cows, through their belches, farts, burps and manure production, are contributing to global warming in a major way. Last year, the United Nations came out with a study detailing the methane gas produced by cows. Methane is the second most significant heat-trapping greenhouse gas after carbon monoxide, and it contributes significantly to global warming."

"Where the hell was global warming this past winter when I needed it?" John asked.

Gretchen refused to be intimidated by John's sarcasm. She continued on about the danger cows posed to human survival. "Also, the ammonia in cow manure contributes to the problem. That's why conservationists are urging people to eat less meat. If we decrease the demand for beef, maybe we can save the rain forest in Brazil, currently being destroyed for cattle grazing, and halt the melting of the polar ice cap."

"Let me see if I understand you. I thought you were sent here to improve our income; but now I see you want us to run fewer cows … or is it no cows? … so we can preserve the polar ice cap and the rain forest. Maybe Mr. Devlin and Rigby are concerned about the polar ice cap, but I've not heard them complaining to me about melting icebergs. It's the cities that are the polluters, not ranches like this one. Yes, I'm concerned about it, but you need to remember that I make my living, just like my parents and grandparents, raising cattle. If you're suggesting we run a cattle ranch without cattle, I'm not certain I've heard an alternative. Yaks, buffalo, ostriches? Sure cattle fart, belch and burp. But so does Rigby in New York and, no doubt, the President in the White House. You should visit the hardware store in town and sit in with the Circle of Knowledge after a dinner of pork and beans. By your scientific standards, their methane production should have melted the Arctic ice cap years ago. Will I soon have to report monthly to the EPA on the frequency and volume of cow farts on the Diamond J? Let me tell you one thing. Those scientists you admire for all their studies don't earn their living raising cattle."

"Now that's about as dumb and uninformed a response as I've heard in a long time," Gretchen said, with an angry intensity that matched John's.

John wasn't in the mood for an argument, "Let's say I wasn't hired for my I.Q., especially when it comes to fertilizers and inorganic chemistry, or a cow's rumen production and the study of organic chemistry. Other than our uses of chemical fertilizers and our destruction of microorganisms, the polar ice cap and the rain forest, how else have we screwed up around here?" John asked.

"I should have my report together by Thursday evening. I plan to leave on Friday and report back to Mr. Rigby. But before I do, I'd like to review the report with you."

"A most thoughtful gesture," John replied as he moved towards the porch of his house with his groceries.

John called the feedlot manager to inquire about the yearlings. They had recovered much of their lost weight from the storms, but the cattle futures kept dropping. If, as planned, they sold in two weeks, the loss would exceed the $225,000 John had calculated and had reported to Rigby.

After supper, he called Trish in Durango. "I'm thinking of taking a two- or three-day break from the ranch and driving down to Durango. Would I be welcome?"

"I can't speak for the Chamber of Commerce, but I'd be thrilled. I have to work Friday, but I have the weekend off."

"I'll be there by mid-afternoon on Friday. Can you get me and Julia a motel room? Also I'd like to take that train ride from Durango to Silverton on Saturday. It's been years since I did that."

"We can do the train trip on Saturday. If you promise not to bring Julia, you can stay at my place."

"Julia will be sorry not to meet you; she's heard so much about you."

"I'm sure. Is she still wearing her spurs to bed every night?"

"She's already worn out one pair. You should see my flanks; I look like a wounded watermelon," John replied in a voice suggesting self pity.

"Come to the railroad office when you get to Durango. It's on the south end of town next to Mr. McDonald's golden arch. You can't miss it."

John conferred with Josh about his intended trip to Durango and what projects needed to be attended to in his absence.

"Josh, I need to get away from here for a few days. Cattle futures are headed south again and seem to have a life of their own; nothing I can do will change them. And to be around Little Miss Muffitt will only get me in deeper shit than I'm already in."

Josh offered, "It would do you some good to get out of here. Should I turn the water in the pasture after I get that head gate set in the ditch?"

"You bet. But you may need some help setting that head gate alone. If so, wait until I get back on Monday and we can do it together."

"John, what's this I read in the paper about Mr. Devlin hosting a conference down near Durango to save the West. What in hell does he want to save?"

"I'm not certain but I don't think he has you or me in mind. But I'm thinking of an alternative. I can't talk about it now, but I'll know more when I get back from Durango on Sunday night. I may need your help. Also, you'll be happy to hear that Little Miss Muffitt will be leaving tomorrow to make her final report to Rigby.

"I know how much you'll miss her."

"Well, I'll manage, especially since I'll be getting away for a few days down to Durango where I'll see Trish." Josh had heard about Trish from John, who had described her as "a number 10 and a real free spirit." Given the frequency of their phone conversations, Josh could tell the relationship was something more than a casual business connection.

As John expected, the mid-morning meeting with Gretchen disintegrated from the very beginning. Her arrogant, know-it-all attitude, always supported by some sort of professional study published in an obscure scientific journal put him on the defensive. Not even two beers could improve his attitude over the course of the two-hour meeting in John's kitchen.

Gretchen started off on the fertilizer kick once again. John ended that topic's discussion with, "You come up with an alternative that will double my hay production, not take me the entire spring season to apply it, and costs less than what I'm using, and then I'll consider it."

Her next issue was the wasteful amount of irrigation water used on the ranch. She lectured John: "I've figured that the amount of water this ranch uses for irrigating the hay meadows is enough water to supply the needs of a city of 40,000 people."

"We have every legal right to use all that water. I can show you the deed to that water if you want. No one has ever complained about the amount of water we use. Besides, it doesn't cost us a dime, except for the cost of the head gates on the river. That water is put to good use on our meadows, as demonstrated by the hay tonnage we produce. As much as anything else, it's our most valuable asset."

"If you used less water, you could sell the excess at an amazing price to downstream users."

"Much of the water we're required to let flow by our head gate ends up in Arizona. How many golf courses do they need? And how do you suggest I use less water and grow the same hay tonnage?" John asked.

"You could save water by lining your irrigation ditches with either concrete or plastic, or use plastic pipe. That's what they've done in the vegetable farms in California. You'd find you'd use almost 15 percent less, according to a published report from the Extension Service at Colorado State University."

"And did you tell them the combined length of all our irrigation ditches so that they could calculate how much it might cost to line the ditches with concrete or use plastic pipe?" John asked.

"I figured about three miles," Gretchen responded.

"Try twice that mileage, plus one. By my simple third grade arithmetic, that equals seven miles, and that's only the main ditch, not counting the feeder ditches. You might want to get with an agronomist or a water engineer and they'll tell you that's one hell of a lot of concrete. I doubt if $200,000 would cover the cost. Suggest that to Rigby and see if he doesn't throw something at you. Now what else do we have on your conservation agenda?"

"Why is it then that other mountain ranches here in Colorado can afford to use plastic pipe?"

"I haven't a clue." She had done her research, John had to admit.

"There's the issue of 'harvesting' the wildlife on the ranch. First off, you generate no income for the ranch by allowing friends and neighbors to come in and hunt free. Second, there is a major liability issue here for Mr. Devlin. And third, if you and your friends kill off the deer and elk, you eliminate one of the major ranch attractions for Mr. Devlin and his guests. And yes, poisoning prairie dogs is certainly a quick and effective way to rid them from the ranch. But when a hawk or an eagle eats one of the poisoned dogs, the raptor too is poisoned. That poison works down the food chain." Finally, mercifully, Gretchen concluded with the observation: "And do you realize that some of the medicines you use on the cattle, like penicillin, also enter the food chain and build up human resistance to the drug?"

John held his tongue for 10 seconds before responding as calmly as possible. "Have you any idea how much the deer and elk on this ranch consume in the way of grass? We probably have 400 elk, all of whom, by the way, fart and belch methane. That's like an additional 400 cows. These elk return us nothing except that two of them fill our freezers each year. Maybe you can get the Colorado Division of Wildlife to reimburse Mr. Devlin for all the grass they eat, or hay they destroy in winter. Don't be surprised if they throw you out of their office like they do to me every time I ask for reimbursement."

John was only getting warmed up. "As for the liability issue, I've already talked with Mr. Devlin about it. We won't be allowing non-ranch employees to hunt on the ranch anymore. So we've already pissed off our friends and neighbors who, in return for their help at critical times, kept the elk numbers to a manageable size. But that seems to be of no concern to either Rigby or Mr. Devlin. As for poisoning the prairie dogs, we haven't done that for four years now. I either flood their holes with water when possible, probably a waste of water in your book, or I gas them out by running a hose off my pickup's exhaust pipe and placing it down the prairie dog hole. A waste of gas you say, but not if it prevents a horse injury or the loss of irrigation water diverted by dog holes."

Then John summed up: "I use practices that we know work here, Gretchen. These may not be practices that they teach at the university or work back east in Central Park. But they work for this ranch that, I need not remind you, is a cattle ranch not a playground, or a golf course or a city park, and definitely not a conservation research lab. You probably think your ideas will somehow save this ranch from polluting the earth and melting the polar ice cap. But I can assure you this ranch will survive," John concluded, "and so will the planet earth without your advice and my stupidity."

"I can see by your attitude, John, that nothing I recommend will be implemented. Rigby warned me about your attitude, but I thought maybe we could work together to improve the conservation practices on the ranch and its profit margin."

John wanted to suggest that if she was so concerned about saving the Arctic ice cap, maybe they should consider putting the entire ranch under a black plastic tent during the winter. The methane emissions from the cows would keep everyone toasty warm, save fuel and some icebergs. God could continue to cause fury and devastate other cattle operations with blizzards, but not the Diamond J.

"Look Gretchen," John replied with some frustration while at the same time trying to appear sympathetic to her good intentions, "Believe me. I recognize the dangers of global warming. I don't want to see this ranch turn into a desert any more than you do. I'm willing to try anything that is environmentally friendly and has been proven to work. You should remember that a good textbook conservation measure does not always mean it is cost-effective in all environments and circumstances. I can try to rid this ranch of weeds by using an environmentally friendly spray, and I've done that, but the results are mediocre and the costs outrageous. I'm not certain that protecting our prairie dogs will help save the polar ice cap.

"Provide me with solutions that'll give me a profit, not a headache. Remember, I'm only a dumb dirt bag cowboy hired to take care of 700 cows and 100 heifers. My job description and instructions from Mr. Rigby and Mr. Devlin, as I understand them, are to raise cattle profitably on this ranch. But until such time as my practices—such as the use of water, fertilizer and an occasional rifle—are considered illegal by Washington, I'll continue to use what is best for this ranch operation." When Gretchen stood up abruptly, John knew the meeting had concluded.

Early the next morning before breakfast, Rigby called.

As usual, he dispensed with the small talk. "I talked with Gretchen last evening after you two had your meeting about her report. She sure didn't appreciate your negative attitude. Everything she recommended you argued with, 'no solutions, only nasty negativism' to quote her. Gretchen's solutions seemed reasonable to me, and I'm certain they'd be reasonable to Mr. Devlin if he were here. As always, you seem unwilling to change your ways to improve the ranch's operation."

"Look, Rigby, anyone can come out here with half-assed ideas on how to run this ranch and save Mother Earth and the Arctic ice cap, but that doesn't mean I have to listen to them or agree to them. Did she give you an estimate of the cost of her recommendations, like lining all the irrigation ditches with concrete? And did you know that Mr. Devlin's cows are responsible for global warming? Yes, they're methane producers—they fart too much. I suppose she's recommended to you that I be asked to stick a cork up the ass of every cow and calf on the ranch! Gretchen talks about her wasted time. What about my time? Do you have any idea how busy we are here in the spring? I'm trying to make the ranch profitable, not a conservation clinic. This ranch has run for almost a century without a conservation advisor and I suspect it will survive another century without one, regardless of who owns it."

"I'm sorry that you couldn't work with Gretchen; she seems to have made a positive contribution on two other ranches, but your lack of cooperation has prevented her from assisting you to the extent of her professional training."

"If that's professional training she's carrying with her, I suggest you send her back to school for a Ph.D, which translates into a post-hole digger in my world, and some common sense to go with her advanced degree. Then send her out here again with her tennis racquets."

Rigby had patiently waited for the opportune time to fire John. He never liked him from the very beginning, ever since he tried to put Rigby on Dynamite. Yes, he knew how to run a cattle ranch but never at a profit. The death losses at the ranch and the feedlot costs, the inability to put together a reasonable budget and live within it, the lack of any positive suggestions on how to make the ranch profitable, topped off by a wise-ass attitude, were reasons enough to get rid of John.

"I'm tired of your negative attitude, John, I'm sorry to say this, but I don't think the Diamond J has any more use for your services. You seem incapable of working in a cooperative manner with Mr. Devlin's advisors or with me. I've leaned over backwards to assist you, but it hasn't worked. You'll have a month to gather up your possessions, leave the ranch, and get settled elsewhere. You will, in the meantime, be carried on the payroll if, and only if, you are helpful in the managerial transition. When you see Josh this morning would you have him call me at my office? I'll be appointing him interim manager until we find the right person."

"So you're firing me, is that it?"

"I'm the one who makes the personnel decisions for Mr. Devlin on his properties. I think I've made myself very clear. I will report my decision to Mr. Devlin, after he returns from Argentina, and explain the reasons," Rigby said. "Goodbye."

John made good time driving to Durango. He stopped at a local sporting goods store to purchase a Forest Service map of the area. He was particularly interested in learning if the main north-south highway into and out of Durango came close to the rail line. He also wanted to learn if there might be a trail from the highway to the rail line. Afterwards in Durango, he had no trouble locating McDonald's golden arch adjacent to the train station. The town was very much as he remembered it—a busy downtown of galleries, shops and restaurants that serviced the tourists who came to Durango to ride the train or travel by car to the area's leading attractions, Mesa Verde National Park and the Southern Ute Indian reservation south of Durango, and its gambling casino.

John found Trish's office at the railroad depot as a train disgorged its passengers. Those who had ridden in the open observation cars brushed coal dust from their clothing; others posed with a conductor or the engineer for a photo opportunity in front of the old steam locomotive.

In the administrative offices above the depot building, Trish jumped up from her desk chair and threw herself at John as he entered her small office. John, a bit surprised by the enthusiastic greeting, managed a wet kiss in return.

"You made it down without trouble?" she asked.

"The trouble started before I left."

"What trouble?"

"Can we talk over a beer?"

"Give me a moment to tidy things up here, and then I can leave."

"I'll be down on the platform looking over the train."

"See you there in 15 minutes. Promise."

John walked down the stairs to the depot to look around. Next to the ticket counter, on the information stand, he picked up a guidebook that included an excellent map of the rail route to Silverton and a description of what to look for at each mile marker along the way. He walked outside to look over the old locomotive, a hulk of black steel with its large round boiler, the source of steam that powered the large pistons and the rods that transferred the driving power to the four large iron wheels on each side of the locomotive. The train's conductor stood on the platform in front of the locomotive.

"How many passengers do you carry?" John asked, wanting to strike up a conversation.

"Normally anywhere from 275 to 300 in 12 cars—8 enclosed coaches, the 2 open gondola cars, a concession car, the combination baggage-passenger car and sometimes a VIP parlor car."

"How many employees does it take to operate this outfit?"

"You've got the engineer, of course, who sits up in the cab and is in charge of the train's locomotion. He's assisted by the fireman, who is constantly stoking the firebox with coal, as much as seven tons, and one shovelful at a time, for the round trip to Silverton. Then there are usually two brakemen, depending on the number of cars, who are responsible for the braking mechanisms on the train. Also, we'll have an attendant in the fancy parlor car, two workers in the concession car, and finally, the conductor, that's me, who's in overall charge of the train."

"So you're the chief honcho, if anything unusual happens to the train?" John asked.

"That's my responsibility."

"If you break down, how do you get help?"

"We carry two radios. I've got one at my desk in one of the enclosed coach cars, and there's one with the 'pop cart.' That's the little one-man car that follows each train, looking for any fire that might have been started by a cinder from the locomotive. We added that car last year after the fires we had around here from lightning."

"Why not cell phones? My experience is they're more reliable," John commented.

"Not in these mountains. There are a lot of dead spots up there. It doesn't make any difference which service you use or the type of phone you have, it's mostly dead space from Hermosa, five miles north of here all the way to Silverton, with a couple of exceptions, where cell phones work but not many. That's why we use two-way radios on our own frequency, and a backup frequency."

"What happens if some crazy Texans think they are banditos and decide to rob the train? You guys have guns?" John asked.

"No. We are not authorized to carry weapons. As for the passengers, weapons are prohibited," the conductor explained. "You only see the holdups in the movies, like Butch Cassidy and the Sundance Kid. In the real world today, Butch, Sundance and their gang of five would have never pulled off the robbery," the conductor declared with air of confidence.

"I haven't been around steam locomotives since I was a young boy. I've always wondered how the locomotive carried enough water to make steam."

"The water is carried in a water tank inside the tender, behind the locomotive. The water is transferred to the locomotive and its coils by way of that there hose," the conductor explained as he pointed to the 4-inch thick rubber hose. "To refill our water supply, we make two stops at water tanks on our way to Silverton and one stop on the return trip."

"I'm going to take the train tomorrow," John said, "so I'd better leave my cell phone and pistols at home. Will I see you tomorrow?"

"There'll be two trains running tomorrow; I'll be on the later train," the conductor responded.

"You mean you run more than one train a day?" John asked.

"In the height of the season, usually July and August, yes, we'll run three, even four if we're really busy. We'll run two tomorrow because, as I understand it, there's a special picnic party on the first train. The weather forecast is for a sunny day but there may be a chill in the air. I'd bring a warm jacket. Have a good trip," the conductor said to John.

"Thanks." About that time Trish walked out on the platform. She greeted the engineer by name, took John's arm and led him towards the parking lot.

"How about we have a cold beer back at my place? I'd really like to wash up and relax before we go out to dinner. By the way, where's Julia?" Trish asked.

"She's still back up at the ranch oiling her body in preparation for my return," John responded.

"Poor thing. Did she offer you any useful advice regarding conservation measures? That's what she was there for, right?"

"She turned out to be a useless pain in the ass. I'll fill you in with the details at your place, OK?"

"Sure. Let me drive, you relax. I'll have you a beer in 10 minutes," Trish said in a soft voice.

CHAPTER TWENTY-ONE

Trish drove her battered Toyota four-by-four to her small, one-bedroom apartment with a view of the Animas River. A Siamese cat greeted the couple as John carried in his bag and Trish headed for the refrigerator. The living room, with a comfortable lounge chair and a foldout couch facing a TV, opened to a small dining area off a modern kitchen. Book shelves and artwork covered the pale blue walls. Trish's literary tastes centered on modern novels with a few classics mixed in. The artwork consisted of watercolors and oil reproductions of local landscapes.

"Here's your beer, and it's cold," Trish said, handing John the bottle and a glass. He set the glass down and proceeded to drink from the bottle.

Trish picked up his small bag and carried it towards the bedroom.

"Where are you going with my life's possessions?" John asked.

"Into my bedroom. OK?"

"I'm accustomed to a couch, if that's your preference."

"It is not my preference, thank you very much. I prefer to sleep with an injured watermelon."

"I'm available," John climbed into the lounge chair as if it were a saddle.

"Now tell me about your problems at the ranch with what's her name?"

"It's Gretchen from Connecticut, and I can assure you she's no relation to Julia Roberts."

John went on to relate Gretchen's weeklong stay at the Diamond J, her incessant questions about the ranch's operation and the ridiculous reforms she had recommended. "I must admit, from the very beginning we really didn't see eye to eye," John summarized. "And then when she called Rigby in New York, that's when the shit hit the fan. Yesterday, Rigby fired my ass. Never been unemployed in my life."

"Just like that," John said with a snap of his fingers.

"Rigby suggested he was acting on Mr. Devlin's behalf. That must be the way they do things in New York." John continued.

"I can't believe it. That ranch has been your life," Trish answered. "But you won't have a problem finding a good job."

"I know, but to be honest I don't want to leave the ranch. Hell, it's my HOME, Trish. Don't you understand? Wherever I go and whatever I do, the place will always be with me—the land, it's like I'm connected to the meadows like a blade of grass. And those cows, I know the history of every one of them and the calves they've had. Some have grown to be producing cows in the herd. We even have five cows that have granddaughters. The memories of my family are tied to the ranch. I can't wipe away all that personal history of the Diamond J. It's part of my DNA. Whatever self-dignity I've been able to muster in my life comes from my work on the ranch. Now Rigby and Devlin have taken it away from me. To have to leave the ranch and my work will, I know, alter me in ways I can't imagine. You know, I have relatives buried on the ranch. Who is going to care for their graves? Rigby? The Devlins? I doubt it."

Trish noticed his eyes watering from where she stood by the lounge chair. She leaned over and took his hand, squeezed it and then kissed his cheek.

"Can you talk with Mr. Devlin?" she asked.

"I'd have thought he would have called me to say he agreed or disagreed with Rigby, but not a word. My guess is that he and Rigby must have some understanding. If Rigby wants someone gone, he's gone. Devlin probably goes along with his decisions when it comes to the ranch. He wants Rigby to do his dirty work for him. Neither of them has the decency to meet face to face with me. They don't want to confront the unpleasantness that might result. Gutless wonders, that's what they are."

"You could call Devlin and plead your case. He is, after all, the owner."

"He's probably in Argentina. Besides I'm not about to get down on my knees and plead my case to anyone. They know what I can do on the ranch, and I'll be damned if I have to remind them," John said with some anger.

At dinner, John talked about the lessons he learned from his grandfather, and the rough edges of his father, and how he once thought he'd escape from his father and the ranch after his service in Vietnam. "I would have, except for Dad's health. I couldn't leave him after my brother couldn't work with him. Dad would have worked himself to death in a year. As it was, it took him another 20 years. My mother tried to help him, and she did, but in the end the ranch was too much of a burden, even with me to help. What we needed was more cash income. Instead, we substituted our labor for cash. My dad worked himself to death like his father before him. We couldn't get out from under heavy debt. That's why Devlin has the ranch, and I'm the hired help. Like the miners always say about their work, "The owner gets the gold and the miners get the shaft."

"I bet Devlin's going to have a hard time replacing you."

"Maybe. He's hiring Josh as the temporary manager. Josh's a damn fine worker, and loyal too, but he doesn't have any idea of what a manager needs to do, either on a day-to-day basis, or season to season. He's always had someone make the decisions for him, like me or his parents."

"Certainly, Devlin will come to realize that Rigby made a big mistake," Trish volunteered.

"I'd rather talk about you than Rigby. Tell me how in hell you ended up in Durango from Indiana?" John asked.

"I think I told you I had my heart set on a dance career?"

"Yes, and you flunked out because of your gorgeous breasts," John replied with a smile.

"Didn't so much flunk out but came to realize I'd never gain a lead role given my figure. Also, after almost four years in the ballet corps I didn't have the drive to practice for hours and hours each day and be dieting at the same time. An injury to my knee made it harder and harder." Trish pulled up her dress to show John the long scar that circled the inside of her left knee.

"But to work under the master choreographer, George Balanchine, was a great experience. Soon after I left the ballet corps, I met a man I thought I loved. He clerked in a bookstore. That relationship never worked out. After that, I dated another man, about your age, who worked in insurance and finance. Then his company transferred him to Denver and then to Durango, definitely a downward career cycle. I wanted children. He wanted a better job and some freedom and chose New York over marriage, while I decided to stay here.

Durango is a very friendly town, much like the one where I grew up in Indiana. I've worked for the railroad for 10 years now, ever since I moved down here from Denver. It's a good job. The owner of the railroad gives me plenty of responsibility but, I'm sorry to say, the salary is not commensurate with it. But I love this country. I hike, fish, raft and ski and have some really close friends I'd miss if I left here for a higher paying job. Also, I'm not certain Hamlet, the cat, would agree to a move. He's got some girl friends in the neighborhood, and he's a father, I'm sure, to half the feline population of Durango."

"Your job at the railroad, it's special events like the one you're arranging for Devlin? John asked.

"Yes. For the most part, interesting work but some events are a real headache."

"Can you fill me in any more on Devlin's conference?"

"I think I told you everyone arrives Thursday evening, the second week in June. Mr. Devlin said we'd get better attendance in early June than in late summer or early fall. There'll be 275 guests, including spouses and speakers, and your buddy, Rigby. Thursday night there'll be a welcoming reception in Durango—sign in, pick up packets, mix with the other attendees, cocktails, that sort of thing. On Friday morning, everyone boards the train with their luggage and a box lunch. The train heads up into the mountains to a picnic site north of Tamarron, where the conference will take place. At the picnic site, Cascade Canyon, a beautiful spot where there's a large meadow, we'll have tables set up for the guests with refreshments, wine and beer. Here, the train will turn around at what is called the "wye." After the picnic, the train heads south to the Rockwood Station, where there'll be buses to take everyone to Tamarron, a short distance away. Right now, I'm still trying to locate enough buses for everyone. We expect the guests will be settled in at Tamarron by late afternoon, time enough to clean up, rest or maybe take a short hike before cocktail hour. In the convention hall, there'll be gambling tables and a live auction of some spectacular Indian artwork. I've seen some of the items—jewelry, rugs, and pottery primarily—and they are museum quality. The proceeds from the gambling and auction, after paying the Indians who'll be running the gambling, will go to Devlin's National Conservation Coalition. A fancy dinner completes the evening."

"Why are the Indians running the gambling? I thought gambling was illegal in Colorado, unless it takes place on an Indian reservation," John said.

"It is. But we received special permission from the county commissioners and the Colorado Department of Revenue. Devlin made a nice gift to the new city library and quite a few of Devlin's guests made some big contributions to the governor's recent reelection campaign. So that helped us with the gambling permit. The Utes have their own casino and know how to run the tables. Unfortunately I've had more trouble with the Utes than the politicians."

"In what way?" John asked.

"They demanded a guarantee of $30,000 from the gambling tables. Plus, they said they wouldn't accept personal checks or credit cards from the guests. They told me, they didn't know any of Devlin's party, and had no way of collecting if someone passed a bad check or a stolen credit card. If they insisted on the $30,000 guarantee, I told them, we'd have to find someone else to run the gambling. Also, I tried to assure the Utes that Mr. Devlin's invitees, mostly millionaires, were not the type who'd pass bad checks or stolen credit cards. The Ute elder told me: 'We don't trust energy companies or conservationists.' So cash it will be. Finally, after a lot of arguing we settled on a $15,000 guarantee."

"Can't say I blame the Utes," John responded.

"The conference sessions start Saturday morning, and go all morning. After lunch, there'll be free time so the guests can hike, bike, golf or do anything they want. Then another cocktail party before a very fancy dinner."

"It sounds to me like they won't have very much time to save the West. A couple of hours on Saturday morning and the plan is complete—an easy chip shot—and then onto the more difficult work of golf. If you could get me on the agenda for Saturday, there are a few things I'd like to say to these folks."

"Sorry, but after your sessions with Gretchen, I doubt you'd be considered a conservation leader."

After dinner, they strolled through downtown Durango. Laughter and music spilled out from the bars along Main Street. The tourist's shops, too, did a brisk business—T-shirts, Indian jewelry, western wear and some postcards for friends and relatives back in New Jersey and Iowa. A motorcycle roared through town, followed by a blinking police cruiser. A tour bus, delayed by roadwork on a 10,000-foot pass north of Durango, delivered its weary tourists to the Strater, the town's largest Victorian hotel. Loiterers, outside the hotel bar listened to the piano player bang out requested ragtime melodies as the patrons celebrated their hard-earned vacations.

Trish and John walked back to the apartment arm in arm, talking quietly beneath a clear sky that served as the backdrop for Orion. Once home, the lovers undressed each other and moved gently into bed.

"Don't be alarmed if Hamlet jumps up on the bed. He always sleeps with me," Trish announced.

"How do I earn the same privilege?" John asked.

"Purr like Hamlet."

"That's easy when I'm with you."

By the time John finished showering the next morning, a bacon-and-eggs breakfast awaited him. Trish said, "Sorry to rush, but we need to be at the railroad depot in 15 minutes. I called this morning to confirm our tickets, and the dispatcher asked if I'd give up our seats on the train to Silverton and instead take two seats on the picnic train. Seems there was some mixup with reservations. You'll see as much country from the picnic train as the other, plus it makes for a much shorter day. Three hours up to Silverton and another three hours on the return trip is more than enough train time for me. I've ridden it at least 50 times. That's enough cinders and smoke for a lifetime."

They drove to the depot, parked, and climbed aboard one of the coaches, as the conductor shouted, "All aboard." The engineer let go two long whistle signals from the cab of engine #481. The nine-car train chugged slowly out of the depot exactly at 9:30 a.m.

John paid particular attention to the location and duties of the train's staff. He walked through all the cars and noted the two-way radio on the conductor's desk in the enclosed coach car directly behind the tender car. He carefully studied the map he had purchased at the depot detailing the train's route, estimated the train's speed at 15 miles per hour and confirmed by the conductor. The train chugged through uptown Durango and into the Animas River valley along the edge of a small cattle ranch. The cows gave their full attention to the lush grass, accustomed as they were to the train's smoke and rumble. A long whistle blast indicated the train was approaching the old town of Hermosa. It moved past an abandoned water tower, and began its ascent out of the valley.

On a tight turn, John noticed the small, open-air maintenance car following about a quarter of a mile behind the train—the one-man, gas-powered pop cart. "He'll tag along throughout our journey and radio back to Durango if he sees the beginning of a fire," the conductor explained.

John's thoughts turned to the possibility of robbing Devlin's train in June. John felt like an Army scout, as he was in Vietnam, scoping out his target before the attack. He needed to prepare for the attack in the event he decided to go ahead with it. John wondered how he and Josh could immobilize the train, including the crew of seven, rob the passengers and get safely away without harming anyone. The two radios, John figured, could easily be made inoperative, and the robbery of the passengers, he believed, did not present any overwhelming problems unless, of course, one or more passengers carried weapons. Unlikely, but nevertheless possible. What about the crew, including the pop cart driver? Did they carry weapons? The conductor told John they did not, but was that enough assurance? John spotted no weapons on the train crew or the pop cart operator. He figured that the crew had the capability to repair any minor damage John and Josh might cause the locomotive. Maybe even get to a radio on the train, at a location unknown to John, and send an urgent message, reporting the robbery from the disabled train and calling for immediate assistance.

Also, John realized he had to select an appropriate site on the rail line where the train could be stopped, immobilized if necessary, and robbed, allowing the two men to make their escape by horseback to the west and eventually to Highway 550, where they would have parked their truck and horse trailer. The spot of the robbery needed to be as far away as possible from any known human habitation or telephone, but also close to an escape route. What was the best way to halt the train? John wanted to avoid a major accident or injuries. He wanted to give the engineer time to recognize a boulder or a dirt slide ahead on the track before bringing the train to a safe stop at a strategic location out of sight of any highway or cabin, and within a dead spot for cell phones. John studied his map.

About that time, almost an hour and a half into the trip, John heard a single whistle blast as the train slowed and came to a stop at a water tank alongside the track on the east side of the Animas River. Before the brakemen and conductor jumped off the train, they instructed the passengers to remain in their seats. The engineer and fireman pulled the water hose attached to the large metal tank and connected it to the water tank in the tender car. The pop cart pulled up right behind the last coach. John checked his cell phone. "No service available." John stepped from the train to inspect the pop cart, particularly its fuel tank and the radio mounted in a wooden cradle on the car's front panel.

The operator walked up to John, who was giving it a careful inspection. "Can

I help you, sir?" the operator asked, suspicious of the train's passenger.

John looked at the operator, who appeared unarmed, and said, "As an engineer myself, I'm interested in how this little cart is motorized."

"A small gas engine, like on a lawnmower," the operator said, pointing to the back of the cart. As John thanked him for the information, he made note of the radio's frequency. Fifteen minutes later, the engineer blew two long whistles and the train proceeded once again on its northern journey.

The water stop, the perfect place for the holdup, John thought. They wouldn't have to disable the train. The crew could easily be rounded up at gunpoint while the passengers sat immobilized by fear, or more likely, snapped pictures and rolled their video cameras to catch the entertainment intermission before the lunch stop. John and Josh would have already disabled the two-way radios. After the armed and masked men handcuffed the eight crew members to the metal-ladder railing on the water tower, they'd walk through each car announcing the robbery.

John believed the passengers would sit frightened as Josh walked down the aisle collecting their cash in a black plastic garbage bag, while John stood at the rear door of each car with his pistol drawn. They figured to collect on average about $1,000 from each passenger. After they had gone through all seven passenger cars, the concession car and the parlor car, they'd mount their horses and make their way across the river to the west and onto the old toll road that led to the highway and their truck and horse trailer. John figured they'd have enough lead time to be into Montrose County, well to the north, before the authorities received word of the holdup. John figured the entire escapade could be carried out without any injuries to passengers or damage to any railroad property, with the exception of two radios and the pop cart gas tank.

John reviewed the details once again. There are some serious problems to overcome, he thought. The water tower site is on the east side of the river, which meant Josh and John would have to cross the river on horseback from the west side and their best access off the highway. The river would be too high with the spring runoff to allow the horses and riders to cross the river twice. Also, the Tall Timber Resort was only a half-mile north of the holdup location. Certainly, they'd have a telephone or at least a radio that any passenger could reach within 10 minutes following the robbery. How could two armed men, John asked himself, contain all 275 passengers on the train without someone escaping? No, this scenario will not work. Should he expand the number of bandits? He was careful to exclude Trish as an accomplice in the event they were caught. He purposely shared no plans with her, only her friendship and company on the train. Josh could be trusted, but except for his brother, no one else.

John continued to study his map while Trish looked out the window. "What's so interesting about the map? You're missing some absolutely gorgeous scenery. Look at those mountains over there, still with all that snow in April."

"I always like to follow where I go with a map, and the guidebook gives some useful information about points of interest along the rail line."

"We should be coming to our picnic spot soon," Trish offered.

Within five minutes, the train came to a stop. Once again the brakemen and conductor jumped off with flags. The train sounded three short whistles, and then backed up. Trish pointed out the U shaped track onto which the train moved in reverse. Once all the cars had backed into the U, the train moved forward onto another track that connected with the main north-south track. The train had turned around at what the map identified as the Cascade Canyon wye. The train pulled forward, allowing the pop cart to pull in behind it, and then on the signal of one short whistle blast, the train, still in the wye, stopped at a covered pavilion, the Cascade Station, identified in the railroad guide. The conductor came through the cars and announced the lunch stop. "Everyone please leave the train on the right side of the train. Be sure to take with you your picnic box and all personal items. If you need to use the facilities, use those on the train. We'll be here about 45 minutes."

The crew unloaded the cold refreshments from the baggage car and carried them to the picnic tables, where all the passengers had seated themselves. They immediately dug into their picnic boxes. The entire crew, including the pop cart operator, sat at a separate table from the passengers. John counted the crew: the conductor, a brakeman, the two concession-car attendants and the parlor-car attendant, the engineer, and the pop cart operator. Only the fireman was missing from the group assembled at the picnic table. He remained at his station between the locomotive and the tender car, stoking the locomotive's fire box with coal to maintain the train's steam pressure. As the conductor had warned John the day before on the depot platform, the air was quite chilly, particularly at the picnic spot in the shadow of tall spruce trees. On his Forest Service map, John identified the three-mile-long trail leading from their present location to U.S. Highway 550, the main route to Durango from the north. After finishing a sandwich, John asked Trish if she wanted to walk up the trail with him.

"Thanks, but I think I'll stay here and have some more iced tea. You have a good walk. I'll be here when you get back."

"Promise?"

"Don't be too long, or the train might leave without you," Trish warned.

John took off up the rocky trail and walked on for about a quarter of a mile. A good serviceable trail, John thought, but steep and somewhat dangerous for the average hiker, though not for a horse.

By the time he'd returned to the picnic area, the conductor had announced, "All aboard," three times. He checked to see that all the passengers had left the picnic tables, and then waved to John to get aboard as he emerged from the trail.

Minutes later, with two long whistle blasts, the train rumbled south towards Durango.

On the return trip, John paid more attention to the scenery and less to his maps and guidebook. "I could sure use a cold beer about now," he said to Trish, "and maybe even a nap."

"I can arrange both in about an hour. How're you enjoying the trip?"

"Wonderful. Those vertical canyons we passed through are spectacular in their color, and that high bridge over the river does take your breath away. I read in the guide how various avalanches wiped out portions of the track. And that it cost $100,000 a mile to build the entire line. It's amazing to think how workers chipped and blasted a path around this mountain. I last rode this railroad with my dad almost 30 years ago. Can't say I see much that has changed, except the passengers and crew."

John reached over and took Trish's hand. "What a wonderful day, thanks for arranging it." He kissed her on her cheek. "The day's been pleasant enough to make me almost forget and forgive Rigby and Devlin."

"Almost?" Trish asked.

"Almost but not quite," John replied.

Trish squeezed his hand and held it tight as she put her head on his shoulder.

CHAPTER TWENTY-TWO

After brunch with Trish, John departed for the ranch. In Montrose, he stopped at Walmart and paid cash for two ski masks and three pairs of handcuffs. Between Josh and John, they had an ample supply of ammunition at the ranch for Josh's .38 caliber revolver and John's 9 mm, semi-automatic pistol.

John's thoughts turned to the work ahead of him, particularly the branding scheduled for next weekend. How in hell can I conduct a branding without the help of neighbors, and all because of Devlin's fear of a lawsuit. And how can I find a crew of 10, John asked himself? This year there'll be no roping and dragging to the fire, where a team of young, strong flankers wrestle the calves to the ground and stretch them out for vaccination, branding and castration. Not enough youthful manpower, John recognized. Yes, Johnny will come down from Cheyenne, and hopefully bring a stout friend who I'll pay by the hour. But I can't expect them to flank 700 or more calves. We'll have to use the old rusted calf table. There'll be problems with it even if I lubricate every moving part with a gallon of WD-40. With a smaller crew there's no alternative. The boys will have to load one calf at a time before flipping the table so the calf is on its side ready for castration and branding. Someone else with experience will have to administer the shots to the calves when they're in the alley or on the table. I could offer to pay one or two of my neighbors who've learned from the Circle's grapevine that no one works on the Diamond J unless they're employed by me, but, they'd find the offer of cash insulting. We'll get by, but it'll be one hell of a long day. John thought, I wish Rigby could be here to suffer through the fatigue that sets in after about 400 calves. No, he'd probably seriously injure himself. I'd love to brand him with the Diamond J, John thought, and then for good measure give him a shot for black leg. Where the hell are you when I need you, Rigby, you little bald, pudgy, son of a bitch?

John arrived back at the ranch at supper time. Outside, he noticed the steel head gate box, which indicated Josh wasn't able to set it alone. We'll get it in the ditch tomorrow, John thought, and then repair some fences up on the forest, assuming the snow's melted.

He entered the shop, where Josh had the Dodge truck's carburetor disassembled on the work bench. John put a frozen dinner in the microwave, sat with a beer and sorted through some mail. Six-hundred and fifty dollars for a new set of tires for the Dodge pickup? The bill will not improve Rigby's sense of humor. And the monthly feedlot charge of over $4,000 will only add a long fiery footnote to his intemperate response. Rigby, John thought, could be as tight as a bull's asshole in fly time.

Josh visited with John after supper.

"I've been thinking, we're going to be short-handed at branding time," Josh said as he flipped open the Coors can offered by John.

"It will be one hell of a long day," John responded. "As usual you'll be the cut man. You'll also have to keep an eye on the propane stove to keep the irons hot. Mary will have to be responsible for refilling the medicine guns and keeping track of the cow book. The other responsibilities I've got figured out." Josh didn't ask for details. If John said he had it figured out, that's all Josh needed to know.

"I understand Rigby appointed you interim manager yesterday. Congratulations," John said as he grabbed another beer for himself from the icebox.

"Yeah, and I'm not too comfortable with the promotion, if that's what it is, because they fired you. If it weren't for the $300 a month salary increase, which I can sure use, I'd tell Rigby to stuff the offer up his ass. I don't like being put in a situation where I'm profiting by your misfortune."

"Don't you worry about me," John replied. "You and your family need to eat like the rest of us. Also, I know these dick heads fairly well. My guess is your position is only temporary until they find someone who'll lick their asses and do their bidding. So I'd strongly suggest that you take their money while you can."

"Rigby did tell me my position was only temporary, but I could apply for the permanent position. I talked it over with Mary. She said, since you're leaving, we should also leave. No telling who'll replace you, probably some rodeo cowboy Rigby saw on TV. You've been the best manager I could ever hope for."

"Thanks for the loyalty, but you need to think about your own future," John said.

"Mary and I talked about it. You think we'll be offered severance pay? A few ranches offer it."

"Unlikely. They made no mention of any severance pay to me."

"If they're not offering it to you, I doubt they'd be offering it to me," Josh responded.

"I do have an idea, however, about how we might collect some severance pay."

John then went on to explain in some detail about Devlin's conference and how the guests, all loaded with cash, will be riding the train from Durango up to a picnic and then to their lodging at the Tamarron resort. John rolled out a map and spread it out on the table. The two beer cans provided the weights to each end.

"I plan to rob the train, and I'd like you to help me with the holdup. It won't be dangerous," John assured Josh, "and if it works the way I have it planned, no one will get hurt. We'll take only cash, no jewelry, cameras, watches or other personal items, just plain green cash. I expect we should get away with at least 135 thousand and maybe as much as 250 thousand."

"What in hell you been smoking in Durango? Did Trish put you up to this?"

"No she didn't. Look, I've had it with Devlin. We've worked like hell, saved his ass in the blizzard, and not a word of thanks. Then he sends out Little Miss Muffitt to give us a little coaching on how to do things. And now he's invited his arrogant, hypocritical conservation friends out here to 'save us.' If they're all like little Miss Smart Ass, and I suspect they are, I'd rather burn in hell. And then there's Rigby, everyone's favorite ranch know-it-all. They all want to save this, save that, but not save working people and their jobs. Hell, they're turning our valley into a recreational colony with their second homes and "designer" ranches. If we can scare the shit of them, maybe they'll stay put back east. Besides, Johnny needs some money to go to college."

"Have you mentioned your plan to anyone else?" Josh asked.

"No, and I'd also appreciate it if this conversation went no further than this kitchen. Another beer?"

"Sure," Josh said, as he thought about the idea John had thrown in his direction along with the Coors.

"So what do you think?" John asked.

"I think you're fucking crazy, that's what I think. But I do like the idea of $250,000. With a portion of that, I could sure retire. I have some questions. We'll be armed, right? What about the passengers and crew?"

"The crew carries no weapons, I've checked; and the passengers are informed by the railroad that no weapons are allowed and if found, the passenger will be arrested."

"How in hell do the two of us stop a train? I know how Butch Cassidy and the Sundance Kid accomplished it. They had at least four other guys helping."

"We don't have to jump the train like Butch and Sundance, take over the engineer's cab, and then disarm the crew. The train will have already stopped at the picnic spot. Everyone will be off the train, including the crew, when we strike."

"That's fine, but someone, probably Rigby, will surely use their cell phone to call for help."

"Well first off, cell phones don't work at the picnic stop, and the train's two-way radios can easily be disabled. Also, I'm thinking about taking Rigby hostage as you go through the crowd with a burlap bag. Anyone who doesn't pony up, I threaten to kill Rigby," John said with a faint smile.

"You forget, there may be some folks on the train who'd love to see that son of a bitch dead. Why in hell do you get to do all the fun things? Why can't I hold Rigby by his hair and see him squirm?"

"He's as bald as a musk melon, that's why."

"If you think we can pull it off, I'm with you." Josh said. "But won't someone recognize us, like Rigby, Devlin or his wife?"

"That's why we'll wear ski masks," John said as he pulled two masks from the Walmart bag and handed one to Josh. "It's yours to wear if you promise to join me. We split the proceeds 50/50."

"Count me in, Kemosabe, but only if I get to wear the red ski mask," Josh answered.

"Tonto, you'll look handsome in red picking up your severance pay."

"Brilliant. But I'm not comfortable if you insist on riding that white mare of yours."

"Why the hell not?" John asked.

"She's a real bitch with other horses when we have work to do. And probably, like the Long Ranger, you'll want to wear double holsters with two pearl-handled pistols loaded with silver bullets," Josh said with a faint smile.

"You got a better idea?"

"Isn't the Ute reservation close to Durango? How about we both dress up as Indians. The passengers will think the Indian robbery part of the lunch entertainment. Also, the conservationists will love the Indians. The country's first conservationists—nature's children—tree huggers all, except when on the warpath. The police will, at first, immediately head south to the reservation while you and I, with our stash, speed north in the truck. Isn't that the American way? Blame all violence on the Indians? If we're going to do this right let's do it like the old-timers."

"Folks would think that if the Indians wanted to rob the train, they sure wouldn't be dressing up like Indians," John observed.

"True for the Durango Police and the La Plata County Sheriffs' office but not for the passengers. They've seen too many Hollywood westerns to think otherwise. Believe me. I've watched a lot of western movies on TV. If by chance they figure we're not Indians but still intend to rob them, they'll be scared shitless. They'll hand over their money faster than we can say, 'We want your cash now!"

"Josh, you can be one smart dude when you want to be."

The two men went about their chores. Josh worked over the truck carburetor. John saddled up and rode through the cattle. Patches of snow still lay in the cedars' shadows above the irrigation ditch. In the meadows, the sweet smell of new grass signaled the arrival of spring. The cows attacked every emerging fresh sprout, oblivious to their calves all stretched out on the drying ground to absorb the warming sun.

By late morning, John and Josh had set the new head gate in the ditch. John noticed Josh's serious mood, not his usual jovial self. John noted, "You look like you've lost your favorite horse."

"I can't get this robbery out of my mind. Keep going over the details. Suppose one of Devlin's guests has a gun, for instance? What then? I'm not into shootin' anyone."

"There won't be any shootin'. Devlin's guests are not the type to be carrying side arms. About the only thing they'll be packing is cash to gamble with and their cameras. Can you imagine the president of Exxon carrying a loaded pistol, or the head of the Sierra Club wielding a six-shooter? They're more likely to pack a water bottle than a weapon. I don't think the head of the Audubon Society or some big-shot New York banker would want to test the gun law, or worse, see his mug shot in the local paper, even if it is Durango." Then John added, "Still, we need to be aware of the possibility that one of the crew members may be armed."

"Are you sure you can block the radio frequency the railroad uses? Also, they probably have backup frequencies," Josh noted.

"I don't plan to block their frequencies but to disable the radios altogether. We cut the cables connecting the antennas to the radios. It is easily done with a pair of heavy-duty wire cutters. There will be one radio on the train and another on the pop cart."

"Any more concerns?"

"Yeah. After we rob the passengers and make our escape, won't the crew and passengers climb back on the train and make it back to Durango before we've driven very far north in the truck?"

"I forgot to mention, we'll disable the locomotive by draining the water tank in the tender car. We open the valve, drain the water, or cut the connecting hose, and the engine is without a source of steam. You can figure that the train isn't goin' anywhere without steam. As for the pop cart, we'll puncture its gas tank, so it won't be goin' anywhere either. But as a precaution I'll carry a stick of dynamite, a cap and a fuse, in case something unexpected turns up," John answered.

"Like what?"

"How in hell can I predict the unexpected?"

"I thought Kemosabe had all the answers."

"Look Tonto, trust me, OK? Now let's get some work done. Remember we're branding this weekend. I've already ordered the medicine from the vet. How are we on needles and ear tags?"

"How the hell can you think about branding while you're planning a robbery?"

"It's called mental dexterity; it comes from drinking a lot of beer. Now, about needles and ear tags and other supplies?"

"We need both. Also, we could use two new glass cylinders for the medicine guns—they're both cracked. I could use a new sharpening stone for my knife. It's about worn thin as a wafer. And the portable propane tank should be topped off," Josh said.

Then Josh remembered there'd be no neighbors helping at the branding. Josh wanted to know in detail "how in hell can we manage?"

"I'll call Johnny in Cheyenne; He'll come down with a friend. Also, I'll get Matt Corcoran; he's done day work for us before and worked at our branding two years ago. He might be a good hand for you to hire in my absence."

"We'll see," Josh said, clearly without any enthusiasm, and then added, "How about Devlin? They're his damn calves."

"I'll give him a call. He did tell me this winter that he'd like to be at the branding with his family."

Early that evening John called Devlin at his apartment. Amanda answered the phone and asked who wanted to speak to her husband.

"This is John Marlow in Colorado," John said.

She responded as if she didn't recognize his name or voice and then said in a frosty tone, "I'll get him."

John explained to Devlin about the upcoming branding and how short-handed they'd be because of his new rule about outside help on the ranch. John had hoped that Devlin might reconsider his prohibition against neighbors coming onto the ranch, given the labor situation. Devlin only asked about the number of calves to be branded. He did not offer his own services, such as they were.

Then John made the suggestion: "I remember you said awhile back that you and the family would like to attend the branding this spring. You could come up here before your Durango conference. We could use your help, and the boys might enjoy it; branding is a fun occasion. It's not dangerous if everyone does their job right. Also, I have a new horse for Mrs. Devlin; she might like to try him out," John said, expecting the invitation to be met with some enthusiasm on the other end of the line.

"I'm afraid the branding this year won't work for us. Mrs. Devlin is in charge of a large dinner and dance to benefit the Nature Conservancy here in New York. It is something that has been long planned, and I have to be present to introduce the after-dinner speaker, Henry Kissinger."

Kissinger, John thought, the former Secretary of State whose lingering negotiations with the North Vietnamese in the early 1970s almost had John killed as he and his platoon waited for Kissinger to decide if he was going to sit at a square table or a round table to negotiate a peace settlement. And wasn't he the guy who wanted to defoliate all of Vietnam? An environmentalist?

"Mr. Devlin, I wouldn't want for you to give up an evening with Henry Kissinger so that you could brand a bunch of shit-squirting calves."

"That's thoughtful of you, John. Maybe next year," he said without mention of Rigby's decision to fire John, except to say, "I also appreciate your staying on at the ranch for another month until we have a new manager in place. I've asked Rigby to involve you in the search process," Devlin answered.

No mention of severance pay or compensation for the week's vacation not taken.

"I assume from talking with Rigby you have another position nearby. I hope I get to see you in early June after the Durango conference. I'm coming up to the ranch with Amanda and some guests. Please let Rigby or me know where we can contact you. I'm guessing you'll have no trouble finding another position in the valley. Also, you can count on a good recommendation from me if you need one." And then Devlin said he was being called to dinner and would have to end the conversation. His last words to John: "I do hope the branding goes well."

John was pissed when he hung up. The tone of Devlin's comments suggested he wanted to wish John a pleasant Caribbean vacation.

The next day when Josh asked if the Devlins would be at the branding, John replied, "No, he has to go to dinner with Henry Kissinger."

"Did he explain the firing?"

"No, the twerp couldn't manage to be direct and tell me why he agreed with Rigby's decision. That might lead to an unpleasant conversation, a verbal confrontation that he, obviously, wants to avoid. He demonstrated such exquisite manners, everything but directness and honesty. He doesn't understand, with all his money and security, that he's ruined my life, maybe forever. It's like being thrown out of one's home for having told the truth. Maybe it's that New Yorkers switch jobs as often as they change wives and homes."

Next week, John drove into town for his errands. He first stopped off at the service station, where he filled up the portable propane tank and then asked the mechanic if he could clean and reassemble the carburetor Josh had failed to repair. The veterinarian had the medicine for the branding. He and John swapped war stories about the calving season. John proudly announced he didn't have to perform any C-sections this spring, and was able to save three calves in his newly designed hot box. The vet reported that a new virus had turned up in the valley but he knew of no medicine to control it.

It was late enough in the morning that John thought the Circle of Knowledge would have concluded their daily session at the hardware store. But not so. When John entered, the Circle's total membership was still huddled around the cold potbellied stove as if they'd all contracted an advanced case of frostbite.

"So what's happening out at the old homestead, John?" someone asked.

"We got through spring OK with not too much sickness. The weekend after next we'll brand. And the last week in May we'll move everything to the forest."

"What's this we hear that you've been let go? Immoral behavior with that underage redhead, I bet."

"No, I can't satisfy the boss. Expenses too high and income too low," John explained. He didn't want to get into a long discussion about the conservation advisor's recommendations and his response to them.

"Well, that's ranching. What did he expect—to make millions in the middle of a winter blizzard? You need to take him to school, John."

"I can't believe you'll be leaving the Diamond J. Hell, there've been four generations of Marlows on that place; it's your home and your folks are buried there," said the history teacher, less to remind John of his landed heritage than to remind other Circle members of the ranch's history.

Another Circle member, the former manager of the county dump, who survived on his sale of discarded refrigerators and broken furniture to newcomers, joined in. "Someone's got to knock some sense into Devlin. And about this conference he's got planned. If he's really serious about saving this place and us hayseeds who make this valley our home, he'll sure as hell need a little help from above. But as we all know when God shows up around here, it's not to improve things, but usually to mess things up. Next time your boss is out here from, where is it? … Chicago? New York? … Bring him in here, John, for an introduction."

"Are there any rumors we can start that might help you, John? Like we saw Devlin humping a sheep in the back of his pickup last winter?"

Slim Warren jumped into the conversation. "As Jake suggested to you last time I seen you in here, I'd sure think seriously about putting a hit on that train your boss is filling up with those rich dudes out of New York. If I were 10 years younger, I'd gather up some boys from around here and give those city folks a real scare. I'd take their cash and retire. That's what I'd do. A lot more security if you ask me, than that there Social Security."

"And I'd join you," the ex-teacher chimed in. Others around the stove nodded in agreement.

"If you plan to do it, let me know. My brother-in-law works on the train. I've got some suggestions for you," Jake volunteered, "so you don't get caught."

I don't plan to get caught, John almost answered.

CHAPTER TWENTY-THREE

Josh and John loaded their horses into the trailer in the gathering light of what the weatherman predicted to be a warm and clear day. John estimated the driving time at four hours from the ranch to the trailhead site, where they'd park the truck and unload the horses. He allowed for an additional 15-minute gas stop, another 15-minute appearance at a bull sale, and an hour to ride their horses from the trailhead on Highway 550 to a hiding spot near the picnic site, where he wanted to be at 11:45 a.m. The train would arrive, according to Trish, at noon. By John's estimate, it would take 15 minutes for everyone, including the crew, to exit the train and settle in at the picnic tables.

Josh kissed his wife goodbye, saying that he and John were off to a bull sale outside Gunnison. In the truck they carried their two ski masks, a full-feather Indian bonnet John had bought off the internet, a jar of cinnamon-colored makeup cream, two holstered pistols with ammunition belts, a stick of dynamite with an ignition cap and fuse, a hack saw, wire cutters and a pair of white Converse basketball shoes. They dressed in frayed work clothes—faded Levi jackets and mud-splattered jeans, silk bandanas, and brown leather gloves. Their horses had small feathers woven into their manes, their brands were covered by a thick coating of red paint and their flanks and hips displayed with what John and Josh thought to be authentic Indian designs—bolts of red lightning.

As they drove along discussing every conceivable detail of the robbery, John looked over at Josh. He had the basketball shoes in his lap with a bottle of red nail polish.

"This is a hell of a time for a pedicure," John remarked.

"I did the pedicure last night. I plan to wear these with my headband with two eagle feathers. Give me a minute and I'll show you."

"See, here it is." Josh pointed to the side of his dirty white high-top basketball shoe that displayed in huge letters, "UTE PRIDE." What do you think? Josh asked.

"Brilliant, Tonto. I hereby appoint you my first deputy."

"Thanks, Kemosabe. So do I get a raise?" The attempt at humor hid their nervousness.

"That comes later," John said with a wide smile. Then in a more serious tone he said, "I think during the holdup you should call me 'Chief' since I'll be wearing a chief's bonnet. Look in the box behind my seat."

Josh pulled open a box and looked at the long, double trail of feathers floating down from a beautifully crafted, beaded headband.

"Very nice, Chief. Since you've changed your name from Kemosabe, I want to change mine."

"To what?" John asked.

"How about Squatting Dog?"

"That's not a name. Besides it's insulting. I hereby anoint you Two Feathers."

"I like that, Chief. Thanks!"

On the road ahead of them they saw the sign advertising the "Monarch Herefords" bull sale and the entrance to the ranch. They pulled into the corral area that held the sale bulls. Josh walked over to inspect the bulls while John went to the sign-in table to obtain his auction number. Josh thought to himself, what a sorry set of breeding stock. Back in the truck with John, he said, looking over at the pens, "One-thousand pounds of hair and, at most, 10 pounds of muscle. I'm glad our alibi doesn't mean we have to buy one of these sorry-looking critters."

John responded, "I wish we had time to stay for the Bar-B-Q lunch." The two men walked from the bull pens to their truck and trailer and headed south towards Montrose on their way to Durango.

As they approached Montrose, Josh asked: "Do you think we'll get away with this?"

"Of course," John replied. "Why? Are you having second thoughts?"

"Sort of. You know, if we're caught and I have to go to the big house again, this time for armed robbery, what will happen to the wife and kids? That's what I worry about. Plus, I'll only get to shower once a week."

"Hell, she'll probably be happy to be rid of you. But maybe out of sympathy she'll put a metal file in the chocolate layer cake she sends you at Christmas."

"And you, what will you receive?"

"Probably a tuition bill from Yale University."

"Isn't that where Johnny is headed next year?"

"Yep, if we can pull this thing off, and by God we will! I know you're nervous. So am I. It's like before I went out on recon missions in Vietnam. I'd sweat bullets, chain smoke, and take a piss about every 10 minutes. After I was outside the barbed-wire perimeter, the anxiety, or fear, sharpened my senses. Hell, I could smell a sniper's breath 75 meters away. If you're nervous, you'll perform all the better for it, believe me."

It was not the first time John had lied to provide false confidence to a comrade in the face of danger. John thought of the lead soldier he placed on point for a scouting mission. He'd assured him the only danger was far distant from the platoon's location. Almost immediately after taking up his position, the soldier took the brunt of a 'Bouncing Betty' land mine. It tore through his testicles and an artery in his thigh before he died of blood loss. John, close behind him, was lucky to get away with only an ankle injury and evacuation to a comfortable field hospital.

"I don't want to fuck up," Josh said.

"You're not going to, Two Feathers. It's only another day at the office."

"But what if I have to say something to one of the passengers? I don't speak Injun."

"If you'll remember, all the Injuns you and I know speak English, maybe with a slight accent, and it ain't always perfect. But there won't be much for you to say, except maybe 'hand over your cash, pale face, and I mean pronto.' With a.38 caliber in your hand, I don't expect there'll be much to talk about."

When they stopped in Ridgway for gas and a cup of weak coffee at the Texaco station, John looked at his watch and said, "The train should be boarding in Durango about now."

"John, are you sure we want to go through with this?"

"Damned right we do. I want to scare the shit out of these eastern bankers, lawyers and CEOs. Send them back home with their tails between their legs and without some cash. If you think about it, Josh, they affect our lives in so many ways. They pull the chair out from under us and then send us off into oblivion without jobs. They have the safety net of wealth while we're one horse shy of the county poor house. They see us through a Hollywood lense— romantic cowboys, totting guns in a world where justice prevails. But you and I know we're only a bunch of dirtbags trying to make an honest living lookin' after some cows every day. All I want to do is even the score, or at least try to. So yes, I do want to take what is ours while we have the opportunity."

They drove on through the Uncompahgre Valley past cattle ranches, once part of the larger Ute reservation. Hereford and Angus cows nursed their new calves on the greening pastures, once the home for Indian horses. Tractors with their V blades cleaned the ditch arteries, soon to be filled with irrigation water.

As the men drove through the mountain town of Ouray, named for the distinguished 19th century Ute chief, Josh turned to John and volunteered. "I can't wait to meet Rigby face to face. Can you smell him yet?"

Devlin's guests had assembled at the 19th century wooden train depot with their luggage at the appointed hour of 9:15 a.m. Most everyone appeared in their new "outdoor" outfits, looking as if they had stepped out of an L.L. Bean catalog. The few who were in their city clothes appeared more comfortable than those guests who had squeezed themselves into tight jeans and high-heeled cowboy boots or new, stiff hiking boots. A few latecomers emerged from the Ralph Lauren outlet store next to the depot, dressed in the designer's latest western fashions and carrying bags of other sale items. Two overweight men could be heard to complain about the altitude and their shortness of breath. One conservationist, who flew in to Durango on his corporate jet, remarked to an acquaintance standing with him at the depot about the number of private planes parked at the municipal airport last evening. "It looked like an Air Force base out there. I understand from my pilot, who phoned me this morning, that the airport doesn't have enough fuel for all the planes. They're calling around to other local airports for assistance. They think they'll have the problem solved by the time we fly home on Sunday."

"I hope so. I wouldn't want to spend too much more time here in Hicksville."

"I don't expect we could get a *Wall Street Journal* here? We should probably consider ourselves lucky to have phone service," responded the acquaintance, who carried a laptop computer and had attired himself in new stiff jeans that he'd tucked into his high-topped sharkskin cowboy boots. His black Stetson angled down and covered the top half of his protruding ears, both of which held a hearing aid.

Soon the 10-car train arrived at the platform and let out four short whistle blasts, a signal to the crew to board everyone. Immediately, an announcement came over the station's loudspeaker:

The platform filled with general excitement as riders selected either an open car or enclosed coach. Charles, with Trish by his side, answered questions from the riders and helped escort them to a rail car. One gentleman suggested to his wife, "Dear, I think you'll be more comfortable in an enclosed car rather than in one of the open observation cars. You know, less smoke and soot."

"Oh, the soot won't bother me. I do want an uninterrupted view of the beautiful scenery as we pass through it."

"I think I'll sit inside," he said, in a tone of resignation.

Some of the corporate executives sat together on the train trading information, including some rumors, and talking about the economy and the president's proposed new corporate tax plan.

"He's going to kill the golden goose," said the CEO of a major steel producer facing severe competition from China.

The head of a prestigious Washington law firm broke into the conversation. "If he goes through with his tax plan, you can be sure he'll lose the vote of the U.S. Chamber and all of its members."

"I've been invited to have dinner at the White House with the Saudi Foreign Minister next week. I hope to have a private conversation with the President on this tax matter," the head of Chevron Oil reported. "I suspect he'll change his tune when he realizes the bitter opposition to his plan from some of his major contributors."

In the parlor car where Charles and Trish hosted the VIPs, two executives engaged in the details of a buyout offer they planned to make for a medium-sized chemical company in Louisiana.

John reviewed with Josh, and for himself, the details of his first task at the robbery site. "If the fireman remains in the cab, and he should be since he's suppose to stay on the train to keep the fire stoked in the locomotive's fire box, I'll ride to the back side of the train when it is stopped, I'll capture the fireman at his station between the locomotive and the tender, take him at gunpoint off the train to the rear of the tender car, handcuff him to the bottom rear step, and then gag him with my bandana. Then I'll run to the front of the tender and with the hacksaw cut the hose that connects the water tank in the belly of the tender to the locomotive. I figure it's got about 3,500 gallons to drain. Mounted, I'll move to the coach car with the aerial and cut out a piece of the coax cable connecting the Motorola CM200 to its antenna. Then I'll ride back to the pop cart and do the same with its radio, and drain its gas tank. If there's no drain valve, I'll puncture the tank with the nail in my pocket and a rock. I figure I can accomplish all of this in nine and a half minutes at most. You will be entertaining our guests with rope tricks as you await my arrival. Then the fun begins. If you need help while I'm disabling the train and the fireman, shoot once into the air. Got it?"

"Se comprende, Chief."

They kept to their time schedule as they crossed over Red Mountain, Molas and Coal Bank passes and dropped down towards the trailhead. At exactly 11:45, they backed the truck and trailer 50 yards deep into the timber-covered trail and out of sight from traffic on the highway. To avoid the possibility of any hikers wanting to use the trail, John tacked a handmade sign to a tree close to the highway: "Trail closed due to maintenance. USFS." They unloaded their saddled horses. Josh put on his gun belt, loaded with .38 caliber bullets. From a jar of makeup, he took a handful of the cinnamon-colored cream and covered his face, hands and neck. Over his ski mask, he put on the beaded headband with its two eagle feathers. He placed one of his dirty white converse basketball shoes into the left stirrup of Butch, a dun-colored gelding, and swung himself up on to his horse. He checked his rope to ensure it was properly tied to the side of his rough-out saddle. "I'm ready, Chief."

After locking the truck, John snapped on his gun belt with his holstered 9 mm. He checked in his jacket pocket for the two extra clips of ammunition. His saddle bag held the wire clippers and hacksaw, a stick of dynamite with its cap and fuse wrapped in a cotton T-shirt, a sharp four-penny nail and two pairs of handcuffs. He re-tied a loose chicken feather onto the mane of his stout gelding, Bando, applied some colored makeup to his hands and neck and then put his flowing chief's bonnet over his ski mask. He swung up into the padded seat of his hand-tooled saddle. "Time to move out, Two Feathers," John said with emphasis and a smile.

They rode slowly down the steep, rocky trail towards the picnic spot in the dappled light that filtered through the 100-foot-tall Engelmann spruces. When they were in sight of the grassy area with the picnic tables below them, John guided Josh in behind some large oak brush bushes that were surrounded by a grove of shimmering aspens. The two men dismounted and took swigs of water from John's Army canteen. Within minutes, John noticed the train's smoke in the distance, about the same time as Josh complained, "Damned if this mask isn't one hot son of a bitch."

"Pretend you're skiing with Paris Hilton," John suggested.

"I don't see no snow, and anyway I doubt if she skis. She don't look like the athletic type to me, except maybe in bed," Josh said, awaiting John's response.

"Look, pay attention to what we're doing here, all right? Forget I said anything about skiing. Just practice your roping skills."

"Sure, Chief."

Within two minutes they could hear the train and after another minute, they saw the black locomotive puffing its way north in their direction. As the train approached the wye, it slowed to about five miles an hour. John noticed an aerial on the roof of the coach car directly behind the tender. Good, John thought, the car with the radio. The pop cart followed right behind the 10-car train. It backed first into the wye, and after a series of short whistle blasts, the train then backed in. They watched the brakeman signal with a flag to the engineer when to stop. With the reverse completed, and after another series of whistle signals, the train moved forward in a southerly direction. Right on schedule, it came to a stop at the Cascade station platform. The brakeman and conductor jumped out first to help passengers off the train and direct them to the picnic tables. "Don't forget to bring all your personal items with you," the conductor shouted above the hissing noise of the locomotive's escaping steam. The pop cart operator, with the assistance of the engineer and the fireman, unloaded two carts of sandwich boxes from the baggage car, and six-packs of water and soft drinks.

Trish and the attendants from the concession car and the parlor car helped passengers off the train and guided them towards the picnic tables. Charles with his wife could be seen walking about, chatting with their friends while looking back at the beautiful canyon scenery they had passed moments ago.

"They're all seated, including the crew. Let's mount up. Check your cinch. Remember, you'll have to entertain these folks with your rope tricks for less than six minutes now that we know the fireman has joined his crew at a picnic table. Thankfully, I won't have to deal with him on the train. If there's any trouble and you need me, remember, shoot once into the air."

"How will I identify Rigby?"

"Forget about Rigby, I'll take care of him. Now let's start a hoopin' and a hollerin' and ride fast down the trail and up to the tables."

The two Indians charged out from behind the oak brush, down the last 30 yards of the trail right into the picnic area. Hollering all the way, they circled the tables. As John had expected, the guests thought their appearance to be a part of the picnic entertainment. Cameras and cell phones immediately appeared. The happy guests stood at the picnic tables clicking away with their Japanese technology. One man shouted to the Indians to repeat their galloping entrance and provide another photo opportunity.

"What in hell is going on," Trish said to herself? As she turned to look at Charles and his big smile, she figured he'd probably arranged for this Indian entertainment without informing her.

As John rode off towards the train, Josh greeted the guests in his best Indian accent. "Me Two Feathers, a Ute," Josh said, and then held his right hand up as if he were taking an oath of office, and shouted, "How." A few picnickers answered with a "How." Josh, shaking his head and still holding his hand to his ear said, "Let me hear you now, 'HOW.'" The crowd roared in unison, "HOW." Josh and his audience all shared the same Indian stereotypes.

"That better," Josh responded as a smile came to the ski mask.

One picnicker leaned over to her husband and asked, "Who are the Ute?"

The husband responded, "They're an Indian tribe. I learned that in a recent *New York Times* crossword puzzle: 'A three-letter Colorado Indian tribe that begins with U.'"

Josh pointed in the direction where John had ridden off and announced, "Chief, he go to get more braves and some squaws for this show. Until he come back, I do rope tricks, OK?" Josh dismounted with his rope.

"Yes, yes," came the loud response from some of the attentive guests. Charles, who found this entertainment interlude a wonderful addition to the picnic, smiled and clapped loudly with his guests. Josh pulled down his rope, fashioned a loop, and swung it a couple of times over his head, and let the rope go in the direction of a man with his back to Josh.

He caught him in mid-bite of his ham and cheese sandwich. Loud applause.

"Put bottle on stump," Josh said to a picnicker while pointing off to his left. Josh remounted and galloped fast by the stump and roped the bottle as if it were a calf's head. More applause. Next, Josh dismounted, made a large loop and spun it inches off the ground, as he jumped in and out of the loop. When inside the loop, Josh twirled the rope up and down his body, careful not to touch his two head-feathers. Cameras clicked and videos rolled. One guest asked Josh to pose with his lasso. Josh obliged, standing tall, holding with his rope like a rodeo star.

John had to control himself from laughing when he joined Josh after riding up from the train.

"OK, Chief?" Josh asked.

"Ugh, Two Feathers," John muttered loud enough for his audience to catch his Indian response.

John pulled his 9 mm pistol out of his holster and pointed it at the assembled picnickers who, upon seeing the weapon, giggled as they anxiously awaited a new scene in entertainment performance.

"OK pale faces, the fun's over. This is a holdup. You conservationists are a bunch of phonies. All you want to save are your taxes and vacation homes on land stolen from the Utes. The environment is for you something from which to suck money. As for all your talk about biodiversity, I don't see no Indians, blacks or Latinos here. All I see are pale faces, and old ones at that."

John fired his weapon at the bottle on the grass where Josh had left it after his roping exhibition. He smashed it with a single shot.

"Now, put away your cameras and cell phones and take out all your cash. And I repeat, all of it. Two Feathers here will go to your tables with a bag. Put all your cash in it. No jewelry, watches, cameras, plastic cards, just plain cash, the kind made in Washington by the Great White Father."

Josh noticed that cameras continued to flash and click away. Most of the guests, he thought, hadn't taken seriously the threat of a holdup. How to move their heads from entertainment to fear?

"Listen up, you dumb fucks. Chief here said put down cameras, and put up cash." He pulled out his revolver and fired two shots into the air. "Believe me, those weren't blanks." Josh could tell the shots, or maybe his language, shocked everyone out of their entertainment mode and back to reality. Charles' wife began to sob; men grabbed their spouses' hands to provide comfort. Trish, whose hands shook nervously, stood up and pleaded with the Indians not to hurt anyone, and then shouted to the picnickers: "do what the Indians ask, please, for the protection of all of us." Then John leaned over to Josh and whispered,

"Two Feathers, you one smart Injun, you sure got their attention. That was my friend Trish who just spoke to us."

"She one pretty squaw, Chief."

John eyed the table where Rigby sat with a white pork pie hat shading his pasty complexion. He headed towards Rigby, making it appear Rigby was a random selection, and came up behind him and grabbed the collar of his plaid shirt. With little effort John pulled him to his feet. Taking Rigby's arm, John twisted it behind Rigby's back and asked, "Pale face, what your name?"

"Fred Rigby," he said in almost a whisper.

"Louder, so everyone hear."

"Fred Rigby," he blurted out in a voice loud enough to be heard throughout the picnic area.

With a gun pointed at Rigby's head and his arm twisted behind his back, John marched Rigby to the front of the picnic area.

"Any trouble from anyone and Mr. Rigby here will be off to his happy hunting ground." John then placed his weapon up close to Rigby's left ear, and said to emphasize his message, "If trouble, we scalp him and then shoot him." John then removed Rigby's hat, and looking at his bald head in amazement, said: "No scalp, just shoot."

Looking out at his audience, John continued: "The Great Spirit says we take all your cash. If you make the Great Spirit mad, Mr. Rigby and maybe others go to not so Happy Hunting Ground. Understand?"

John watched Devlin's countenance gradually transform itself from one of happiness to sheer terror. Devlin thought of standing up and saying something to the Indians, but thought better of it. Instead he grabbed his day pack and took out a thick envelope filled with cash. Soon everyone, who could see Charles, took their lead from their host. Trish, who stared at the terrified Rigby, dug into her back pack.

As Josh made his way around the tables with his burlap bag that had stamped on it, "Ute Mills," Rigby suddenly struggled to free himself from John's uncomfortably tight grip on his shirt collar. As he jerked his head to the right, John lost his grip and the glove on his right hand fell to the ground. John immediately leaned down to pick up his glove with the pistol in his hand. Once again, he put pressure on Rigby's arm behind his back.

In a soft voice, John leaned into Rigby's left ear. "If you make one more move like that again, or one peep, I'll put bullet in your left ear that will go out other ear. Anyone looking in one ear will see only a weather pattern after I finish with you. Got that?" John then tapped Rigby on his right temple with the butt of his pistol.

Rigby, terrified, said nothing as he relaxed his muscles under John's grip. Be calm, don't try to be a hero, and follow instructions, Rigby said to himself, a reflection of his usual passive behavior when working for Devlin.

John watched as Josh made the rounds of his collection. He noticed with pleasure that even Trish made a contribution to Johnny's college tuition fund A number of guests stared at Josh's dirty-white basketball shoe with 'Ute Pride' painted on its side, and the burlap bag with the stencil "Ute Mills." Josh had stopped at the side of one man and John could hear him say, "Now Mr. Turnbull, your nametag say you the Big Chief at Exxon Mobil. And all you give is $30. Mr. Turnbull, you look again in your bag. I bet there more cash." Mr. Turnbull, his hands shaking, with a .38 cal. revolver pointed at his temple, reached into his daypack and pulled out a wad of cash. "You one good pale face, Mr. Turnbull," Josh said, as he patted him on the shoulder.

John, in an attempt to strike additional fear into Devlin's guests, put a gag in Rigby's mouth, handcuffed him and walked him over to Bando. He took the rope from his saddle and tied it around Rigby's handcuffed hands. As Josh approached with his bag of cash, John mounted his horse and dallied the rope to the saddle horn. Then he turned to Josh, who came up to Bando and announced, "Two Feathers, I think we need to take Mr. Rigby with us for everyone's safety." Josh responded, "OK, you the Chief. I ready to go." Josh mounted up, lashed the bag of cash to his saddle horn and the two horses and riders took off at a slow trot up the trail. Rigby found it difficult to run alongside of Bando without falling behind. He knew if he stopped running he'd be dragged by his tied hands across the rough, rocky ground.

A low branch clipped John's bonnet. It fell off to the side of the trail as the men made their way towards their truck. John made no attempt to retrieve his bonnet. But he did notice Rigby breathing hard and tiring faster than expected after running only 30 yards up the steep trail and out of sight of the picnickers. He'd gained his goal by terrifying Rigby, but he didn't wish to make him suffer any additional pain. He stopped and cut the rope. Rigby immediately fell to the ground trying to catch his breath through the gag of silk bandana. He struggled to free his hands from the cuffs without success, but did manage to get both cuffed hands to his head and remove the gag with his thumbs. He wanted to shout something to the two riders but couldn't catch his breath. Then Rigby took three steps down the trail and collapsed in excruciating pain.

Back at the picnic site, the train conductor ordered the fireman to go up the trail as fast as he could to reach the highway, where he could summon help and get a message to Durango. But in less than five minutes he returned out of breath, with the Chief's feathered Indian bonnet in his hand and announced in a loud voice, "Rigby's lying unconscious up on the trail." Everyone immediately assumed the Indians had killed him, though the fireman did say Rigby had a pulse and, as far as he could tell after a hasty inspection, didn't have a mark on his body.

A half-hour after they cut Rigby free, John and Josh had loaded their trailer, pulled out from their hidden parking spot and headed north on Highway 550 towards home.

"I think we did it," John said, pulling his mask off and facing Josh with a wide grin. "It went a hell of a lot easier than I thought it would," Josh commented. "Why the extra treatment for Rigby?"

"Only wanted to give him a little scare and some exercise to slim him down."

"He sure looked scared out of his wits to me," Josh answered. "Do you think he recognized you?"

"I don't think so. When I lost a glove, fortunately it was the right one, not my left. He'd have seen the missing finger."

As they sped north along the empty highway, Josh asked, "Can I count the cash?"

"Let's wait till we get some miles under us," John said as he focused on his driving, glancing nervously from time to time in the rearview mirror.

At the picnic site, Charles ran over to where Trish sat writing in a small notebook. "Did the Utes give you any indication they were planning a robbery? I thought you had it arranged for them only to run the gambling tables. Then they show up on horseback with guns. What in hell is going on?"

"They never hinted or indicated in any way that they planned a robbery. I don't know what ever got into them. They were annoyed that we rejected their demand for a $30,000 minimum take at the gambling tables. But when they agreed to $15,000, they appeared satisfied with the figure."

"That didn't seem to be the issue with them. They had something against environmentalists. Can't imagine why," Charles said.

Charles broke off his inquisition of Trish when he noticed two excited guests run up to the fireman holding the Chief's feathered bonnet. They wanted to inspect what they knew to be a piece of critical evidence as to the robber's identity and their tribe. The first man to grab the bonnet was a corporate lawyer from New York, a nationally known expert on Native American artifacts whose generous donations to the Museum of the American Indian enhanced considerably his reputation. He gave the bonnet, and particularly the beadwork, a close inspection. After inspecting it, he said in an authoritative voice to the small assemblage of guests crowded around him, "It's an Arapahoe Chief's headdress. I can tell by the beadwork and its design. I have one in my private collection similar to this." Another elderly guest, who also considered himself an authority on Indian artifacts, stepped forward and inspected the headdress. After about 30 seconds, he announced with an air of supreme confidence: "This is not Arapahoe, the size of the feathers are too large. I recognize the beadwork, and this is Pawnee.I believe they have a reservation somewhere near here."

The train's conductor appeared and said he'd like to keep the bonnet for evidence when he meets with the sheriff. The New York lawyer handed the bonnet over to the conductor, who held it as if it were a wounded duck. He looked it over carefully, impressed both by the beadwork and beautiful bald eagle feathers. He then turned the beaded headband inside out and after reading a small label, announced, "It says 'Made in China.'"

"Chinese Indians, I see. They sure came a long way for the heist," the conductor commented, glaring at the two bonnet specialists in attendance.

"More than likely, the Pawnee had the Chinese make it for them," the bead expert said.

"Sure, and they sent their laundry to China to have it cleaned," the conductor responded. He continued, "Did anyone notice one of the robbers wearing a pair of sneakers with the message 'Ute Pride?' And on the burlap bag used to collect the cash, 'Ute Mills' appeared. Looks to me like these guys were Utes."

Those who had crowded around the conductor shook their heads in agreement, except for the Arapaho and Pawnee experts.

Back at the picnic tables, Charles stood up on a table and announced in a loud voice, "May I have your attention. Please gather over here by me. Thank you." The guests moved quickly into a tight circle while talking among themselves. Charles continued, "Can I have your attention please? The engineer informed me he would radio to Durango to inform them of the robbery. The railroad will also inform the state police and the local sheriff's office." About then the engineer appeared and said in a loud voice, "They've disabled the radios on the train and also on the pop cart." At about the same time, the brakeman approached Charles. "I have some other bad news, Mr. Devlin. The Indians cut the water hose to the locomotive and emptied the water tank. We can't move without water and there's none immediately available. Even the pop cart is disabled. They drained its gas tank. Looks as if we'll be here for a while."

Charles repeated the message to the guests.

One guest spoke up in a loud voice. "What about a cell phone?"

"No service right here," the engineer answered. There's a spot about three miles up the line where it'll work. Also, about an equal distance to the south is the small resort, Tall Timbers. I believe they have phone contact with Durango."

Many of the guests were visibly upset, less by the money they'd lost, which they knew they could replace, but by the fear that the Indians might return and cause further havoc, including the Hollywood stereotypical Indian specialties—scalping, rape and murder—and not necessarily in that order.

"Do we have any weapons to defend ourselves in the event the Indians return?"

No one raised a voice.

"How about extra food and water?" Someone asked.

"Only a few extra picnic boxes and some bottled water," the engineer replied. Four of the guests immediately rushed to the other picnic tables and collected partially empty water bottles and some lunch boxes that appeared to be untouched.

Charles announced from his perch atop a table, "Please, let's not panic. One of the crew members is already on his way by trail to the highway about three miles from here. We could all walk out on that trail but, I understand from the conductor, it is steep and very dangerous. I have an alternative solution. I'll ask a few of you with cell phones and their spouses to collect themselves over here to my right. Everyone else please move here to my left."

Charles talked quietly to the train's conductor and then continued. "The conductor tells me he'll accompany the group with cell phones up the rail line, north about three miles to the spot where he knows there to be cell phone service. The brakeman here will accompany the rest of us south to Tall Timbers where there's a phone line to Durango. Every group should have a leader. I'll lead the group north. We need a leader for the southbound group." Surprisingly, there were no volunteers. Then Charles asked, "Anyone here with military experience?" When no one responded, Charles realized they'd probably all avoided service with a college deferment, as had he.

"Anyone here with extensive outdoor survival experience?"

A middle-aged man announced he'd once been an Eagle Scout.

Another said that for three years he'd been a senior counselor at Camp Mohawk in the Catskills back in New York.

Charles remained unconvinced that leadership skills could be so lacking among his guests.

"Certainly someone here must have had some experience in the wilderness."

Only the young man from Trout Unlimited raised his hand.

"DeWitt, you're the leader of the southbound group. When you get to Tall Timbers put a call into the Durango-Silverton Railroad Company. Their number is …." Charles looked at the conductor who said "nine-seven-zero, two-five-nine, six-five-zero-five."

"Report the robbery, and tell them we think they were Utes who took off with a considerable amount of cash, probably headed towards the reservation. Report also that one of our party, Mr. Fred Rigby from New York, is seriously injured and requires immediate medical attention. Durango needs to know we're stuck here, no radios, no working locomotive and little food or water. We have to be rescued immediately," he said with emphasis. "Does anyone wish to stay here rather than walk along the rail line?"

No volunteers. "Off you go, Dewitt, with your group. We'll try and call you at Tall Timbers when we find cell phone service. Good luck. The engineer has just reminded me that my group heading north will need to cross a long trestle, 100 feet above the river. Most of you will want to crawl across it rather than walk since there's no handrail." Charles made it sound as if they were off on a dangerous adventure through snake-infested jungles of Africa. Immediately some in Charles' group, where most of the techies had congregated with their phones and Blackberries, slipped unobtrusively over to Dewitt's group heading south.

Both groups shared the fear of spending cold nights and countless days without food along a desolate rail line at 10,000 feet in the isolated heart of the San Juan National Forest.

CHAPTER TWENTY-FOUR

As John and Josh made their way north, they stopped for a sandwich at the Subway shop in Montrose. Three hours had passed since the holdup. Word of the robbery and the injury to Rigby had already reached the railroad. They immediately called the sheriff's office, which requested the Durango hospital helicopter to evacuate Rigby from the picnic site. The department's radios buzzed with the news, all of which was picked up by radio scanners at the *Durango Herald.* The paper immediately dispatched the entire newsroom to the story. By mid-afternoon, the Associated Press sent out a three-alarm news bulletin across the western United States announcing the train's robbery by two suspected Ute Indians. Josh and John heard the bulletin on the truck's radio as they finished off their sandwiches and coffee.

"Two Indians today attacked at gunpoint over 250 passengers on the Durango-Silverton Railroad in Colorado. They robbed the passengers and made off with an estimated $200,000. The passengers, mostly from out of state, were headed to a conservation conference at a resort north of Durango. Authorities reported some minor injuries but no known fatalities. One passenger suffered a heart attack and is resting comfortably at a hospital in Durango. Governor Rover is scheduled to arrive in Durango this evening to coordinate the search conducted by federal, state and local law enforcement agencies brought in to apprehend the robbers."

"Damned if we didn't get some attention. I had no idea we'd cause such excitement," Josh commented. "I think we evened the score with Devlin and Rigby and all those folks who wanted to save us. You think Rigby is the one who had the heart attack? He sure didn't look too good to me after you cut him free. Laying there on the ground, all red in the face, and gasping for air through the bandana in his mouth. He probably did have a heart attack. I hope he survives. If he passes on to his 'Happy Hunting Ground,' we'll be in a shit pile deeper than the one we may find ourselves in."

"Yeah. I'm sorry to think he may have had a heart attack. But to think that Rigby may reproduce himself is enough to put western civilization at risk," John responded. "I have a feeling those Eastern folks won't be returning West anytime soon to save us. As for Rigby, he may have recognized me, not by my finger but by my limp."

"Hell, I know hundreds of Indians with limps. And when you held that gun to his head, I was surprised if he didn't shit in his pants. I doubt if he had the presence of mind to add two and two, much less put you and the limp together. If we don't get away with this, we'll be charged with assault and armed robbery. That's probably a minimum of 20 years in the slammer," Josh reminded his partner.

"And that's why we need to hold our story together. In the meantime, just calm down and take pride in what you pulled off. Luck was with us today. The radio says we got away with 200 grand. To occupy yourself, why don't you verify their estimate," John suggested, throwing his head in the direction of the burlap bag behind his seat.

They continued their drive north and arrived back at the ranch two hours before Charles called his guests to an assembly at Tamarron.

The Utes had already disassembled the gambling tables and taken away the auction items. At Charles' urging, the Indians finally relented to accepting credit cards at the tables and auction. But the guests, after the events of the day, produced little enthusiasm or money at either venue. And after the Utes agreed to take their reduced cut of 10 percent, the evening's proceeds barely exceeded $5,000. The head croupier, a senior Ute tribal leader, almost got into a serious fight with one of the guests, who asked him, "Which one of your God-damned cousins robbed the train?"

Not all the guests appeared for Charles's late-night announcement. Seven guests had to be taken to the Durango hospital for treatment for minor injuries—sprained ankles, cut hands and feet. Those who wore cowboy boots learned quickly and in many cases painfully, that riding boots were not the best footwear for a three-mile hike on and across railroad ties. Many of the folks in their new hiking boots discarded them along the rail line when painful blisters hindered their progress. They walked in stocking feet only to pick up splinters from the wooden ties. The non-hospitalized guests limped into the noisy hall. Also present were members of the La Plata County Sheriff's office, the president of the Durango-Silverton Railroad, two investigators from the Colorado Bureau of Investigation and the supervisor of the San Juan National Forest.

The sheriff stood up and walked to a podium. "May I have your attention, PLEASE?" he shouted over the conversational noise of the gathered group. "I'd like to say a few words, before handing over the meeting to Mr. Devlin, your host. First off, I want you to know how lucky you are to be here tonight without any major injuries or loss of life. Mr. Dunbar's railroad and his crew exhibited superb leadership in getting everyone safely here. Your train's brakeman, once he made it to the highway, luckily encountered a state patrolman who called for a medical helicopter from the county hospital. He also called the railroad dispatcher in Durango. The hospital sent its helicopter to the picnic site where it picked up Mr. Rigby and airlifted him to the hospital. The train dispatcher in Durango immediately sent a relief train down from Silverton. That train had departed Durango with a full complement of tourists an hour before your departure. It was scheduled to return from Silverton at one-thirty but the dispatcher in Durango held up its departure because he couldn't make contact with your train, fearing the rail line might be blocked. Finally, when the dispatcher learned of the situation at the Cascade picnic ground, by way of a phone call from the Tall Timbers resort, the dispatcher contacted the conductor of the Silverton train, told him to unload all of its passengers and proceed immediately south to pick you up and collect your baggage. The reason the recovery took so long is that many of you were scattered out along the rail line for close to six miles north and south of the Cascade picnic area. I don't know who told you to split up, but it was a very unwise decision, given the dangerous situation. Fortunately, the relief train was able to recover everyone safely.

"Ambulances, ordered by the railroad, waited at Rockwood station to transport the seriously injured to the Durango hospital. Thanks are owed to Mr.

Dunbar, the president of the railroad, and his staff for the efficient and orderly way they conducted your recovery." The sheriff was interrupted by some applause. "Now I know Mr. Devlin would like to say a few words."

"First, I want to sincerely apologize to all of you for what happened at lunch today. Fortunately no one was seriously hurt. I really thought we'd have some major accidents when our northbound party had to crawl on hands and knees over the trestle 100 feet above the Animas River. I commend you all. That took some courage. Just to update you, nine from our party have minor injuries and have been taken to the hospital in Durango. Also, Mr. Fred Rigby, my accountant from New York, suffered a heart attack after his capture by the robbers. Thanks are due to the railroad's young fireman, who first discovered Mr. Rigby on the trail and had him carried back to the picnic area, before he ran three miles up the trail to the highway to find assistance for our party. Despite having to wait over an hour and a half from the time of his heart attack until he received medical attention, Fred is resting comfortably in the Durango hospital. After further tests, I understand he is expected to be released in a few days." Charles looked at some notes in his hand and then announced: "I see from our attendance sheet that we have not yet accounted for Mr. and Mrs. Thornberry."

"We're here," a loud voice shouted from the back of the room. Loud applause and whistles greeted this announcement.

"We're glad you're safe and sound, Jerry and Barbara." Charles continued his announcements. "I hope everyone has retrieved their luggage from the front hall. The relief train that brought you to Rockwood station picked up your baggage from our disabled train and transferred it to the buses. Not all of it made it on the first round of buses, but I believe all the bags should be here by now. If not, please inform the front desk and we'll locate them. Also, if anyone needs any medical attention, we have a doctor present. Sandwiches and drinks are over on that table, and most importantly, the bar will remain open until midnight." The last item generated loud applause. Someone shouted above the din, "Well done, Charles."

Charles smiled and then continued. "You're probably wondering about the money you've lost. We've contacted all the police and military authorities in the area. I've talked personally with Governor Rover, who many of you know from New York, when he came east to raise money for his upcoming reelection. He assures me he will personally take charge of the search efforts. As we speak, he's meeting in Durango with FBI and representatives of other law enforcement agencies. Colorado National Guard helicopters have already circled the Ute reservation throughout the afternoon in search of trucks hauling a horse trailer. I've been told that state highway patrolmen aided by Colorado National Guard SWAT teams have stopped and questioned several trucks this afternoon and early evening, and have taken into custody 10 Utes for questioning. When we find the robbers, we're certain to find the money. Which reminds me, each of you who lost money this morning, please make a note of the amount and with your name and drop it off at the front desk. We'll then know how much cash was stolen and, after the recovery of the cash, how much to return to each of you."

Someone interrupted with a question." Does the railroad have any insurance for such a robbery?"

The president of the railroad, Mr. Dunbar, responded: "No, we have no insurance for such an event. A rail accident, yes, but not a robbery. There's never been a holdup on this rail line in over a hundred years that I'm aware of, except in the movie "Butch Cassidy and the Sundance Kid."

Another question popped up. "Why wasn't security provided by the railroad to prevent the occurrence of a robbery?"

"Again, sir, we've never experienced a robbery, so we saw no need to provide security."

"By God, I'm going to get my money back if I have to sue your railroad. And not able to use my Blackberry. I lost some important clients today because of your railroad's primitive communication connections."

"Sir, we and the authorities are doing our best to recover the cash. And when we do, your money will be returned. I can assure you."

Another hand went up. "How could the train be so easily disabled? Looks to some of us like it was an inside job."

"Sir, it looks to us also that the robbers knew exactly how to disable the train and its radios. As for this being an 'inside job,' the four Utes we have working for the railroad are in custody as I speak and are being questioned by deputies of the La Plata County Sheriff's Department."

The railroad president's response did nothing to placate another passenger. The wife of an oil company executive from Colorado stood up, her bleached blond hair frozen in place by two aerosol cans of tornado-proof hair spray. With her blood red finger nails slashing the air like swords, she announced, "Don't misunderstand me, some of my best friends are Indians, but sometimes I don't understand their antics. We set them up on comfortable reservations with hospitals, schools, plus huge welfare payments and they're still not satisfied. I can't understand why they hate whites so much. They're ungrateful, that's what they are." Many in the group nodded in agreement.

"Charles, will we still follow the conference schedule tomorrow?" someone asked.

"No I think everyone's exhausted, I know I am. We need to sleep late. Recover our health and relax in this beautiful setting. The session leaders, who are expected tomorrow morning, will be available for informal presentations right after breakfast. We'll post the location of each gathering in the morning. We do expect beautiful weather tomorrow, so for any of you wishing to play golf, the course has been reserved for our use. For those of you who didn't bring clubs, I understand the golf shop has over 30 sets to rent. We'll eat together tomorrow evening, and then on Sunday morning, we'll take the train back to Durango."

Charles continued quickly for fear that some guests would slip off from the meeting. "One further item. These men here," Charles said pointing to the investigating authorities, "would like to question anyone who might have information that can help locate and apprehend the robbers. Have a good sleep and see you in the morning. Call the front desk if you need any assistance."

Along with Charles and Trish, about 25 guests stayed behind, all of them men except for Trish. The sheriff immediately announced that the press would be barred from the question and answer session with the authorities. "Why?"

asked the reporter for the Durango newspaper. "Because any leads we pick up from the victims would become public knowledge, thus hindering our investigation and search for the robbers." The reporter grumbled but offered no argument.

Once the press left the room, the sheriff continued: "So that I have an accurate account of the sequence of events, can someone review for me the events leading up to the robbery?" Charles answered in some detail, including the time of departure from Durango and time of arrival at Cascade and the time of the robbery.

The sheriff continued. "Someone please describe where the robbers appeared from, and also their physical description."

The Exxon-Mobil executive spoke up. "The two Indians appeared suddenly on horseback, galloping down the trail leading to our picnic site. They wore ski masks; one Indian wore a war bonnet and the other one a headband with two feathers. The chief with the bonnet called him, 'Two Feathers.' At first we thought the sudden appearance of the two Indians was for our entertainment but when they pulled revolvers and shot into the air we quickly learned otherwise."

Someone interrupted. "Not two revolvers—a revolver and a dark-colored pistol. They spoke broken English, but other than their headwear, they didn't dress like Indians. Also their horses had Indian designs painted on them."

The questions continued.

"Where did they appear from?" Much agreement.

"Color of the horses?" Some disagreement.

"Were they wearing saddles?" Again more disagreement.

"What about the physical size of the robbers?" No consensus.

"Any identifying marks?" "The 'Ute Mills' burlap bag and the Ute Pride painted on the dirty sneaker," someone volunteered. Another passenger said he thought that one of the robbers had a slight limp.

"Anyone threatened by the robbers?"

"Yes, Mr. Rigby," Charles shouted.

"Is he here?"

"No he's in the hospital after suffering a heart attack."

"Who collected the money?" Again, some disagreement.

"After the robbery, where did they ride off to?"

"Up the trail leading to Highway 550 and dragging Rigby with a rope, gagged and handcuffed," again Charles responded.

"Did they seem to have it out for Rigby?"

"They took him as a hostage in the event we gave the Indians trouble. It appeared they selected Rigby at random. It could have been any of us." No disagreement.

The police authorities took notes from the sheriff's questions and the answers given by the "victims," as they were now identified.

One of the victims, the Indian artifact collector from New York, asked, "Could it be possible the robbers were not Indians? After all, the bonnet worn by the one who called himself Chief was made in China."

The sheriff responded, "Possibly. But we do know that many Indians tribes, like the Ute, obtain some of their ceremonial gear from overseas, primarily Taiwan and China. I don't know about the Utes. They may be exempt from environmental regulations that make it a crime to kill eagles, the source for their feathers."

Further questions, often with conflicting answers, lasted almost until midnight. The sheriff, himself exhausted by the events of the day, finally brought closure to the session. "I know you are tired after a very stressful day. So let's call it an evening. We may want to talk with you further tomorrow. In the meantime, we very much appreciate your assistance in this matter. The governor will be down here to talk with you tomorrow. He's already called out the National Guard for assistance and has alerted every county sheriff's office in Southwest Colorado to be on the lookout for the robbers. The Colorado Bureau of Investigation is hard on this case, and has already called in the FBI, because the robbery occurred within the federal jurisdiction of the U.S. Forest Service."

The next morning at breakfast, Governor Rover appeared. He spoke to the assembled victims.

"On behalf of the State of Colorado, I want to extend our sympathy to all of you for what you've had to experience in the last 24 hours. You must consider yourselves fortunate that no one was seriously injured. To update you on our efforts to capture the robbers and bring them to justice, I met with the FBI last evening. They tell me, after some lab tests, there is the distinct possibility that the robbers were not Indians as they pretended, but probably eco-terrorists seeking money to fund their activities in the West. They've caused considerable damage in Colorado in the past and will stop at nothing to attain their radical goals. For example, the Earth Liberation Front believes that mainstream environmentalist advocates have sold out to oil, timber and mining companies, in addition to the banks that support these activities on federal and state lands. In short, they're an organization committed to violence." The governor could hear the assembled crowd collectively inhale upon hearing the shocking news.

He continued as he looked down at some notes. "Yesterday afternoon and evening and again this morning, I have been in contact with various law enforcement agencies. The National Guard will soon have 200 troops here, including pilots, mechanics and spotters for two Kiowa observation helicopters, two Hueys and three Blackhawks. I've alerted police authorities across our state, New Mexico and Arizona. The FBI has called on 10 counter-terrorist specialists; the Colorado Bureau of Investigation already has investigators in the area; the Colorado National Guard has in place two SWAT teams, pilots, crew members, ground support personnel, including a bomb detonation squad, and specially trained personnel to man listening and observation posts, and a special response team. Also, the highway patrol will send extra patrolmen to this area, three helicopters and their emergency response teams, including bomb technicians and police tactical experts. Finally, the Ute Tribe and the Navajo Nation have volunteered to provide armed personnel from their tribal police forces. The Navajos will also provide their expert dog tracking team."

The governor continued, as his audience gave him their full attention. "As of this morning, in an area of 500 square miles, we have closed rivers to rafters, fishermen, hikers and tourists. Highways in and out of Durango are closed except to residents, as are the main roads into and out of the Ute and Navajo reservations. I have placed Durango on a security alert, and, you may have noticed, for the last 12 hours we've had roadblocks in place manned by armed soldiers and search dogs. So, I think you will agree that we are taking all necessary precautions in the event we are dealing here with terrorists.

"I'd also like to announce that at Mr. Devlin's request, we are allowing all of you with private planes to leave tomorrow to free up some needed space at the county airport. I've also arranged for a commercial carrier to come to Durango and transport those of you needing to return to Denver so that you can make your connecting flights home."

One of the victims stood up and thanked the governor for his fine leadership and prompt response to the robbery. "We are in your debt, Governor, and I'm sure the nation is looking at Colorado as a model of how to respond to terrorists."

The governor certainly did not want to be perceived as soft on crime. His quick and forceful response to the threat would, he hoped, attract national attention and elevate his chances for gaining his party's presidential nomination in four years. Certainly, he could take pride in the public's response to his "timely executive decisions," as reported on the CBS network's Evening News.

By Tuesday, however, three days after the holdup, complaints began to surface. Between the multitude of military units and the civilian investigating authorities, coordination was almost impossible. The state police, for example, continued to trip over National Guard units on the highways. Nor could sheriffs' departments make contact with the National Guard because of uncoordinated radio communications. The Associated Press characterized the Durango area a "war zone," a report that circulated across the country.

At the local level, the *Denver Post* reported that bookings for Durango motels had come to an abrupt halt. Shop owners complained that sales had fallen off sharply. Restaurants served only to soldiers and civilian law enforcement personnel. The city put up $50,000 in reward money leading to the capture and arrest of the robbers. The roadblocks continued to scare local citizens, and tourists were warned to stay out of the Four Corners area. The *Durango Herald* reported that at one roadblock site, "an armed soldier frightened a truck's occupants when he stuck his rifle in through the open window. When a dog jumped out of the back of the pickup and took a chew on the soldier's leg, the soldier shot the dog in the head. The driver had to be restrained and handcuffed until he regained his composure." In another reported incident, "an air spotter noticed smoke rising from a field at a small isolated ranch off the Dolores River. Thinking that it might be the hideout of the terrorists, the airman called in a helicopter gunship. When it landed, men dressed in black jumped to the ground, with automatic weapons at the ready. They discovered a terrified rancher burning some old fence posts." The paper also reported that just north of the Ute reservation, "one innocent hiker wearing an old floppy Vietnam-era camouflage hat was ambushed by three Special Forces troopers, themselves clad in camouflage. They handcuffed the surprised hiker, knocked him half unconscious and dragged him off to a clearing, where the soldiers called in a helicopter for what they referred to as 'a dust off.'"

After the governor's call for assistance on Sunday, a number of police forces across the state sent at least one, and in some cases (Denver and Colorado Springs) as many as five representatives to both assist with the search and learn from the experience. The *Denver Post* reported that almost 200 law enforcement officers showed up from various jurisdictions across the state. With smaller police forces, the paper also reported that crime actually declined in most counties, a statistic that no police official could explain.

After three days, officials at the search headquarters in a Durango middle school tried to put a positive spin on an otherwise perplexing, frustrating and downright embarrassing situation. "We should have this thing wrapped up by the end of the week," the official state spokesman told the *Denver Post*. Police armed with search warrants, quickly authorized by a local judge, scattered throughout the Four Corners area. They had, however, no leads on where and what to search. The paper also estimated that the search was costing the state about $400,000 a day, plus an equal cost to the federal government.

Back in Washington, Colorado's senior senator, Edward Barlow, secured a pledge of $250,000 from the Chairman of the Senate Appropriations Committee "as a reward for the capture of the outlaws who continue to threaten the local residents of Durango and impose a significant burden on Colorado's law enforcement resources." The press release went on to say: "This reward, along with the outstanding efforts of local, county, state and federal law enforcement officers, will help bring these criminals to justice more quickly." Through a press release, the director of the FBI announced that his agency was offering "an additional $50,000 for information leading to the arrest of the robbers," and then went on to say: "I am committed to having the FBI support this manhunt until the perpetrators are found, and we will provide whatever resources are necessary to bring it to a safe and successful outcome. We will be adding these two men to the Ten Most Wanted list, even though we haven't identified them yet."

After the FBI learned from the railroad that Trish had made most of the arrangements for the conference and its guests, they questioned her in detail about any calls or inquiries she might have received that would be helpful to the robbers. "No I can't remember any such inquiries."

"Did you ever hear any Indian, or anyone else, threaten to disrupt Mr. Devlin's party?"

"No, but a Ute leader did express real anger to me when I, after conferring with Mr. Devlin, said we'd find other operators for the gambling tables if he continued to insist on a $50,000 guarantee. He agreed to a lesser amount but wasn't happy with the outcome, I could tell."

"Again, any inquiries from individuals or groups wanting to know about the details of the train trip, the conference, or its participants?"

"Only the Durango newspaper in response to our press release."

"Thank you Ms. Jackson for you assistance. If you think of any additional information that might help us with the investigation please contact me." The agent handed Trish his card with his cell phone number.

Also on Tuesday, three days after the robbery, doctors at the hospital gave the FBI permission to question Fred Rigby, whose strength and overall health continued to improve. The FBI agent entered the light and airy hospital room with a tape recorder and his notepad. The room looked like an annex to a greenhouse, the agent thought, with Rigby barely visible behind a barricade of flowers sent by fellow victims. He had to remove a giant arrangement of red roses to have an uninterrupted view of the New York accountant outfitted in a blue hospital smock.

"Mr. Rigby, I understand from your doctors that you're making a fast recovery from the trauma you suffered three days ago."

"Yes, thank you. They tell me I can be out of here by the end of the week and home for the weekend."

"That's great news. I do want to ask you some questions that might help us identify, locate and capture the robbers." After confirming some of the of the robbery details, the agent volunteered: "There are some investigators here, particularly the FBI, who believe the robbers were not Indians, but possibly ecoterrorists seeking to collect cash to fund ongoing terrorist attacks throughout the West. Do you have any thoughts as to that scenario?"

"I think I'd agree that they were not Indians, Ute or otherwise." Displaying his own prejudice of Indians, Rigby added, "Besides, they're too damned smart to be Indians, knew exactly what they were up to. Also I didn't smell any liquor on their breath. Whether they were ecoterrorists, I can't speculate one way or the other."

"Do you know anyone who'd like to see you or any of Mr. Devlin's guests harmed in any way?"

"That's a damn good question. In fact I do. And that would be Mr. Devlin's ranch manager, who we fired a few weeks ago. His name is John Marlow and he's at the ranch until we find a permanent replacement for him."

"Why was he fired?"

"Insubordination and always acting like a wise ass," Rigby said with some authority. "One other thing," Rigby continued, "This Marlow fellow walks with a slight limp, and so did one of the Indian robbers, the one dressed as the chief."

"Right or left leg, do you remember?"

"Yes, it was his right leg."

"You're certain it was his right leg?"

"Positive," Rigby said without hesitation and then added as an afterthought: "Of course I am by no means certain it was Marlow. He's not smart enough to have pulled off the robbery. And I have no idea who the other robber might be."

The agent asked a few more questions just to confirm the testimony of other witnesses as to the holdup itself, and the robber's escape.

"One further question, Mr. Rigby, and we'll let you get some uninterrupted rest. Did the robbers say anything to you at any time during your ordeal?"

"The Chief said to me, after I broke loose from his grip, he'd put a bullet through my ear and out through the other ear if I tried a move like that again. He also referred to our group as a bunch of wimpy environmentalists. When he cut me loose on the trail I overheard him say in a soft voice to his companion, "Let's get out of here and get going south. And then the Chief looked at me and said, 'Don't forget to floss.'"

"What was that supposed to mean?"

"I haven't a clue unless they were dentists. But it doesn't sound to me like something an Indian, or even a white dentist, would say to a complete stranger."

"Nor would I expect a terrorist to offer such advice," the agent said, and then added, "I think I need to find Mr. Marlow and have a talk with him." The agent reached over and turned off his tape recorder, shook hands with Rigby and went to find Charles Devlin.

CHAPTER TWENTY-FIVE

FBI special agent Colin Fallon located Charles Devlin at the Durango fairgrounds, the control center for the massive manhunt. Here, Charles was answering calls from the press, and two unpleasant calls from guests on the train.

"Charles, you have to return our money. This is ridiculous. Besides the danger, my wife was scared to death," the head of a major New York bank said to Charles with some anger.

The banker continued. "If you can't get this properly settled, you and I know Goodman's business is certain to suffer."

"Look, Barton, I'm doing all I can. I've contacted the governor and he's called in additional law enforcement officers plus the National Guard. The feds are here with investigators, plus their own law enforcement contingent. Durango looks like an armed camp. What else can I do? Also, Barton, I don't appreciate your threat to Goodman's business."

"I'm not threatening anyone. All I want to see is the Indians, or whoever the hell they are, brought to justice and my money returned. Do I make myself clear?"

"Of course," Charles replied to end the conversation.

Charles, with Trish's assistance, made calls to the other guests to assure them that massive efforts were underway to capture the robbers and return the stolen money.

The governor diligently attempted to coordinate the search efforts. Finally on Tuesday morning, he established a unified command under the direction of General Paris, the head of the Colorado National Guard, a decision the Feds reluctantly agreed to. The governor also managed, with considerable difficulty, to convince the senior commanders of the search units to share radio frequencies. The need occurred when a National Guard gunship and a State Patrol helicopter nearly collided after a sheriff's deputy radioed for an emergency medical evacuation at a road junction in Ignacio, the headquarters town for the Southern Utes.

As the governor explained to Devlin when the FBI agent located both of them at the fairgrounds, "Everyone wants to be the first to arrest the robbers and take credit for their capture. It's been a military nightmare down here ever since I arrived late Saturday evening. But now I think I've brought some coordination to the search efforts. Plus, my damned back is killing me. Why must all motels have mattresses made of granite? I need to get home to my own bed. I'm flying back to Denver later this morning, where I have a three o'clock cabinet meeting, never an easy gathering, followed by a talk at the Hispanic Man of the Year dinner. Tomorrow morning I must welcome the National Association of Morticians at the Denver Convention Center. Haven't a clue what to say to them. Any ideas?"

Charles responded, "Keep it light and lively. You might start off with a remark I always use: 'I feel a bit like Elizabeth Taylor's sixth husband. I know where I am, but I'm not certain what to do.' That should get them into a less moribund mood. From there on, governor, you're on your own."

"Maybe you'd like to substitute for me?"

"Thanks for the invitation, but I'm flying up to my ranch this afternoon. I've already provided the authorities with all the information I can. My presence here won't speed up the search, and with my guests safely gone, there's little for me to do here. By the way, Governor, my guests very much appreciated the arrangements you made to allow them to fly out on Sunday."

"I could tell some of them were really pissed and wanted nothing more to do with Durango, railroads or Colorado, for that matter."

"Yes, we had a few hot heads. The press reports I've read seem fair and balanced, for the most part, except for that *Durango Herald* reporter who called our efforts a military three-ring circus, naming you as the circus master."

"I saw that. I'll have a word with that reporter after we capture those Indians or whoever the hell they are."

Leaving Trish behind to coordinate the guests' transportation to Denver and their connecting flights to the east, Charles and Amanda encountered two roadblocks on their way to the airport. At the second, Charles' pilot was being held for questioning. Charles provided his identification, and to clear the pilot, he called the governor, who was himself on the way to the airport. At the roadblock, Charles and the governor once again bid each other farewell.

"Good luck with the morticians," Charles said cheerfully.

John greeted the Devlins at the Gunnison airport and asked if they needed to shop in town.

"We'll need some food," Mrs. Devlin responded.

"I've taken care of that," John answered and then asked, "What about the guests you were bringing?"

"They've had enough of Colorado after our incident on the train. I'm guessing you've heard what happened. It's been all over the press and national television."

"Yes I've been listening to the radio. You're both OK, I assume? Have they caught the Indians yet?"

"We're fine except for the embarrassment of it all. No they haven't caught the robbers yet, but they will, I'm sure. They may not have been Indians but ecoterrorists."

"No place is safe anymore, especially here in the West," John volunteered. "And to think that your friends, who truly wanted to help the West, were attacked and robbed at gunpoint by some wild Indians or ecoterrorists, it's unbelievable. I heard about Mr.Rigby. How's he doing?"

"He's on the mend." Mrs. Devlin chimed in.

"Things going well at the ranch?" Charles asked.

"As well as can be expected given the turmoil."

"Yes, we need to talk about that over dinner," Charles responded.

To change the subject, John said, looking at Mrs. Devlin, "I found you a fine horse. He's saddled and awaiting your arrival. He's a young, handsome, gentle quarter-horse gelding. I've been working with him, but to tell you the truth, his former owner did a beautiful job with him. He can do about anything you ask, except maybe for swimming across the river. You can rope off him, run barrels, trail cattle, and he doesn't mind a dog running around his heels. I think you'll like him."

"I can't wait to ride him. As for the swimming part, I much prefer to find a bridge. Does he have a name?"

"Buster."

As they pulled into the ranch headquarters, John pointed towards the nearest corral. "There he is now to greet us."

The handsome bay, already saddled, danced around the post where he was tied, impatient for attention and to be free from his hold.

Mrs. Devlin jumped out and exclaimed about his confirmation, particular his muscular hind quarters. "Darling, where are my riding boots? I want to ride him right now." Charles fetched her riding boots from a duffle bag in the back of the truck. Within three minutes she was mounted on Buster, with John at his side to adjust her stirrups.

She walked and then trotted the horse around the ring. On the second revolution, she put Buster into a soft lope, brought him to a swift stop and had him back up. Then she made a quick dismount, dropped the reins, picked up Buster's left front foot, inspected it and quickly remounted. The horse didn't move a muscle, except for his ears. She leaned over his neck, gathered the reins and put Buster through additional maneuvers. She trotted up to her husband and said, "Oh darling what an adorable horse; he's gentle, smart, quick and has a wonderfully soft trot. And look! He's not even sweating after this short workout. John thanks so much for locating him. Can you find Charles and the boys horses like this?"

Her skillful ride on the four-year-old impressed John. "You handled him with real skill," he said to Mrs. Devlin, and then turned to Charles. "I've been lookin' for another like Buster but horses like this don't come along every day, at least at a good price. I lucked out and found Buster from a friend for whom I made a saddle."

"I didn't know you made saddles," Mrs. Devlin said.

"He's a man of many talents," Charles answered. Knowing how much Amanda wanted to continue riding Buster, Charles suggested, "To get a little relaxation after the recent events, let's all ride up to see the site for the new house. The one with the mice. It's just a short ride, right, John?"

John nodded.

"But Charles, you know we can't build there. The federal authorities have already notified you by letter," Amanda offered.

"Yes, but I'm sure we can get rid of them either by poison or coyotes. The feds will never know. If we can't rid them ourselves, I've asked Senator Barlow to see if he can't arrange for us to have an exemption," Charles responded.

"But the mice contribute to biodiversity," John countered, using one of Amanda's concerns.

"And what do they contribute?" Charles shot back.

"Food for the coyotes," Amanda answered.

"If they have mice to feed on, why must they feed on my calves?" Charles countered.

Coming to Amanda's defense, John added, "That's the whole point, Charles. There aren't enough mice for the eagles or the coyotes, so they go feed on your calves."

"This sounds like a circular argument to me. So OK, let's go look at the other site," a suggestion he knew would placate his wife.

As John proceeded towards the corrals, Amanda volunteered, "Let me help saddle the horses."

Within 15 minutes, the three riders were mounted—Charles on Ginger and Amanda on Buster—and were riding across the meadows filled with cows and baby calves. At the edge of the meadow, they encountered Cabin Creek as it flowed through the ranch. On the other side of the fast moving stream, a rough trail led through the timber to the house site. They stopped at the steep 15-foot bank on the near side of Cabin Creek. A similar embankment appeared on the opposite side of the creek. John stopped on top the bank and instructed the riders to follow his path, one at a time, down the bank, across the stream, and up the other side. Bando, John's horse, stepped off the embankment, slid part way down on its hind legs, trotted across Cabin Creek and then galloped up the far side. Amanda followed, except that Buster jumped the creek before galloping up the far side. Charles led his horse, Ginger, to the edge, holding a tight rein and looking down at the creek. John shouted at him to let up on the reins and give the horse a little kick. Instead, Charles held tight to the reins, holding the horse's head so high it couldn't see to judge the grade of the embankment. Charles kicked his horse hard, and Ginger responded by stumbling to her knees just over the bank's edge. As she did, Charles fell forward over the saddle horn onto the horse's neck. Simultaneously, his right foot slipped through the stirrup. Charles kicked the horse with his left foot, hoping the horse would regain its balance. And as it did, Ginger leaped towards the creek, jumped the stream and galloped up the far bank with Charles hanging off the right side of the horse and his right ankle caught in the stirrup. As Ginger emerged from the bank, she trotted towards the timber with Charles bouncing like a rubber ball along the ground beside her. His screams for help caught everyone's attention and then the yells stopped as Charles lost consciousness. John immediately kicked Bando into a gallop, rode up on Ginger's left side, but couldn't find a rein. He leaned out of his saddle and caught the leather throat latch just below Ginger's chin, bringing her to a quick stop. John quickly dismounted and went for the ladigo strap that held Charles' saddle to the horse. Unbuckling it, he threw the saddle off the horse towards Charles, to relieve the pressure on his entangled leg. Amanda dismounted and rushed over to where the horse and Charles had come to a stop. She noticed a nasty gash on his hairline, the source of the blood that covered the right side of his face. As John carefully disentangled Charles' leg and ankle from the stirrup, he regained consciousness. Amanda, in uncontrollable tears, said through her sobs, "You'll be alright, dear. Just stay calm and try not to move." John had run to the creek, removing his outer shirt and then ripping off his undershirt and soaking it in the water. He returned to Charles, now sitting up, and wiped the blood off his face and wound.

"It's only a scalp wound," John said to Amanda, "but they'll bleed a lot." He went over to the saddlebag on his horse and returned with a small plastic tube.

"What's that?" Amanda asked.

"A disinfectant I always carry for a wire cut on a horse or a calf."

"Does it work on people?"

"We'll see," John said with a smile.

John turned to Charles and told him, "this medicated salve is going to burn like hell, but it will disinfect the wound. I know. I've used it on myself on numerous occasions. If you feel like yelling, go ahead. Or I can get you a stick to bite on."

"I'll take the stick."

John found a stick while Amanda, holding the wet undershirt to Charles' wound, tried to comfort her husband.

John applied the salve on Charles' wound. Amanda watched the white jell take effect as Charles tightened his jaw on the stick and his eyes watered. After a few minutes, the medicine numbed the sting from the cut.

John asked Charles if he could stand up. With Amanda and John's assistance, he stood uneasily on both feet, an indication that Charles had neither broken his right ankle nor his leg, as the three of them had feared.

"You're one lucky rider, Charles. A scalp wound and nothing broken. If Ginger had galloped off into the timber with you, you'd have bought the ranch right then and there. Sit still and I'll go wash the blood off this shirt so we can use it as a bandage until we get back to the ranch."

John led the horses back across the creek and then returned on foot to help Amanda and Charles down the bank, across the stream and up the opposite bank.

"Think you can ride back to the ranch?" John asked Charles.

"I feel fine. My ankle is a bit sore thanks to that god-damned unmannered horse. I hope she'll behave herself on the way home. As I remember, she acted up on me the last time I rode the bitch."

John held his temper. He wanted to give Charles an earful on how to follow instructions, like giving a loose rein to the horse so it could look down and see the steep bank. John wanted to ask Charles: How would you like it if I blindfolded you at the top of a steep staircase, put a 175-pound pack on your back and then gave you a hard kick in the ribs to get you moving. Do you think you'd make it safely to the bottom?

Charles said nothing more as he turned away from John and walked towards Ginger. He looked at her as he would an enemy soldier on a battlefield, but nevertheless made a feeble attempt to mount her. John, seeing his difficulty, went over the assist him. Amanda mounted Ginger without trouble or comment, and the three rode slowly back to headquarters.

Josh was the first to greet them. Noticing the bloody shirt wrapped around Charles' head, Josh asked, "What happened, Mr. Devlin? You look like you're coming off a Civil War battlefield."

"Ginger had a mind of her own," Charles snapped, "bucked me off and then dragged me by the stirrup up a steep bank."

"Ginger? Hell, she's the gentlest thing on four legs."

"Not today she wasn't."

Josh looked at John who rolled his eyes. Then John suggested, "We better get you inside to patch you up. I can put a butterfly bandage on you and you'll be good for other 10,000 miles."

Amanda immediately jumped in. "No, Charles needs to go to the hospital to be properly attended to. Maybe that ankle is broken, or he has a concussion or, god forbid, some brain damage."

"The ankle is not broken. See? I can move it. A bump on the head does not translate into brain damage. I've suffered brain damage in New York and Argentina, my dear, and I know what brain damage feels like. I'm not going to the hospital," Charles said with a slight smile but in a firm voice. "What I need is a drink, not a doctor."

John walked Charles over to the tack room, where a first-aid kit was located. "Sit here," John instructed Charles, "and I'll make that bandage." He fashioned the bandage quickly, with the skill of an Army medic, and then washed the wound again, splashed it with some mild disinfectant and applied the bandage. Amanda was struck by the efficiency of John's medical applications.

"Sure you don't want to go to the hospital?" John asked.

"What do you think?" Charles asked.

"Since you asked me, I think you'll be all right. But if, after supper, you have a bad headache, I think we need to drive to the Gunnison hospital." Amanda nodded her approval with the plan.

"OK. But right now, I want to go to the cabin, wash up, and have a drink. Join me."

"I'll see you over at my house around six for dinner. Nothing fancy, I can assure you."

"See you at six. I'll bring a bottle of Scotch," Charles said as he walked with a decided limp to the homestead cabin accompanied by Amanda, who had her arm around his waist.

After a change of clothes, Charles walked alone to John's house with the bottle in his hand. "John, Amanda is ecstatic with Buster. You've made her week. She'll be over in a minute after washing her hair. How about we have a drink? I can sure use one." John pulled three glasses from the cupboard and filled them with ice.

"I'm mighty impressed with the way Mrs. Devlin handled that horse—like a real pro."

"A lot better than my horsemanship today," Charles responded. "But I know if I'd ridden a better horse, I'd not have lost my balance and would have held my seat in that situation. I've ridden in and through worse circumstances in my life."

Charles poured three fingers of Johnny Walker Black label into each glass. "Cheers," Charles said, raising his glass in John's direction.

Charles continued. "I've been thinking about Rigby's decision to let you go. It's obvious to me that you and Rigby don't get along, for whatever reasons. But I do realize how well you know this ranch, how to manage it efficiently, and with only one other person. I've come to learn, talking with friends who have cattle ranches, it takes three and sometimes four men to operate a ranch this size. So I can tell this is a well run ranch, despite what our conservationist advisor might say. I recently talked with her in New York, and I must say I found her extremely opinionated, and a bit arrogant. I know I couldn't work with her if she were at Goodman. By the way, she was Rigby's choice, not mine, and he became angry when you argued about her usefulness. Normally, I leave all personnel decisions to Rigby, but in this case I think Rigby made a mistake by relieving you as manager in my absence. I admit I was slow to recognize his mistake, but I'm asking you now, and so is Amanda, to stay on. Also I'd like to raise your salary by $200 a month."

John took a large swallow of scotch and water, let it burn into his throat and said, "Thank you Charles; I'd like to stay on. It would be nice if we could do something for Josh. He's one hell of a fine worker, been here long enough to know every aspect of the ranch's operation. Besides, he knows cattle as well, if not better, than me."

"What do you recommend?"

"Same raise as mine."

"Consider it done. And one other thing—see if you can't work things out with Rigby. In so many ways he's my right-hand man. He's just a bit headstrong at times." John wanted to add, "and a fucking asshole at other times."

After the steak dinner, the Devlins talked about their plans for the new ranch house. Devlin put some drawings on the dining table and explained to John the various spaces in the stone and log structure. The five bedrooms, six baths, a library finished in African hardwoods, a modern kitchen attached to a dining room that appeared to John to be the size of the ranch corral, plus another corral-sized area—the living room that Devlin called "the Great Room," a wine cellar adjacent to a workout room and a heated three-car garage together totaled close to 20,000 square feet. A swimming pool, two tennis courts and a skeet range would all be within walking distance of the house, Charles explained. "I'm hoping we can get started this summer," Devlin said, looking at John.

"I don't see why not. It will depend, of course, on the contractor's schedule."

"I've already talked to one back east who can bring his own crew out here next month. I do want to look at the house site again tomorrow morning before we fly out in the afternoon."

About the time John and the Devlins finished their meeting, a phone call came from the FBI's chief investigator in Durango. Fallon said he'd be flying up in the Bureau's plane tomorrow morning and expected to be at the ranch around nine o'clock. "I'd like to ask you and Mr. Devlin some routine questions surrounding the recent events in Durango." John hoped he didn't display any nervousness when he relayed the message to the Devlins.

"Damn there goes the time we wanted to spend at the home site," a disappointed Charles commented.

"Don't worry. I'm sure we'll have time before your afternoon flight to get up there by truck and walk around," John responded, and then added, "But this time we'll leave Ginger behind." Charles sat stone-faced silent.

The couple said good night, and with the aid of Amanda, Charles limped back to his cabin.

The next morning, the FBI agent arrived in Gunnison at seven-thirty, rented a car and drove into Silver Valley. He stopped at the first gas station to get directions to the Diamond J ranch.

"Couldn't help you," the attendant said to the agent. "You might ask at the hardware store, just down the street from here on the left side. They do business with all the ranchers in the valley. They'll know the Diamond J."

"Do you know a John Marlow who works at the Diamond J?"

"Recognize the name, but I can't say I know him. Again, I'd ask the folks at the hardware store. Like I said, they're bound to know him."

The agent located the hardware store, and walked into the smoke-filled front half of the store. The Circle had already assembled and was engaged in a spirited discussion over the subject of the day: spring floods.

"If it gets any warmer real soon, we'll see the river break through those sand bags up near Danny's garage and come fast down Main Street. The last time it flooded over the banks, back in the '60s, the river sure gave the town a good enema."

Another member broke in. "'Bout time we could use another one, including this shit house."

"Just one minute," Jake, the owner said, "What you got against this store? I provide a meeting spot for you, plus coffee, and then clean up after you and the other slobs here. So what's your fucking problem?"

"Now you just calm down, Jake, I appreciate your hospitality, always have, but your prices kill me."

"Well, just take your fat old ass down to Gunnison and see if you can do any better. I give you a 10 percent senior discount. See if they do that in Gunnison or Montrose, for an 80-year-old geezer who's slow to pay his bills."

"Jake, calm down. He's just pulling your leg," said a voice from near the stove where the Circle had gathered.

When the agent walked in, everyone turned towards the door. Conversation came to a complete halt, less because the Circle failed to identify the new customer but because of his dress —a coat and tie—an outfit they associated with a wedding or the more common event, a funeral.

Jake walked to the counter. "Can I help you, sir?"

"I'm looking for the Diamond J Ranch."

"I'm Jake Dolan, owner of this store, and you, sir?"

"Colin Fallon, FBI" The two shook hands. Having never encountered an FBI agent before, Jake gave him a close and suspicious inspection. Fallon looked to be in his mid-40s, well built, with a trace of gray around the temples, and no evidence of a sidearm.

The mention of the FBI immediately changed the Circle's attention from floods to the more serious subject at hand.

"FBI? Is that what you said? You got business up at the Diamond J?" the ex-sheriff asked.

"Let's just say I need to talk with some folks at the ranch. Does John Marlow work out there?"

"Last I heard he did," Jake injected, "and a damned good manager he is. Comes in frequently for supplies … you know, wire, staples, posts, medicine, things like that. Sometimes he'll buy a big ticket item like a generator. The ranch is a good customer for us and it pays its bills on time, unlike other folks I know." Fallon noticed everyone around the stove, shaking their heads in agreement.

"I understand the ranch is owned by Mr. Charles Devlin?" The agent asked.

"That's correct." And then to solicit some information from the agent, Jake continued.

"He's the one that hosted that gathering of conservationists down in Durango last weekend we heard about on the radio. Those holdup guys, whoever they are, sure cleaned their clock alright. What's this we hear it might have been Indians, and now the papers say it could be ecoterrorists. Which was it? You must know. I'm assuming, of course, that you're investigating the Durango train robbery?"

"That's right. I can't say for sure at this point in our investigation who was involved. I'm here to gather some background information," Fallon responded. "A witness to the holdup said one of the robbers walked with a slight limp, and worked around here ... someone by the name of John Marlow, Anyone here know him?"

"If you're singling out John Marlow because he's got a limp, you're making a big mistake, Mr. Fallon. There's got to be about 3,600 folks in this valley, take out the 400 kids in school and you got 3,200. Figure that half of them are male which leaves 1,600. Right? Of that number, I'd estimate that about 20 percent are walking around here with a limp. A lot of horse accidents in this here cattle country. So what's that leave? Jake, you got the calculator."

Jake pulled a small calculator out of his pocket and shouted out "Three-hundred and twenty."

"That's 320 folks walkin' around here with a limp, and that's just in THIS valley. And Marlow is just one out of that total. So you can see that a man with a limp might rule in as many folks as it rules out. Fallon, you got yourself a lot of work to do. Hell, you might as well take up residence in Silver Valley."

"That's for sure," another member added, as he glanced at the nodding heads circling the stove.

Fallon's frown, however, signaled his disbelief of the Circle's probability model for injuries in Silver Valley. Later, I'll take a different tact to the investigation, he thought to himself.

"Mr. Fallon, what I want to know, now that the robbers scared off the environmentalists, is: who the hell goin' to save the West? I kinda looked forward to what they had to say and what they planned to do with towns like ours and us dirtbags that live here," the old ex-miner said.

"You'll just have to wait for another conference, but I'm sure you guys will survive."

"But for years we've been told we've been shitin' our nest and we needed to clean up our act. Now there won't be no one around to advise us. Woe is us."

The agent couldn't miss the sarcasm and refused to get caught up in further discussion. To change the focus, he asked: "When was the last time someone from the Diamond J ranch came in here?

"Just last Friday I believe," Jake spoke up. "Marlow was in to buy some supplies for branding next weekend. When I asked him why not this weekend with the good weather, he said he had to attend that bull sale down near Gunnison.'"

"What sale is that?" the agent asked.

Jake directed the agent to the sale flier still tacked to the bulletin board hanging by the door.

Fallon inspected it and took some notes, and then asked again for directions to the Diamond J.

"Go out of town heading east, and after two miles look for County Road F heading north. Take that four or five miles and you'll run right into it."

"Thanks, Jake, and you guys take care," the agent said as he headed towards the door.

Once the agent drove off, everyone around the stove forgot about floods and focused on John.

"What's he snooping around here for? Thinking maybe that John did the job in Durango or maybe Devlin himself?"

"I thought the TV said a couple of days ago it was those Durango redskins."

"Yeah, but now they say it may be some hippy group who call themselves ecoterrorists. Wouldn't bother me one bit if they capture the whole bunch of them there hippies and send them to California and clean up Colorado."

Again, the nods signaled general agreement. Everyone around the stove had decided for themselves that John had pulled off the robbery, and by doing so, had sent the environmentalists home with their tails between their legs. No one dared talk about it or even hint at it, not even within the private confines of the Circle, for fear of putting John in further danger. Didn't John just last Friday morning buy some water soluble red paint and a small brush? Also two horse shoes, size aught. And didn't a news report say that the horses had Indian designs painted on their flanks in RED paint? I'll have to delete those items from the invoice, Jake thought.

"How in the world could the FBI ever imagine that John was involved in the holdup? Hell, he's the most honest guy in the valley and without a violent bone in his body," the old miner announced.

"Isn't that the truth," the former teacher volunteered.

"Yeah, yeah," they shouted in unison, as if taking a vow of silence together.

Agent Fallon made his way out to the ranch and pulled up in front of the shop. John walked out to see an unfamiliar car and face.

"Is John Marlow anywhere around here?" Fallon asked.

"He's around right here," John said, pointing to himself. "What can I do for you?"

"I'm Colin Fallon of the FBI and I'm here to ask you and Mr. Devlin a few questions relating to a train robbery in Durango last weekend."

"I've been reading about those wild Indians in the paper. Why don't we go over to my house and talk over a cup of coffee," John suggested.

As they walked to the house, Fallon noticed John's slight limp in the right leg.

In the kitchen, John brewed up some of his strong coffee, offered a cup to Fallon and asked, "Cream, sugar?"

"No, I'll take it black, thanks. Let me get right to the point, Mr. Marlow. I'm trying to locate everyone who might have wanted to disrupt Mr. Devlin's conference in Durango last Saturday and also rob his guests. I talked with Mr. Devlin's accountant, Fred Rigby. You know him, I assume?"

"Yes, I know him."

"Rigby tells me you were fired as ranch manager shortly before the holdup in Durango."

"That's correct, but Mr. Devlin just rehired me last evening. You might want to check with him."

"Can you tell me where you were last Saturday?"

"Yes I was at the Monarch bull sale down towards Gunnison."

"All day?"

"No, we left right after lunch. We stayed for the beef Bar-B-Q."

"Did you buy any bulls?"

"Not a one."

"Why not? Isn't that why you went there, to buy bulls?"

"Mr. Fallon, you being from the FBI, I'm guessing you don't know much about cattle. If you did and went to that sale, you'd have seen a bunch of thousand-pound hairballs walking around on spindly legs, without an ounce of muscle. Bulls are raised to breed cows; that's about their only function in life. Oh, that some us were so lucky. But these bulls had peckers the size of pencil stubs and balls smaller than roasted peanuts. So with hardware like that, I'd be wasting our money and selling a bunch of open cows in the fall. Josh, my hired man, and I came home in the afternoon with an empty trailer. We'll find our bulls elsewhere—probably in Three Forks, Montana, where I have a line on some good Angus bulls."

"Can I see your horses?"

"Sure. They're in the corral right now."

The two men walked over to the corral. John's white mare was standing next to Buster. The other horses stood across the corral at the water trough. "That's a beautiful horse," Fallon said, looking at Buster.

"Yeah, he's new. I just purchased him for Mrs. Devlin. A lot more handsome than this white mare of mine."

Fallon walked over to pet both horses and then went behind the mare to look at the horses from the opposite side.

"Fallon, look out," John shouted, "that horse of mine will kick!" And just as John finished his sentence a white leg flashed from the underside of the mare, barely missing Fallon's leg.

"She's not very well mannered," Fallon commented nervously, as he looked for any remnant of red paint on her white flanks.

"That's a mare for you," John casually responded.

The men walked over to the horses at the water tank. Fallon again looked them over for any signs of red paint.

As they walked out of the corral, the agent thanked John for his time and shook hands.

Fallon caught up with the Devlins sitting outside the homestead cabin drinking coffee, and said he wanted to follow up with some questions that had occurred to him since their meeting in Durango. Charles got up from his chair and walked over to shake Fallon's hand. The agent immediately noticed the limp and the head bandage. Charles was quick to explain, "a horse accident yesterday." And then added, "Pretty common around here."

"Let me immediately get to the subject of why I'm here. Do you have any reason to believe that Mr. Marlow might have been involved in the train holdup?" Fallon asked.

"You must be joking. John's as loyal as they come, and a terrific manager. And, I can assure you, he's not a holdup artist," Charles responded.

"Your man Rigby suggested to me in the hospital that one of the holdup men could have been Marlow."

"John told me he attended a bull sale near here on Saturday. Besides, Rigby doesn't know what in hell he's talking about; I'm sorry to say this, but he can't always be relied on for accurate information, except maybe when it comes to numbers." Fallon asked some other questions of Devlin, and the answers agreed with the information he'd gathered from the victims in Durango.

Just as Fallon drove off, the phone rang in the Homestead cabin.

"Charles Devlin here."

"Mr. Devlin, this is Rigby. I'm still in the hospital but expect to be released tomorrow. As you can imagine, I've been giving a lot of thought to the robbery and who might have been involved. I'm more certain than ever it was Marlow."

"And why do you think it was Marlow?" Charles asked.

"He's the only person I can think of who had it out for you. Also, from previous conversations with Gretchen, the conservationist advisor, John detested environmentalists. Mr. Devlin, you must get the authorities to investigate John's whereabouts last Saturday. I've never trusted Marlow from day one. Get the FBI or whoever to arrest him and ask questions later."

Rigby, just calm down. I've already talked with the FBI. They'll catch the robbers. They always do. Just back off and let them do their job. OK?"

"Ok but the FBI should keep an eye on him."

After Fallon left the ranch, he drove to the site of Saturday's Monarch Bull Sale, and introduced himself as an FBI agent. The owner confirmed John's attendance, and to corroborate the inquiry, he looked in the register and said to the agent, "There he is, signed in," pointing to John's signature, "and with the bid number of 129."

"Do you remember if he stayed throughout the sale?" Fallon inquired.

"Can't rightly say, but I think I remember seeing him and his hired man at lunch."

"What did you serve for lunch?"

"Same as every year, Bar-B-Q. What'd you expect at a bull sale, catfish?"

Fallon ignored the comment and asked, "Did he buy any … bulls?" He caught himself before he said "hair."

"Not a one," the rancher said with some disgust.

"Thank you, sir, for your assistance," Fallon said as he walked to his car.

Fallon had forgotten one item he wished to verify. Instead of heading to Gunnison and his plane, he backtracked to Spring Valley and Jake's hardware store. He arrived at noon, the time the Circle normally adjourned. When they saw Fallon once again, however, they immediately reassembled around the stove.

"Back again? I bet you need some irrigating boots," Jake greeted him.

"No, I just want to thank you guys for all of your help. I found the ranch, also Marlow and Devlin. They too were most helpful with my investigation. There is one thing I forgot earlier this morning. Jake, may I have a word with you?"

Over by the stove, the old miner leaned over to the ex-sheriff and asked in a soft voice, "You think Jake's a suspect now?"

"These FBI guys, you know, aren't the sharpest nails in the store."

Fallon asked Jake if he could see the receipt of John's purchase on Friday.

The owner went into his back office and within a minute or so he returned with the yellow copy. "It looks like he purchased two rolls of barbed fire, some medicine, a new bit for his post-hole digger, assorted nuts and bolts, two rolls of duct tape and two boxes of castration rubber bands, plus 10 heavy-duty rubber bands."

"I see something is scratched out here," Fallon said pointing to the middle of the receipt.

"Yes, I did that when I mistakenly wrote a box of heavy-duty rubber bands. He said he only needed 10, so as you can see I only charged him for those."

"Why the duct tape?"

"It's what keeps our ranches held together around here."

"And the heavy-duty rubber bands?"

"John says he uses them on the testicles of young Angus bulls."

Fallon wasn't certain he understood the explanation but didn't think he needed one.

Fallon asked Jake to make a copy of the receipt and then bid farewell to the Circle once again.

"Hope you catch those banditos," the old miner said, as Fallon approached the door.

"We always get our man."

As Fallon departed Silver Valley for his plane in Gunnison, he mentally wiped John from his suspect list. He knew he'd have to refocus his investigation on the Chief's partner, Two Feathers, or the ecoterrorist with the roping skills. Damned if he had time to hunt up over 300 limping cowboys.

Jake stood at the counter with a broad grin as Fallon's car headed in the direction of the airport.

"Fellas," Jake said, "You know what I think? We can save the West from right here. We don't need no more folks coming out here to tell us how to save ourselves. We got the materials here—an ample supply of genuine, down-to-earth rumors, some duct tape and rolls of barbed wire. What more do we need?

EPILOGUE

Three months after the robbery, Johnny entered Yale, aided by a satchel of small bills he counted out at Yale's bursar's office. By the end of his first semester, he'd set the college's single-season passing record for a freshman quarterback. In the classroom, he gained the Dean's list as easily as he earned all-Ivy League honors on the gridiron. His pine beetle research in the biology lab became the scientific foundation for the introduction of a South American bird to the western United States that thrived on a diet of pine beetles and their eggs. Johnny's professor, who took credit for his student's research, increased his scholarship by $250.

Up on the burial site of John's relatives, the Preble's jumping mice tripled their population in the six months after the robbery. John kept them well fed in grain over the winter, paying cash at the grain mill for their rolled corn, dipped in delicious molasses.

Rigby recovered from his heart attack and returned full-time to his work for Charles Devlin at the same time Johnny threw the winning touchdown pass to beat Harvard in Cambridge. During a late November trip to the ranch, John managed to convince Rigby that Dynamite did not properly describe the equine's sweet gentle disposition. Rigby's subsequent ride on the horse proved to himself, John and the Devlins that God never intended for Rigby to mount a horse. A compound fracture of a leg, a broken arm, and a concussion kept him at home most of the following winter and spring and, to John's delight, away from the affairs of the ranch. In preparation for Rigby's summer visit, and knowing that Rigby would never again choose to ride Dynamite, John spent much of the winter looking for his replacement, but one with Dynamite's temperament.

Charles maintained his position as Chairman of Goodman Samson with the personal intervention of the President, who Charles had assisted by bundling $15 million of campaign donations from Goodman partners for the president's forthcoming reelection campaign. And the Secretary of the Treasury (the former Goodman Vice Chairman) pressured the IMF to match U.S. loans to Argentina. The loan package assisted the country through its economic troubles and, within 18 months, towards full recovery. The Argentine recovery helped increase the value of Goodman's stock and Charles' stock options. Charles managed to pay down his ranch mortgage to a serviceable size. It also allowed Charles, in his personal account, the luxury of not having to sell his Argentinean bank stock at a loss, while he waited out the country's economic recovery. Goodman Samson's loss of $200 million was more than recovered by the bank's ability to withstand the temporary loss, as it too waited for the U.S. Treasury and IMF loans to take effect within the Argentine economy.

The Devlins completed construction of their 15,000-square-foot ranch house the following year at the "least desirable site," while saving the Preble's mice and the Marlow cemetery. Amanda spent more and more time at the ranch assisting John and Josh, riding through the cattle in the summer and feeding them in the winter. Central Park appeared to not suffer in her absence.

Much to Amanda's distress, if not envy, Trish moved in with John after quitting her railroad job, assisted by John's improved "cash flow." She headed up the remodel of John's house, including the expansion of the one-person shower stall in the master bathroom. The appearance of the front yard was immediately improved with the removal of weeds and the planting of grass. The "god-damned" dogs learned to eat and find cover outside and away from the mud-room, itself cleaned to the basic sanitary standards expected by western civilization.

Josh surprised his wife, Mary, on their tenth wedding anniversary with a new washing machine, paid for with cash. He again shocked her with a new refrigerator, another cash transaction, for Christmas. That winter, Josh helped his parents locate and pay for a warmer home near the university hospital in Aurora, outside of Denver. Josh also awarded himself a new three-year-old mare out of a champion cutting horse, which he planned to train and breed within the year.

When the old miner's dentures stopped chattering, Circle members dressed themselves in clean jeans and borrowed ties for his funeral service. One of the members gave a eulogy in which he said, "Phil was always a bit windy, but constantly entertained us with his Walmart clappers." The Circle debated for weeks on Phil's replacement, until they finally decided on Pete Martinez, recently retired as the girl's soccer coach and janitor at the high school. As one of the members said to the Circle, "We could sure use some cleanliness and bio-diversity within this dirtbag organization." The vote was unanimous.

Later that summer, the number of riders on the Durango-Silverton train increased by 30 percent, with tourists wanting to visit the holdup site. The following summer, a holdup occurred on the Georgetown Loop Railroad, west of Denver. It ended with the arrest of two armed Texans who, involuntarily, moved their residence from Plano, Texas, to Canyon City, Colorado, the home of the state penitentiary. John finally convinced Charles to rescind his ban on neighbors helping on the Diamond J. Relations much improved when they took 15 elk off the ranch during hunting season.

That same season, two Ute hunters on their reservation sought cover in a thunderstorm. In the cave where they took refuge, they discovered the remains of a human skeleton. Retrieved by the county sheriff's office and examined by the county coroner, the press release in the *Durango Herald* announced that the "victim had suffered a gunshot wound to the forehead that, according to Sheriff Delaney, 'probably killed him.'" The Sheriff added that, "after a DNA check, the young man proved to be an Anglo" and, jumping to an unsubstantiated but publicly accepted conclusion, "was probably one of the holdup men from the June train robbery. The reward money continues to go unclaimed." Delaney went on to announce that his office "could no longer continue the search for the second robber. We have exceeded our budget by 30 percent, and the county commissioners are reluctant to call for a tax increase in next November's election.'"

ACKNOWLEDGEMENTS

I learned quickly that writing fiction requires different skills from writing history, my usual venue. To help with this transition, I'd like to thank Susan Carey, Robert Westbrook, Kent Nelson, Steve Horn, Anne Price and Betsy Armstrong. For assistance with the physiology and sex habits of the Preble's jumping mouse, I must give credit to Harry Sinnamon. My good friend Ed Barlow offered useful suggestions regarding New York's financial world. Only a lawyer like Gene Rooke could think of ways to disrupt the rural retreat of an arrogant investment banker. And to Al Harper, President of the Durango & Silverton Narrow Gauge Railroad I owe thanks. When I presented Mr. Harper with a draft of the train robbery, he responded, "That's not the way to rob my train. Let me tell you how to do it…." Readers are advised not to replicate my fictional account of the robbery.

My friend and neighbor, William (Willy) Matthews, the premier watercolorist in the West today, created the cover and to him a special thanks!

Richard Ballantine and Robert Whitson at the Durango Herald Small Press and Lisa Atchison at Atchison Design assisted with the book's production. And throughout the process of writing, I received the encouragement and imaginative suggestions of Bill Adler. In the end, my wife, Deedee, provided positive criticism and, as always, her loving support.

PETER R. DECKER was a professor of history and public policy at Duke University before becoming a Western rancher in Ridgway, Colorado. He served as commissioner of agriculture for the state of Colorado, is a director of the renowned National Western Stock Show in Denver, and serves on the board of trustees for Fort Lewis College in Durango, Colorado. He is the author of *Old Fences, New Neighbors*, a book about the transformation of a Southwest Colorado community into a tourist destination, *Fortunes and Failures*, a study of San Francisco's nineteenth-century merchants, and *"The Utes Must Go!"*, the story of the expulsion of Colorado's first residents from the state.